THAT DEADMAN DANCE

BY THE SAME AUTHOR

True Country
Benang: From the Heart
Kayang & Me

THAT DEADMAN DANCE

a novel

KIM SCOTT

BLOOMSBURY

New York   Berlin   London   Sydney

Published by Bloomsbury USA, New York

All papers used by Bloomsbury USA are natural, recyclable products made
from wood grown in well-managed forests. The manufacturing processes
conform to the environmental regulations of the country of origin.

LIBRARY OF CONGRESS CATALOGING-IN-PUBLICATION DATA

Scott, Kim, 1957–
That deadman dance : a novel / Kim Scott. — 1st U.S. ed.
p. cm.
ISBN-13: 978-1-60819-705-7
ISBN-10: 1-60819-705-0
1. Nyunga (Australian people)—Fiction.   2. Aboriginal
Australians—Fiction.   3. Western Australia—Social life and
customs—Fiction.   I. Title.

PR9619.3.S373T43 2011
823'.914—dc22
2011014163

First published in Australia by Picador, an imprint of
Pan Macmillan Australia Pty Limited, 2010.

First U.S. Edition 2012

1 3 5 7 9 10 8 6 4 2

Typeset by Westchester Book Group
Printed in the U.S.A. by Quad/Graphics, Fairfield, Pennsylvania

To Reenie,
For all these years.

THAT DEADMAN DANCE

PROLOGUE

*K**AYA.*

K   Writing such a word, Bobby Wabalanginy couldn't help but smile. Nobody ever done writ that before, he thought. Nobody ever writ *hello* or *yes* that way!

Roze a wail . . .

Bobby Wabalanginy wrote with damp chalk, brittle as weak bone. Bobby wrote on a thin piece of slate. Moving between languages, Bobby wrote on stone.

With a name like Bobby Wabalanginy he knew the difficulty of spelling.

Boby Wablngn wrote *roze a wail.*

But there was no whale. Bobby was imagining, remembering . . .

Rite wail.

Bobby already knew what it was to be up close beside a right whale. He was not much more than a baby when he first saw whales rolling between him and the islands: a very close island, a big family of whales breathing easily, spouts sparkling in the sunlight, great black bodies glossy in the blue and sunlit sea. Bobby wanted to enter the water and swim out to them, but swaddled against his mother's body, his spirit could only call. Unlike that

1

Bible man, Jonah, Bobby wasn't frightened because he carried a story deep inside himself, a story Menak gave him wrapped around the memory of a fiery, pulsing whale heart . . .

On a sunny day, walking a long arm of rock beside a calm ocean, you see the water suddenly bulging as a great bubble comes to the surface and oh! water streams from barnacled flesh and there is the vast back of a whale. You are enclosed in moist whale breath.

Barnacles stud the smooth dark skin, and crabs scurry across it. That black back must be slippery, treacherous like rock . . . But you see the hole in its back, the breath going in and out, and you think of all the blowholes along this coast; how a clever man can slip into them, fly inland one moment, back to ocean the next.

Always curious, always brave, you take one step and the whale is underfoot. Two steps more and you are sliding, sliding deep into a dark and breathing cave that resonates with whale song. Beside you beats a blood-filled heart so warm it could be fire.

Plunge your hands into that whale heart, lean into it and squeeze and let your voice join the whale's roar. Sing that song your father taught you as the whale dives, down, deep.

How dark it is beneath the sea, and looking through the whale's eyes you see bubbles slide past you like . . .

But there was none of that. Bobby was only imagining, only writing. Held in the sky on a rocky headland, Bobby drew chalk circles on slate, drew bubbles.

Bubelz.

Roze a wail.

He erased the marks with the heel of his hand. It wasn't true, it was just an old story, and he couldn't even remember the proper song. There was no whale. And this was no sunny day. Instead, the wind plucked at Bobby's small shelter of brushwood and canvas, and rain spat on the walls. In the headland's lee immediately below him the sea was smooth, but a little further from land—a few boat lengths, no more—it was scuffed and agitated, and scribbles of foam spilled in a pattern he was still learning. Rain made sharp silver thorns, and then there was no sea, no sky and the world had compressed itself into a diagonally grained grey space before him.

Bobby heard the heavy tread, and Kongk Chaine thrust himself into the little hut. Hardly space for the two of them beneath this roof, these three flimsy walls. Bobby smelled tobacco and rum; if Kongk breathes in deep, stands up straight, this shelter'll explode. Chaine steamed with rain and body heat and ruddy health; water cascaded over the brim of his hat and gushed from his bristling beard.

You need a fire here, Bobby.

He looked out across the angry ocean as it reappeared, and at the rain racing away.

Nothing, huh?

They sat, each in the smell of the other, and despite the warmth of the body beside him, Bobby felt the cold seeping into his bones. His fingers were chalk, but with loose and wrinkled skin. He drew on the wet slate with his finger.

Fine we kild a wail.

Chaine barked. Laughed. Bobby felt the man's arm around his back, the tough and calloused paw squeezing him.

I hope to kill myself a whale, my boy. More than one, come to that. More than one. But right now I wish for sunlight and a clear sky.

Bobby grinned and nodded. Dr Cross might be gone, but Geordie Chaine lived on, another new old man.

Hug.

Bobby wanted to be the first to sight whales, but he knew the Yankees or even Froggies would likely see them first, since they had sail and all. A tilting tip of mast and sail could point out a whale spout he'd not yet seen.

Bobby kept a sharp lookout. He wrote on slate and showed it to Kongk Chaine to read. No matter if weather-watching, whale-watching or writing, Bobby Wabalanginy was always ready to shout and come running soon as he saw what they all sought.

Fine, he wrote now. Again wishing, imagining.

Fine no wailz lumpy see.

He erased the word *fine*, and straightaway a crowd of water drops rushed across the crest behind him: tiny footsteps slapped leathery leaves, ran heavily across the granite and were drumming loud on the canvas all around them. Bobby shouted with surprise and joy, but even Chaine right beside him could not make out a word, could not hear his voice, only the pounding of tiny feet and hands, and water gurgling, chuckling. The two of them looked at each other, mouthing unheard words as a thin sheet of water ran across the granite beneath their feet.

They were out of the rain, out of the worst of the wind in a pocket of shelter, but still the spit and fingers of wind touched them. Bobby's kangaroo-skin cloak and the oil and unguents rubbed into his skin kept him warm. Life tingled in his very fingertips.

A trail of silvery spikes ran across the sheltered water below their headland and disappeared into the wind-chopped sea beyond the island so close to shore. All along the southern coast the bellies of clouds were being dragged over just such rocky headlands and islands.

Chaine shivered, farted. Grumbling, he made his way carefully down the slope to the beach.

Bobby wrote straight from his mother and father's tongue to that of Chaine.

Kongk gon wailz cum.

There! Bobby saw a sail, a mast change its tilt, and then, sunlit among the grey and white tufts and tears of ocean, a spout of spray. Oh. Lotta spouts, a clump of silvery bushes blossoming in a great trunk of angled sunlight out there on the wind-patterned sea. For a moment he thought of sails, of a great fleet of ships rolling in from the horizon. But no, this was whales. Bobby, arms and legs windmilling down the sandy track, yelling out, yelling out, voice pricking men into action. No time just then, but he wrote it later.

Thar she bloze!

Bobby wrote and made it happen again and again in seasons to come, starting just here, now.

Kaya.

PART I

1833–1835

RETURNING ON A ROPE

ONCE UPON A TIME there was a captain on a wide sea, a rough and windswept sea, and his good barque was pitched and tossed something cruel. Wan, green-skinned passengers dabbed their mouths, swallowed, and kept their eyes fixed on a long and rocky strip of land seen dimly through salt and rain and marked by plumes of foam rising into the air each time the sea smashed against it. The captain—his ship bashed and groaning, the strained rigging humming—sailed parallel to this hint of haven and the mostly bilious passengers resigned themselves to whatever fate offered.

Drenched with spray, Bobby Wabalanginy stood at the bow with a rope tied tightly around his waist. He bent his knees, swayed from the hips in an attempt to maintain his poise as the ship leapt and plunged. A lunging wave swept him across the deck with nothing to cling to and only the rope to save him. Laughing in fear and excitement, he got to his feet and, hand by hand along the rope, thrust his way against the elements back to where he'd begun. Through the soles of his feet and within his very ribs he felt the vessel groaning. He sensed the sails, possessed by an unearthly wind and stretched tight enough to burst.

Gulls shrieked and called to him, and clots of foam or cloud were caught in the rigging and then flung free. Cold and shivering, too scared to free himself from the rope in case he was swept overboard, Bobby slid to and fro across the deck like he was about to become a dead man, with no flame of consciousness or desire and a very barren self.

And then the ship heeled over the other way, came around between headland and island and into the lee of a towering dome of granite. Its dark mass was a comfort, and yet the sunlight was still on them. Bobby stretched out on deck like a starfish, already warmed.

Every passenger felt the change, the transformation from the southern side of land to this, how the same long strip of land battered by sea the other side gave shelter here. Between towering headland and island they entered a great bay and found sandy shores within reach.

Yes, there was a captain, and even as his passengers adjusted themselves to the wind no longer roaring in their ears and buffeting them, and even as the salt dried on their faces, the captain and his sailors were remembering other, leafier shores—warmer climes and bare-breasted, dancing women. Small waves slapped teasingly against the hull.

There was a captain with a telescope to his eye, and frustrated sailors sighing, and passengers stretching on the deck and breathing deeply in the relief of the settling sea and oh how the wind had dropped soon as they came around this corner of land. The sun shone upon them and upon rock immediately to their left that rose straight up from the deep blue ocean.

A little further the other way the swell broke on the outer side of the island, and foam periodically leapt and hung in the sky. Behind the comfort of one another's voices, they heard the loud and regular boom and boom and boom of ocean upon rock, and the shrill caw and call of birds, rising and falling with the spray as if they were the musical score of this shifting, irregular and atonal song of welcome.

So they talked all the more, of what had seemed trees of stone, forever bent by the wind forever sweeping across the headland, or—moving further into shelter—how rock rose majestically from the sea, or boulders balanced high above, some perversely shaped, some rounded and ready to roll, and huge slabs sloped to the very water's edge. The passengers looked around nervously, wanting to recognise the scent of land, of soil and earth. Smelled only salt and eucalyptus oil.

The dark figure of a boy in the rigging.

They anchored in a great and protected bay, close to one of its high arms of land. Had entered its embrace.

King George Town people call this place now.

MENAK

MENAK'S CAMPFIRE would have been invisible from the ship, yet his view took in the inner harbour, the great bay, the islands and the ship coming around the headland. The ship seemed to skim the ocean surface, and even after all this time Menak was reminded of a pelican swooping from the air, landing in water. But of course a ship's canvas wings hold the wind, and keep that wave tumbling and frothing at its sharp breast as it slices and pushes the sea aside. Such power and grace, and there is that milky scar as the sea closes again, healing.

The ship settled, its sails furled. Menak had seen ships come and go since he was a child, had seen his father dance with the very earliest visitors. Not that he really remembered the incident, more the dance and song that lived on. It worried him that these visitors didn't live up to the old stories, yet they stayed so long.

At Menak's back the granite boulder was warm with the morning sun. Comfortable, he thought of the close air of the buildings further down the slope, and how their roofs were made of timber from the whispering trees around, and their walls were a mix of twigs and the same white clay with which his people decorated themselves.

Menak was not a young man: his chest was decorated with parallel ridges of scars and his forehead was high. Bright feathers sprang from his tightly bound hair and the bands around his upper arms, and his skin glowed with oil and ochre. Calling his little white dog, he stepped down the steep, narrow path to the white buildings squatting beside the sea and entered the hut where clean trousers and shirt were kept for him. He washed his hands, continuing the ceremony—their ceremony—for greeting people when they came from beyond the horizon. He looked forward to greeting his nephew and Dr Cross, and the other people Cross wished him to know.

Menak had been absent from this, his heart of home, for some time following his brother Wunyeran's death, and as he went through the peppermint trees and blossoming paperbarks to the white beach of the harbour, his little white dog trotting beside him, he thought of what close friends Wunyeran and Dr Cross had been.

So many of Menak's people were dying and, although Cross was a friend, Menak did not think they needed more of his people here. Yet here they were. True, they had things to offer, and few stayed long. And, if nothing else, they might be useful allies against others who, to Menak's mind, were sometimes little more than savages.

Yes, Menak looked forward to seeing Wabalanginy again. Bobby, Cross and the others had named him, Bobby Wabalanginy who'd been born the sunrise side of here and, having seen ships arrive and sail away again over his whole lifetime, had now sailed away and returned. Only Wooral and Menak had done as much, and not for so long. He was a clever boy, Bobby Wabalanginy, and brave.

Wooral was in the pilot boat now, heading for where the ship rested, its wings folded and tied. But it is a ship, not a bird, Menak reminded himself again. He gestured to his dog, and the animal leapt into his arms and fixed its attention on the ship as if the sight stirred some memory of scurrying after rats below its deck.

Menak stroked the dog. *Alidja, Jock. Noonak kornt maaman ngaangk moort.*

Look, Jock, your house father mother family.

CHAINE

GEORDIE CHAINE GRIPPED a timber rail caked with salt, his nerves as tight as any rigging, and speared his attention to the immense grey-green land beyond the shore. Empty, he thought. Trackless. Waiting for him. A few columns of smoke were visible inland. Even as his wife touched his bicep and insinuated herself into his arms, Geordie Chaine ground his teeth beneath his tam-o'-shanter cap.

The pilot boat pulled alongside. One of the crew, a dark and wild-haired man, naked except for some sort of animal skin tied around his waist, threw a rope to a sailor on the ship. Chaine moved his wife behind him, to protect her from embarrassment. Their son held his father's hand, their daughter touched her mother lightly but stood away.

Dr Cross, who had advised Mr Chaine to take up land here rather than at the Cygnet River colony, introduced him to the pilot, Mr Killam, and the two men shook hands most effusively.

My wife, Mrs Chaine.

Killam was indeed pleased to meet Mrs Chaine, and of course the children, too.

You are a lucky man, he said.

But Geordie Chaine knew it was more than luck.

And what are you bringing with you, Mr Chaine, if I may ask?

Geordie Chaine had two prefabricated houses. He had money and stock, tools and enterprise, which he'd been promised was enough for him to be granted land. But all the land of any quality at Cygnet River was gone and, what's more, hopelessly surveyed and divided. This land looked no worse than that of home and he'd heard that—unlike Cygnet River—there was plenty to be had. Geordie Chaine was on the make and no privilege of class would hinder here. As he liked to say, every bucket must sit upon its own arse.

Alexander Killam thought much the same, but duty called, and so he did not take the time to explain that he was done with soldiering, and proud—despite limited experience—to be both harbourmaster and pilot at this most sheltered of waters along the south coast. It was not a demanding role because few ships called into the harbour. But he thought that might change.

Geordie Chaine immediately realised Alexander Killam's advantage: the pilot was first to board each vessel and therefore first to know what cargo was aboard and who was trading. He would know what those on shore needed. No doubt rum was in demand.

The men agreed that, with this wind and fading light, it would be unwise to attempt getting the ship into the inner harbour; a fair wind was expected tomorrow.

Dr Cross arranged for the Chaine family to accompany him ashore with Killam.

Bobby was already in the whaleboat and had taken the oar from Wooral. Cross sat down in the boat and spread a handkerchief across his knees—a strange gesture to those watching—and the young man whose oar Bobby had claimed lay his head upon Cross's handkerchief and was asleep as soon as the rhythm of the rowlocks was established. Mrs Chaine studied the greased and ochred face of the young man, the matted hair held by a headband of fur, the body thickly smeared with oil and reddish clay, the scanty belt of woven hair or fur. Her husband pointed away somewhere, somewhere there in the coiled bush, the granite boulders . . .

Was that the settlement?

And then they were in a narrow channel, grey rock sloping either side and ribbons of seaweed waving from a fathom or two below the sea's skin. There were figures on the shore, and a white sandy beach, dense and willowy trees . . . A few grey-roofed, white buildings huddled in the cleft between two hills shone warmly in the last moments of a falling sun.

Bobby Wabalanginy and Wooral sprang from the boat and held it fast while the others—those who in the old stories had always danced so sharp and precisely—staggered, heavy-footed and clumsy, onto our seashore.

Bobby would have liked to help carry Mrs Chaine, especially when her husband, stumbling on sea legs, almost fell with her in his arms. Or perhaps the children, but they had turned to the arms of sailors. And of course he was too small yet.

The sun dropped below the low hills on the other side of the harbour. Further up the slope from the settlement a thin stem of smoke rose to the low, pink-tinged sky, and all the differing greys of cloud, smoke, granite and sea began to merge . . . White sand glimmered and little lapping waves broke brightly in the failing light. It was a subtle rhythm, and Bobby gently moved his hips and knees, sinking his feet deeper and deeper into the wet sand. Settling, having returned, he recalled his departure . . .

His people calling goodbye, the boy Bobby Wabalanginy had sailed through the narrow gap in the granite and out toward the islands. Looking back, he watched the sun touch the land and sink, and the white sand of the beaches persist for a time but soon that, too, was no more—he had gone deep into the sky.

Stars shone all around him. A splash, and half the sky exploded.

Of course, Bobby knew it was reflections in water, not sky, and he never shook and trembled like the stars and moon that, so slow to reform and settle, were lulled only long after the anchor—now silent and somewhere else altogether—gripped and held him tight.

He lay beneath furled sails, one ear to the deck, listening to the ship breathe and sigh. Waves slapped the tight timber boards and yet, even out here so far from land, something hulked close by in the darkness. Bobby made himself relax, pulled his kangaroo skin close around him. Slept.

He sighed and opened his eyes. An island loomed solid in the vast blue of sky and the many shifting, tilting surfaces below. Only ever an ethereal thing at the sea's horizon, the island was now close enough for Bobby to sense its mass, reach for its shelter, see its tightly curled and clinging tangles of sapling and shrubbery.

He turned: the distant shore and, more distant still, a thin stem of smoke.

The sails fell, caught the wind and the boat came around the island. Beyond was only ocean. A small swell moved up and down bare rocks at the end of the second island, not breaking.

Beneath his feet the bow tossed foam and water like scattered applause, and the swollen sails were all pride and power. It must have been some fluke of wind and the proximity of the island, but Bobby was given—took it greedy and grateful—one last breath of eucalyptus and leaves, of earth and sun-warmed granite before the boat set itself into the swell angling around that jutting dome of headland, and the islands, the very land of home itself was sinking away behind him, and too soon there was only ocean, only horizon, only the boat and those upon it.

Bobby Wabalanginy felt very alone.

Where we going, anyway?

He leaned over the side of the ship, emptying himself. All at sea, he was being turned inside out. One moment the boat was in a valley between mountains of water, the next it was cresting a ridge and held against the sky. Despite the undulating swell, the surface of the water was smooth, and Bobby bowed again and again to what seemed a great fathomless eye, holding him in its gaze.

*

Many days later Bobby was very glad to get off the ship. Dr Cross felt the same, Bobby knew, even though he never said. The anchored ship pitched unpredictably, the waves reached for them, wind shrieked in the rigging. This was not the harbour at home with land all around like a mother's arms, this was like being a cloud out in the blue sky and sea and the wind threatening to tear you apart.

This was Cygnet River, Dr Cross said, where there were friends from his old home. Menak and Wooral will be here, too, from *our* home. Bobby smiled with him.

They rowed from a cluster of restless and anxious ships into the mouth of a river among surging waves that feathered but never crashed. In places it was very wide, and snaked so that sometimes they went into the wind, and sometimes with it. Around midday the wind dropped, and in moments began blowing from the opposite direction, and when they put up a small sail the boat came alive. Warm in his clothes and the sunlight, Bobby fell asleep against Dr Cross and when he opened his eyes the sun was much lower. He fixed his gaze across the wide, brown river on a spot on the bank not far from where a sheltering cliff towered above the water. Soon the boat nosed up to that sandy spot among rushes and paperbark, exactly where Bobby had been looking.

See? He didn't even have to write it down; just think it, spear his mind there and it came true. Dizzy, he hesitated with each step. After so long on deck he kept expecting the earth to move under his feet. But it did not. Not that he could trust it.

Dr Cross knew this place. It was like home to him.

Bobby looked for signs. Not many birds. No little animals. There were some horses, a cart and, further back, bigger buildings than he had seen before. And there, in among some paperbarks along the bank, a man in a kangaroo-skin cloak and woollen trousers. Wooral!

Bobby ran, and they hugged one another.

*

Bobby and Wooral followed Cross and his friends. Bobby was full of his experiences onboard the ship: the pleasure of it, the fear, too, waves like mountains rushing at you. He realised that, just as on the ship there had been paths where only the Captain could walk and even Dr Cross was not allowed to set his feet, so it was here. As they approached the big buildings it became clear that Bobby and Wooral were to rest among the straw and the horses. Menak was there, waiting for them. He did not speak with Dr Cross.

Dr Cross returned later with his friend to see that they were comfortable. He had rum, and explained that food would be sent to them. Tomorrow they would meet some of the Noongar of this place, and he wished them to speak of how it was at King George Town. He had, at Menak's request, brought kangaroo-skin cloaks from home.

Tell them, Cross said, how in King George Town we are friends.

Menak looked around them, scowled.

Winja kaarl? Fire? Wooral asked.

Cross began to explain, but then saw that despite the straw, there was a fireplace and chimney. He lit the fire himself and left. Wooral swept a small space of the earthen floor clear. So they had a small fire, were out of the wind, and had a roof if it rained. Food was sent to them and, although they would have liked more, they were content just to be together, and spent much of the night talking and getting to know the horses, too. Making a home.

Wooral and Menak's experience of the sea voyage had been quite different to Bobby's. They passed over it quickly, but the problem had been the weather, and their clothing had become wet. They'd wished to anoint themselves with oil to keep off the chill, but there wasn't much so they had taken whale oil from the lamps. Wooral did most of the talking and then sang some of their old songs, their stories of journeys and transformation, and individuals returning home as heroes. He reported he did not like it here.

They keep us at a distance, are so cold and stand away.

Bobby had never known Menak so quiet, so sullen.

Hungry as they were, they saved some of the lard from the mutton to rub into their skin, because without it they knew the clothing they'd be given would not keep them warm once it became damp, not if the sun was hidden and the wind kept blowing so strongly. Even now a dry wind was moaning around the chimney. They built up the fire, reassured by its cough and lulled by the soft chatter of its many tongues; if they were to meet these strangers tomorrow, it was as well they went with Dr Cross and his friends with their guns.

*

The morning was hot. Better even to be naked, but since this was ceremony, they draped the kangaroo-skin cloaks over their shoulders, letting the breeze find its way across their flesh that seemed so strangely tender and naked without oil and ochre.

With the white men, they followed an earthen path broken up and crossed by wheel tracks and the hard feet of horses and sheep and scattered with horse and bullock shit like that of giant emus. There were many footprints: bare feet, not boots. The camp Cross had told them about must be up ahead, but there were no footprints they recognised.

Bobby was surprised to see so few signs of birds and wallabies in such a place, although there were plenty of yams: enough to feed many people and they would soon be ready for digging. He wondered why fire had not yet been put through here. When they saw the camp they stopped so the strangers could make their way over once their presence was noted, but Cross and his friend kept walking.

Bobby felt isolated and very discourteous. Menak sat on the ground, on a small rise so that he would be seen from the strangers' camp. They might have followed Cross and his friend, since they were the only people here they knew, but Menak said wait, and soon Cross returned to bring them to where a group of men awaited their arrival. They were also clad in kangaroo-skin cloaks and had spears, held in the proper formal way of greeting strangers.

As we would at home, thought Bobby. Wabalanginy, he said to himself. He'd given them that name, not Bobby.

Bobby hung back behind Cross and his friends, but Menak and Wooral strode ahead to the heavily scarred Elders.

Menak unpinned his cloak and offered it to one of them. *Kaya. Ngayn wardang didarak . . . Ngan kwel Wooral maadjit koonyart . . .* He offered a greeting, some words of where he came from and how he was known. The younger of the Elders accepted Menak's gift, and the two men each put their cloak across the other's shoulders, pinning it at the throat.

The others stood and watched, far removed and ignorant of how it was for the two men enclosed in one another's scent.

Wooral exchanged cloaks with another man, and then the two motioned Bobby forward, with words of explanation for his youth. Bobby remained silent as the men went through the names of families and lands between them, searching for connections. Though understanding one another, neither could quite relax in the other's dialect.

The men led them away from Cross and his friends and they sat between small fires talking. As the shadows shifted, they performed aspects of what they recounted.

An old woman embraced Menak. She laughed and patted Wooral almost like he was a child: pinched his nose, and held him playful-like. Her smile washed over Bobby like sunlight when he was cold, shade when he was hot. Bobby thought of old Manit, Menak's long favoured companion. It would be good to have her here now.

Nitja wadjela. Your friends? the old woman said, no longer so friendly and playful. *Tjanak!* Devils! Smile to your face but turn around and he is your enemy. These people chase us from our own country. They kill our animals and if we eat one of their sheep . . . they shoot us. *Baalap ngalak waadam!* The very smell of them kills us.

Not this one with us, Wooral replied. He is our friend. He needs us.

But Menak listened carefully to what was said.

Wooral and one of the other men took turns throwing a spear at a rolling disk of bark, using the spears of different men in the group until the disk began to fall apart. Bobby was surprised; the other man's spear struck the bark many times. They ate, and Menak, particularly, was given the choicest of what was available.

In the afternoon, Dr Cross and his friends took them to a piano in one of the huts, and the music rose and fell over them like a waterfall, like a wave that kept rising and yet fell so surprisingly gentle and made them feel fresh. The pianist's hands danced across black and white, and that hand-dance made the music and did not just follow the sound. They drank tea from small cups and sat in their soft chairs, and the talk all around them, the furniture, the spoons and cups: sharp sounds, tinkling. As is only right, Menak and Wooral sang and danced in turn; they didn't do the Deadman Dance, but. Too special altogether that one, and a dance for home only. Bobby explained a little of what the dances were about and sang some songs Cross had taught him.

Their audience afterwards agreed they had found it very entertaining. The young boy's command of English was remarkable—a tribute to the good relationships at King George Town—and he was confident and charming, quite precocious, in fact.

Dr Cross's words passed among the crowd: there is land available at King George Town. Good land at King George Town.

*

Cygnet River Colony was a strong wind blowing all morning from land, the rest of the day even stronger from sea. Menak and Wooral were rowed out to where the anchor-snared ship jumped and pitched like an angry beast but soon the sails fell and swelled and the ship was away on the wind. Shore was windy, too, was grit in your teeth and the terrible glare of white stone. Bobby stayed with Dr Cross and together they followed the long brown river inland among scowling, rocky brows back to the buildings and the horses and sheep and cows.

Bobby, a child-stranger at Cygnet River, saw people looking at him from a distance and caught smiles intended for Dr Cross. Sometimes there was handshaking. Bobby kept at his lessons and stayed in a hut, just as if he was Dr Cross's own family. Such a closed-in life made Bobby ill, and for a long time he saw the trees and sky only through the frame of a window or doorway.

He could not breathe properly, and the wind moaned with a voice that might almost have been his ailing own, circling in his head. He wrote down the sound, *wiirra wiiiirra wiirrn* . . . Sleeping, his thoughts and breath bounced from the walls. The paper of his lessons was old skin beneath his fingers.

Waking in the night, the darkness all around him was un-formed spirits pressing for his attention and reaching, ready to snatch him away to where he'd never get home again. Sometimes Dr Cross's kindly face floated before him, a lock of red hair hanging beneath his hatbrim, his eyes like tiny pools of ocean, his handkerchief at the mouth.

Bobby heard a repeated call, just two notes: Uh-oh.

*

Eventually, they sailed back to King George Town, Dr Cross's cough as familiar as the creaking timbers, the slapping sail and rigging, the ocean's foam and wash. That cough came on the wind, disembodied, like the calling of seabirds. That cough sought out Bobby, wound its way to him within whatever enclosure of the ship he had buried himself.

A man joined them on their return voyage, Mr Geordie Chaine, a tall, stout man with buttons down his chest and belly, and whiskers either side of his face. He had a wife and two children—a boy and girl—who the mother shepherded close. The children and Bobby exchanged glances while Bobby roamed the boat as independent as the first mate. Twins, the boy and girl seemed sufficient unto themselves and did not speak to him.

Compressing his lips, Dr Cross played the fiddle, and Mr Geordie Chaine skipped on the same deck Bobby roamed. The heavy Mr Chaine went up on his toes, lifted his feet and lightly stayed just above the surface of the deck, bobbing. Bobby had no match for it, had never seen a dance like this. He was still learning the rhythm of being on deck, the steps to take as the ship hurtled across the sea's skin, bucked and fell, tackled each line of swell, was caught and released by the wind, again and again.

The twins held one another, hand to hand, and skipped in circles to the music but they were clumsy, too. And the boy suffered badly from seasickness.

Doctor's cough kept on. In his sleep Bobby braced himself, breast foremost like a ship's figurehead against the never-ending swell. And rose each time, buoyed above that persistent barking breath but the long call, the searching wailing of the fiddle remained higher still, somewhere among the clouds the sail or wind or whatever spirit propelled them.

Dr Cross coughed. Dr Cross dabbed his lips. Dr Cross would bring his wife and family across this sea, to live where land enclosed a small part of this vast ocean and people had everything you might need.

Dr Cross coughed.

*

Bobby liked being on deck: the smell of fish-soup sea, wet canvas and rope; the sound of waves slapping, of groaning timbers, and oh his bare feet treading the humming boards as he was buoyed along, looking up and thinking mast and sail cling to them clouds we trail sweeping the sky across.

Sailors looked to the sky and sea, reading.

Bobby wanted to read all things.

Sailors went barefoot.

Bobby liked being barefoot.

Bobby was a sailor.

His language grew and his thinking shifted the longer he was at sea. Gunnels and galley. Thwarts and 'midships. Tiller and keel; shrouds, mast, sail.

Whales and dolphins slipped beneath the surface, waved as

they rose again. Land lay like smoke at the sea's edge, and then was gone. It formed and faded, reformed, rose and sank, as if not always remaining there just beyond his vision.

Bobby learned the swing of a hammock, how to hold a plate or spoon on a table lest they slide across it . . . and look! The water in a glass made a tiny horizon, tilting with the boat.

And the loneliness?

He attended to his conversation and lessons with Dr Cross, but the older man's cough kept him to his cabin and with no one to do introductions and help him make his way, few seemed ready to speak with Bobby.

Because he was a black boy?

Bobby pulled his cuffs, adjusted the buttons of his waistcoat. He rolled his trousers to his calves, simply to walk on deck like that.

CROSS

D R CROSS SAT AT HIS CABIN desk, quill hovering. The pen lowered itself to the inkwell, rose into the air, lowered almost to the paper, rose again. Not an easy letter to write. How to tell a wife he had not seen for years that he had retired from service. That he was proposing to make a life for them here in this most isolated of colonies. That he could not promise to keep her as she was accustomed, that she might join him here with their children of an age to begin their careers, because here there were opportunities unavailable at home. He had land aplenty, and to develop it and increase their capital they needed only energy and initiative. And courage. In his letter Cross didn't say he had those qualities, couldn't really explain what compelled him to stay.

He heard the sound of quick light steps descending the companion ladder. The door opened, a dark head appeared around its edge, pulled back. The door closed again, and Cross smiled as knuckles rapped the timber.

Come in, Bobby.

Sunlight spilled in as Bobby entered; it must have been some coincidence of the ship's angle on the swell, a door ajar upon the deck, the placement of sun in the sky. Cross blinked, smiled once again at the boy's enthusiasm, his bright and cheerful spirit. Bobby scanned the desk.

Later maybe?

Thank you, Bobby. I really must complete this. He waved his hand absently across the desk. Coughed. My wife and family.

The door closed quietly, the quick footsteps ascending. Cross's hovering pen. This letter to write, then another seeking confirmation of his land grants. He would explain to his wife that he'd resigned as military surgeon once the garrison had been ordered to return to Sydney. He had been granted land as per the capital he'd bring to the colony—thanks to his wife's recent inheritance—and perhaps having at one time been Ship's Surgeon to the newly appointed governor had helped.

His wavering pen . . . There were things he could not explain, even to himself. Past the middle of his life and having survived the war against Napoleon and the many years away from his family, why did he now offer them this risk? His experience and knowledge of the fledgling colony and his acknowledged good relations with its natives only seemed to diminish his personal sense of authority. Now he had encouraged others to come live among them.

Cross listened to the water rushing along the hull. Appreciated the cabin's low ceiling. Thought he might curl up in a ball.

SHIPS AND HOME

O H IMAGINE SAILING ON one of those very fine days on the ocean. Clear sky, sun and bright air, foam and bubbles at bow and wake, and taut, swelling sails. Bobby felt like a bird, rising on a sweep of air; he felt like a dolphin slipping easily in and out of the wave face.

The deck tilted mostly one way, and its regular beat at that angle put a rhythm to Bobby's step, a walking-uphill-downhill thing that, even with no music and no one singing out loud, made him want to dance. A flourish of limbs embellished the rhythm and energy of the boat as it fell from wave crest to valley; different steps were needed when it wallowed, or balanced on the peak of a rushing ocean ridge.

Dr Cross had his violin, and while his breath came hard, and he could sometimes not speak for coughing, the violin's voice soared and swooped, spiralling on and on with no pause. The new man, Mr Chaine, danced. A jig, they said, his feet springing up from the deck again and again, as if he did not want to be there at all. His children laughed and clapped their hands, and jumped up and down, too. And beneath all this the steady accompaniment of the wind, the sea, the boat's passage.

Bobby grinned, laughed out loud with the joy of it all; the bubbling foam in his blood, the salt air in his lungs, the differing rhythms. And now this jig. The shifting deck made it impossible not to be moving; the rhythm of it set his muscles trembling, gathered energy to show these people, this strangely dancing man and his children.

The violin stopped. Cross was hacking into his handkerchief, the violin and bow held out in one hand . . . Chaine was puffing and red-faced. Bobby let his feet take him, let the boat and the ocean beneath it set him in motion. His arms were the sails of a ship, the wings of a bird; his legs lifted him into flight, swooping, rising, swooping. He put his own voice to it.

A lone seabird, white, trailed the boat, following its milky white path from above. A group of whales came close by, each great glistening back a flowing arch beneath its spout of vapour. Bobby felt his own shoulders begin to rise and curve, his own form merging with that of the whale even as his little audience's attention moved away from him to them.

Over the shoulders of what had been his audience, Bobby saw giants each side of the ship, breathing. Dr Cross turned and Bobby, catching his eye, danced a little of that Chaine jig but there was nothing in it now, no energy. The whales, though, there was energy there, and this was a path they followed, year after year. A watery path that was hard to follow yet was that of their ancestors and his own, too, since he came from ocean and whales. That was why Menak gave him the story and the song that took the whale from east of King George Town along the coast to its very shore. The whales were close now. He heard them breathing, that rhythm.

The blonde girl, Chaine's daughter, asked Bobby the blackfellow word for dancing. He gave her the word all the sailors knew, from Sydney. Corroboree, he said, laughing. Oh, her very earnest face. The twins, Christopher and Christine. You know, named for Christ. Who died for us and came back from among the dead.

Then the weather turned, and the wind blew them to the shelter of King George where Bobby felt his toes sink in the sand.

*

Dr Cross folded a letter, the ink barely dry. The first recipient of land at King George Town, he was a man endowed with curiosity, compassion and—as was now being displayed, albeit so late in life—considerable ambition. He had written to his old ship's commander, the newly appointed, inaugural governor of the infant Cygnet River Colony and, having congratulated Governor Steeling on his appointment and foresight, immediately applied for a land grant at King George Town. His application detailed the extent of capital he had recently acquired through his wife's inheritance and, in arguing that King George Town become an adjunct to colonial headquarters at Cygnet River rather than be completely abandoned, he had outlined the benefits of the place and, in particular, his relations with its people:

> *They refer to themselves as Noongar . . . are very friendly and often assist the settlers, several of them preferring European frock and trousers to the scant kangaroo skin and a good house to the cold bush . . . the person who arrogates to himself the title of King of the tribe, Menak by name, and his brother, Wunyeran, who served more especially as interpreter before his unfortunate death, have often lived with me.*

This, his most recent letter, offered advice on the transition from military garrison to colony, and factors crucial to its success. First and foremost was its population, which at present was something over thirty people, fifteen of them soldiers, four with wives and children. One of the soldiers—Sergeant Killam, recently retired from active service—had set up a small public house. It was likely to be a lucrative business. Killam was also

pilot and harbourmaster. A ticket-of-leave man—Skelly—had
good building skills, and was likely to be in considerable demand. There were two other settlers, and a number of absentee
landlords—maritime men mostly. Itinerant sealers had proved a
nuisance in the past, but because of the depleted seal colonies
there were not so many sealers today. However, there were a
great many whaling ships along the south coast, and because the
crew of each was greater than the population of the fledgling
colony, there was ample potential for trouble.

Cross did not elaborate on his plans, save to say that he believed
agricultural development was both inevitable and necessary, and
could only be achieved with the assistance of the natives. The
real problems of the colony centred not so much on its small
population, as on its character. The colony needs people, wrote
Cross in a sudden rush, who are willing to explore the surrounding country and able to rise above torpor and timidity so
that they might . . .

> *aid and assist each other, create a mutual demand and supply, and extend
> themselves into the interior, or with capital to beat the enormous expenses
> of first improvement. Security against want, and extravagant prices
> of the necessaries of life, would do much to attract the labourer, who is of
> paramount importance.*

This Chaine, thought Cross, although no labourer, seemed
just the sort of man the settlement required. Again, that cough.

*

Gritting his teeth, Geordie Chaine was already aware of the
shortage of labour. Cross had helped him enlist labourers, natives among them, but there were too few, and some had wandered away before they'd even begun. At least his sheep, having

swum to shore, had been shepherded to safety. Boxes and chests were still being carried across the white sand to the edge of the grove of peppermint trees.

Watching his cargo pile higher, Chaine noticed two natives, both in European clothing, reclining in the shade of the peppermint trees. He moved his vantage point so that he could keep an eye on the man and boy as the unloading of his property continued. The sun glinted from a wall mirror being carried ashore and the boy ran from his older companion to wait a few steps ahead and waved at his reflection as it went past. He ran a few steps further, repeated the performance and then, laughing and tumbling, came back to his spot in the shade. Chaine recognised him as the boy who'd danced on the ship. And just then his own children, Christine and Christopher, along with another young child—the daughter of one of the settlers probably— ran up to the natives, offering something from their cupped hands. The native boy became very animated and theatrical, made a great show of tossing whatever it was they had given him into his mouth, chewing and swallowing in such an exaggerated fashion that the children squealed and clapped with delight. The little dog barked and might have snapped, but a gesture from the man made it sit quivering on its haunches.

A woman appeared, grabbed her child's hand and hauled her away. The boy from the ship turned to the approaching Chaine and shrugged his shoulders. Surprised that his attention had been noticed, Chaine was surprised a second time when the boy held out his hands, palms up and with his fingers closed. Chaine paused. His children held their hands clasped before them and could barely suppress their laughter. The native boy opened one hand. A golden beetle sat on his palm. Looking Chaine in the face, the boy put the beetle into his mouth, and swallowed. Christopher and Christine shrieked, Oh Papa! Giggled. Then the boy opened his other hand and offered Chaine the second golden beetle.

Chaine swallowed it with barely a grimace.

Man and boy grinned. Geordie Chaine gave them a nod, took his son and daughter in hand, and walked away.

*

A day, two days passed and still the unloading of the Chaine family's belongings had not been completed. A horse cantered past as Chaine strode away from the harbour, and he cursed the boy who'd been riding to and fro most of the morning with just a basket or small bundle under one arm.

The horse lifted its tail, and Chaine altered his path ever so slightly.

There were only a handful of buildings in the settlement, none could be called substantial, and Cross's hut seemed ready to collapse. Two lengths of rough bush timber propped up a flaky wall and Chaine, concerned at its frailty, hesitated as he was about to knock, and instead called out.

Dr Cross!

The man was barefoot. Without embarrassment, Cross explained the hut's construction: layers of white clay worked into dry twigs of wattle shrub formed the walls, while the roof was made of slats of local timber. They had used bark initially, he said, but she-oak—*casuarina*, in an aside—was more permanent and quite attractive. Chaine agreed it had a humble charm; the roof had weathered grey on the outside, but inside remained a warm, honey colour.

This fireplace, said Cross from the hearth, was built from bricks manufactured on site and local granite. My friends among the natives sleep here, he said, hands opening and indicating the hearth and adjoining floor almost as if he were scattering petals.

It must at times be hard to maintain your feet, said Chaine, for the room was small.

Cross smiled.

There was something of resignation in his smile, thought Geordie Chaine. Something of regret?

They have entrusted me with a child, a boy, Cross continued, although in truth the boy comes and goes as he pleases. He is family, so Wunyeran told me, but whether nephew or some relation more distant I do not know. Almost everyone seems related, in one way or another. Even to birds and animals, and plants and things in the sea.

The boy aboard ship? asked Chaine. I've seen him since. He's helped with my stores.

Cross nodded. It's their custom to have uncles (though they use the term more liberally than might we) oversee a young boy's education. Wabalanginy is the name he goes by, although my tongue cannot do the sound justice.

Chaine did not attempt to say the name. And it means? he asked.

Something to do with 'all of us playing together', so far as I can tell. He is a creative boy, of that there is no doubt, and I suspect has wider talents still.

Quite suddenly they shifted to the problem of labour, especially acute now the prisoners were gone. One, whose term had expired, remained. They would have to pay for his labour.

He is a skilful worker, said Cross. Though there may be other possibilities. The natives are happy to bring firewood and will accept food—ship's biscuits—as payment. They like rice, too. And treacle.

They serve as labourers? asked Chaine.

In time, I believe.

As he took his leave of Cross, the cheerful nod and hello of an approaching native caught Chaine by surprise. The man was quite elegantly dressed, despite his bare feet, and he and Cross greeted one another with the warmth of long acquaintance. Chaine hurried away, and then, remembering he had previously met the man, turned his head to look. The two were already deep in conversation, and had no interest in him.

Menak handed his clothes to Cross, took on his kangaroo-skin cloak and hair belt and, walking along the path which led from the settlement, paused where a couple of men were widening an old and narrow path. As he studied their work one of the men clicked his fingers, trying to entice the dog. The dog looked to Menak, who gave the men a nod, and continued on his way.

Feeling their gaze on his back, Menak smiled. His thoughts flitted from one thing to another; the phrase 'Man Beetle Ate' recurred again and again, and he played with the sounds and the structure. He thought, too, of his brother, Wunyeran, now dead and gone, and of his good friend Dr Cross. In his heart he was glad there were no longer men in chains.

Ex-Sergeant Killam saw Menak halt, and the little dog wheel around and run to him. It slid to a stop on its haunches and then, at a gesture from the man, leapt into his arms. Killam and Convict Skelly met eyes. Skelly had yet to assert the importance of his labour to this little annexe of a new colony, and Killam was still in the habit of commanding him. Killam lifted his chin, and Skelly lifted the shovel.

THINGS TO DO

Months on, and Geordie Chaine had made little progress with his list of things to do:

Store goods
Find rental property (The Farm?)
Pasture stock
Call upon society (?)
Choose land
School children (?)
Lease island for rabbits (?)
Erect First Prefabricated House . . .

The list went on and on with oh so many question marks. Altogether too many 'firsts' might be required. People arrived, intending to settle and most—even some of those who nodded agreement as Chaine outlined the possibility of partnerships in potentially lucrative opportunities—sailed away on the next available ship.

Chaine visited Killam's public house. Not much more than a crude shelter under canvas with a low-ceilinged construction of the ubiquitous wattle-and-daub at its centre; its customers were mainly soldiers—Killam's old colleagues—and visiting sailors of one kind or another: a rough clientele. The floor was limestone except at one end of the bar, where a rough timber floor became part of a solid, secured chest in which Killam stored his wares after closing time.

Despite the trading advantages available as part-time Ships' Pilot, Killam expressed reservations about investing, let alone remaining, in this tentative settlement. It was rare for more than one or two ships to visit the port in any given week. The settlement could easily fail. Why, if the government should withdraw support . . . It seemed the sort of talk the soldiers favoured, but Chaine noted that for all his pessimism, Killam had begun a new enterprise—the grog business. There are opportunities, he said. He had put in a tender to build a decent road out to The Farm. If more ships visit . . .

Chaine invited Killam for a drink. Still under canvas, Chaine nevertheless had help and fine crockery. Good port and tobacco, too.

I see opportunities for a merchant such as himself, he told Killam.

The harbourmaster or pilot, Alexander Killam replied, is the first to know what each ship carries, and what she needs. And as you know, I am harbourmaster and pilot both.

Geordie Chaine made a mental note to add a schooner—a whaleboat, at least—to his list. And to cultivate Killam's acquaintance.

Mr Geordie Chaine asked about the natives manning the pilot boat.

They are surprisingly able, these savages, Killam told him. No boats of their own, but happy to use ours. Some with a fancy for the sea have already learned our swimming strokes. They are quick to acquire new skills, Geordie Chaine heard, nodding.

The wind came cold across the harbour, rattled the stiff canvas around them. Chaine dismissed his servants early.

If you want land, Alexander Killam said, follow the rivers inland to the mountains. That's what Cross did. Why Killam himself, if he had the capital . . . Cross must've been last to get a grant, and he had chosen some very good land indeed upriver from Shellfeast Harbour. It was his native friends who showed him.

Yes, an expedition could be arranged. Several of the natives are quite experienced guides, having helped Cross. They know where the water is, can supply your meals. You'll never get lost, and they'll deal with any other natives you meet. An expedition need last only a few days, maybe a week.

*

Geordie Chaine took time fitting out his expedition. Made another list, then another. He packed a tent-fly to keep off the heavy dews of evening, provide shade in the heat of the day and shelter from any rain. The old hands of the settlement explained that the topsy-turvy seasons of this part of the world meant rain could fall at any time. He packed a small axe and spade. Guns also. They were but three, he told his companions. Who knew how many savages out there might oppose them? He packed oilskins and tin saucepans for cooking. And tobacco and pipe, brandy, flour, biscuit, pork, beef, rice, sugar, tea, cheese, butter, salt . . . He wondered if they could get by without horses.

Soldier Killam (as even Chaine now knew him) came by and reduced the load. Not so much food, he advised. We'll give something like that—needn't be good quality— to the native boys when we return. If we're short they'll feed us out there. But all the same, we'll need someone to help us carry the gear. Your horses still not arrived?

*

Next morning, Geordie Chaine, Soldier Alexander Killam and Mr William Skelly set off together. Skelly was a stocky individual of rough garb and carried a larger pack than the others. An observer might have recognised that he was not much of a conversationalist.

Wooral and Bobby appeared. Chaine saw two natives, a young man and a boy, brimming with what he called 'animal health', their skin shining and their bright smiles dazzling. The man, grinning and holding out his hand as he approached, seemed particularly pleased with himself. Prominent scars lined his chest, and he wore a small bone through his nose.

This is Wooral, said Killam, and Geordie Chaine found himself shaking hands with what must have been a savage, yet one who spoke perfectly understandable English, and who gripped his hand firmly and looked him in the eye.

The young boy also held out his hand.

Delighted to meet you again, Mr Geordie Chaine, he said. His words carried Cross's accent; it might almost have been Cross talking. *Kaya*, we say. The boy would not stop shaking Chaine's hand. His smile was infectious. You like to eat beetle? he asked with that remarkably clear enunciation.

Chaine had some trouble with the boy's name.

Bobby, Skelly interrupted.

Ah. Chaine remembered him now. His tongue had no trouble with that name.

Yes, that a mooring for me, the boy said, grinning. And shook Chaine's hand once more.

Alexander Killam had brought along a set of clothes. He had none for the boy, but a prepubescent boy's nudity was acceptable. He would need clothing on future occasions, though, unless Killam was a poor judge of a boy's development.

Wooral sniffed the clothes and held them up for inspection. Boots? he enquired.

Chaine held the kangaroo skin Wooral had offered him awkwardly, fingering the small piece of bone used as a clasp when it was worn across the shoulders. Well-worn, oiled and softened, the animal skin seemed too intimate an item of apparel.

Wooral rolled the trousers to his calves in sailor fashion and, seeing Chaine nonplussed by the kangaroo skin, attempted to help him. Chaine shook his head and passed the cloak to Killam who, after some fussing, also declined Wooral's offer of help and returned the cloak because Skelly laughed, and waved it away. Wooral looked at Bobby and nonchalantly put it back on his own shoulders. Bobby put on the shirt, so large it could've been a coat, and bunched up the sleeves. Then, with a tilt of heads to indicate direction, he and Wooral set off.

Chaine, Killam and Skelly glanced at one another, shouldered their heavy packs and followed.

A distant mountain range rose before Geordie Chaine as he crested the hill that marked the boundary of his knowledge of the settlement. The mountain stood like a stage prop in a vast, grey-green plain—a blue cutout against the horizon.

Wooral pointed out a few thin and lonely columns of smoke in the distance as he led them along a well-worn path, putting people's names to them. Smoke merged imperceptibly with haze, the vastness of sky.

We alright?

Chaine had a compass, and Killam said the mountains were further confirmation; this was the direction they'd intended. No harm following Wooral while the going was so easy.

They followed a path, rocky and scattered with fine pebbles that at one point wound through dense, low vegetation but mostly led them easily through what, Chaine said, seemed a gnarled and spiky forest. Leaves were like needles, or small saws. Candlestick-shaped flowers blossomed, or were dry and wooden. Tiny flowers clung to trees by thin tendrils, and wound their way through shrubbery, along clefts in rock. Bark hung in long strips. Flowering spears thrust upward from the centre of shimmering fountains of green which, on closer inspection, bristled with spikes.

Sometimes Wooral addressed the bush as if he were walking through a crowd of diverse personalities, his tone variously playful, scolding, reverential, affectionate.

It was most confusing. Did he see something else?

Soldier Killam gave Chaine the names, pointing out not only peppermint and tallerina, but also paperbark, she-oak, banksia . . . Blackboy, he said, and Chaine saw the very thing in a grass skirt, standing on a hillside and silhouetted against the sky. Chaine admired what was called Australian mahogany, although sometimes the branches were an erratic, almost wriggling growth with little cup-shaped seedpods scattered among its foliage.

Skelly stayed to the path, looked ahead, did not contribute to the conversation. Perhaps the dry, serrated leaves of banksia provoked him; perhaps their bristling blossoms seemed manufactured, and not the soft nature he knew from the forests of the manor he'd once known. Perhaps he was at home with such bristling spikiness.

In the course of the day their path (and inevitably, as they approached, Wooral's singing) led them to springs and water holes, often concealed under overhanging rock, covered with a slab, or in one case filled with pebbles.

So it don't evaporate, suggested Skelly, surprising them with his voice as well as his insight.

Skirting a clearing demarcated by a recent fire, Geordie Chaine wondered what had stopped the flames so suddenly. A change of wind?

Woody flowers rustled, strips of dry bark peeled from branches, leaves rotated slowly as they passed and red sap oozed from trees.

It was a physical relief when the forest thinned, the trees retreated and the path faded as they entered a plain scattered with clumps of trees and a soft and fine grass. A continuing gully was marked by trees winding across the plain. Almost a cultivated landscape, said Chaine.

Wooral showed them where Dr Cross had slept when he travelled with them.

You seen Mr Cross's book, Mr Geordie Chaine? asked Bobby. His voice had shifted again. You gunna write a Journal of Expedition?

Chaine looked around, and Killam nodded. Skelly was already busy setting up camp. They carried their own shelter and food, and Killam said their guides were more than able to find each of these, wherever they might travel.

We'll continue in the morning, Chaine said. He looked to the mountain range in the distance, now beginning to retreat as the tongues of flames gathered his attention.

Wooral caught Bobby's eye. This was not like with Dr Cross.

Well fed, Chaine, Killam and Skelly toasted the success of their first day. Evidently, there was good grazing land to be had. The campfire flames, barely noticed, leapt and crackled.

*

Next morning, when their guides had still not returned, the three men decided they must continue at least as far as that clear, blue mountain range. They had food and water enough for several days yet, and surely it would take only a day or two to reach the mountains. In the future they would arrange for horses, and have no need of guides or assistants who were unwilling to carry the party's luggage and deserted them as soon as this.

No matter.

Unlike yesterday, there was no clear path to follow, save that leading back the way they had come, but the mountain range beckoned them. They could see its valleys, its ridges and peaks, and the open lower slopes inviting their tread.

*

Some hours later the mountain was no longer in sight.

They had come across what they believed to be a path, but after a time it disappeared, and they could see no further than a few yards in front of them. They were soon reduced to pushing, then hacking their way through dense shrubbery. The sky above was clear, but they had no view ahead or behind. It might have been a maze that held them, except there was no easy going, no way to take even a few steps without forcing. Initially they tried to steer by their compass, but soon resorted to the least difficult way (no way was easy) through this infuriating, frustrating scrub.

Hack and push.

They tended to follow any slope downward and so, pushing their way through rushes, found themselves knee deep in water and mud and with no choice but to retreat, regroup and— glancing at the compass—try to find better ground. They had no clear view, not even of sky.

All day they worked to escape the confinement of scraggly, twisted, pressing scrub. It was as if a great many limbs restrained them, disinterestedly; as if thousands of fingers plucked at their hair and clothing. Tree roots tripped them.

They climbed trees to get a vantage point, but they bent under their weight, or were too short, or had branches far up the trunk and out of reach. They had no clear sight of anything but the scrub which trapped them until, as daylight was fading, they stepped into open space. There in the foreground was the smaller mountain range and, further beyond and visible to the right, an apparently still larger range. The latter remained blue with distance, but across a small, grassy plain scattered with a few clumps of trees, the earth rose rocky and gnarled, a heavy mass against the sky. An eagle circled.

They had hardly wandered off course at all!

After a day struggling with scrub the party was relieved to have space about them, a place to camp and their goal in sight. They stretched out on sandy, level ground, and their gaze moved from the dying sun and burning sky to the disappearing mountain range, and finally into the heart of their campfire. Banksia cones, they agreed, burn like the coal of home and hold their shape, even as ash. Skelly reached out with his boot and touched one. It collapsed into the ashy bed.

Rain and a powerful wind woke them deep in the night. They tossed and turned in their bedding as their canvas slapped and snapped restlessly until finally, convulsing like a terrified thing, it tore itself from the ground and flapped away on panicking, pale wings. Soon, each man lay in a pool of water. Oh they *tried* to jolly themselves through, joking of the convenience of bath and bed being one and the same, and resting on elbows and knees with their backs to the sky, but still their skin wrinkled and thinned where bone touched the earth, the rain drummed on skull and shoulders, and their dripping noses only added to the puddle within which they lay. Voices drowned by the sound of rain, of trees creaking, of the roaring wind itself, they crawled to a single tree and huddled in their dripping wet bedclothes. Toward dawn the wind dropped and, shivering, they tried to relight their fire.

They were still trying as day came cold, with a grey and washed-out light. Drops of water fell in clusters from the straggly trees and prickly shrubs with a sound like tiny footsteps rushing and dancing all around them. The low cloud and misty rain thinned, intermittently showing the waiting mountain range.

A high-pitched barking pricked their attention. Bloody Menak's dog, said Killam, and they watched it scamper back to a group of figures who had apparently coalesced from the clouds, who wore anklets of water drops as they stepped across the plain until they stood in a rough circle around the three shivering men, their sodden bedding and smoking pile of twigs. Dark figures in short cloaks of animal skin moved closer to the three men and Wooral's hand emerged from beneath his cloak holding a warm and glowing banksia cone. The circle of men brought out similar burning cones from beneath their cloaks, and Chaine and Killam and Skelly felt the warmth enclose them.

Proper fire not far, said Bobby.

The warmth, perhaps even the company, revived Geordie Chaine. They waded through a number of small creeks until eventually the men, as damp as if they were themselves made of clouds and rain, were led to a shelter among towering granite rocks. Their boots crunched dry, coarse sand and a couple of fires warmed a natural enclosure of overhanging walls of stone.

You eat beetle, Wooral told Geordie Chaine, smiling. Now *bardi*, unna? He held out curls of seared meat on a sheet of paperbark.

With a nod from Wooral, Soldier Killam replaced his wet shirt and jacket with the shirt he'd earlier given his guide. Dry and warm, it was scented with the fire's sweet smoke.

Killam and Skelly slept. But Geordie Chaine circled the rocks of the shelter. Bobby followed the sound of his crunching boots. See, he said, pointing at an old cowpat which, having dried, had now almost disappeared because of all the moisture in the air. Nearby, Bobby indicated a hoof print, protected from the wind and rain by the wall of granite beside which it was so closely imprinted.

The little dog sniffed the cowpat, looked up at Bobby and Geordie Chaine and wagged its stump of a tail.

Bobby wondered if he could explain what his people were saying. Could he? Sheltered like an insect among the fallen bodies of ancestors, he huddled in the eye sockets of a mountainous skull and became part of its vision, was one of its thoughts. Moving across the body, journeying with the old people, he drank from some transformed, still-bleeding wound.

Bobby Wabalanginy and his Uncle Wooral heard the frogs and the birds singing and the voices and even the drooping leaves, and the sky told them there was rain to come, that they must be moving inland.

Wind and rain hide the hunter while the kangaroo scratches his chest, rotates his ears inward and looks away, awaiting the spear. Birds nest. Striped emu chicks appear. There are possums everywhere in the tall trees.

The plains run with water, streams joining old paths leading all the way to the sea, not just to King George Town where those people camp all the time now. Not everything or everyone moves that way.

But these new prints in the earth came from there, these prints made by the bellowing, blundering devils the horizon people brought with them. What they want? What they offer?

*

The Chaine party were shown a creek, and were told it would lead them to the coast close to King George Town. They never really left the mountains behind because they saw them from each hilltop and agreed that, although quite unremarkable in the country of home, they made a grand impression here, floating like blue islands in this otherwise flat landscape. They crossed plains of dense mallee and areas of long, rippling grass, and the creekbed offered knotted groups of trees and deep pools of water at irregular intervals.

Good for kangaroos, Wooral had said. Bullock, too.

There were many small, dry and obviously intermittent tributaries and patches of soggy, recently burned land. One creekbed, descending a rocky slope, became a sequence of small deep pools stepping from one level to the next. An eagle in a large tree beside one pool, its nest surprisingly close to the ground, returned their gaze.

Perhaps it was fatigue. Geordie Chaine moved in some other atmosphere: the air moist, the light thick and honey-coloured, and his breathing so shallow he wondered if the air needed to be eaten, swallowed rather than inhaled. The many and varied voices of frogs, the harsh rustling vegetation and the wind moaning in trees, the impertinent, abrupt birdsong, the improbably bounding wallabies . . .

He heard a cow bellow, the sound strange in this wilderness, then a high-pitched barking. Chaine fell behind the other two men. He smelled roasting meat, and blundered on until he heard someone coughing and then there was Dr Cross sitting by a campfire outside a small hut, Wooral and Bobby beside him, Killam and Skelly on their feet looking back over their shoulders at him, Chaine.

He scanned the clearing: a cow, tied to a tree and with a bell on its neck; a rough pen full of sheep; a tiny hut with its crude door of kangaroo skin. A vegetable garden. The strong smell of shit. Something tapping in the wind.

I've taken this land, Cross said. My land. The three at the fire got to their feet and Chaine and Killam shook hands with them all. Skelly stepped back, but the Noongar man and boy held their hands out to him and when Cross followed their lead he shook all their hands.

Bobby shook hands with Wooral, with Cross and Wooral again.

Skelly kicked at a chicken scratching near his feet.

A SINGLE HEART BEATS

A LEXANDER KILLAM AGREED with Skelly's judgement—agriculture was not worth the effort and trouble. Poor soil, the topsy-turvy seasons. The natives think stock is theirs to spear, and there is the trouble with the fires they light that can race across country like charging cavalry.

True, his pilot duties did not keep him overly busy; he'd been able to take several days off just now, hadn't he? On average, only about one ship a week came into the inner harbour, although others anchored in the sound and still more at other sheltered bays along the coast. That was the key. Already he had smuggled rum ashore, and sold or exchanged fresh vegetables for things he knew would be valuable.

There were plenty of whaling ships. Perhaps Mr Chaine should put his mind to that enterprise? Alexander Killam had the Sailor's Rest. Not that there was much rest to be had, unless you counted being dead drunk and laid out in the gutter to one side of the steps. But the whalers who came into the harbour found it amenable enough. The crew of a whaling ship pretty well doubled the population of the community and although they reckoned they found the settlement quiet, it nevertheless provided them with a diversion after their long days at sea. They'd delight in occupying one of the drinking houses, looking for excitement, a fight, women.

The Sailor's Rest was the sort of place you had to stoop to enter, and even having done so many would be obliged to remain stooped, so low was its ceiling. Its walls often failed to prevent a drunken body crashing through in a cloud of old clay and twigs. The air was usually a fug of grog and tobacco fumes, and thin shafts of sunlight striking across the room showed smoke coiling and collecting, unable to escape. Of an evening a couple of oil lamps and the open fire were the only illumination.

Its customers—rough men, soldiers and sailors mostly—were inclined to fight among themselves. For anything else, say for singing, and certainly for women, they'd go to one of the native campfires beyond the edge of town.

It was often hard to remember how you got there, as both Skelly and Killam knew.

*

Cross sent Bobby for Wooral and Menak, but only Wooral came. Bobby didn't know what was wrong with Menak, or if he was grumpy with Cross and all his people, these new ones who had arrived with the latest ship. Cross said, No matter, but we need a dance performed, a corroboree. These visitors are our friends and we want to welcome them properly, make them feel at home. But only you, our Noongar friends, can truly do that.

Chaine laughed.

A lot of Noongars were in the settlement. Well, at the edge of the huts, really—Cross's bed was closest—where the old people and women and children camped when Wooral and the other young men stayed with Cross. There was space there for the fires and the dancing. People readied themselves with ochre and oil and stories, and waited.

Chaine and Cross and their friends from Cygnet River arrived just after sunset. The fires were alight, the men painted-up, and people sat in groups, apart. But Menak and old Manit were still not there. Dr Cross and Chaine—those good friends of Wooral and Bobby—brought tubs of sweet rice. Wooral explained that this was for *after* the dance, and they waited and waited still for Menak and old Manit to arrive. That old woman, Manit, was their best singer. And Menak knew the best dances, the best songs. They knew how things were done properly.

Bobby and Wooral built the fires higher and higher, but still Menak and Manit never came. Cross and his friend sat down, and the Noongar were happy to have them there, but Chaine was rising up and down on his toes, looking around. He beat two of the boomerangs together, laughing loudly, and tried to get everyone to start.

The dancers were nowhere to be seen. And then people began moving, arranging themselves. Voices fell away as Menak and Manit walked across one edge of the circle of firelight and went to Cross and Chaine. Dr Cross was seated on the ground, and Manit held out her hand to help him up. She waited for Menak to shepherd Chaine, whose voice was loud in the relative quiet. The two old ones led the men to where they might sit, waving their hands at the guests so that they might also be properly seated among the group of people, a little while ago seemingly chaotic and now so orderly, organised by a combination of age, gender, familiarity and, it seemed to the alert Dr Cross, what they had to contribute. Cross was closer to the edge than the centre of those who were watching, Chaine and then the newer settlers a little further again, all of them grouped together at the outside of the circle. Menak and Manit went to sit with the ones too old to dance, but in a position that showed their centrality.

Now the young men appeared from behind some bushes, standing in a line just like in that dance from over the ocean horizon, that Deadman Dance. It was very quiet, the wind and the waves hushing them all. Wooral and Bobby were in the middle of the line of dancers, and Bobby the youngest.

Then came the singing.

Emu dance first: the men did it together, sat back and took turns, each man with his arm extended, bent at the wrist, and moving like the neck of an emu. No special dances, and not the Deadman Dance, though many were thinking of that one, hoping this important friend might lead them in something like that. And after the dance where men show their strength, standing on one leg, almost motionless but for the muscles quivering under their skin, Bobby started playing. He did his shipboard dance: the rise and fall. The boys caught on, bobbing like things floating in the water and the wave moving along them; and Bobby took little steps side to side, like on the deck of a ship. The men lay down, and Bobby walked across their moving bodies, like the boat in the harbour going from ship to shore. Walking on the waves, see? And then he was staggering side to side and mimed lifting a bottle to his lips: that dance the sailors do.

The singers tried hard not to laugh, and sometimes took up the rhythm and sound of some other dance, some safe dance, to get everyone back to a less cheeky repertoire. Time and time again they took the dancers back to the test of strength, one man standing motionless with the muscles quivering under his skin while the others stomped the ground, releasing all their strength into it.

Bobby improvised as soon as the singers relented, sang for himself until the Elders took it up, and in his dance was rolling side to side, awash on the deck. Then he was walking, plodding—all the young men joined in, a single line behind, doing the journeys Cross took them on, walking walking walking ever outwards and away. They gathered around Bobby like curious spirits as he plucked flowers and feathers, and turned the pages of a book. Faces turned to Cross, and he did look embarrassed, too. And after each improvisation, everyone still laughing at Bobby and his cheek, the singers brought the dancers back, and again it was Bobby everyone looked at, standing on one leg, his muscles quivering and jumping under the skin. Bobby stayed and stayed and never moved from that one spot until the singers finally released him. All that concentrated power, and he just a boy.

Menak was very pleased with him, everyone could see.

The singing and dancing stopped, and the crowd became like water again, moving and collecting, and Dr Cross as if following some tiny gully rolled away on his own.

*

In the morning and the days to come there was not a Noongar to be seen.

They are a mobile people, Dr Cross tried to explain to the new settlers. And there is an order to their movements, according to season and the laws of their society. They do not yet need us. They will return, he said, and later wrote it down as if for reassurance.

Sailing, sailing just the same almost on the land as on the sea, Bobby came back on a dry wind and found the water holes drying. He went with his Elders as they set fire to the reeds, then a day or two later walked easily to the water for the frogs, tortoises, gilgies, the ducks and swans. The wind swung and brought family from further inland, and fish came close to shore as if to meet them. There were salmon in the face of waves, cobblers and flathead against the ripples of sand. Possums distracted one another, male and female, and were easy game. Kangaroos and wallabies and quokkas and tammars, heavy with young, came to where the grass sprang up with the first rains after Bobby made fire.

They were easy, too. There was never trouble with food and shelter, and even less now that the sailors stayed longer ashore. Bobby had seen them back away from a wall of flames, and heard how they thought it a miracle when the flames turned back on themselves and died. Sailors, who should be able to read the wind.

Bobby waded in the shallows of the harbour, eyes scanning the sand ripples beneath the water, his vision at that in-between space, ready for the contrast, the counter movement, the shadow or flick of a tail that broke the pattern. He believed it was on an occasion like this, the same coincidence of natural rhythms—movements of sun and wind, of fish, birds and animals—that his uncle had died. He formed the name inside his skull. Wunyeran. Him and Cross like brothers. And Dr Cross? Dr Cross was coughing same as Wunyeran did.

Dimly, Bobby remembered his own mother, coughing.

Dr Cross's cheeks and nose were flushed. Bobby had seen blood on his handkerchief and a lace of pink foam on his lips. Dr Cross was a wave, breaking just a little, and what was inside and beneath was spilling out.

The marri trees oozed their red gum, were heavy with flowers.

A ship under little sail moved into the harbour, slowly, and anchored way over the other side in the deep water beside the huts. Where the horizon people stayed. Horizon people? Some of them been here forever now. And Bobby had been over the horizon himself, hadn't he? Again and again, had sailed away and back from between the islands, from where the sun rises and the whales also come. Him and Menak both.

Dr Cross's sheep huddled together, their collective back to the wind and rain. Chickens ruffled their feathers. And although it was daylight and he had many things to do, Dr Cross lay curled in the corner of his little bush hut, coughing. This was his new home, his homestead. *Kepalup*, the Noongar called it, because of the spring filling the river: the place of water issuing forth, water welling.

Cross's body shook with each cough and he pulled the rough woollen blanket more tightly around him. He lay on kangaroo skin, a kangaroo skin was his door, and he thought of his wife and children arriving before he'd built a hut big enough for them to live in, let alone to store all the goods he'd asked they bring. The price of skilled labour was exorbitant. And perhaps they would not want to live out here by the river, so far from the settlement.

They would not.

He'd made a mistake. How could he provide for his family once they arrived, and not simply fritter away his wife's inheritance? Yes, he had land—good land—and sheep arriving by ship. His friendships with the natives would help enormously, but there must be give and take, not all the benefit going one way. But his strength was going and so, too, his interest, motivation . . .

What had possessed him? Now men bragged of the land they'd been granted, and never thought that it was seized, was stolen. Why must it matter so much to him that the lives of the natives would be altered forever and their generosity and friend-liness be betrayed? He could not change that; what made him think he could do anything, or show another way to go about it when he would not even be able to make an independent life for himself and provide for his own loved ones? He had friends among the natives. He was barefoot, was dirt, grime and pale, peeling skin. He was cold, even though he'd greased himself as Wunyeran might. His fire gave off more smoke than heat. Had he the strength, he would have taken his violin from the chest where it lay among so many other discarded things, and played himself back to health.

If I should die, he'd told Chaine, bury me with Wunyeran.

And were that to happen he'd arranged that Chaine buy his land—they'd agreed on a price—so that at least Cross's own wife and children might benefit, for someone must benefit from this enterprise, this grabbing and selling of land.

Cross had thought to be part of a new kind of society, but his wife and children would be better off to never go aboard a ship, and if it was too late for that, to turn around and sail home at their first chance, sail back to money in the bank and away from here.

He was not strong enough for this.

The trees in the misty rain looked like drawings: trunks and limbs darkly shaded one side and their leafy, drooping heads dissolving at the edges. Cross drifted, buoyed by the rain, and moved by currents as if the heavy damp air was in fact ocean. He was far beneath the surface and did not know up from down as darkness moved in around him. The sound of his coughing was very distant and faint, although his body continued to shake with each loud, plodding heartbeat.

PART II

1826–1830

BOBBY NEVER LEARNED

L AUGHING AND LOVED, Bobby Wabalanginy never learned
fear; not until he was pretty well a grown man did he ever
even know it. Sure, he grew up doing the Deadman Dance—
those stiff movements, those jerking limbs—as if he'd learned it
from their very own selves; but with him it was a dance of life, a
lively dance for people to do together, each man dancing same as
his brothers except for the one man on his own, leading them. It
was a dance from way past the ocean's horizon, and those people
give it to our old people. Used to be an Elder would be on his
own, facing all the others as they stood tight together, shoulder
to shoulder, but Bobby changed all that. Still just a young boy
when he first joined in, he made everyone laugh, but there was
something about the way he danced that made them all move
back and give him space so that he ended up like the Elder, the
only one on his own, the only one standing against everybody
else, commanding them.

The dance? You paint yourself in red ochre, neck to waist and
wrist, and leave your hands all bare. White ochre on your thighs,
but keep your calves and feet bare, like boots, see? A big cross of
white clay painted on every chest.

Each man takes a stick about the size of an emu's leg, and sometimes you wave it about, sometimes carry it on your shoulder as you walk up and down very stiffly, sometimes hold it away from yourself with your arms outstretched. Everybody doing this together, exact same thing on the exact same beat. Everyone in line, and when you move—stepping a fast and even cadence, one after the other and all men moving the same—you stay just an arm's length apart.

Sometimes, even though it's a dance, you just stand dead still while one person out front moves his hand very fast, bends his arm at the elbow until the fingertips quiver beside his face. Then he stops dead still and everyone facing him does it the same, but all together. Over and over again, the many copy the one. And people clap—oh that is a wild and stirring rhythm—and they whistle. All point their stick into the air—like a rifle, of course—and bang bang bang like the boom boom boom of thunder or ocean swell meeting rock. But sharper, and the echoes roll on and on in the silence after.

A bang and a boom end the bright, whistling music. The neat, sharp dance stops. First time ever we saw that dance it was as if dead men had come back to life and, having lost everything once, were more serious and intent and all of one will. Boom, and boom again, coming from the sea.

But Bobby changed all that; he made the dance his own. One day when Menak and his woman companion Manit were leading the music, Bobby stepped out from among the others, stiff-limbed and moving jerkily to the sound of his own frightening whistle; a tune like the one we knew, but different all the same. The singing began to copy his, and all the other men—even the Elder—started to copy his actions, too, but then their minds went blank, their vision barren. They stepped back, they quailed before Bobby, went down on their haunches and clumsily backed away as he went among them, slapping playfully, hardly putting his hands on them, but laughing and grinning like a crazy man. Each man he touched lay down as if he was dead. Dead.

People loved the experience of it. To have had no will of their own but only Bobby's, briefly.

By the time he was a grown man everyone knew it had never been dead men dancing in the first place anyway, but real live men from over the ocean's horizon, with a different way about them. There was difference among them, too, as a grown-up Bobby learned too late, but this was something people argued about.

Different? No, they're all the same.

Bobby would get to know them well; too well, as many said. He knew and was a friend to men like Dr Cross, Soldier Killam, Jak Tar and Kongk Chaine. Not forgetting Brother Jonathon and Convict Skelly. Some names so strange that no one could say them back then, until Bobby showed them how.

And, as an old man strutting around with his boots and gun, Bobby would tell anyone who listened that he was there when they did the Deadman Dance that very first time. Sure, not even a baby, but everyone knew his mother got him when the whale came up on the beach. All the people moving in the water around the still live whale had seen the tiny shadow, that flicker in the water as the light died in the whale's eye, and the old man— Bobby's father—took hold of his stone knife and cut the whale. Even then there were sails upon the horizon.

Bobby said he first saw the Deadman Dance from the ocean, not from shore. Right there, and he pointed to the deep water close to shore where we'd all seen the whales come (but not quite like then, and not so many now). And Bobby was barely a baby in a hammock of possum fur slung from his mother's shoulder, his head rolling side to side with the rhythm of her stride.

Perhaps he was still too young to know that Menak and Manit were with him, or even to know any individual other than his mother, but Baby Bobby sensed the sails and while other babies could hardly see the world beyond their mother's breast, his baby fists clenched and clenched again trying to grasp something else.

So Bobby told it, anyways.

His little cluster of people had travelled with the wind at their backs, touching the earth lightly, buoyed by the journey their old people had made over and over before them. The place was beginning to shrivel in the heat, to shimmer at the edges, and withdraw back into itself: rivers shrank to a chain of pools, frogs burrowed deeper underground into silence, flowers and leaves withered as roots and tubers grew.

Smoke showed the family group's trail, their return to the place of their youngest child's creation and to this very centre of home by the sea's edge. First there was smoke, and then, much later, their figures crested a hill like they were sliding with no feet, like they were gliding on heat waves, moving above the ground toward the water.

The wind swung around as they walked toward their old camp, the clouds gathering in the western sky. The smell of ocean and approaching rain refreshed them and their arrival was like entering an embrace; a ridge sheltered them from the open ocean to the south, and white sand surrounded a circle of enclosed ocean this side. There was a bubbling spring, a river pausing in the sand dunes, paperbark trees waiting like old friends ready to help repair last season's huts.

Familiar.

But something had changed.

A collection of objects lay in a pile beside their old campfire and, even coated with ash, their smooth surfaces screamed. Such hard and bright things—Bobby would learn the words, we all would: *beads, mirror, nail, knife*—were passed around as the rest of the family arrived. Look, feel, smell them; and oh the sharp taste of steel. Some said they remembered them, from the time of the dance. And the footprints without toes.

There had always been a particular rhythm to their visits, and now this new pulse, at first feeble, began its accompaniment. More sails were noted, and more things detected: a cairn of stones, for instance, and within it—once the stones were dismantled—some markings on thin bark inside a container of glass. Smoke rose on the islands, as if a signal by someone approaching.

In later years it would be horseshoes, the remains of saddles, a revolver, buried food and bodies . . . But all that is for the future. Bobby's family knew one story of this place, and as deep as it is, it can accept such variations.

Gifts? they wondered. Then, these visitors? Where they from? Where they gone?

The wind, blowing to the horizon and back.

They danced like dead men, cruel brutal men.

But they were never dead.

Bobby Wabalanginy believed he was a baby then, and still only a very young boy when yet another ship came close and spilled people upon the shore. Bobby spoke as if it had just come to him and was on the cusp of memory, inside the face of a wave of recollection about to break.

Was it really Bobby? No matter who, it was a very young, barely formed consciousness, and watching from some safe place somewhere else.

These men had yet another strange tongue, *oui*, and Bobby Wabalanginy must've gone on their boat with his special Uncle Wunyeran—or perhaps it was Wooral or Menak or some other of those old people—because he remembered that first sensation of the deck shifting under his feet, rolling with the swell. And Bobby made that a dance, too, a small stepping shuffle one way, then the other, to and fro. Not quite the dance of strangers, not quite a dance of this country, people would smile as they shuffled and swayed to Bobby's strange tune.

Some of his extended family learned seasickness from another ship's visit, and something of its speed: how home could recede, and rush back at you again.

Menak and Wooral and Wabakoolit and Wunyeran all went on ships, Bobby would say in his old age, mouthing names that sounded so strange to many of his audience's ears, names of people no one else could remember. White people *asked* us to go on their ships, Bobby emphasised, and Wunyeran was first to wear the sailors' clothes. He went on deck of a ship anchored at the mouth of the harbour, and people stood on either bank calling out to him, and to the sailors, too, but they were deaf, they could not understand anything of what we said, we may as well have been seagulls squawking.

Silly things were traded—a shonky axe for a mirror, a spear that would never fly straight for a hat. Each party was delighted with the novelties, and there was strange food to be tasted.

Bobby Wabalanginy heard the stories so many times they lived as memory, and now he told them as if he was the central character: the gifts, the sails, the Deadman Dance, the whale and his mother, the shifting deck beneath the enclosed wind rushing them out past the islands to the horizon and back.

The most famous journey was that of Menak, a very wise man, said old Bobby, forgetting his own youthful opinion. And he would perform the story of Menak's deception and betrayal and revenge. The character of Menak's enemies was easily shown: he enacted their slaughter of seals (and it was this, the laying out of bodies, that had first inspired Bobby Wabalanginy's version of the Deadman Dance). As his audience listened on the sandy beach inside the harbour, not far from where they'd disembarked—the very place Menak had returned to after terrible days out on the horizon—they could see one of the islands, blue and distant, way beyond the harbour's entrance.

Old Bobby Wabalanginy remembered Menak the storyteller—the old man with his many ridges of scars and his high forehead catching the firelight, sharing his younger self with Wabalanginy, that most avid of listeners.

Bobby Wabalanginy shivered, because now *he* was the old man, and the young ones never listened as he had. Sometimes he was talking to himself, but even then he imagined that he was Menak recounting his adventure. It became Bobby's story to his listeners.

Faces swam back into the firelight, toward those eyes glittering in the dark hollows of old Bobby's face, and Bobby was once again saying he had been out there, out to the islands that—now that darkness had fallen like a blanket over them—his listeners could not see.

And if I tell you about those islands, Bobby said, you know we don't always see them from here, with leaves and trees and rocks between us and them. You know them as well as Menak did then, because before then he had never been out there to see the sun rise from a horizon further away still, and ocean all around and between him and this very shore where we now sit and where he was born.

And old Bobby would kick the fire with his big heavy boots so that sparks leapt into the air. Poke it with his silly old spear. Grumpy old Menak had been right, and it hurt Bobby to admit that to himself again. It hurt to be Bobby Wabalanginy the old man, remembering, but it never hurt to be Bobby Wabalanginy the child or Bobby the young man, or even Bobby Wabalanginy the yet unborn.

Menak always began with the scene of his return, and so

Bobby did too, telling of when he was but a baby and the black man and white man first lived together here in this very place and why he had remained unafraid and been so trusting.

*

Menak fell from the boat, waded in the shallows, stumbled across the sand to the grove of peppermint trees just as quick as he could because he did not know these people who had brought him back from the island. They seemed almost the same people who stranded him out there in the first place. He was confused. Yes, frightened.

With some distance between himself and the strangers, Menak collapsed into the burned-out hollow at the base of a favourite tree. The smooth charcoal, the cool shade and the scented carpet of dried leaves soothed him. He looked back from within the sheltering frame of leaves and branches at the strangers so busy on the shore.

Oh . . .

And as he spoke, old Bobby would reach up and pluck leaves from a peppermint tree, crush the leaves in his palm, inhale and pass his hand under the noses of his listeners so they might share the scent.

Breathe it in.

Oh, poor Menak, one moment lost in salt-grained sunlight, dizzy in sparkling blue sky and sea, then his feet felt beach sand again. He smelled these leaves, Bobby told his listeners, and his pulse come strong straightaway.

Strangers had rescued him, but it was also strangers that left him out on the blue island that when you get up close is solid rock in the middle of water and sky. The sealers took him out there and left him. They killed his cousin-brother, took the women.

Menak had been on boats before, but not so small as this one, and this time some magic had confused and weakened him.

He'd forced himself to swallow the first mouthfuls of that drink they'd shared. Their food had made him thirsty.

He'd trusted them, ate and drank and fell among soft seal-skins singing their songs and embracing them like brothers, faces so close that Menak saw his reflection in the blue eyes of the other.

He laughed as the boats left the shore; even sitting he felt un-steady, perched on the ocean's skin like this. Each surge of the oars unsettled him, but then he got the rhythm of it and when they put up the sail and the power of the wind hauled them along slicing the sea's surface, the bubbles and foam were laugh-ing same as the blood in his veins. His blood was thickening as they approached the island, but Menak sprang from the boat and onto the shore of what he had really only ever known as a blue shape on the horizon. Really, he should have been frightened, shouldn't he?

In truth, it was hard to recall exactly.

Somehow separated from the others, he was on his knees vom-iting. And then the women's screaming sent him rushing, stum-bling back to the boats. To where the boats had been.

His brother's body was floating in the water, too far from shore to reach. The strangers and their boats further again from shore, and the women with them. Menak's woman.

Menak's shouts made no difference, and the boats grew smaller and smaller.

The water around his brother's body was dark and oily. That body, isolated and far from shore. Ocean all around, out on the horizon; like Menak was, too. Like he'd been banished as far as the stars, banished within sight of a home unreachable.

Thirsty, he could find no good water and was vomiting again. Aching head, a furred mouth, a weak and heavy body.

He made fires so his countrymen would know he lived, and the smell of smoke and salt air surrounded him as he followed the body drifting around the island. Suddenly it came alive and began thrashing frantically in the water. Then Menak saw the shark. His brother's body rose above the water and for a moment Menak held the blank gaze, then the body broke apart and disappeared.

A sail grew larger, a ship sailed past. It was as if the sea, the horizon, kept spawning them. This one stopped well inside the island, held by a rope thrown splashing into the sea, and next morning it entered that gap in the land, went onto the flat bed of ocean surrounded by hills, and among the laughing women of that harbour, his home. Menak watched small figures traipse up one slope.

When a second boat nosed onto the beach of the island two days later he knew it was the only way he might return. Apart from those who'd stranded him, the faded men from the horizon had been friendly, but of course Menak was wary. He watched them stand on the beach, looking around.

He had no choice but to go to them.

The sail unfolded, snapped open in the wind.

It was an anxious beginning, but as the shore grew larger he also expanded. Brothers waited for him on the beach, and the boat landed him there and then sailed around to the harbour where the mother ship waited. There was no sign of the boat that had left him on the island.

But where is Wunyeran? Menak asked his people.

*

Where were you, Bobby, what about you? the tourists asked. Sometimes he would throw off his policeman's jacket and heavy boots and drape a kangaroo skin over his shoulders and—since they wanted a real old-time Aborigine, but not completely— wear the red underpants. At night he would set fire to his boomerangs one by one, and throw them into the night sky. As they came spinning back over the heads of the crowd, roaring with flames, the women shrieked and tried to bury themselves in the arms of their flinching partners who stood their ground and grinned in solidarity with the winking Bobby.

One day a statue of Wunyeran gunna be in the main street of this town, Bobby told his listeners. Maybe not in my lifetime, but I say shame on King George Town that it's not there right now, because Wunyeran he welcomed the first white people that sailed here, just like I welcome you now.

And oh yes everyone smiled with Bobby.

He looked around to see if any of his people or the constable or shopkeeper were among his listeners and then, hunching his shoulders and beckoning his listeners closer, he said, This is my country, really. This is my home. Straightening up, in a loud voice, he said, You welcome here. You know, Wunyeran never grew to be an old man. Soldiers buried him just like his black brother Menak told them to, and when Dr Cross died (Dr Cross was like the Boss of King George Town back then), they laid him down in the same grave as his good old friend, Wunyeran. A lot of bad things been done here—we won't speak of them now, my friends—but that was a good beginning.

The old man pointed up that slope, finger quivering at the end of his long, thin arm. That town hall rests upon the hearts of two fine men: Wunyeran and Dr Cross.

He dipped his boomerang in something liquid—whale oil?—touched it to the fire, and threw it at the ground not far from them. It bounced, flame curved in its flight and came spinning back, flames roaring. Even the men ducked and ran a few steps this time.

Wunyeran was a friend of everyone! shouted old Bobby Wabalanginy. He had no fear.

*

It was true Wunyeran had a certain charm, and an easy, soft laugh that was like an arm gently pulling you close.

People had seen the sealers sailing their little boat from shore and to the island. They saw Menak's signal fire and made smoke to answer him. But no one knew how to reach him. And then the ship—not a single-masted whaleboat like the sealers', but a *brig*—anchored in the harbour.

People watched.

Wunyeran went to charm them, see what he could find out. Were they enemy? Would they help?

Wunyeran was a young man then, the bone not long through his nose. (And Bobby would lift his head, flare his nostrils, show the tourists the fine bone nestled in his own.) Not alone of course, not on his own, not after what had befallen Menak and the others. He went along the beach to where the white man camped, and an older man and a baby went with him. They had no spears with them, and the old man carried the baby.

The baby would be all grown up now, of course, old Bobby said.

How old?

He paused, waited until all eyes were upon him and met each gaze. Oh, same age as me, exact same age as me. See, Wunyeran was my very special uncle, like we say *Kongk*, but extra special uncle is *Babin*. My special friend, and already I was travelling and going from friend to friend in my family. But yes, that baby is me, Bobby told them, and made his audience think of how long ago but how recent it was. He offered himself as a fine image of the passing of time.

See, he said, no threat in two men and a baby. Nothing to fear from little Bobby, that's for sure. Sure enough, to be sure be sure, old Bobby would say, winking at one or two in the crowd, Wunyeran was invited aboard and Wunyeran charmed them, amused them, never said a word about his older brother out on the island. Lot of our men liked to go onboard a ship then. But now look what happened! One of the small boats—not a ship, but a smaller one, a whaleboat—took a woman away, and left our men way out on the island. And what did Wunyeran do? He got himself onto the very next ship that arrived.

It was not easy talking back then; you shook hands and grinned, danced and mimed and laughed, but you never knew what the other fellow was thinking, not really (do we ever, dear friends?). Wunyeran was still learning that people on larger boats (people like yourselves) were of a better class, were a different kind of people altogether to those who had only a single whaleboat.

Wunyeran stayed onboard. That was his job, to stay with them, find out what he could. He made himself useful, even went ashore again with a man repairing boats and helped him heat and spread the pitch. Watched how it was done, because everything interested Wunyeran, that's how he was. And he kept very alert.

Meanwhile, as you know, Menak had come ashore.

Menak and a small band of brothers painted themselves up, as people do on important occasions. They grabbed their un-barbed spears and headed for the far side of the harbour where a smaller boat had landed and men were felling trees and collecting water: all morning people had been following the movements of these latest visitors, reporting back.

Menak's party was about the same size as that on the other side of the harbour. They moved off at a jog, calling to Wunyeran from the bush as they passed where he was helping repair the boat.

Wunyeran smiled at his companion, tried to explain that he must leave but he had so few words then, so everything was mime.

He placed his hands palms together against his cheek: I'm tired. Wiggled his fingers in the air: goodbye.

Calm, see. No sign of stress or fear, and no sign that payback was about to happen. But he quickly got out of the way.

On the other side of the harbour the man never even knew they were there until Menak drove a spear through his thigh. The man screamed and fell to the ground, clutching at the spear and groaning. He tried to drag himself away, kept his frightened eyes on Menak and clawed at the soil. Menak watched him, trying to understand. The man was frightened, yes, but how come in so much pain?

The man's companions came blundering through the bushes and pulled up short when they saw Menak and the others. The man slowly dragged his wounded self across the space between the two groups as they glared at one another.

Menak lifted his chin and snorted contemptuously. Turned on his heel and walked away. The strangers reached for their companion, and did not follow.

Good.

Menak and his brothers made their way around the harbour. They saw two strangers walking the water's edge, another repairing the upturned boat on the shore, and one of the speared man's companions running wildly back around the harbour shore to where the ship was anchored.

Menak made his way up the slope to the rocks above the spring. The sun was almost gone and, from where he stood, the water of the harbour was as calm as a rock pool. His eyes followed the narrow and sandy strip of land that separated the harbour from the less sheltered waters of the great, open bay until it met with the rock ridge to the south; that ridge reached out toward the islands to the east and ended in a bald dome of granite. A giant might need only one, two leaps to reach the islands from that bald headland, but would have to swim to get to the land way over the other side of the bay. So much blue, so much water and sky, and the island he'd been stranded on like a whale dying was the knee or heart of a great giant resting below the ocean.

When Menak got back to camp not so many steps later, Wunyeran put his arms around his waist, lifted him from the ground, and turned him around in a circle.

They talked and sang deep into the night, light from their small fires splashing them, shadows like pools in the silvery moonlight, and again and again their words led them across the ruffled ocean by a path of moonlight to the very island Menak had stood upon.

*

Several days later the boat that had stranded Menak returned and went straight to the ship anchored little more than a spear's throw from shore.

It might have been a battle, it might have been a long initiation journey he was about to overtake, such was the discussion and preparation, such was the trouble and ceremony Wunyeran undertook later that particular morning. People sang with him and the scented smoke curled around them as if they were mountain peaks. Then a small group of men walked down the slope, but only Wunyeran went along the beach to where the strangers camped on the shore closest to their ship. He carried no spears and his slim body was bare but for a kangaroo-skin cloak slung over his shoulders and a hair belt circling his waist.

Concealed, his brothers studied Wunyeran's approach.

Hello hello, he called, holding out one hand as he walked slowly toward the strangers, smiling, relaxed and trusting. Brothers breathed with relief to see the strangers lower their guns and shake hands with Wunyeran in the way those people did, and then lead him to a shelter made of sails set back from the shore. Two men came out and they too shook hands with Wunyeran.

He got into a small boat with them, and sat very erect at the bow as it rowed out to the mother ship.

*

Old Bobby Wabalanginy, telling this true story of before he was born but of what gave birth to him, wanted his listeners to appreciate how it was for his Uncle Wunyeran to experience, for the first time, things most of his listeners had grown used to: the boat sitting upon the sea's skin; oars walking across it; the bristling rope ladder; the slap of waves on timber, and being perched high above the water while the space between you and land grew and grew . . . Even paper, he said. Old people never knew what it was.

And if there were townsfolk among his listeners, as there sometimes were, they might have wondered about that battered and oilskin-covered collection of papers Bobby was rumoured to own.

Wunyeran was friendly, Bobby told anyone who listened. He charmed people. He was a *mabarn* man. People loved him—a bit like me when I was young.

The townsfolk would grin and shake their heads. Ah, that old Bobby. Always playing around.

Wunyeran hauled himself aboard and the men who'd stranded Menak were brought before him, tied with ropes and barely able to walk. They had stolen a young woman of Wunyeran's clan, and although she was someone with whom Wunyeran would normally not be allowed to socialise, in these circumstances he nodded to her, trying to appear calm out here on the ship as he thought of what might happen next. Looking at the commander, he pointed to her, tapping his chest to explain she is ours. The woman looked around nervously at all the strange men watching and, after the briefest of hesitations, came and stood beside Wunyeran. They did not embrace or exchange emotions in any way. But even the sailors saw her relief.

The roped men glared and sulked, curled their lips. Even without the evidence of ropes it was clear that they and the men on the ship were not friends.

The woman glanced to the shore, spoke softly and Wunyeran turned his back on the roped men and went to the side of the ship and looked down upon the dinghy that had brought him here.

Soon the woman was ashore, and disappearing among the trees.

It was some days before Wunyeran returned. He told how he met the man Menak speared, and he was like a friend now. It was hard to explain the food, he said. Some of them had tasted it before on ships, but other tastes too and . . . all very strange. There were many things . . . He tried to explain the tube you looked through that brought you close; the scratched markings one of the men made on something like leaves. *Book. Journal*, they said.

They gave him a good *koitj*, he said, and showed his people the smooth axe. He had chipped trees all the way from shore almost to here, and the blade bit deep.

The man scratching and making marks, Wunyeran told them, has hair like flame but keeps it covered. Cross. It was a difficult word to pronounce. Wunyeran was patient, explaining it. Yes, Dr Cross they call him. I slept in his shelter, he said, and accepted the admiration of his fellows. He is a man who scratches in his *book* all the time.

When Bobby Wabalanginy told the story, perhaps more than his own lifetime later, nearly all his listeners knew of books and of the language in them. But not, as we do, that you can dive deep into a book and not know just how deep until you return gasping to the surface, and are surprised at yourself, your new and so very sensitive skin. As if you're someone else altogether, some new self trying on the words.

A MOST INTELLIGENT CURIOSITY

*W*UNYERAN HAS A MOST INTELLIGENT CURIOSITY, Dr Cross wrote. It was a characteristic they shared.

Cross and his superior agreed their colonial outpost needed to build strategic relationships. We are outnumbered, they said. It is their home. And we do not know what is planned for us or how long our colonial authorities require us to remain.

Dr Cross's conclusion that sealers were responsible for the stranding—and therefore the spearing—was confirmed when he met with a group of young men and boys on one of his regular walks. He stood his ground, couldn't outrun them and might have got a spear in his back if he tried.

Wunyeran, he said. The only word of their language he knew.

They smiled and put their hands upon his shoulders. He thought they might still be angry at their companion being stranded on the island, and at the treatment they'd received at the hands of the sealers, but no, the spearing of the carpenter had appeased them. They did not seem to mind him or the camp upon the beach and—not at all frightened—were friendly and curious. The colour of his hair intrigued them, as did the nature of his clothing.

Womany? they asked.

He showed them otherwise, that it was only clothing, then stood, smiling, arms open, as they touched his hair, felt his buttons. He sat at their fire and took off his hat and boots. Then, standing and re-dressing himself, he turned and returned the way he had come.

Wunyeran was not the only one who knew some English and French. Nor was he the only one who'd been on ships, but it was Wunyeran who began to visit Dr Cross and accompany him on his walks. His English improved at an astonishing rate. Dr Cross was an enthusiastic tutor, Wunyeran a capable guide.

Like other learned men sailing the southern hemisphere, Cross had read the journals of Flinders and Vancouver, and references to friendly encounters here. Apparently, there had even been rudimentary trade. Sealers, too, were obviously familiar with the benefits of the place; in addition to the seals which sometimes made the rocks seem a thing of rippling fur, there was fresh water and sheltered anchorages. And it was sealers who'd stranded the man on the island some days before their own arrival, and stolen the women. When their man was speared, Cross and his Commander discussed whether to retaliate and agreed they must continue to demonstrate the difference between the sealers and themselves.

Cross guessed Wunyeran was in his early twenties. He wore a fine bone through his nose, a cloak of kangaroo skin across his shoulders and the belt of woven hair around his waist usually held a small axe or club. Sometimes he wore feathers in his hair or in a band at his upper arm, and he was inevitably coated in grease or oil. It must, surmised Cross, protect him from insects and cold weather.

Cross showed Wunyeran his books and journals, his samples

of flora and fauna and his surgical tools, and Wunyeran and some of the other young men began to sleep in the crude hut Cross had constructed with the help of the prisoners. He enjoyed their stumbling conversations and Wunyeran's playful spirit drew him out of himself.

The natives, who give themselves the name Noongar, are particularly delighted by music, he wrote in his journal, surprised that he was using his violin more than he had for many a year.

Cross formed the habit of a morning stroll to the hilltops above the camp to take in the view: he looked south over the harbour and, turning slowly to his left, saw the harbour enclosed in the east by an isthmus which ran toward him from a rugged ridge extending eastwards into the open ocean and ending at a granite domed headland. He continued moving his gaze left: two islands at the wide mouth of the huge bay, then again a rocky coastline. His eyes followed that coastline back westwards to another harbour, with an equally narrow entrance only three or so hours walking from where he now stood—the Shellfeast Harbour referred to in the basic charts. He could see the two rivers draining into it and a very small island near its centre. Beyond it stretched dreary grey-green scrub until, in quite startling contrast, a mountain range rose. Perhaps it was two, one behind the other.

Dr Cross imagined their military outpost as a dot on a map; although indeed any map of this part of the world was still most vague. Their settlement—its tiny population, its handful of huts, its barracks of mud and twigs, its canvas shelter for the shackled prisoners—nestled between two hills beside this very sheltered anchorage. At this time of the year, the sun rose between the two islands like a golden coin.

They were surrounded by . . . how many natives? Cross couldn't answer his own question. And they themselves were what? Barely fifty-odd people, almost half of them soldiers, and an almost equal number of prisoners. Three of the soldiers had their wives with them, and there were a handful of children.

Wunyeran often slept in Dr Cross's hut. They ate together, walked together, but even so their communication was rudimentary, and so not until after he had met Menak for a second time did Cross realise Wunyeran had been preparing him for the meeting for several days; was perhaps performing some piece of diplomacy.

They were walking together when Wunyeran put a hand on Cross's arm and pulled him up. Menak stood perhaps twenty paces away in a small clearing.

A physically impressive specimen, thought Cross. Middle-aged, perhaps much the same age as himself. His hair was gathered in a knob at the back of his head, and a tightly wound band circling his skull held a bunch of white feathers. Bands around both upper arms held similar crests and raised scarring patterned his chest.

Dr Cross hardly realised he was being manoeuvred toward Menak until they were very close to one another. Wunyeran playfully pushed and pulled Cross with an infectious good humour, while Menak was a picture of indifference, looking away as the two of them approached.

Then Menak turned from his view of the huts and tents scattered at the edge of the wide harbour to face Cross. The heavy scars on his chest seemed to reach out, his crown of feathers to shade them both as he held a hand across the shrinking space between them. Cross grasped it and Menak immediately pulled him into an embrace. He then lifted him from the ground and with his arms around Cross's waist turned a full circle. Eyeball to eyeball: one man in a cloak of animal skin, a hair belt, and with mud and grease smeared over his skin; the other with only the flesh of his face and hands exposed.

Menak released him and stepped back. A beaming Wuny-eran gestured for Cross to remove his jacket, then he unclasped Menak's cloak and slid it from his shoulders. He handed each man the other's attire.

Cross settled the kangaroo skin over his shoulders while Wu-nyeran and Menak struggled with the problem of sleeves. The difficulty was the tuft of feathers inserted in Menak's armband. They unwound the band, and Wunyeran wrapped it around Cross's shirt-sleeved arm, hastily adding the feathers. Perhaps Menak had lost some of his dignity by putting on the old coat. But then, what of Cross?

The surprisingly soft and pliable kangaroo skin hung easily from Cross's shoulders, enclosing him in the smell of another man, a very different man, of course, but a man for all of that. *Noongar*, he remembered. The scent was not so much that of a body but of sap and earth, the oils and ochres and who knew what else of this land.

They walked together, a strange sight: black man in a military coat, white man in a cloak of kangaroo skin with feathers on his arm.

The man—Skelly—who Menak had speared all those weeks ago turned away from the sight, and again leaned into the up-turned boat he was working on.

CONVICT WILLIAM SKELLY

WILLIAM SKELLY WAS TRYING to spread red gum along the whaleboat's keel. He normally used pitch, but there wasn't any. Gum wasn't as good; the first batch he tried had turned brittle and not lasted long at all. It had been Dr Cross's idea to use it.

The Indians use it, he said.

As if everyone didn't know that already, seeing as how they'd all traded food for native hatchets, and knew how the stone was joined to the wooden handle. Same with their knives. Some reckoned their spear throwers had a tooth held in place with red tree gum. A human tooth, Skelly had heard; others reckoned it was from a kangaroo.

Skelly hadn't ever seen a spear-thrower up close, but knew their spears better than he liked.

Pausing in his work, he fingered the scar on his thigh. Had *that* spear been launched by a human tooth? It still made him wild that he—a man innocent of any crime against the blacks—had been the one speared, and that his own country's fighting men had done nothing about it. But Skelly had to admit it had turned out well enough. They'd since had no trouble. Maybe this place would be even worse if they weren't here, with their parrots and jabber and nakedness.

But where were their young women?

William Skelly's sacrifice, his acceptance of pain and willingness to let bygones be bygones had created the friendship of white and black here. Even the Captain thanked him for his forbearance. You could tell they didn't expect such behaviour from a convict. Not that he'd be one for much longer, because his term was almost up.

Skelly believed Dr Cross, for all his funny ways, was a just man, and he'd listened as Cross tried to explain: the blackfellow'd been kidnapped, his friends killed and their women raped. And then they stuck him out there on that island. Of course he wanted revenge. We must all look the same to them. So William Skelly's forgiveness allowed peace. A convict turned the other cheek.

He had been like a Christ not only for these savages but for this entire community. Mind you, he'd still like to drive a spear through the thigh of the man who speared him. He and the good Doctor were on the best of terms these days, if Skelly could believe what his eyes and ears told him.

Of course, Jesus Christ was a carpenter, too. But William Skelly would bet Christ never worked with kangaroo shit, because that's what made the red gum easier to work and less brittle when it dried. The young Indian fellow that hung around all the time had shown him how to mix them together. He liked watching you work, that fellow. He liked *working*, and he kept coming up with good ideas. Because he did more than watch: at first he helped Skelly spread pitch, then manufacture a gum to spread across the bottom of the boat. Skelly was learning from him. The gum was still inferior to pitch, though, even with a pinch of kangaroo shit thrown into the mix.

Yesterday, when the soldiers brought back the boat, Skelly

noticed it had taken in more water than expected. Still, it was doubtful that even pitch would've helped this boat after the beating it took. Skelly'd done a masterful job, even if he was the only one who knew it.

He was proving himself a useful man here, was William Skelly. Anyone can wreck the boats, but who fixes them? Who here could build a house? Shoe a horse? Bill Skelly was a long way from the world he grew up in, but he'd be a free man soon, and then . . . who knows? Maybe he'd stay hereabouts. Lord it over these Indians. A harem and everything.

When you stepped into the water of the harbour, fish rose to meet you. The seine net caught more than anyone could eat, and so they divided it up: soldiers, prisoners, and plenty for the blacks, too, and they made sure some got back to their camps. Wunyeran and some of the others helped the prisoners haul the net in—the joy and energy they brought to it caused even some of the soldiers to lend a hand—and learned to row the boats. They were good at it, too. Young men, see? Life bursting out of them.

Captain even let them use the boats themselves. All of which meant more damage and, in the long run, more work for the likes of Mr Skelly. *Mr* Skelly. Not a convict much longer.

They think they have a better life, the blacks. Not that they're slow to appreciate what we offer.

RIVER EXPEDITION

THE FIRST COMMANDANT was replaced, and then his successor. They were not interested in a place like this, and allowed their ambition and the detail of paperwork and administration—even in a tiny outpost—to preoccupy them. Cross's load was light; the men's health was good, only threatened by their excessive reliance on rum. There were few prisoners, and if they escaped where would they go, anyway? The soldiers' boredom fed their fondness for the grog.

Meanwhile, Cross's own authority grew. He arranged it so that Wunyeran and his brothers not only had use of a boat, but men to accompany them, too. Ever lively, Wunyeran and his brothers took their turn rowing and even mastered the sails. Only Menak preferred to sit, staring at their destination with a telescope whenever one was available, allowing others to oversee the mechanics of arrival.

The boat left the harbour and headed toward the great bald dome of granite at the end of the headland and, watching, Menak saw the smoke of their hunting drift toward the islands and colour the sunlight, merge into the blue sky, the sea, become part of the salt haze . . .

* * *

Wunyeran returned at day's end with fresh meat for Cross, and for the soldiers and prisoners, too. Rum-fed, the red eye and scurvy skin of salt beef and ship's biscuits damned them in a land of abundant good food. Fretting for their diet, Cross recognised that Wunyeran's people were physically fit, supple and strong. And if their tools were less developed, their ability to adopt anything new was obvious.

In return for lending the boat, Cross gained fresh food and a sound relationship with several Noongar individuals. The garrison sat upon their land, but Cross knew of no adequate authority structures to allow a negotiation between nations. And those were not his instructions—that was not his business—he believed the garrison was no more than an insurance card against the French, and would very likely be abandoned.

Dr Cross planned an exploratory expedition along one of the rivers which very likely led to the mountains he could make out from the top of the hills shadowing the garrison. Wunyeran suggested they take the whaleboat around the coast to that second landlocked harbour into which both rivers emptied. Cross had looked over the land between, but had not in fact actually walked it.

They slipped from the narrow channel of the first harbour and, with a fine southerly wind, were soon in the equally narrow entrance to the second harbour, with its white sandy beaches all around. Cross had pored over the journals of maritime explorers of earlier decades, and Wunyeran had recounted going aboard ships. Now he pointed out the bountiful oysters that had so pleased the sailors, laughing again at the thought that people could eat such things.

Yes, he agreed, the sailors chopped down trees for their ships. He pronounced the last sentence proudly. The sound 'sh' still occasionally gave him trouble. 'S', too, was awkward.

Shellfeast Harbour was extensive and shallow, fed by two slow and meditative rivers. The relatively deep water of its entrance tortuously wound its narrow way to the river mouth, at times barely deep enough to keep them afloat. They rowed leisurely, surrounded by very shallow water. Stingrays glided away from their approach and merged with other dark shapes beneath the ripples. In the distance across the wide basin of yellow and blue water, a man stood motionless, spear poised. No one in the boat commented.

The expanse of water began to narrow and, despite the rising tide, several intricate, interlocking lines of stone clearly reached from the sandy shore to their right—the fish traps reported in the ship's journals. A few black figures stepping within the rocky pattern raised their hands in answer to the wave of those in the boat. Cross asked Wunyeran about them, but his answers seemed curt—dismissive of either the question or the individuals searching the traps—Cross was not sure which.

Nighttime, plenty fish.

They had entered the river, at first so wide that the trees could not shade its entire width even early or late in the day, but it soon narrowed and the trees closed and the water grew dark. They came to a stone weir beyond which the boat could not continue. Cross examined it carefully. Man-made? There was a path on either bank, each side of the stones. Cross decided the boat could return to the garrison, and that he and Wunyeran would continue on foot and follow the river or these paths and return over land within a few days.

The soldiers rowed away, and one of them kept his eyes upon where Wunyeran and Cross had been only a moment before.

SOLDIER ARTHUR KILLAM

THE RUM BURNED and cleared a little space in Arthur Killam's consciousness. He'd had his fill of salt beef and peas and his muscles were heavy from the long row back from Shellfeast Harbour.

Oysters, yuck. Like eating snot. He couldn't eat them, and nor could the blacks, which was a tribute to their good sense. Perhaps there was hope for the sawbones and his ideas of civilising them, after all.

Killam had been surprised at Dr Cross's confidence in finding his way back on foot, and by his trust in Wunyeran. The blackfella would slow him down, though, in Killam's opinion, since none of the natives liked to walk too far without a meal or a rest. On top of all that, Wunyeran would still be sore from their race up the hill and back. Killam was sore, too, but the memory made him smile. He'd won. Come to think of it, maybe Wunyeran wasn't as sore, since he'd walked up the hill to save his strength, and only ran downhill, whereas Killam had made a big effort running up, and took it easy for a bit as he began the run back down. He was spent at the finish. Everyone expected the black to win, but it was Killam by almost a minute. He'd made a tidy pile betting on himself. And it was good for morale. Even the Captain had congratulated him on his effort, even though he was unhappy with a race that could have ended with one of his most valuable soldiers breaking a leg. Never thought of that, conceded Arthur Killam. But then, no one had expected him to win, either.

Wunyeran was a cocky blighter. No sense of time, no plan to win, just assumed victory would be his. It was like the tortoise and the hare, 'cept here, they got no hare and they eat their tortoise (like everything else) soon as they sight him.

Arthur Killam's stomach heaved at the thought of fresh meat. He'd never tried tortoise, sometimes ate fish, but the gamey taste of kangaroo was something he could do without.

Sea captains liked their men to get fresh food, vegetables especially. Not that this place was much help in that regard, having very little in the way of gardens. Not yet, anyway, but Arthur Killam was taking responsibility for that. He got the prisoners to do most of the heavy work, but still did a lot himself; liked to be in charge of the harvesting, especially. Potatoes grew well enough, and beans. Fish guts as fertiliser helped.

It wasn't soldiers' work, but he needed something to occupy him. Life could be boring here. There was no fighting, and although he'd wager they'd make short work of the natives, it was also true that they were heavily outnumbered, and once they moved away from their barracks it might be a very different thing. You couldn't see some of these people unless they wanted you to, and the way they hunted showed no shortage of skill—not just in tracking and using a spear or club, but also in teamwork and their use of fire. Killam had seen them casually clubbing kangaroos and wallabies that, blind and confused, rushed from the flames. Fire in their hands moved faster than mounted infantry, and could be more devastating. In his mind's eye he saw soldiers staggering back before the onslaught of fire until the harbour was at their backs, and then armed natives standing up in the shallows where they'd concealed themselves beneath the water.

Fortunately, the prevailing wind was from the south.

At least the natives didn't have guns, though Killam would wager they'd like 'em.

WHERE AND WHO?

BARELY BIDDING THE MEN FAREWELL, Dr Cross turned and followed Wunyeran along an earthen path beside the river. Almost immediately he stopped. Two paths diverged from this one that led from the river crossing—one continued across a patch of quite recently burned earth until it disappeared among the trees; the other led inland along the riverbank. Wunyeran took him by the hand and, chuckling to himself (at my indecision? wondered Cross), led him around soggy ground surrounding some rocks on the riverbank, and away from a spring that fed into where the river was divided by rocks to form what appeared to be a lock such as characterised the rivers of home. Perhaps another fish trap like those they had earlier seen.

The river diminished quickly, and after an hour or two of walking they came to a distinct rocky section, with boulders arranged on each bank, where thin streams ran from water hole to water hole, stepping down a steep slope. At the bottom, beside the largest pool, a tree held an eagle's nest which, despite the height of the tree, seemed surprisingly low to the ground. Not far beyond that a small tributary branched east.

Later in the afternoon, they emerged from shade through

shafts of sunlight and into a clearing. Cross saw a Noongar on the gradual slope leading from one bank, surrounded by small and fresh green shoots springing from fire-blackened earth.

The two men embraced, each putting his arms around the other's waist and lifting him clear off the ground. Turning in a small circle, locked together, their voices were a melody of goodwill.

The newcomer, younger than Wunyeran and probably not long out of adolescence, looked at Cross curiously. Their speech reminded him of the sounds of the river from earlier in their journey.

Wooral, Wunyeran said by way of introduction.

Their new companion turned away from Cross, and a woman emerged from the trees and shrubbery.

Birtang, added Wunyeran.

Mrs Wooral—as Cross named her in his journal—was older than her husband, and seemed a jumble of animal fur with human head, arms and legs. An unusually long cloak hung from her shoulders. Standing apart from their mother, two very young children, a boy and a girl, studied Cross with undisguised curiosity.

*

Me! Me again! Old Bobby Wabalanginy told his listeners. My sister and myself. Not that Wooral was my father, no. And my poor mother passed away soon after like so many of us did then, from all the sickness. True, Wooral was very young and lucky to have a woman like my mother. But read the histories; I am the only Noongar alive today who is mentioned in Dr Cross's papers, published in your own mother country. *Your* mother country, he said to the tourists, not mine because my country is here, and belonged to my father, and his father, and his father before him, too. But to look at me now you wouldn't think that, not with all these people in their fine houses and noses in their rum who got no time to thank me or share what they have . . . They don't know me. They look and think they do, but no. But I know them, and all those pioneers they love and thank, I know them, too. Knew them. They were my friends.

Me and my people . . . My people and I (he winked) are not so good traders as we thought. We thought making friends was the best thing, and never knew that when we took your flour and sugar and tea and blankets that we'd lose everything of ours. We learned your words and songs and stories, and never knew you didn't want to hear ours . . .

But yes, of course, you're right, you're right; my life is good, and I am happy to talk to everyone, and welcome you as friends. The same God and the same good King looks over us all, does he not, my fellow subjects?

*

Bobby Wabalanginy's sister, Binyan, was a bit older than him and already promised to an old man.

Cross was flattered to meet the mother of Bobby and Binyan. He'd never been allowed so close to any other than very elderly women. Mrs Wooral, though senior to her man, was not elderly.

And what was in the other bag she carried? Wunyeran put Cross's question to Wooral rather than the woman. They stopped and she withdrew a banksia cone from somewhere within her cloak and bags.

She was, Cross saw, quite naked beneath the soft fur draped across her. She was, Cross confirmed, not long past the prime of life.

The banksia cone glowed red as she blew upon it. A little smoke, tongues of flame: within moments a small campfire lived in the space between them.

What else might she have in her bag?

*

Old Bobby asked the question again and held up a possum-skin bag. What else would she be carrying, 'cept of course her beloved, darling baby son? But you know, he said, I never needed no carrying once I learned to walk! Old Bobby strutted and swaggered, an old man parading a boy's innocent vanity, and the tourists laughed.

I walked all on my own even when I was the littlest little boy. But seriously, what you think a Noongar woman gunna carry? he asked. Oh yes, she would have her *waanna*—the digging stick she could also use to bash any stray man, or any women who wanted to steal that beautiful little boy of hers. And, tongue between teeth, Bobby waved his stick and the tourists stepped back.

You *wanna* (he dragged the word out, suggesting the stick and an American accent all at once), you *waanna* know what was in her bag? Do you *want to* know that?

Old Bobby unpacked the bag as he continued his story, thinking of Dr Cross's journals which his widow had published. Chaine showed him the newspaper that published the extracts, and they'd read it aloud so that Bobby saw with those eyes and oh . . .

*

There was another banksia cone, a roll of paperbark. Gently, she placed a seashell on the ground in front of Dr Cross. Then a fine piece of what must have been whalebone. The others watched Cross reach for it . . . The edge of the shell against his thumb was as sharp as any razor. He smiled, raised his eyebrows, picked up the whalebone needle. He held each of the objects that emerged from her bag, returning them to the humble display between them.

Wunyeran gestured, and Mrs Wooral presented even more of the bag's contents: a tight bundle of cord—woven from possum fur—and some pieces of dry mud. Ochre.

The other three kept their eyes on him. Waiting? Cross ventured into his pockets. Extracting his notebook, he laid it beside the pile Mrs Wooral had made.

She withdrew what must be food: tubers of some kind by the look of them, and nuts and fruit, though not of any variety he recognised; also some frogs, and a lizard. The frogs were still alive, their legs tied with thin cord.

Cross stood up. Mrs Wooral returned the things to her bag, leaving Cross's notebook on the ground, and built up the fire. Then she and her man moved away across the slope to a separate small clearing. Wunyeran suggested Cross take off his pack and place it beside the fire. When Cross turned back from the sight of Mrs Wooral's lighting a second fire—the glimmer of its small flame, the glow on the tree nearby, her surprising grace—Wunyeran had gone.

He heard the chop of Wunyeran's axe cutting footholes in a tree trunk so he might step up to a possum's lair. Cross fashioned rope and canvas into a windbreak.

Wunyeran returned. *Koomal*, he said and grinned, tossing a possum beside the fire.

Ah, those paws, said Cross, unconsciously flexing his own hands. Blood caked the side of the possum's head.

Wunyeran built up the fire. Sparks leapt as he threw the possum onto it; the fire coughed, and Wunyeran rolled the body around to singe the fur and then hauled the disfigured carcass from the flames. The hands were curled tight, eyes seared; the hungry flames made the growing shadows deeper but for the glow of that other fire, and the occasional glimpse of a figure moving before it.

Cross poured himself a tumbler of brandy and offered some to Wunyeran, who declined. Once the fire was rearranged and the possum laid deep in the ashes, Wunyeran grunted with satisfaction and slipped away again into the darkness. His silhouetted figure approached the couple's campfire, the three of them flickered in its glow.

The moon had long risen and a large pool in the river shone with its light. The trees between the water and Cross were starkly delineated, the grass trees as if drawn with fine inky lines. Cross poured himself another brandy, savoured its burn. The moon, the light reflected from the water; ducks and other large birds flew above and splashed into the water so that its silvery surface was broken and shards of shadow and light jostled, trembled. Cross got to his feet, unsteady. How many brandies?

Wunyeran appeared from among a clump of grass trees, his oiled skin catching the firelight. He brought with him roasted roots and fire-baked cakes that, although appearing crudely made, were tasty. Cross offered ship's biscuits in return, but Wunyeran was removing the cooked possum carcass from the fire. Responding to a gesture, Cross passed Wunyeran the knife. Wunyeran packed the animal's stomach with its internal organs, and broke its limbs. Later, they ate, dipping into the juices collecting in the opened abdomen.

Why trouble with ship's biscuits?

Once again, Wunyeran declined the brandy and Cross, on an impulse, got to his feet and set fire to two grass trees close by. The rushes caught quickly, and the two feasting men were held in a red, flickering glow.

Like chandeliers, thought Cross, chandeliers held up for us. Like a grand dining room. He was staggering, not dancing.

Wunyeran stepped backwards.

He heard angry shouts from the other campfire.

Wunyeran slipped away.

The trees moved in the flickering light of the fire, moved around Cross in a small, shifting group. Approached, retreated.

* * *

They began next day along a path leading from the riverbank, the three men walking abreast of one another, Wunyeran at their centre and translating at least some of the conversation he ensured continued. Mrs Wooral trailed a few yards behind and came no closer than several steps from Cross.

Cross never saw them leave.

Around noon they came to another large pool, its surface a feathery quilt of ducks and swans pressed so closely together there was little water to be seen. Cross rested the long barrel of his shotgun in the fork of a tree, shifting to ensure it was secure. The bark fell away, showing a new surface, still of bark, but quite pink and raw. After so many hours of only the many varied sounds of the bush, and one or the other of their voices, the gunshot was like a blow. The birds rose on the great wave of sound, of frantic flapping wings, feathers and clawed feet beating the water, smothering the echo of the weapon's explosion. Cross staggered back from the cacophony of bird calls and feathered, pulsing hearts; the tumultuous air. One bird remained, splashing in a circle at the centre of the pool. Another, propelled by splashing legs and wings, escaped around the bend of the river.

Cross had flung off his clothes, was pushing through the reeds at the water's edge and splashing through the water. The bird called and called in the distance growing around it. Closing, Cross slipped beneath the surface: thin shafts of sunlight in the tan water, bubbles, the bird's legs working; his own pulse an accompaniment. Then, head and arms above the river, he was breathing again, was breaking the bird's neck.

He saw Wunyeran speaking with some people in the deep shade of the paperbarks. Where had they come from? But when Cross walked from the water Wunyeran was alone.

Cross was dressing himself when Wunyeran pointed to the rifle and tapped himself on the chest. Me shoot gun? His request was uncharacteristically awkward in expression. The river's pool waited, reflective, behind Wunyeran; the mountains rose blue on the horizon, their gnarled and knotted contours clear despite the distance. High in the sky an eagle circled. Cross—dead bird in hand, naked in Wunyeran's generous world—could not refuse.

A willy-wagtail skipped, danced, tried to entice Wunyeran away. He felt the weight of the gun in his hands, and when Cross went to explain its use Wunyeran grinned and demonstrated that he already knew. Because he observed closely.

The walking both tired and lulled Dr Cross. It seemed a dream when, just before nightfall, he lifted his eyes to a well-fed and glossy bullock chewing its cud. It stared right back at him from the grassy bank at the other side of a river which was now little more than a halfhearted chain of ponds. It bellowed (how loud, brown cow) then turned and crashed away through the scrub. The beast was in prime condition. Must've escaped from some ship, or made its way to the ranges and back, following the river. With such a well-worn path leading through it and rolling pasture at regular intervals, this was good stock country.

A day or three after their return, Cross, on his morning walk to The Farm by a different route than usual, saw Wunyeran with some companions. He was entertaining an audience of adults and children with some sort of performance. Cross sat on a log to watch, and to render himself less visible. He could not have said why.

Wunyeran was rowing, his mime made that clear. Then a pause. He mimed . . . It was hard to be sure, the distance and all, but it seemed he was miming someone writing. There was the sharpening of the quill, the dipping in ink, the turning of a heavy page. He mimed what seemed to be a hunt. It was not a silent mime—

clearly he was enacting what he spoke—but Cross could not hear the words and if he had he would still not have understood them.

Wunyeran put a hand to his chin, stared into space, again acted out a pen crossing a page. Now he was someone walking, and tired. Someone unsteady on his feet. Oh, it was a most uncanny skill he had. Now he was setting fire to something, to things at head height all around him. His hands showed the explosion of flames. He was writing again. He was shooting a gun, undressing and wading into water . . .

Cross got to his feet and blundered away into the bushes, making a wide detour around the group.

Wunyeran's performance of the journey was structured in the way of an expedition journal. Or was Cross imagining things? He knew himself well enough, knew that sometimes his perception of the world became very unstable.

*

Cross awoke under canvas, his tent billowing, snapping and straining at its guy-ropes. It was a very small tent, and only when Cross crawled from it did he realise he was on a vast mallee plain. He was still on his knees, forced by the wind to clutch at one of the tent pegs, and the tent was the tallest thing he could see and then it was as if the wind had him, was sucking him up into the cloud-torn sky and his little tent, shivering with the wind, was lit from within. He felt his own round face glowing like the moon, and shredded clouds cobwebbed his vision even as he drifted below them, drawn to the glowing tent. The wind had dropped.

Below him a banksia cone glowed like a piece of coal, the smell of strawberry jam oozed from the pile of kindling; these hints of home. But the Far East scent of sandalwood was in the smoke, and who might be in the shadows around the fire . . .

He saw himself hovering at the tent's entrance, like an insect silhouetted against a lamp. A body in his place, beneath his blanket, was breathing deeply; calm, asleep. The soft light showed Wunyeran's black face and thickly greased hair upon Cross's pillow.

Cross awoke in the grainy light of morning safe in his little hut. The white clay covering the thin walls of acacia branches and twigs glowed, he could smell the clay and the paperbark and rushes of the roof and just then the flimsy door opened, and he saw Wunyeran silhouetted against the early morning sky.

Come in, he said, and sat up in his rough bed. He was so very pleased to see a native, he realised. A Noongar. He wondered where he was. Who?

MEN AT SEA

ACCEPTING RESPONSIBILITY for the settlement's health, Dr Cross insisted a vegetable garden be established as soon as possible. The agricultural possibilities interested him, even though the current population preferred a diet of salt meat with no fruit or vegetables.

He visited The Farm at least twice a week. Strode straight up the hill from the sea in the early morning, pausing at the top to gather his breath and take in the view. Whitewashed buildings, the saucer-shaped harbour, the narrow isthmus dividing it from the sound to the east, and then two islands hovering by the horizon, white foam pulsing at the edge of the one on the right. He went across a granite scalp, and then wound his way down between boulders and wildflowers.

The men had broken up more ground, but the only one there now was the supervisor, Sergeant Killam, who Cross thought a decent but prissy fellow. The man had a passion for gardening, and had been relieved from other duties in the hope he might help provide fresh vegetables.

We got the bull, Killam said.

Some nights ago, woken from sleep by a Minotaur's bellowing,

Cross had rushed to the door of his flimsy hut as a solid shadow sped past in the darkness. He remembered the beast's warm breath and the ground shaking beneath his feet. He remembered its great bulk. The few soldiers pursuing it passed by like ghosts: pale, insubstantial, their footsteps barely detectable.

Killam showed him the enclosure built to hold the animal and Cross was surprised at how quickly it had been completed, and how sturdy it seemed. The work of Skelly, he was told, and Cross once again thanked whatever fate had decreed a craftsman be among the prisoners; he doubted it was the good planning and foresight of their superiors. And he thanked God that Skelly had survived the spear he'd received by way of welcome. The man was a good worker, and tractable. Cross wondered how much of his sentence remained.

And sir, they been into the potatoes again. Killam pointed out the footprints.

But our own people are among these, Cross declared, pleased with himself, despite the evidence of theft. He showed Killam how the large toe of someone accustomed to wearing boots turns inward, and how different this was to a native's imprint, something Wunyeran had explained to him.

Perhaps we should make a plaster cast, he said, and test it against each man's foot. Killam's expression flickered, and Cross glanced down at the man's boots. They were distracted by a high-pitched and excited barking, as Killam's terrier, stiff-legged and sniffing, circled the woodheap.

She's a good ratter, sir. One of the ships' dogs got to her in season. I could give you one of her pups, sir. If you've a mind.

A few weeks later Cross surveyed the evidence of yet another raid on the vegetable garden: just the one small area of digging, and what seemed two sets of footprints.

Wooral, said Wunyeran, with a snort of amusement. Wooral had been in the settlement just yesterday, he explained, was visiting from his country a little further to the east.

Nearby, Sergeant Killam pushed at the spilled soil with the toe of a well-worn boot. He'd like—no, needed—new boots, but who knew when the next supply boat was due? It was as if their settlement had been forgotten, and now even the natives were not taking them seriously, stealing a small number of potatoes each time, just enough to challenge and annoy. Every little thing added to his irritation, his frustration. Killam was a soldier and expected Cross to take command and put a stop to these games. Or order him to do something.

He was all the more irritated because he was putting aside a small amount of vegetables from each crop and trading with ships—whalers generally—anchored at one of the sheltered coves nearby. Ships moored there rather than Princess Harbour so as to avoid pilot fees, and to prevent crew members deserting. Killam was simply demonstrating the very initiative Cross himself kept telling people was necessary for the growth and sustainability of a tiny, isolated settlement like this. An American had wanted to make a bet with him about how many whalers there'd be in a few years. Killam would be happy to lose the bet; some hundred or more American whalers sailing along the south coast would be very good for business indeed. He sold rum to his fellow soldiers cheaper than they'd get it elsewhere in the settlement. Grog, a good garden and a regular supply of fresh meat (kangaroo was popular with the French, he believed) provided a nice supplement to a soldier's income. He reckoned he could better it.

Let the others live for their cards and rum. Killam had too much drive for that, although he understood their boredom well enough. Perhaps that was why the natives were always quarrelling, one family with another. Was that also why they stole potatoes, just a few at a time? Because it was fun? Kept them amused?

Killam was far from amused to be among the soldiers the Commandant chose to pursue the potato thieves, especially when they were told *not* to load their rifles. Far from amused? He was furious. At least Cross didn't give Wunyeran a rifle, too. Killam never liked seeing him heading away from the settlement with a rifle borrowed from Cross, even if he inevitably returned with a welcome addition to the soldier's monotonous diet.

Wunyeran suggested they take a boat straight to the river mouth in Shellfeast Harbour and make up ground on Wooral that way. That path they used, remember? he said. It crossed a bit more upriver, and Wooral would go there heading east. It was a good suggestion, and spared them a long walk. Not only that, but a favourable wind meant they needn't row.

Almost as soon as the longboat nosed onto the riverbank just past where the rocks were laid out in maze-like patterns to trap fish, the wind suddenly dropped and it was strangely quiet; perhaps it was the proximity of the water and stone to the trees that gave the air such a peculiar acoustic quality. Killam heard the sound of the pup he'd given Cross: grown, but still young. The high bark sounded very close, intimate.

It offended Killam that Cross had given Menak the pup. It wasn't the sort of dog natives should be interested in, unless as food! He thought a hulking wolf, a lion or bear would make a better companion, but their dogs were quiet and as likely to sneak behind you as come up barking and snarling. Whereas this pup, the offspring of two small rat-catching ship's dogs, yappy and strutting, demanded attention out of all proportion to its size. Its yap yap yap came drifting over the valley in which the settlement lay: a familiar voice, made alien in this landscape.

Menak carried the dog in his arms more often than not, and Killam had seen it sniffing the air, head up as if it ruled the landscape. He was surprised how calm it seemed; they were usually quite nervy beasts.

Now here was its voice again.

Wunyeran moved to the back of the group, assuring them all Wooral was not far ahead. (As is obvious to all of us, thought Killam, and no doubt Menak is with him, too.)

Killam stepped from a grove of peppermint and redgum, bending his head beneath a low branch, and there was Wooral, at the centre of a small clearing. Killam swung the barrel as Wooral turned and ran, and received the disappointment of a tiny click, no Boom! Killam imagined a wound widening on the native's naked back, but the man was gone. Killam spat, cursed, and was about to race off in pursuit of other bodies running in the shrubbery when Cross called, Halt!

The soldiers glanced at one another. Heart pounding, Killam listened to Cross and Wunyeran speaking in that gladbag bastard language the two of them used together, and then Wunyeran was calling out in his blackfella talk. Half a dozen or so grinning heads appeared from around trunks and rose above the low shrubbery. Within range, thought Killam. The soldiers and Captain listened uncomprehendingly as Wunyeran and the others— Wooral among them—spoke to one another across the distance. The wind snatched at their voices and swept between pursuers and pursued, shaking the shrubs, and bending the small trees.

Wooral and the others began to walk toward Killam's party. Halfway there, Wooral called out and Wunyeran responded. It must've been the answer that stopped them. Wunyeran looked at Cross, and Cross called out, Apprehend them, men!

But the soldiers' quarry knew there was no spite in the gun barrels brandished their way, and although well within rifle range, they were forever just beyond reach of the heavy hands and boots clumping toward them. One moment they were in a circle around the soldiers, showering them with kangaroo pellets, the next they were in one group, leading the soldiers on and waving, laughing. Wind rocked the trees and shrubs, and the Noongar disappeared and rose again, so light on their feet they seemed to glide. Killam thought of men in the sea: diving not falling, waving not drowning. The same branches that alternately supported or concealed them clutched at his jacket, and tree roots tripped him.

Wunyeran had moved from pursuer to pursued, from hound to hare. Killam could hear the puppy's excited barking. Menak must be with them, too, then. It was a game. They thought it fun.

Killam stopped to load his gun.

They had lost all sight of their quarry.

One potato, two potato, three potato, four. Bye bye redcoat, bye bye Jak Tar, bye bye.

The voices fading, and that infernal dog's yapping.

THE WRONG PORT

CROSS WAS RELIEVED the natives had left on one of their journeys, their regular migrations. Feeding them proved a drain on the stores and Wunyeran and the rest often took up a great part of his day, distracting him from other things he could be doing: collecting specimens, recording, instilling in the men the importance of diet. And then—Cross was an honest man—with the natives absent, the awkward issue of his own presence was not always bothering his conscience . . .

Certainly, their absence pleased the rest of the settlement's population. Friendly enough, the natives, but the smallest things could suddenly turn their mood, people said, reminding one another of the times there'd been trouble. The spearing. The theft and lying. The nuisance of them. The prisoners were glad not to be every day reminded of their servitude while inferior beings were free and feted. Those soldiers with families dined at one another's tables. Others kept at their cards and rum and tried not to doze through their days between supervising at The Farm, or maintaining and building their homes, or at the fishing or road works. The prisoners were kept under guard, but not shackled.

Cross dealt with his correspondence and planning, and discussed morale with the Captain. He went on long walks around the coastline.

But a child ran to its mother, sobbing that a black had chased her. A gunshot echoed from the hills around the harbour, and the settlement froze. A soldier had fired at a few blackfellas he'd seen hiding either side of the path ahead of him. The way they flitted in and out of the strange trees you never knew for sure if you were safe or not.

At least with Menak and the rest, you knew where you stood. And they were friendly, they made you laugh. Where are our natives? Menak was a leader and he kept the others away. Wunyeran too, and he was such a happy young man. Had they stayed away so long last winter? Some people thought not. Why so long away this time, then? Yes, they had fought other blacks, but everyone knew they all cooperated at other times. What if they were to join forces against us? What chance would we have?

Heavy rain swept across the harbour, and in the valley between their two hills a stream of water ran back to the sea. Whales came close to shore, and a few whaling ships came into the harbour. Some visiting sailors said they'd seen blacks, and certainly their fires. There was a great crowd around a whale that had been cast up on the beach to the east of here. Hundreds of them.

The soldier's lookout duty was increased.

*

On his own, old Bobby often agreed that yes, he really was important to the way everyone—black and white—had got on so well here in this, what did people call it? This neck of the woods, this isolated seaport, this godforsaken place? Yep. Truthfully, he had been the main man. It wasn't his fault things went bad.

Like mallee or *moort* his roots reached out, and people sheltered close to the ground under his branches, made like a family. *Moort* means family, too.

Dr Cross and everyone remembered the special thing that happened, but they never knew Bobby was right at the middle of it. He didn't remember Bobby from when he was still just a little boy not long on his feet who walked into that settlement set upon the windswept shore where no Noongar had been for a while and lay down beside the soldiers' hearth, lay down upon the soldier's bed to die. But it was Bobby. It was Bobby himself who caused the trouble and who also made the peace.

His sickness was part of the story that was circling round and round in his head, beginning with his own mother and father forgetting how to breathe properly so they could only exhale and cough, always bent over, stooped, moving like their feet hurt from touching their very own earth. They lay down quietly until the flies came around them and went into their eyes and mouth and nostrils. Lay there as the birds settled upon them with their hard and gripping feet and their beaks tore at the softest flesh first. Bobby could not keep the flies away; not the birds, either.

There was no one strong enough to bury his mother and father, or send them on their way properly. So Bobby had wandered away from them and into the soldiers' barracks, into the walls of white clay beneath the roof of thatched grasstree rushes. It was a large inside space, smelling sharply of earth and dried vegetation. He could not speak the language then, only 'hello hello' and anyway there was no one about. The floor inside the big hut was worn and hollowed from the soldiers' sweeping and sweeping, so that he stepped down into what was like swept and packed ash, like soothing talcum powder. The breeze came cool from the harbour through openings on one side of the barracks and out the other, refreshing his hot cheeks. There were no soldiers there, but the beds were laid out side by side to the left and the right. He picked one in the very middle. Sat upon it.

Lay down.

He sank into the bed, the smell of soldier, snuffled at the rough blanket prickling his nose. The smell of soldier who was no longer a stranger. He went very silent and deep into the cave of himself.

When the soldier came in he saw a very young boy soft and all but naked on the bed, and leaking.

Cried out.

And the voices went out, saying a young native boy (it was his old self, Bobby knew, he felt it still) had died. But Bobby was deep inside himself, gone very tiny like a pale mouse and was watching, listening. The voices went away from the barracks that was the centre of this trouble, and his own people were angry, of course, because how could a young boy die just like that? Someone must be to blame. The soldiers, see.

The men came into the settlement trembling with anger, shaking their spears.

Dr Cross went up to them, heading straight for Wunyeran and ignoring the spears. He wanted just to talk, and the other men moved back from Wunyeran, and a few soldiers walked quietly up to stand behind Cross so it was the two men—Cross and Wunyeran—with the others standing behind each of them. Two groups, apart.

Wunyeran was wild, and the soldiers and their prisoners and Dr Cross and the soldiers' wives and children all looking on had known Wunyeran only as a laughing, playful man. They hardly thought him a savage now. But here he was with his people, shouting and glaring at them and shaking spears more than anyone.

Some of Dr Cross's people stepped further back. They were standing close together, their arms reaching inward to one another, wives and children clutching at their men.

Wunyeran strode around, leapt in the air, shouted. His face was terrible to see, and he ripped his *wadjela* shirt from his body and tore it with his teeth. He hurled the tattered thing to the ground and stomped on it.

One of the men, Wooral it was, threw a spear. It only just missed Dr Cross and went right through the wall of the barracks. The soldiers lifted their guns, but Cross called out, No no, don't fire. There were more men with spears than men with guns. Dr Cross kept speaking to Wunyeran, and did not let the soldiers fire. He got one of his soldiers to carry the boy out and then took the limp boy in his arms. Tears on his cheeks, and tears on Wunyeran's cheeks, too.

It was Wabalanginy, Bobby Wabalanginy. Dead. But Bobby Wabalanginy remembered all this, he will talk about it when he is older. Other people will listen, and they will tell it, too. He was only a small boy then, and he was dead in Dr Cross's arms. Cross gave the poor little body into the arms of his friend Wunyeran.

And then the body, Bobby Wabalanginy, sat up while the two men's arms were crossed and still upon him. He sat up in their four arms and then, only a little boy, he climbed up onto the shoulders of Dr Cross, and Wunyeran moved beside his good friend and the boy Bobby Wabalanginy stood with one foot on each of the men's shoulders holding the hair of their heads. Dr Cross's hat fell to the ground.

Those two men, with the tiny boy on their shoulders, walked away from the barracks with the soldiers and wives, their children and the prisoners, too, on one side, and the Noongar men on the other. People had stretched out in a line each side to see the boy and the two men, and spears and the rifles pointed up to the sky as Cross and Wunyeran carried the boy who came to be known as Bobby on their shoulders, carried him between them. He stood high in the sky for everyone to marvel at, and he stood on their shoulders.

Not everyone remembered this story like Bobby Wabalanginy

did, but he knew no fear, see, and knew it was him, floating from the soldier's bed in the barracks and floating forever safe above the long guns and percussion locks and caps and even his beloved family's fighting spears. And he would tell you that he rose even higher into the sky that day, little boy that he was, and saw future graves: Dr Cross and Wunyeran curled together, and two others curled tight, too, a man and a woman: one from here, and one from the ocean horizon. It took him some time, but started then: Bobby looked into future graves, and into some people's hearts and minds, went into the hollows within them, into the very sounds they made. All his friends and their goodness kept him alive. And he never learned fear, because he was not just one self. He was bigger than that, he was all of them.

And no little boy died in the soldiers' barracks, not ever. No, they brought him alive. No little boy died when the soldiers and sailors and Noongar lived together, not ever. No no. Never never never.

*

All my friends, old Bobby Wabalanginy would say to the tourists, in between throwing his flaming boomerangs and holding his palm out for their coins. You, my friends, you keep me alive.

All his friends and family kept that boy Bobby Wabalanginy alive, just by loving him, wanting him, and wanting him to stay where he was. Stay in this place.

*

Menak began visiting the settlement again, Wunyeran, too. Cross made no mention of their previous hijinks, for so the vegetable-stealing incident had become. Indeed, Menak was very popular; those soldiers with wives invited him to dine with them one after the other. Cross wondered at the man's social stamina.

Content after a shared meal, Wunyeran and Cross sat within

the glow of fire and candle, heads close and nodding to one another, gesticulating with wrists and fingers, speaking slowly and softly. There was darkness all around; a darkness Wunyeran seemed to fear and Cross did not know. Anyone looking in from that darkness would have seen them as if held in a sac of yellow light. Cross was drinking brandy: not a drink Wunyeran had learned to appreciate, though tonight a few sips eased his discomfort. He had recovered but was still heavily congested.

We are two men of such different backgrounds, thought Cross and, attempting to fuse them, we are preparing for the birth of a new world.

Without a woman? He would turn in his sleep, restless.

They sang to one another. Wunyeran initiated it, Cross accepting. It was a way to communicate, to say more of oneself than was possible with their limited shared vocabulary. Cross sang pieces from childhood, anthems and ballads, *Auld Lang Syne* and bawdy sea shanties. Nevertheless, his repertoire was soon exhausted, but Wunyeran was enthusiastic to hear them again and again and soon sang along.

Late one afternoon, Cross, Wunyeran, Menak, Killam and some of the other soldiers were together in a hut. Wooral came through the doorway, but hesitated at the edge of the room.

Wunyeran looked up and sang, *Oh where have you been all the day, Billy boy Billy boy?*

There was a moment's stunned silence, then the soldiers' nervous laughter.

Sometimes the hut grew too warm and too close, as if there was not air enough to breathe despite the way, in different weather, rain collected in puddles on the earth floor and chilly air found them however much the fire blazed. On one such stuffy evening, the two men went out under the night sky—not far, because

Wunyeran liked to keep fires or light close at hand—and Cross tried to follow Wunyeran's words of what was in the glittering sky: the origins of different stars, the stories of dark spaces between, the way the sky and its slowly shifting constellations signalled that rain was due, whales would be appearing, emus nesting inland . . . He told sky stories of how things became the truths they are.

The two men sat either side of the hut's doorway, the candles inside flickering, and the dark shapes massed around them—huts, a heap of wood, tents, shrubs, trees—contrasted with the sky, which lowered a net of stars to enmesh and welcome them.

You people in England, they die?

The question came after a silence between them and Cross had hardly replied that yes, they did, when Wunyeran, the timbre of his voice eloquent with melancholy, continued that his own people were dying in great numbers. He coughed and wheezed, mimicking common symptoms. Mimicking, but he knew the symptoms too well. He scratched himself.

And what then? Cross tried to ask. What of a heaven and hell? Angels? A God?

Doctor-Sunday-book-paper?

Wunyeran had politely sat through several church services and now, broken English interspersed with his own language and again with song, he expressed something of his elder brothers the kangaroos, and that trees or whales or fish might also be family. Or so Cross understood. The sun was their mother . . . Cross's face showed he did not understand.

Doctor-Sunday-book-service, Wunyeran said, smiling at the clumsiness of his own language. It was a new language of sorts they were developing. Wunyeran people *dwongkabet*.

Ah, Cross understood. Wunyeran's people were deaf to the church; they did not understand.

Now Wunyeran talk, Dr *dwongkabet*.

Cross nodded, nodded again, and was suddenly speaking passionately, as if he was a young man again and wanting Wunyeran to know his heart, the weave of his inner galaxy, his Christian beliefs. Wunyeran understood something of how individuals died and went to a place in the sky, but when Dr Cross tried to speak of heaven, and chains-of-being, and of a place of constant suffering within the earth where a big spirit-man sent bad people . . . Wunyeran laid his hand gently on Cross's shoulder.

You in the wrong port now, Doctor.

TONGUE AND PAPER

As he waded in the warm shallows at the south side of the harbour, each of Wunyeran's shins momentarily became like the bow of a boat pushing a tiny wave before it, or the point of a spearhead. As his weight shifted onto the foot, the water eddied, and suddenly there was no wave, no bow, no spearhead. He stopped, wriggled his toes and sank deeper into the sand. Calves, ankles and feet were slightly to one side of where they should be. Below and above the sea's skin did not quite match. As if there were two people, not quite the same, one visible only below water, one visible above. These legs, so dark and thin, might be spears, oars, gun barrels, even.

Wunyeran weighed the spear in his hand. He was wading in seawater, and yet there was land all around except the one small gap way over there toward where the sun rises and the boats slide through onto the white sandy beaches like lost whales. And those boats come and go, come and go with their oars and gun barrels and oh the things they bring.

From up on the hills this land-encircled ocean looked like a lake, a plain of glass: a great pane of glass, a looking glass, even. And Wunyeran, up close now, motionless, waiting for the water to settle, saw part of his reflection but also, behind the reflection, that the sand was not white, but coloured like bark or ochre. Why? Because the water is dark. Why? Is the bush staining this shallow part of ocean? Or is it the smoke, colouring the light and therefore the water, too? The questions you ask, learning a new way of speech. How it drives your thinking.

He had begun to collect leaf, feather, bone and, pressing some of them between sheets of paper, to mark the days by them. Why?

Smoke, way up there: someone hunting along the ridge between him and the open Southern Ocean. More wind up there, and his brothers would be poised at the edge of tendrils and thick loops of smoke, the fire roaring and crackling in the scrub, and bodies crashing, rushing to meet their spears.

And why he not with them?

He had run across the hot burnt earth in boots, with shirt and trousers sticking to the ochre and oils and sweat of his skin. Naked now, but. Barefoot and wading in sunlight and salty water with the weight of a spear in his hand.

He gazed at the rippling water, the ribbon weed barely swaying at his feet and sometimes the sandy ripples marking the ocean bed. Lifting his eyes, he saw high above and in the smoky light the clouds spread across the dome of sky in the same pattern as the sand beneath his feet. But the clouds were edged with blood. All the things you can't collect and press, that won't slip between sheets of paper. Today the light was smoky, and the water, and so, too, the sandy floor of this shallow ocean with its shape of the water's movement made solid enough to look at and study. But the sand could no more record his passing than could the water, the air or clouds.

His footprints disappeared.

And these words hold barely a trace of Wunyeran's voice, yet so much of the others who came as strangers and were surprised more than once at what marks could be found and what could be realised from them. Just as no mark of his passing remains in the water, so there remains little trace of his tongue in the air, or these hills around him and sky, these clouds . . . But surely if we paused, listened long enough . . .

Wunyeran and his brothers, his fathers and uncles, waded here at night and, separated by darkness, the light of their firesticks shimmered and danced on the water; laughter bubbled, a fish plashed. Sounds—a tiny voice, disembodied, an invisible dog barking—skimmed across the surface from the far shore, that scatter of tents, the huts of timber and pale mud, the boats straining at their ropes. Here, Wunyeran and his family were held within the hum of fire, within the sputter and cough and tiny tongues of flame. The lapping and chuckling ocean ripples.

Today there was sunlight and high open sky and space all around Wunyeran—like being in a boat at sea but for the rhythm of his step and his breathing. The land was close behind him, its tall trees and stony ridges keeping the wind mostly high overhead, but every now and then it swoops down, whispering, ruffling the water's surface.

They call this place *harbour*, this body of ocean surrounded by hills and held within earth hollowed like a grave that their boats sail into. They collect on the other shore, blown there by the wind.

Boats, clothing, dogs and guns . . . Even the food they eat. Interesting. Wunyeran's lips and tongue shaped their words now, and their songs, Oh where have you been all the day . . . ?

Heads snapped up when he sang like that. Surprise, and hurt, too, shows on their faces when we walk like them, fold our arms, cross our legs. Speak their way. When we be like a looking glass, and show their way back at them.

Across the lapping sea, at the mouth of a harbour, Wunyeran saw the fine mist, silver in sunlight, of a whale's spout.

Something moved across the patterned sand at his feet.

Kitjel don.

His spear missed.

DEATH AND SPIRIT

THE NOONGAR WOULD COME and go; for weeks on end there would be no one, and then suddenly Cross's hut was full of Wunyeran and his brothers. This time, Cross heard Wunyeran's coughing well before he ever saw him. He stayed a night, went away and returned a few days later, almost carried by Menak and that young boy with them again. For several days he lay beside the fireplace, shivering but hot to touch. Now and then he spoke very rapidly, or sang, but not to anyone in the room with him. And sometimes there were several there to listen, because elderly men of his own community and even some of the soldiers came to see how he was, show they cared.

Cross tended him as best he could, while Menak watched closely. Menak wanted to take Wunyeran back to his own people and, presumably, their own wise people's attention, but he could not travel just yet.

Early one afternoon he rolled his head to gaze at Menak and Cross. And said something, Wabalanginy, perhaps? Then his head lifted from the pillow just a little, and his eyes rolled back under their lids: one moment alive and focused on Cross and Menak, the next like glass. Was that goodbye?

Dr Cross watched as Menak, sighing deeply, placed his palm against his brother's cheek. He arranged the body: raised the arms and crossed the hands near the neck, tilted the head forward, drew the knees up to the chest. Finally, he pulled the lower legs and feet closer against the thighs, rolled the body onto its right side and wrapped the blanket completely around it.

Menak turned to him demanding, Peer, peer.

It took Cross a moment to understand; Menak wanted to spear someone as payback for his brother's death.

Of course, Cross could not allow that. After all, who might he wish to spear?

Menak signalled the sun's path across the sky to show he would return the next day, *benang*. He wanted the body to remain just as it was, until the burial. Then he left.

Cross remained by his friend and prayed that a merciful God might admit so refined a soul through the gates of heaven, despite the many—not knowing him—who would say heathen, and insist he was but an uncultivated savage. What good was Cross's science when it could not save his friend? What good was it to be civilised, when he could offer no more help than could this poor fellow's own brother? Wunyeran had returned here to die, not to be healed.

Did God watch over them all?

Cross stayed by the body for hours. He prayed, he read the Bible. He sipped rum. Prayed again. Got to his feet and stood swaying. He could not stay beside this body, all that remained of he who was Wunyeran.

A little boy peered around the corner of Cross's wattleland-daub hut, clad only in an adult's cast-off shirt, and mouthed the very prayers he heard mumbled. He slipped away from the doorway a moment before Cross stumbled through it, and even though it was now dark, and many of his own people would've been wary of leaving their campfire, Bobby followed Cross's assistant to the hut and so saw—his lips parted in horror and wonder—the man straighten the limbs and lay the corpse out flat, in the European way.

Bobby was there again in the morning, learning the curses Cross uttered as he tried to return his deceased friend to his original position. But the limbs no longer moved the way they had, and the body was not as it should be. Cross wept. Cross swore and cursed and sobbed so that his body shook and the sounds came from deep within. Watching, the boy moved his limbs like a dead man, tried that style and so began his mastery of the Dead-man Dance.

He was a good man, Dr Cross. But no wonder Wunyeran's spirit never departed the proper way.

Morning. Soldiers carried Wunyeran up the slope and deep into the shadow of the hill where the rising sun had not reached. They gently laid the blanket-wrapped body upon the ground, and soldiers' shovels, directed by Menak, cut the earth to make a sharp-edged hollow the size of the oldest Noongar graves.

Menak had them shovel the soil to the southwest corner and, when they stood back, he crouched and carefully shaped it with his hands. Bobby looked at the harbour further down the slope and the hills on the other side; looked from harbour to grave and back again. One echoed the other.

Menak got the soldiers to fetch certain bushes, and he and the Noongar men put these in the grave, and then laid Wunyeran's body on its side upon this bed of bush, facing the sunrise. Menak pushed soil from the lower, northern side of the grave and it spilled over the body until the grave's surface sloped gradually for the morning sun to warm it and the cold wind to pass over. It was like a good camping spot, although a small one.

Menak swept the grave with a branch and laid a broken spear upon the smooth surface. Pushed a spear thrower upright into the earth. Made a little fire. He and the other Noongars sang in the smoke, the white men stood with heads bowed, mumbling as the shadow finally receded and sunlight flowed onto the grave so that the flames disappeared and the smoke looked so thin . . . Everything there and not there, all at once.

They went back to the Captain's hut, soldiers and Noongars together, and ate ship's biscuit and a little salt meat.

That boy? Cross asked, seeing him all of a sudden though he'd been there all along. Bobby?

Yeah, Menak said, Wabalanginy mummy daddy they finish. That grave one now? He uncle him.

That was how people said the words, then. Them days.

There were small piles of clothing where the Noongar had been. They had shed their English dress; were gone.

The soldiers had their barracks, the prisoners had theirs. One was of wattle-and-daub, the other of canvas, and although this should have made it the lesser construction it was the prisoners who had erected both under the supervision of William Skelly, and perhaps the tent was the better protection. Skelly thought so. So, it would seem, did some of the blackfellows, since one or two of them would sometimes share its shelter.

No Noongar had slept there for a long time, though. Skelly, for one, didn't mind, and was glad not to have to listen to the soldiers boasting how their blackfellow friends were ready to share women. He reckoned they lied, and tried not to think about women, anyway. But even a hinge, even drilling or fitting timbers together could bring women to mind.

He was working now, though he'd got himself well out of the rain, and was happy to turn a blind eye to Skelly's workmates also keeping clear of work when they could. It was Skelly who'd command them when he needed their help. He worked, even in the rain, sheltering in an old oilskin he'd won in a card game with one of the drunken soldiers and then managed to hold on to, despite the man's protests next day, with the support of many—soldiers and prisoners alike—who'd witnessed it. The oilskin helped, but the rain still reached him so that after a few hours he'd be chilled if he didn't keep working hard. Might've been the rain that made him notice them, as much as anything, since he thought they must surely be very cold, out in this weather. And just the two of them. They'd appeared almost as if they'd dropped with the rain, Menak and that very young boy. They were both in kangaroo-skin cloaks and Skelly, out in the weather himself, noticed how the cloaks were turned fur inward and how large drops of water caught in their hair; the grease they use, he told himself.

Then he realised there were white men trailing behind them. He pushed himself back from the window frame he'd been making, but they didn't notice him. Menak winked, but never turned to face him, and the heavy-footed men he led just kept walking, a couple of thin horses with their heads held low bringing up the rear. The other men never even saw Skelly, and wouldn't have said hello to the likes of him even if they had.

He went back to pushing twigs into the rough timbered wall frame he'd made.

Cross joined the commandant to talk with the little group of men who had arrived overland from Cygnet River. Sun-bronzed and foot weary but arriving in persistent rain, they said they'd made good time and come across excellent grazing country. The land awaits development; there is fine hinterland. We had heard of your natives here, they said, and indeed if not for them . . . and skated over the tensions within their group and how they had become so confused as to their direction. We were helped on our journey, the black people led us here. They are friendly, indeed.

Good grazing country, they said, repeating it among themselves. And they rested, dined and made plans to explore the country all around this port. Land would be granted here, too, they insisted, to those with capital and without need for the purse strings of government. Men like themselves, with initiative and courage. There would be no military outpost and no prisoners but it would be a self-sufficient colony.

Dr Cross had not heard anything of such plans. He would have to leave or stay and consolidate his presence. He declared himself unwell, and retired early.

Bobby Wabalanginy was with Menak and Wooral when they had led the white men into the settlement. They had called on Dr Cross, but could not find him and so they talked with the soldiers and were welcomed. Menak and Wooral let them be, to make themselves known to one another in whatever way they had. Bobby came looking for Dr Cross again the next day. It was mostly young men who came to the huts, not boys, and especially not one as young as Bobby. But Bobby came in, alone.

Where is Dr Cross? he asked a soldier, and the soldier, recognising the boy, tried to explain.

Dr Cross is unwell . . . We had visitors . . . They did not lay down to sleep until sunrise this morning.

Then came Dr Keene, one of the visiting expedition party, a medical man like Dr Cross. They shared a name because of that. Dr Keene had a red face; blood vessels rose above the skin of his nose and his breath was like a soldier's. Oh, you are the boy Bobby? he said. It was not really a question. Dr Cross is unwell, he also said. Could he help? He spoke the same language as Dr

Cross, and Bobby knew they were of the same people, but it did not always seem so. Bobby did not really know this man, Doctor, but told him his uncle, someone like a brother for Menak, was sick. Snake bite him. Doctor said I can help, I heal sick men. He was not the one Bobby came for, but he kept on and on wanting to be taken to the sick man and so Bobby took him for a walk saying, Oh I think it was here, or here, oh I dunno now, and they walked and walked and walked but Bobby could not remember where his sick uncle lay. Sorry. He was only a boy, after all.

Could Bobby really trust this stranger, Dr Keene, who grunted and barked when he spoke?

Dr Cross was at his hut later, and Menak joined them as he and Bobby set off, saying he was glad because he had been coming to get Dr Cross, too. Menak easily led the way to where Uncle was and of course then Bobby Wabalanginy admitted he remembered it. But Dr Keene could not come because this time he was the one unwell. Lying on his bed he'd smelled like those soldiers who fell down on the ground from rum-drinking. A group of men sat with Uncle, and two women were at a campfire just a little walk away.

Doctor said he was sorry and he sat beside Uncle with the other men and Menak lay beside the sick man with one hand under his head, comforting him. Seeing the mark of a snake bite on Uncle's hand and how sick and tired he was, Cross said soft words. I think you know the problem better than me, he said, because I do not think I can help this man. But he bandaged the hand, anyway.

*

Dr Keene came with them the next day, and could only get down on the ground with difficulty; he was a man whose belly overbalanced him and whose legs would rub together as he walked, so he moved with his feet wide apart, rocking like a sailor. He took Cross's bandage from Uncle's injured hand, and rubbed the hand vigorously. Vigorously, he said, you must rub it vigorously. He looked at everyone sitting around and again said the hand must be rubbed to take away the poison. But none of them understood this way of healing, and people were crying because this was not as they would do it. Why had Dr Cross brought this man to help? Dr Keene gave Uncle something from a small bottle, and Uncle sat up straight, breathing deeply and casting glances at all the people around him. So it seemed good.

As they walked back to their own huts, Dr Keene talked to Dr Cross angrily. He said these people do not seem to care enough whether the man lives or dies, and his family cannot be bothered to take a little trouble or expend the energy required to heal him. He didn't seem to care that Bobby trailed along with them some of the way and might be hurt to hear such things.

In the morning Dr Keene again came with Cross to the sick man's camp. Bobby joined them along the way but when they arrived Cross knew no one there. It surprised him, because the Doctor had told Menak and the others to sit by the patient's side, give medicine and rub his hand. Once again Keene took off a bandage that was tied very tightly, more on the wrist than the hand. Then Cross followed little Bobby, walking for an hour or more until they reached Menak's side.

Why, Cross wanted to know, had the sick man been left alone?

Menak told him Uncle would not take the medicine, though they tried and they tried. After a little time he suggested, to reflect the view of those who were closest to Uncle, that the medicine might work good for you people, but it was no good for a Noongar. And my cousins said they would sit with him.

Cross decided to return to the sick man, and Menak and some of the others went with him, moving quickly along a well-worn path. They had not yet reached their destination when a cry—very lonely it sounded—halted them. Menak called out straightaway, and when that was answered everyone but Cross and Keene broke into a run. Stumbling after them, Cross saw a man at the head of an approaching group throw himself to the ground, and the others stop beside him until Menak's party reached them. By the time Cross and Keene arrived, people were crying and wailing, and already bleeding about the head from hitting and scratching themselves.

Fat Doctor cried out, For the love of God we have no time for this, take us now to the man, we do him no good to dally!

But Cross knelt quietly beside the man lying on the ground and sobbing into the earth and said his name. Menak. And those two men clasped hands. And our Bobby Wabalanginy stood with a hand on each man's shoulder. Menak's woman, Manit, noticed, and though she was upset and known for her temper, she gently pulled Bobby away and left the two men to share their sorrow.

Isolated, Dr Keene cursed and walked like an angry duck all the way back to his hut.

Sniffling and sobbing, Bobby scratched his cheeks and struck his forehead so that blood and tears flowed together on his cheeks same as they did on Manit's. The old woman, a moment ago so self-possessed and assured, fell to the ground with the force of her sobbing. And look at Dr Cross, crying too.

Menak made a space for Dr Cross beside the dead man's feet. Tears streamed down Cross's face. Bobby was made to stay with the children and women, a little away from the men, but he could hear them, and some wanted to spear the fat man Keene, or one of the other white men. The fat man was to blame for this death, and since he wasn't here . . . A man got up and grabbed his spear, but Menak pointed to Cross, crying among them.

The men carried the body to bury, arguing about who to spear, who to blame for this death. Bobby heard Menak again protecting Dr Cross and his friend. They tried to help, he said.

And then Bobby touched the dead man, and the dead man sat up. He came alive and got to his feet, saying how very tired he was, and went to his woman. Her hair was wet with blood and her face smeared with tears and he took her hands in his.

Menak cried out because where the dead man had been there was a little boy, Bobby Wabalanginy. And now he seemed like the one who was dead. But as Menak and Dr Cross touched him he sat up like a sleepwalker, and the two men lifted the boy as they rose to their feet together, and Bobby Wabalanginy climbed until he was standing on their shoulders with a hand in each of theirs. All the people at the camp moved into two lines and joined their voices together and raised their eyes to Bobby as he went between them.

He was very spirity, Bobby Wabalanginy, even in these years before he reached adolescence.

SPEARS AND GUNS

Mr Killam—already he was calling himself Mr, looking to the day when he was out of uniform—lowered his head over the records, making sure everything was in order. He was careful to secrete away only a little of the stores at a time. Some rum had been put aside, of course; his fellow soldiers could never get enough of that. Salted beef, too. Ship's biscuits, sugar and rice; the blacks like this stuff and he'd seen the good Doctor ingratiate himself with them by such means. It was more than a month now since he'd reported a theft, although of course no culprit had been found. He thought if he arranged it so that a couple of the prisoners escaped he could make it seem like they'd raided the storehouse before they'd scarpered.

Trouble was, the new storehouse, built by that fellow Skelly, was not as easy to get into as the last one. Killam didn't want to 'overlook' locking it and then have his own competence questioned.

Tolja!

He looked up from his books. It was the chief of the blacks, but dressed up like he thought he was one of us.

Bikket.

They're taking us for granted, Killam thought. As if we are

only here to keep them fed with ship's biscuit, rice and sugar. He shook his head, No, and walking out of the storeroom closed the door behind him. The two men stood very close, face to face. Killam was glad of his height. He smiled, wanting to appear relaxed. The black was smiling right back at him.

Killam looked to the ground; it helped somehow to see those bare feet. He turned around and, chaining the storehouse, stepped away. Friendly like, he motioned to the door. If you can open the door, you can have some biscuit. Some bikket.

It amused him to watch the savage pull the door and have the chain stop it. Next, predictably enough, he tried to reach through the small gap, but to no avail. Mr Killam had his measure. Menak—that was the blackfellow's name, one of the Doctor's favourites—stepped back and, after studying the door for a few moments, gripped each side and lifted it clear of its hinges.

Damn. Killam should have realised. He went to pull Menak away, but one or two steps from the door which now rested in the frame, the man placed a hand firmly on Killam's chest. Well, his orders were to avoid conflict wherever possible . . . Killam stood back. Let him do what he will.

Since the door was still chained, Menak opened it from the hinge side and the chain itself became a sort of primitive (well, of course it had to be in such hands) hinge. Yes, it was just as well they didn't all carry weapons because otherwise Killam might've shot this rogue in the chest right there and then and blasted him to kingdom come or wherever it was they went. But no, Killam kept his head and since he knew everything was packed away in chests—save for some biscuits that were too weevil-ridden to inflict upon even the prisoners—he offered some of these to Menak. As (still smiling) he opened the box, that boy everyone had once thought dead ran into the settlement with some women, all of them angry and yelling and obviously agitated. In a moment they were gone, and Menak with them.

Killam turned from the vexatious problem of his door and saw the Doctor following the natives' path.

Curiosity, eh? Well, everyone knows where that leads.

*

Young and still weak, Bobby drifted along behind the others. It sometimes felt as if he moved in water. His heavy limbs, see? Blurred vision and the pulse pounding in his ears, and yet—like coming to the surface, like having come through the membrane between one world and another—there were these startling moments of clarity.

Spears were proper flying. Most of the men had a woman beside them picking up fallen spears, and they had to be just as alert. Bobby loved this sort of thing: the dancing and dodging more than the throwing, and the throwing of insults more than spears. And the women were best at this. He was excited at old Manit's voice, at what she shrieked from among the kangaroo-skin cloaks her young men had cast off so they could move more freely.

It was that topside mob again, coming south to the coast. Another one of them musta died, and they reckoned it was our fault. Why they gotta come here making trouble? Menak had claimed he knew most of them, and they were almost as bad off as his own family with so many dying from the coughing and scratching that soon there might not be enough left to collect as well as throw the spears.

Spears whispered through the air, cutting to and fro, and voices called their exultation. Another miss; oh the excitement of it all. Wooral seemed almost motionless in the flurry of spears and arms, he swayed slightly to avoid a spear yet scarcely seemed to notice it, and then launched one of his own, and his spear-thrower seemed an organic extension of his arm.

Someone went down with Menak's spear in their thigh and it was like a storm settling, the wind and sea dying down. Menak's touch yet again, his power, see? Blame was not to be found here. The wounded man lay while his family snapped the spear off, casting resentful glances at Menak and the people around him. They dawdled away muttering, not quite enemies, the lame one half-carried, half-leaning on his brothers.

They would be back, and if not them then one of the other families surrounding them here, this womb of their home. And Menak wondered again if it was wise to allow these other strangers to remain so long, these pale horizon people. True, they chose to camp where Menak or anyone else would not—beside the water in the coldest winds and yet where the sun does not reach until late morning. The water is deepest there, too, but a poor place for spearing fish. They had been there a long time, with the air in their huts growing stale, their food old, and shit spilling from the ground around them. These men, from the ocean horizon or wherever it is they come, they do not leave even when the rains come and that wind blows across the water right into their camp. Yet they would have our women, Menak knows that. Perhaps when the whales and cold again return, perhaps they will leave. Or offer a little more.

He had retrieved most of his spears. Their guns would be good. A fine skill, shooting. And only the quickest can dodge powder and ball. These pale horizon people will help us. Thinking aloud, he said as much to little Bobby.

Yes.

A NAME AND MEMORY

PEOPLE TALKED ABOUT BOBBY WABALANGINY, and not only his own people. Even Skelly knew of him, if not yet by name, and in truth Bobby did not yet have the name he would come to be known by. And Skelly, who knew his time was almost up and was nearly a ticket-of-leave man, had heard that a new colony had begun this side of the continent, somewhere further up the west coast at a place they were calling Cygnet River. He reckoned he'd go there if this place was abandoned. Not back to Sydney. Not back over the sea. Something must be built here. A village, and I at its centre. He occupied himself with such thoughts most evenings, wearing a mental path toward his dreams.

Skelly was at The Farm some days later, minding sheep. Killam was there as well, and that was alright to Skelly's mind since Killam was the best of the soldiers, but sheep—and particularly shepherding—was not work he enjoyed or, in his own opinion, where he was most useful. Still, it was time alone. Killam said he'd best keep an eye out for the natives; he'd fired at some a few days previous because it was the only way to keep them clear of the stock and the garden. Fired over their heads like, and shouted to wave them away, as he was within his rights to do so, whatever the Doctor might say.

The sheep had more idea than Skelly where they wanted to graze—he just followed, his main aim to ensure he was back by day's end. Just before the plain began to slope there was a wide expanse covered with holes. Must be them digging for roots, Skelly realised, and so close to our own vegetables, too. It was alright for Killam saying how he'd taken a shot and all, but what was Skelly to do? He didn't have a gun. He'd not be going far, you could count on that.

He kept walking, though, since that lulled and stopped his thoughts tying themselves in knots the way they did until he got angry with himself and anyone crossing his path. The sheep did not move fast, there was plenty of grazing, and except for the middle hours of the day when, despite the season, he needed to rest in some shade, he spent the day plodding with them. Trying not to think.

Making his way back, not yet able to see The Farm but knowing he was close by the lay of the land, a spear landed in the ground beside him. He stopped. The spear swayed a little, but stayed upright. A dark wood, he noted, oiled and well handled. His heart leapt and raced. They don't need to land no spear in me, my heart will just stop if any spear comes closer than that besides which I've had my quota of spearing. He thought to run. Glanced over his shoulder. A group of natives, all with spears at the ready, were some distance behind him. Not so far as he'd like. He looked ahead at the sheep, kept walking. His limp was worse.

A few steps later the black men were in his peripheral vision, on either side and no doubt behind him, too, but he was not turning to look. What was the point? He had no weapon to fight with and maybe they were the kind that didn't take to spearing a man in his back. Those were very long spears. Not that he wanted to see them. He could hear the men talking to one another, hear their bubbling laughter. He stopped walking. Spears pointed at him from either side. Skelly faced ahead, not moving, only his eyeballs going rapidly side to side.

Then—it must've been the veering sheep that alerted him—there was the boy, the boy that came in with Wunyeran. He walked up to Skelly, talking, and took him by the hand, still talking. Skelly could make nothing of it. Did he hear names? Menak? Wunyeran. Swore he heard 'Cross'. The boy led him away by the hand.

Dr Cross's boy, he said, tapping a hand on his chest. We spear you, already, *kaya? Nitja baalapin waam.*

But Skelly could not understand, could not speak. The sheep scattered again, suddenly startled. He saw a sheep fall slowly to the ground, its legs folding beneath and a spear waving from it like a mast in a stormy sea. He squeezed the boy's hand. They kept walking.

Spear you already. Spear*ed*, Skelly realised. The boy knew he had been speared. Skelly saw the clearing and buildings of The Farm. Was it only he and the boy now? Yes? Skelly was striding out, trying not to run as the sheep scattered before him, but he did not let go of the boy's hand; he held tight to that hand.

Why the boy had been in the vicinity and come to Skelly's assistance was a constant source of conversation among the settlement's population. Not that there was a shortage of subjects attracting attention. This business of Cygnet River, for instance.

Yes, Cross answered Sergeant Killam, who had interrupted Skelly's account of how he'd been saved by the boy, Wabalanginy. Yes, Cross said, colonial headquarters for this side of the continent will be Cygnet River, not here. They are sending a party overland from Cygnet River, we should expect them in some days. No, he did not know what was to become of this place. He believed that people would be granted land here as at Cygnet River according to their capital. Investment is a measure of commitment, he said, why, at Cygnet River Mr Peel plans to . . .

Even Killam, so long away from the mother country, had heard of this name. He who has created law and order in London? he asked. Peel's Bobbies?

No, not he, not him. But yes, Peel is the name behind those men of law and order. Those Bobbies.

The three men glanced at Bobby Wabalanginy, sitting by the fireplace.

Nevertheless, you are well informed, Sergeant Killam. But we have our own Bobby here, do we not?

Wabalanginy was the centre of their attention, then. He returned their look, wanted to know, Who these Bobbies over the ocean?

The name stuck from then. Bobby.

*

Menak suggested the boy Bobby stay with Cross for a time. Learn things from him and his friends. The one that died, he said, brother for me, he Uncle for this boy. You Uncle-friend too? *Babin*, we say.

Dr Cross had not seen his children since they were babies, but had his own ideas of what a youngster needed. The boy was quick to learn, fed himself and kept himself clean. Bobby Wabalanginy surprised Cross with how quickly he mastered things, not least the alphabet. They began with slate and chalk, and although Bobby soon proved himself adequate to quill pen, ink and parchment, Cross kept him to the slateboard. There was a shortage of paper so far from home. They sat outside his hut, usually in the morning sun. At other times they worked by the fire, although Cross's eyes were not always good enough for such light.

Within a few months Wabalanginy spoke English better than Wunyeran ever had, and of course it was English he was learning to read and write, even though very early in their consideration of phonetics and letter patterns they tried to reproduce some of the sounds of his own language. But that is no easy task.

Even his name:

Wabarlungiyn?

Warbarlung-in-y?

Bobby.

Bobby could soon make out words even in Cross's journal, but put them differently in his own hand. From trying to write his own language he used phonics.

A most intelajint kuriositee.

We haf taked ther land.

Deseez and depredashen make them few.

Not then quite fully understanding the meaning of the words he wrote.

No, laughing and loved, Bobby Wabalanginy never learned fear, least not until he was pretty well a grown man. He never really had no sense of a single self, because . . . Well, he was young and he was like a spear, thrown and quivering in the air and only the pointed tip, that very spirit of a spear, remains still.

Bobby never knew himself then as do we, rapidly moving

backwards away from one another, falling back into ourselves from that moment when we were together, inseparable in our story and strong.

He was born, reborn, took on new shapes around the one spirit that need never fear an ending. Then that one name stuck.

As a much older man on the harbour shore, Bobby Wabalanginy sometimes wore a policeman's hat—a bobby's hat. It took him some time to get hold of such a thing; not until the first steam ship slunk into the harbour in the dark of early morning and moved across the still water, clunking and groaning enough to terrify people. Bobby made a trade with a retired policeman on-board: a boomerang for his hat.

Tourists smiled at the hat perched above Bobby's white-ochred face as they disembarked, and in his performances he would sometimes bend at the knees so that the returning boomerang knocked the hat clean off his head. Oops, he'd say, grinning. *Kerl kaart baaminy.* And then stand there twitching and looking around as if another flaming boomerang might come out of nowhere. Like a fool, perhaps, but all eyes were on him, and he was in command.

And although he was a clown—perhaps *because* he was such a light-hearted, laughing fellow—he could sometimes take his audience and turn their mouths down, furrow their brows and squeeze their hearts until tears welled. But it was never good business to stray too far from laughter.

He talked with the tourists, grateful for their ears. Staring down their smiles, he told of himself and other pioneers of those who were once his friends and though at the time he did not understand them or know their thoughts, he does now. He understands them now.

I was raised to be proud and to be friendly, he says. My family thought we could be friends and share what we had.

After the tourists, after the ships—some with sails, some driven by steam and almost spouting like a whale—old Bobby goes to his little humpy on the hill to the west of the valley in which the town sits. His women and children have gone away, and he has no real friend or family in the white man's camp beside the sea to welcome him. Only tourists. He can only talk. On a bad day he grabs people, insisting they understand what he is saying, but they look at him and do not.

Once upon a time he danced and sang for people, but that was no good, and talk is less. He sits in camp and talks in his head (since no one understands him anyway) of long ago when he first saw the big boats up close, and had hardly seen such a boat before . . . But now there are too many of them . . . He looks all around. So many things have gone.

Women no longer see an old man like him.

He has a language for the real story inside him, but it is as if a strong wind whips those words away as soon as they leave his mouth. People say he twists words, but really it is the wind twisting and taking his words away to who knows who will hear them.

Too many people in this camp and this town should not be here.

Once he was a whale and men from all points of the ocean horizon lured him close and chased and speared and would not let him rest until (blood clotting his heart) Bobby led them to the ones he loved, and soon he was the only one swimming.

After a time of darkness with only heartbeat and humming in his ears, there came light and bubbles, and then he walked across beach sand and among wattle and peppermint trees. Barefoot, he breathed the air and opened his eyes properly. There were no more of his people and no more kangaroo and emu and no more vegetable. After the white man's big fires and guns and greed there was nothing.

Old Bobby sits and shivers; he and summer wait for one another.

One day, flesh and bones folded in dark wool and warming in the sunshine, old Bobby looks up to see he has visitors. Has to blink, blink, look again. White folk come to see him? Oh, the grown daughter and son of Jak Tar and Binyan! Sent by their mother.

They ask is he well? Looking around at this place where he lives they say, How might we help you?

Bobby finds himself telling of when he was a young boy on lookout, scribbling not what had happened but what will. Why, he still has the old oilskin-covered journal in his hut. He and the grandchildren of Binyan and Jak Tar turn the yellowed pages and study the faint lines of ink. There is nothing of how he sang and danced on a whale's back as the inside of the sea spilled all around him. Nothing of the people he had known, nothing of what they were seeing, thinking. And although their children are here with him, Binyan and Jak Tar are not the only ones he is remembering.

PART III

1836–1838

ONE DAY NOT YET NOW

B FOR BOBBY. The name given him.

Bobby had taken to his letters easily with Dr Cross, liked the feel of chalk on slate and made patterns, drew small footprints of animals and birds and the shapes of different skeletons. Some sounds had a shape on the page, too, he learned. The alphabet might be tracks, trails and traces of what we said. He copied things from books, from Dr Cross's journals and letters, even. That helped him improve his spelling, though not the words of his first language.

Mrs Chaine took over as Bobby's tutor. It is our moral duty to do so, her husband suggested, to help him move toward civilisation, and our friend Dr Cross established it as a priority, to help and save him.

She could only agree, and it need only be a few hours each week, at most. She looked at his work. Some of it seemed most peculiar, and then she realised he was trying to write his own name—not Bobby, but his native name. And the name he gave his mother he also gave his father, and the same name for Dr Cross, as well. She saw it was no-name, a name for loved ones who'd died, and most of Bobby's loved ones, including Dr Cross, had died coughing. In his rare sad times, Bobby would also cough and once she saw him by the looking glass doing that cough—a wheezy breath, the slow collapse—and once he lay down, and waved non-existent flies away from his open mouth and eyes.

A lot of his people had died, Mrs Chaine was coming to realise. Our arrival means their death though we do not lift a hand. We help, she whispered, but even then only in her mind, pushing away scenes from near her husband's public house. You have lost many of your family, Bobby, she said, wrinkling her face in concern.

Yeah, Bobby said, but there was too many family everywhere, and he belonged here, never came from nowhere else.

She corrected his speech. He was a quiet boy, at least with her. Quiet, but sometimes she heard him speak and it could have been Dr Cross. It frightened her to hear a voice from beyond the grave. He had a remarkable ability to mimic, and this came through in his anecdotes, when he was recounting dialogue. She had heard him reproduce her husband's voice also, swearing and all, conversation overheard at the public house no doubt. Quiet, but who knew what he was like really, or what he was like with his own kind, because there were long days, weeks, when they hardly saw him.

W for Wabalanginy, that was his first name. It had taken Dr Cross some time to master that sound and Mrs Chaine never quite got her mouth working properly that way when she began to tutor him.

Being so young, Bobby Wabalanginy was used to being around women. Loved them. And Dr Cross, let alone Mr Geordie Chaine, had always been too busy really to be properly teaching any boy his letters. So Mrs Chaine took him in hand.

A few years later Bobby hoped maybe her daughter might do the same. Christine, that was the daughter's name. There was a son, too. Christopher. Twins, see? They were all learning the play of putting their thoughts and sounds on paper together.

Bobby Wabalanginy had been mentally composing a letter to Dr Cross's wife. First chance he got he wrote it down all in a rush.

Dear Missus Cross,

I hope you to read this.

Just think, your dear husband teached me to write and now I send this to you too. We meet soon I think, and also you and Mrs Chaine who now shows me my letters. Mr Chaine is building a fine house.

I hope you will soon come to where your husband lays and we remember him. Your dear husband gave me my letters, and took me for trips on ships.

Once upon a time a man on a deck on a boat was talking King George Town (that is what they call the huts and where the sailors stay). A great banishment to be sent there, he said.

That is not true.

I did not ask him what he meant, and he did not look to see me speak.

He said they live on salted meat, and nothing grows but rocks and stones, and claimed no one took the trouble to catch the fish of the bay. I do not know what they are doing, he said in a very loud voice. And nor do they.

I spoke up then with my name and handshake and surprised him I think. Mr Godley, I think he said his name. He was more laugh than beard, and more squeezing my hand and keeping me away than meeting me.

He speak loud and look to the others for them to nod and say he speaks true. They stand with him and not with me like many people do when they speak to a black boy.

The rocks and stones I told him are the beauty of the place and he laugh and speak big and very loud. I could not think what to say but that the climate is good and he looked at me then and said, 'Oh, you are right in that, it is the best.' I did my best and did not speak rudely. I did not say flowers and parrots too. I did not say stars, moon, the waves and leaves and campfires I thought after. I did not say you handshook the wrong people.

A strange thinking came to my mind from his eyes. He was angry at me, I wonder. We did not speak very much the rest of the trip, and I felt quite on my own.

Another man I met on a ship trip was Mr Chaine. Mr Chaine, that is the spelling of his name. He is at King George Town now. His family too. I learn my letters with his children and the help of his good wife.

They would all like to meet you and I look forward to our handshaking and Menak and Manit and Wooral too. One day not yet now.

Your friend, Bobby

Having corrected his spelling, Mrs Chaine spoke. It may be that Mrs Cross will now not ever arrive, Bobby. She folded the letter. But I think we shall nevertheless send your message by the next ship.

THE GOVERNOR FAMILY'S TREE

THE GOVERNOR SIR CAME in a ship of his own, Mrs Chaine told Bobby. In a ship of his own, Bobby overheard many of the people of King George Town pronouncing it: in a ship of his own he came with a wife and nine children. He came with:

Servants (two black boys among them)
Sheep
Bullocks
Chickens . . .

He had a longer list than Mr Chaine! The new governor-resident brought so much with him he needed a second ship. Fruit trees and tools and wheelbarrows and glass panes and mirrors, too . . .

He had servants, including two young men who were, what? Not quite servants, not quite family. Bobby wanted to talk with them, but they turned away from him on the heels of their well-worn shoes. Their scent was very sweet, and they did not understand Noongar language, only English, which they spoke very like the Governor, who wanted them to have nothing to do with

Noongar people and barked at them to get away. And they seemed quite happy to be standing with the Governor's family, the littler children like emu chicks beside the protective legs of their father, all of them together looking at we people. A red-haired son, not a lot older than Bobby himself, among them.

When the Governor and his family first arrived they had nowhere to sleep unless they remained aboard ship, and they longed to be on land. Chaine said he might put them up. He had a house where his men often stayed, he told them. Where your predecessor, the good Dr Cross, resided.

The Governor and his wife, after so long on a shifting deck, accepted Mr Chaine's hospitality and stayed in a little hut by the grey sea in the shadow of a hill. The cottage sagged as Geordie Chaine pulled the door open and the Governor and his wife both saw how he lifted the door as he pulled it. One corner was propped up with poles, outside and in. There were insects in the walls, no garden to speak of, and white sand everywhere.

Chaine showed them how their fire might be lit; he set the flames himself. Servants were very hard to come by, he said. Told them their luggage would arrive soon. They were very quiet, and so he kept talking, saying there is no coal, but the timber burns well, see? Warm. Unlike coal, no need to clean.

With two ships at anchor in the inner harbour and two public houses keeping many sailors' lips wet, it was a long way from the genteel welcome to the country that a good man's wife and family might have expected.

The grey shingle and whitewashed cottages are a picture and so subtle in the soft afternoon light, the Governor and his wife said. And to overlook the harbour like this . . . They shivered, pulled their cloaks closer about them. The harbour waters held daylight, or so it seemed because look how it glows blue even though the sun has gone and the sky is darkening.

Voices came from close by, loud in the still, chill air; voices singing, drunken and raucous.

We are not many, Mrs Chaine told them, wanting to speak so those voices would not be heard. All her husband could say was these sealers and whalers and sailors are mostly our guests.

You must dine with us, said the Chaines.

I see we will need to adjust ourselves to our new circumstances, the Governor's wife afterwards said to her spouse.

The Chaines took Governor Spender and his good wife Ellen to the little bush hut Cross had built at Kepalup which did not even have the wattle-and-daub walls and she-oak shingles of his building in town. They made the journey in Chaine's new whaleboat (of local timber, he could not help but proudly say, and built by one of my men) and the Governor and his wife pulled in their chins and shrank as they passed the fish-traps and the thin figures with their spears and went to where the river water was so dark. And where, just upstream from where Bobby met the boat and secured it to the bank, a small weir made fine sinews in the river, and a thin trail of foam and bubbles, like someone's hacking cough had left spit and phlegm in the water. But the river on the rocks sounded like someone laughing softly. Chuckling. As rivers and people do. The same.

The Governor politely spoke of the trees, the grassy bank, this quaint path . . . The path maintained, he heard whispered, by many bare feet before us.

Chaine clumped his feet on the ground. And now our own boots, he added. But we are not enough, and will put down stone and with hatchets make a future for already they grow few . . .

Bobby was watching.

The coughing has taken very many away.

The Governor looked at this boy, past him. His pale eyes took in the little hut and Bobby, twisting, trying to look with those same eyes, saw the sheep held in a pen of rough posts and limbs and twigs, the leaves still drying. A fence which scratched and rustled in the breeze. The yellowing, scraggly vegetable garden.

Skelly was at work and, trudging heavily, seemed like a bullock. With arms outspread and moving as if signalling with flags, Chaine indicated the timber frame Skelly had erected, the trees that had been felled, the wall down at the riverbank—there— that held water from a natural spring deep enough for stock to drink their fill. His eyes sparkled, and it seemed he wanted to break into laughter but Bobby, following people's gaze, saw Mrs Chaine turn away from her husband and glance sideways at the Governor and his wife. She is sad, thought Bobby, as her eyes, again sliding away, caught his gaze for a moment.

Their guests looked away from Skelly and Chaine and their achievement, and at the trees standing all around them. Talked of King George Town.

We walked to the top of the hill above the village, they said, and saw we were surrounded, one side by ocean, and the other by grey-green bush rolling as far as the eye can see. You might drown in forest, sink and never be seen.

Such delicate wildflowers we have seen there, they said, taking comfort in detail that, isolated, might be pressed between the pages of books.

Chaine thought the whaleboat would sail them back, and they left late afternoon. The sky was low and grey, and the water of Shellfeast Harbour was grey, too, with some yellow hue of sunlight trapped in the shallows. The wind dropped, and Bobby saw there was rain in the ladies' hair and bright drops on the wool of their clothes. This fine rain—*mitjal*, meaning tears—jewellery drops reflecting the moonlight when the clouds lifted. They rowed and rowed and thought they could see the dark mass of shore across the water. But the wind came up and blew at them, and the ladies were seasick, even though this was quite sheltered water, and it seemed they would never reach that shore, let alone arrive back at the sand and briefly cobbled streets of King George Town.

Finally they reached solid, gleaming sand, but were still inside the mouth of Shellfeast Harbour. Seeing as how the ladies recovered once their feet were ashore, Chaine thought they might walk and he instructed his men to take the boat as best they could to King George Town Harbour. He expected he would see them in the morning, and they would have a late night themselves because there were still a few miles yet to walk. The Governor's old war wound meant he could not walk even that distance, and he went with the men in the boat.

Perhaps it was the difficulty of their journey from Kepalup, or they may have strayed from a straight path, but the ladies stumbled, and it was understood that they must rest. Geordie Chaine spread his long coat for them, and they lay together, the Governor's wife saying, Please do not leave us, Mr Chaine, you have been too kind, sir, but really I must lay myself down . . .

Perhaps she also thought Chaine was like a rock. You could break against him, cling. A thing of strength, that nothing could shake.

Bobby had slipped away, but the cold made the women prefer to be on their feet again walking, and they found themselves moving closer and closer together, and held one another for support, and stumbled again and again, bushes sprinkling them with silver drops like confetti. Not until dawn, just before sunrise with the sky lightening and space growing all around, did they walk down into the valley of the settlement, and the harbour was a great shallow bowl glimmering before them.

The wind had again dropped. The boat had arrived before

them, after all, and here was the Governor, fully clothed, asleep in a chair in their hut.

Still numb and sleep-thickened later that same day, Chaine showed them a mound of earth and a cross newly erected on one slope of the valley that led away from the harbour. A Dr Cross cross. Solid, freshly whitewashed timber. A timber rail around that. Letters that had been neatly chiselled and darkened:

DR CROSS.

A FOUNDING FATHER.

PASSED AWAY 1837.

The man you succeed, Mr Chaine said. The Governor's wife may have given a little shudder. Chaine did not say it was a shared grave. That the man had asked to be buried with a native, Wunyeran. They saw how the Governor had looked at Noongars, and stood away. How could they explain?

Bobby, hardly noticed and with them again, realised Wunyeran's name was not on the cross. Why?

*

Governor Spender moved out to The Farm and away from the community of King George Town. With so many people in his family it was almost like he made another little town altogether separate from King George Town out there where Soldier Killam used to live nearly all the time on his own. Most of the people at the port walked out to The Farm for a special occasion of flag raising and firing guns and planting trees. A tree will be planted, the Governor said in his speech and pointed. Although it was only small, you could see the storybook shape of it already. Norfolk Pine, the Governor named it. It was only a small crowd really, Governor Spender and his people, Mr Chaine and his, an old soldier, a cobbler, a few merchants and sailors and landowners, ex-soldier Killam and ex-convict Skelly, some wives and mothers and children . . . A group of Noongar people, too. Governor Spender was accustomed to public speaking and, taking his time, he looked around the small crowd and saw Bobby. The Governor beckoned him, and for once in his life Bobby was slow to understand and so did not respond. The Governor put down his shovel (he did not use it like the other men) and walked toward Bobby. Some people wondered what he was going to do. Was he angry? He brought Bobby back with him and together— both pairs of hands lifting, each taking a turn on the shovel— they planted the tree.

A memorable day, Governor Spender said. I am the King's representative and . . . He gestured at Bobby Wabalanginy and everybody started clapping. Bobby gave a bow, and the applause increased. Bobby smiled as big as he could, looking at the Governor's son and his two black servants (is that what they were, those two?). He felt very proud.

When Bobby was a very old man he would tell tourists to go look at that towering tree. And shake his head.

I was only a little boy, he said.

*

Geordie Chaine took charge of the bar of the public house he'd hired Mr Killam to manage. He even shouted a round of drinks when Mr Killam returned to celebrate their new business arrangement.

It was a low-ceilinged and dark place, cramped enough to suit the habits of the seagoing folk who were its main customers. It did not yet have the great whale jawbone within which Chaine in later years would stand and command his clientele, but there was a fireplace at one side of the room, and at the other a bar and wall of stone. A grid of wrought iron attached to the wall could be folded over the bar to make the grog safe from the hands of the many who would walk through any wattle-and-daub housing presumptuous enough to think it alone could stop them.

And Mr Geordie Chaine now also had a farm managed by Mr William Skelly (who swelled with pride when addressed as such by Geordie Chaine, and then despised himself). The farm, Kepalup, was out of town just beyond the edge of Shellfeast Harbour, on a river leading inland to the mountains, a branch of which apparently ran to yet another sheltered bay to the east.

*

Early morning, and Bobby lay half-asleep. An easy day, a lazy day. He imagined the sun beginning to show above the horizon, emerging from the sea between the islands, where the whale paths ran. He'd come from the ocean that same way, and been borne by the wind like a bird. Now he was earth and stone. He could not see the sun, but the pale sky was opening, light expanding from right there between the islands. His world opened around him, each day grew a little more.

His feet could not take him as far as his eyes might lead . . . Oh, far enough, but. His piss steamed in the thin morning sunlight. Dew caught the sun. The dark tree trunks, and all around him on leaves and twigs and grasses the water droplets sparkling, so that he was like a spider at the centre of his web.

The blazing orange magic of Christmas tree, they called it. He stayed clear; a branch fell, a feathered-thing flew heavily from the tree, wings straining in the air as it called *Nyu! Nyu!* and turned a very human face to Bobby. Its long legs dangled and swung in the air as it flapped away.

The thin gnarled trunks and crimson blooms of . . . bottlebrush. For a moment the word returned him to a ship's door, to a bowl of soapy water and glass bottles. Bobby missed climbing the mast and, like an eagle, looking to the horizon, seeing all, being unseen.

He wandered to where the view was of limbs of land laying in the ocean, and the islands peeping up saying, me too, me too. All spread like gifts before him at the centre of this sparkling morning.

He heard footsteps, something rolling toward him. Was stopped dead in his tracks. Felt like he'd been slapped in the face.

There was a long whiskered face, its tall ears turning and a quizzical expression directed at him. A mule; and the man astride it wore a long coat, bright as a flower, but fading. He had a tall three-cornered hat, shining medals against his chest, and a sword bumping against his side as he went by, unaware of Bobby.

Bobby stepped back, thin branches fell across his shoulders like comforting arms, and prickly fingers tried to shield his eyes.

Despite the hat, coat, medals and sword, the Governor's hair and skin seemed like nothing, almost as if they were made of the sunlight dappling his clothes, and about to be drawn back through the thin and fragmentary canopy to the sky.

Behind him, two more mules pulled a cart in which two women—mother and daughter?—balanced precariously on chairs. A sharp, sweet scent and stale body odour followed the party. Bobby turned to watch them rattle down the slope. Two young men—dark like himself—sat on the back of the cart, feet dangling. They stared at him, but offered no greeting. So solid, so solemn. Who?

Standing between them, bracing himself with a hand on each of their shoulders, was a boy not much older than Bobby himself; a red-haired boy who poked out his tongue. Frowned.

After they were lost from his sight, Bobby listened to the group proceeding down the slope until they were lost from his hearing, too. Later he saw them emerge on the beach below.

A boat left a ship that was anchored in the harbour. Bobby

had not seen this one arrive. The boat rowed to the sand, and its men lifted the women from the cart and mule and carried them through the shallows. They bore the Governor on their shoulders. As they reached the ship a thin, cracking thunder reached Bobby's ears. Wisps of smoke trailed from among the masts.

Shooting at the Governor?

Oh, they must be shooting into the sky just to say hello.

A YANKEE CHALLENGE

M R KILLAM WAS LEARNING what it was to have someone move in on what you thought was your very own home. He thought it was the last straw. The very last. He was back under canvas, and the Governor was planning the rooms he'd add to the main building; a building Cross had constructed especially for the Cygnet River's Governor's summer home, and which Killam had later claimed as his own. And now the new Governor's family was right there, watching the garden ripen. No surplus to hide away now.

Killam never thought he'd miss the barracks and the company of soldiers and he wondered if he'd done the right thing handing in his resignation. And staying here? It was bad for business having the Governor at The Farm, and how was Killam gunna make his way? And now he had these black boys of the Governor's. Chaine couldn't stop grinning when he brought them to Killam and said the Governor wanted them made useful, trained to be capable working men. They'd work for keep, the Governor had said, until they prove their worth. Train them to be useful, they are simply a burden upon me at present. He thought he had enough mouths to feed in this colony and its precarious supplies, without another two.

Jeffrey and James stood with downcast eyes, dressed in fine clothes which, although shabby, were beyond those to which any working man might aspire. They nodded their heads in reply to Killam's greeting and listened to Chaine's plans for them and their life with Killam.

A solid working life. The Governor wanted them trained to be useful and to have a place in society as workers. Meantime, Chaine said, and it might take some time, we'll have their labour.

Well, Killam knew that they'd have to learn to hold their tongues first of all. He didn't want them talking to the authorities, and best if they never knew the difference between what was legal and what was more in the way of a grey area. If they were clever enough they'd soon realise what could be gained from helping him, and remaining dumb. There was more and more work in this grey area. The reluctance of captains to pay the fee they were charged for entering the harbour meant they anchored outside, and that increased the possibility for tax-free trade. Some called it smuggling, but neither Killam nor his employer, Mr Chaine, used such a term. It was easier to work for Chaine than starting from nothing. And Killam admired Chaine's ingenuity, his pluck and energy.

*

Soldier Killam . . . Well, he was no longer a soldier. Just a man trying to make his own way. Trying to advance his-self.

Easy enough to say every man has to sit on his own arse if, like Chaine, you had money to pad the seat of your trousers, but Mr Killam couldn't afford sitting-down time and had taken to patching his trousers lately. If he wasn't careful, he might soon be as bare-arsed as the blacks hereabout. Not that these boys of the Governor's were bare-arsed; a couple of dandies, were Jeffrey and Jimmy. They'd have to prove their worth, and prove they could earn the food he was obliged to give them. The Governor got here with his notion of showing how the natives could be trained to fill the role of working white men, but suddenly realised he might struggle just to feed his own people.

Big-hearted Chaine stepped in yet again, so soon after buying a dead man's property just to help out the poor widow. Killam wished he'd had the chance—and capital—to do the very same thing. Chaine thought Killam could help train the two black boys.

Killam knew he needed more than his own two hands to properly advance himself in this part of the world. It was handy to have Chaine's backing, at least until he got some capital behind him, some friends and contacts of influence but—as Chaine showed—he needed to offload labour whenever possible. These two might yet prove useful.

They were rowing now. Having left where the curve of sand met the rocks in the very lee of the headland, the boat slid softly across the sea's skin. The boys rowed satisfactorily, and after several brisk strokes of the oars they were beyond the rocky point and the ship's light was once again visible. Closer still and the ship was an almost menacing presence: a squatting coagulation of darkness that the ocean lapped against, that disturbed the wind.

The three in the boat were tense. This was a risky business. The oars dipped, the ocean accepted them. The moon lifted its large and yellow self from the dark silk sea. So calm out on the ocean, and warmer than on land. Tomorrow this ship would lie in the harbour with other Yankee whaling ships.

It would be grand to have a tavern like Mr Chaine. Lucrative too. There'd been enough money passing over that bar the last few days to make up for any high-spirited hijinks the sailors and whalers got up to. But Killam didn't have a tavern, though he'd once sold grog in a hut. He may once have helped ships into the harbour, and called himself harbourmaster and pilot, but when those positions were made official and put up for tender, he'd not won them. Why? Because he didn't have his own boat, and maybe they thought he wasn't good enough with small talk. Maybe because he didn't have the right connections, the right way about him. Chaine wanted to be first onboard each ship and reckoned he was sharp-witted enough to take best advantage of that—to meet the captain or whoever was best able to strike a deal. Then he gave the task over to Killam, paid him a wage.

Killam knew he was sharp-witted, too, but all he had was his own brain, brawn and near enough to bare arse.

He shifted about on his buttocks. Put up a hand. Shh.

The boys held the oars in the air.

No one had time to notice water drops, silver with moonlight, and the stars dancing in the sea.

Drifting on the silky waters of the sound under a bone-coloured moon, Killam was here on unofficial business. Something overheard, initially, about men wanting to desert ship. The captain had kept too close a watch on them while they were ashore, and let Chaine know he didn't want any left behind; he was low on hands as it was. For all of that, Killam had managed to lend an ear to a couple of the men who wanted off. Chaine had suggested he might help such men escape, might hide them away, too. There was a need for *skilful* labour, Chaine had said, looking at the two black boys.

So be it. The escapees had promised him a reward, and had tobacco to bring ashore. Chaine would reward him, too, at some future time, if things turned out well.

Here now, the first of them, sliding down a rope ladder he'd swung over the ship's side. Now, the second . . .

Killam grunted in pain. Something (an anchor? a grappling hook?) plummeted into the boat, glanced against his leg.

Seize him! A voice of authority, he thought, even as he tried to throw off the hands that obeyed it. He saw someone slip into the water, quiet and fast as a seal. Then, dazed from a clip around the ears, he was aboard ship, lamps swinging and shadows shifting. Unsettled, frightened. Face to face with the captain.

Throw 'em in irons.

Jeffrey and Jimmy were sobbing out loud. Begging for mercy. Praying. To our God, thought Killam.

I am a British subject, sir!

They kicked him below deck.

*

Daylight found Killam tied to the rigging; an insect to the captain's spider. Shirtless and bound, he could only turn his head a fraction from side to side. His mouth was gagged, otherwise he would have shouted, The whole settlement is beside me, this is sovereign land, sir! Squirming and twisting to try to catch someone's merciful eye, he chanced to see a many-ended rope, thin and knotted. He realised the crew had gathered, that there was a watching crowd.

The captain made a speech. Any man who tries to escape, or any man who helps him . . .

There was a silence. Killam heard the noise of the rigging, waves lapping the boat. The wind is coming up, he thought, incongruously.

And then felt the first blow. Killam had been a soldier, a fortunate soldier, obviously, because until now he had never known pain like this.

After what seemed a very long time, the captain untied his gag. Up close, he looked into Killam's face. Then moved away, it seemed as if on wheels.

Any man, or any man that helps him, desert my ship . . .
The flogging continued, and Killam cried out, cried out.

They lay him in his own boat, and Jeffrey and Jimmy rowed to
shore. The boys were sobbing still and Killam, knees on the floor
of the boat, was sprawled across a thwart with his back open to
the sky.

The Yankee captain would have left if he could, no doubt, but the
wind kept him anchored just outside the harbour mouth. The
pilot boat came out once again with Geordie Chaine aboard to
take the captain ashore.

The Governor and appointed magistrates heard the Yankee
captain. They listened to Mr Chaine, noted the distress of Mr
Killam and were of the opinion that the Yankee captain would
need to be sent to Headquarters—Cygnet River—on trial for
assault. They placed him in the town gaol.

There were several American whalers at rest in the harbour,
waiting on a shift in the wind, and those Yankee whaling men
had little affection for British law. Bobby Wabalanginy liked
their accent and listened close whenever he heard it, and now he
heard a loud voice saying they should take possession of an English barroom at a little port like King George, strike up 'Yankee Doodle', and break down in genuine fore-and-after.

King George Town had been a disappointment. No pretty
barmaids, although some found comfort with a local native lass.
There was more life in the blackfellas than the townspeople, for
they'd try to trade you a parrot, a spear, and yes, a woman sometimes. But all in all it was a dull place, and now this damned
easterly wind held them and threatened to hold them longer. So

when the American whaling ships heard one of their captains was imprisoned, their crews were excited. Adventure!

At the time, the population of King George Town was mostly unaware that a party of Yankees braced with pistols confronted the Governor. Some, if not many, would have been delighted to hear that the Governor—whose eyes Bobby once thought were dissolving into sky—had no way to stand against them. It was unlucky for the Governor that he was not at The Farm, the population gossiped, and although not pleased that the authority of their colonial outpost had been so lightly dismissed, they enjoyed hearing of the Governor's trials.

His eyes watered with helplessness, humiliation.

His voice blustered, faltered.

He insisted that a fine be paid.

A trifling thing, the Yankees told him, laughing, and tossed coins into his lap. You have a man of ours who absconded.

The Governor insisted that he could not spare resources to help track down every missing sailor.

Wooral was in the room, dressed in the livery the Governor required. The American party walked in, and Wooral's body softened as the exchange developed so that he was overlooked, forgotten. There was no need to step out of his shoes, because he was barefoot—the shortage of footwear in King George Town meant even the Governor could not have servants costumed as he preferred. Wooral dissembled his stance from that preferred by the Governor and, leaning back into the corner of the room, slid down to his haunches. He wanted invisibility; wanted to watch things unfold, was impressed by these men.

Ah by crikey, those blooming Yankees look after their own people, unna?

JEFFREY AND JAMES

JEFFREY HATED THE WAY people always considered James and himself as if they were the same and quite inseparable from one another. Well, they weren't. Weren't inseparable, weren't twins, weren't even brothers. He couldn't remember his own parents, and the people who he'd thought of as his mother and father had all of a sudden disowned him. That was such a long way from here, a long time ago: years and years, and many ship journeys. He still thought of them there in New South Wales when he wanted comfort; actually, not of *them*, but of *being there*. He remembered the oven radiating its warmth and smells, the pages of the Bible turning, rough voices singing hymns and eyes looking down on him. Memories from when he was little more than a baby, he realised.

There were no other children to begin with, only him. Then they had brought James into their home. He came with no name, and they gave him James. Jeffrey remembered no resentment at having to share his foster parents, at least not on that occasion. He liked having baby brother James, liked caring for him and helping Mother with him, in between lessons and Bible study and all the chores children can help with on a farm. In fact, he took over many of Mother's roles so she could care for the child, since he, as they kept telling him, was a big boy now.

James had taken on many of those chores at an even younger age. So, between the two of them, they milked the cows, tended the vegetable garden, made butter and bread, washed dishes and clothes, steamed sheets in the great copper and hung them out on the propped line, and helped with fencing and shepherding . . . Two young boys, they were trained well, and did their jobs so diligently that Father rarely had reason to strike them. They were close, Jeffrey and James in those years. But even then, not brothers, not really.

And then Mother became pregnant. Had a shitty baby. A baby that got all the love and their eyes and hugs even, and just gave vomit and tears and crying. Neither boy liked to dwell on the years from then, and they never talked about it. Their bedding was moved to the shed, their meals increasingly eaten apart from Mother and Father and baby. There was still the Bible, but more and more work to be done, and only orders and punishment from Mother and Father. They still came into the house for hymns and Bible readings. The boys knew Mother and Father liked their singing, and when their voices joined in it was almost like old times, before the baby, before . . .

It was James who chased the old cow. Firstly because it was a bossy one, always hard to get into the milking stall and likely as not to kick if you strayed behind it. When he quite suddenly grew out of the fear of it and realised his mastery, he liked to tease. But Father never saw James chasing the silly cow, oh no, it was Jeffrey he saw chasing it, making it do that clumsy run with its eyes rolling and udder swaying side to side.

Father punished him like a child. Put the gangly boy across his knee and beat him with increasing energy and ferocity. Which was partly why seeing Killam tied up and flogged had upset them so. That was what made them blubber, even though they were grown up now, Jeffrey almost a man.

He smiled to himself, thinking of the hair under James's arms and the quickly stiffening snake in one another's trousers that they knew so well. Smiled again. Father to thank for that, too, when you come to think of it. Him coming back to Jeffrey in the long night after the flogging, with ointments to salve the raw, hot flesh. And coming back nights and nights after that, to lie with him; it excited Jeffrey now just thinking of it.

Father thought he was a sinner, you could see the change in him because sometimes he could not look at Jeffrey, but other times Jeffrey might just touch him or brush up against him, and then it would soon be that the man could not get close enough. Then rush away.

Jeffrey taught James what he'd learned from Father. So not brothers, more like lovers almost. And just as well, because they only had one another now that Father and Mother had children of their own.

At church, when they had been talking of the civilising influence of Christianity on the blacks, and Mr Spender said he was on his way to the most isolated of shores at King George Town to administer a small colony amid hordes of savages where he would likely suffer a shortage of servants on the token salary offered, they invited him to take their own well-raised boys to accompany and support both him and his family. It would continue their Christian education also.

Spender paraded the boys as products of his own endeavours. Said he had trained them to dress, moulded their manners and made them so very useful. It could be done with all of the blacks, he said.

And so Jeffrey and James were paraded and locked away for their own sakes, to spare them from the temptations of civilised life. But even they noticed their clothing was shabbier than it had been, Jeffrey wearing his a little longer before they were handed down to James. Then they arrived at King George Town where there was no one worth parading before. Were they really such a drain on finances?

Spender lent them out to Chaine, and he to Mr Killam. Who they watched receive a cruel flogging tied to a ship's mast, and then rowed to shore in the sparkling sunlight of early morning.

*

Killam lay facedown. Jeffrey and James had tried to help him, but were only able to weep and flutter ineffectually, whereas his good friend—in fact, who would have thought him such a friend?—his good friend Mr Skelly had really come to his aid. Skelly bathed Killam's flayed skin with calloused but surprisingly gentle hands. Killam winced and made little yelping sounds. Skelly told him the story of the Governor's surrender; it was all around the town. Killam would have liked to see the familiar face that accompanied these gentle hands and the voice, but it hurt to turn around.

And that sailor, did he stay away?

Skelly had heard nothing of any sailor. He went out of the hut to speak to someone and when he returned said, Yes, that escaped sailor Jak Tar was with Mr Chaine apparently. On his way out to the river property.

Kepalup.

JAK TAR

JAK TAR SAW NOTHING for him at home, no reason to return. On his way down to the waiting boat he'd heard some warning shout and so, instead of sliding into the boat, he slipped into the water with barely a splash. As soon as his head rose above the surface he knew something had gone amiss and he was treading water in a sea of trouble. He duck-dived and swam beneath the dark mass of the ship, swam underwater with the faces of the captain and first mate in his mind until his lungs were bursting, then surfaced to stars like thorns in his wet vision, gasped, and went underwater again. His thudding heart. Rose to breathe and took his bearings best he could. There must be land not far—he saw the absence of stars, swam toward that. Underwater he took off his jacket, his heavy jumper. Lean and smooth, neither fur nor feather nor scale, he rose to the surface like something made for water, or so he told himself. Took another breath. Slipped off his boots.

The sound of men's voices carried across the water. Their shouts and their rage. Was that his name he heard? Next time he surfaced he was in the moon shadow of that small isthmus not far from the mouth of the harbour. An island close by, barely a stone's throw from the beach.

He swam without a splash, his face barely above water until he reached the rocks. The beach shone white in the darkness and he dared not cross it, felt as visible as a shadow puppet on a screen. Water was warmer than air. He was a seal hauling itself up moonlit rocks with hardly a limb to help him, and dreading the club of some swift-footed, cruel man. He stumbled, crawled to where seaweed was piled high and sand met rock and bur-rowed deep into salty, ribbony stuff. Pulled it over himself for warmth, for the hiding in.

It hid him well enough. But warmth?

Jak Tar was pink and purple wrinkled skin when he rose up stiffly, hobbled with cold, and shook the seaweed off, patting and plucking at himself to be free of the last fleshy ribbon or bauble. He moved away from the rocks, across a corner of squeaking white sand, fine and soft as powder and over succulent fingers . . . Here, his toes gripped one such fleshy plant finger and shivering in the pre-dawn light he scrambled up a smooth granite shelf. Sunlight fell upon him, and the scent of peppermint trees. His skin was still tender and wrinkled, and he imagined it tearing from him, caught and hanging in seaweed-like strips left on the spiky scrub. He smelled smoke and ash and by the warmth realised he'd almost crawled into a still glowing campfire. Live. Red.

Whereas he was wet, grey, and dressed in damp rags and sea-weed and his skin stung in patches. He lay down and almost curled around a pile of embers, lay at the very edge of soft ash and felt it coat his cheek, moving with his every breath. Oh warmth. His back was cold and hard, brittle, but he could not turn over. Why go from boat into deep water?

Opened his eyes. Darkness bled away.

Oh, a boy there, looking at him. Black boy. And two small fires, one either side. The boy had a pouch on the hair belt around his belly. Wore a skin cloak, a pair of sailor's breeches.

Ah, my man Friday, the wide-eyed boy said. Clear English like a dream surprising Jak Tar. The boy was at the mouth of a small rounded hut, rubbing thick oil into his skin. He glowed warmly, cast his own light, was his own sun.

A little dog, a Jack Russell with its head tilted to one side, close-up staring at Jak Tar.

THE HEART OF HOME

T HE HOUSE AT KEPALUP was built as easily as Geordie Chaine had hoped. Two men pressed its pieces together—click snap nail—almost like a child's game; indeed, the boy Bobby saw it as exactly that and would've leapt in and helped if Chaine hadn't warned him off. Chaine wished his own boy were as keen or, for that matter, possessed some of the energy and interest of the daughter. She—Christine—and the black boy Bobby were presently coiled at the outer perimeter of Chaine's consciousness, only springing into the range of his attention at irregular intervals. Where was his son? It irritated him.

The house went up, the two men toiled and Chaine, rising up and down on his toes like a buoy bobbing on the ocean swell, watched them. Neither man seemed inclined to converse with the other, which was for the best as far as Chaine was concerned. So long as the work went well.

Bobby knew the workers by name, and would have insinuated himself into the project but for the presence of Chaine and his countervailing wishes.

Nevertheless, Bobby called out, I say, Mr Killam.

His pronunciation was formal, a near copy of the vowels of

Mrs Chaine, and he seemed able to adopt different ways of speaking at will—from the mixed-up English most of the natives used, to high formality. But it was a child's voice for all that. And there was something in its timbre; call it a dark voice?

He spoke again. Mr Skelly.

The smaller man glowered at him, but there did not seem much malice in it. True, the social class implied by Bobby's voice irked Skelly, the more so because its source was a black boy, but Skelly wanted to impress Chaine with his work ethic and desire to get on with the job. He'd been very grateful when Chaine had asked him to manage things at the farm. They looked an unlikely combination, Killam and Skelly: one stocky and apparently careless of his appearance, the other so tall and neat, all spit and polish and grooming except for the habit of pulling his shirt away from the skin of his back.

Chaine turned, and sailed away.

Geordie Chaine allowed the boy Bobby many liberties because he was a fine boy, and it was only right that he be given every chance to better himself. Geordie was proud to let him into the bosom of his family, like he'd promised Dr Cross. It was part of the pact they'd made, along with seeing the good Dr Cross's wife given every assistance. By now she'd be home.

His own wife, Mrs Chaine—Grace—was a cultivated, cultured woman. She cared . . . Their new house (prefabricated, so easily erected) would've been the envy of the tiny seashore settlement, if only it had a population capable of such discernment.

Grace Chaine tutored her own children, since any help—hired or conscripted—was best applied to the many other things that needed doing in these, their altered circumstances. She guessed Christine and Christopher were a bit older than Bobby, but were obviously more advanced in their studies and social development. They were generous children and their proud mother observed the signs of their moral superiority: their helpfulness, and the allowances they made for Bobby. They were nearly always looking out for him. And why not? They'd known him from since before they ever got here—remember, he rowed them ashore himself—and how could they ever forget their teeth crunching into golden beetle? They'd be looking out and Bobby Wabalanginy would suddenly appear: come leaping over the crest of a hill; or when their papa took them down to the seashore there he was, standing on rocks at the ocean's edge where just now a wave had collapsed.

They were twins, but Christopher was still finding his feet, still getting his balance after that long sea voyage from home. Christine could barely remember leaving; her earliest memories floated on ocean, and she felt as though she had surfed to shore. But Christopher was a buttoned-up, hands-by-his-side sort of child who would now and then stand to attention with his fringe straight across his brow like a helmet, his mouth a thin line. Christine had tended him when he was seasick, emptied his bucket of vomit, wiped his brow. Not that she was a servant to him, or obsequious. No, she was the leader, but she cared for him. Was it at sea then that their relationship had set, or had it always been that she was always the one who decided a direction and reached back to grab her brother, made sure he came, too, so they could later share the talk of it? Like they shared the one room in their new home, its walls of twigs and clay.

She remembered, not so long ago perhaps since she herself was so young, when their home here at Kepalup had a door of animal skin. One day a native swept it aside and stood proud and tall with an axe and boomerang stuffed into his hair belt. Dangling at the front was a piece of fur and his thingy. He peered into the room, and spoke, but all she understood was,

Cross Cross. Children and mother retreated into the tiny enclosed space, but Bobby walked at the man talking blackfella
lingo. Outside, Papa had his rifle in hand, raised.

Bobby laughed, brushed past the man and stood between
him and Papa, his back against the barrel of Papa's gun. Bobby
stood between and against them both offering their names to
one another and, switching from one language to another, was
so animated, so cheerful and delighted in their company that he
soon had everyone smiling.

The naked man went away with Papa's hat pulled tight onto
his head. And he never came back no more.

Anymore, Christine heard her mother say. Didn't come *anymore*. Didn't return ever again.

Yes, Missus Chaine tutored Bobby, too, of course. Strange,
but at first Bobby was shy, since he didn't know how he should
be with her: look into her face, keep his back turned or what?
Whose relation was she?

She thought Bobby shy. Sweetly took his jaw in her hand one
time. Look at me, she said. Look at me when I talk.

He smiled. Saw how giving his smile meant a lot to her and
that, therefore, so might not giving his smile. But it was the same
for him, because he wanted to please her, too. She liked him to
look at her, but sometimes watched him closely with Christine.
Even though he was a boy himself he was formal with Christine,
like he was a grown man and she was forbidden him. So he
thought, not yet understanding the force that can drive a man
and woman together. He was still a child.

And pleasing Missus Chaine helped him learn the words; the
reading and writing of her sound and what those marks might
mean. And even painting; he liked the feel of those things, the
paper more than the slate. And then, slowly, he came to need
the feel of all those small and intricate movements required to
build up a picture, a story, a permanence. Came to need the ritual

of it, the absorption in the doing of things, and then—stepping back—oh look what had been brought forth. It was like you froze things, froze the fluid shift and shaping, held it. Like cold time. *Nyitiny*. Like a seed in cold time, and when the sun came out the waters rose.

Roze.

Roze a wail.

*

The notes went from the piano, through the window, and joined the trembling light which lay over the harbour. Awestruck, Bobby watched Mrs Chaine's hands closely as she played and then, when she left, sat with his hands splayed above the keyboard, humming, touching, softly moving his lips. Soon he was playing simple pieces by ear, matching sound to the keyboard pattern.

Mama, called Christine, as was her way, and she rushed to fetch her mother, the two of them delighted at Bobby's achievement.

Grace Chaine was also a watercolourist of—as she herself said—some small accomplishment. She took real pleasure in it. Mother and children and their little friend painted pictures from books first, then from nature. They made washes of grey-blue skies, clouds billowed on the paper, clouds that had bellies heavy with rain. And when Bobby made a solid stem, a dark cloud joining ground to sky, and explained it in his own mother tongue, they worked out that the English words for it would be *a leg of rain*.

That afternoon three children strode the earth, giants of all creation. On slate boards they played at spelling. But Bobby's name! His real name. Who could spell that?

There were few servants, and very little labour available. Mr Chaine had found a man with carpentry skills, best of all one who could work in stone and even metal. Skelly was capable at a blacksmith's forge, and could also make a boat.

Now, from inside the house, Geordie Chaine saw movement at the edge of his vision. Three children, Christine, Christopher and black Bobby leaping in the flaws of his window glass, bent and sliding down toward the river over the other side of a patch of open, grassy ground. Damp ground, good soil, and with small holes dug all over it even in the time Cross had been here. It had caught fire in that time, too, just this patch. The children ran, Bobby out front, skipping backwards and facing Christine as she ran up to him. It pained Geordie Chaine to see his boy, pale-haired Christopher, trailing the other two. What playmates were there for his son? What young man might he become in this new land? As for the girl . . . But they were children yet. His daughter turned to hurry her brother and Bobby scanned their surrounds while he waited. Those blank windows at the house.

The children ran through soft grass, followed a natural pathway, a path any visitor used after crossing the river. They ran past the fence being built around the garden, its upright posts of Strawberry Jam Tree; the saplings just the right size for a fence post, needing only the weedy branches trimmed. It burned to a fine ash, too. Further down the slope a bubbling spring fed a pool, made a creek, flowed into the river. Chaine planned to build a wall around that spring, make a well.

I come back from the islands out there, Bobby told his friends, pointing. I come back and speared him in the leg! I rode a boat with a gun in my hand. I stood on the old men's shoulders and waved down at the soldiers!

Bobby told them stories, sometimes nearly the same ones Papa told them. Nearly, but different.

Skelly bringing them sheep back, said Bobby, and he got old Nelly on a lead, (he mimed holding the lead, the weary horse) and all of a sudden all these Noongars standing all round him.

Spears *mirrel*, you know, ready to spear him. He proper scared then, like he gunna mess himself and I, said Bobby, never too modest, I go up and say, This is my friend Mr Skelly and Dr Cross he's my friend, too. Then Bobby grabbed Skelly's gun and said, This rifle my friend, too, and held the gun and his hand up like a governor or soldier or Geordie Chaine so they knew he was a strong man.

Christine laughed at him. Oh yes, so you say.

And Bobby said, Yes, I say. You know, I jumped over the top of all their spears and over the moon, too, still holding Mr Skelly's hand, and when I landed I put Skelly on my shoulders and took off. Running like an emu.

Bobby held his arm, hand up, making it look like an emu's head and turning around, just a little bit frightened and watchful, looking back as he ran.

And Skelly sitting on my shoulders backwards so he could watch their spears flying after us, and tell me run this way, that, to dodge them. Skelly on my shoulders backwards, said Bobby, giggling, his feet knocking on my back, his thingy in my face . . .

Christopher laughed out loud, Christine opened her mouth, Oh yuck . . . but Bobby was gone, running down to the river and they ran after him. Bobby pulled rushes from a grass tree beside the spring, and the twins helped him make a carpet of tiny criss-crossed spears. Together they walked barefoot across to reach the edge of the pool.

The trees were women leaning to the water to wash their hair, and when the children stood under their limbs they were among loved ones. Christine looked up to a magpie, just above her, a grey fuzz of downy feathers on its chest. A parent bird, glossy black and white, landed beside it. They were close, just beyond her reach, and their gaze held hers. The birds warbled and Christine tried to answer with the sound they made, but they looked at her quizzically. From close behind came the voice of another magpie.

She turned and there was Bobby, at her shoulder, magpie-talking, liquid sound bubbling from him. The birds turned their heads, each keeping one eye on them. And stepped along the branch a little closer.

Bobby sang one short phrase. Christine tried to repeat it, but her mouth was stone and wood, her tongue cloth. Close together, face to face like this, music continued to spill from Bobby's lips and tongue and bright teeth and then from feathers and sharp beaks, too, as the magpies joined in, their songs merging, swelling, buoying them all.

At a distance, the bubbling music spilling over him, Christopher crouched by the riverbank. Fins and tails of mullet broke the surface, trees shifted and whispered reassurance among themselves, and the river flowed over stone weirs with barely a sound. The fish here, Christopher saw, could move neither upstream nor down.

The three children spent most of that afternoon throwing crudely made spears into the water. Twice there was a small spear moving sideways, upright on the surface, twice it toppled from fish flesh before they could grasp it. Small groups of mullet, frightened, eventually leapt from the water, over the stone, out of the pool. Each time it happened the group of mullet in the next pool was a little larger. Yet this pool was smaller than the first, and so the fish even easier to spear. Bobby grinned when Christine tried her spear there.

Trees bent over them, bowed each side of the sandy pathway Bobby led them along, then straightened again and rose higher as the humans passed. At another bend in the river there was a tiny tributary and Bobby, crouching, plunged an arm below the surface and came up with a handful of red clay. A few steps away he did it again, but this time it was white clay in his hand.

Christopher was tiring, was too mature for ochre dabbed onto his skin. The bubbling spring held him, how it fell from granite onto sword and sedge, along a cleft running down to the pool. His father, he knew, thought to fatten sheep and cattle beside it.

They made letters of ochre, three-dimensional at first, then smeared large on bark and rock. Finally, they used their fingers to make letters in the sand. Bobby showed them footprints; did they know the animals that made each mark?

Alitja, look, he said, showing them some scratches not far above the base of a tree. Possum writing, laughed Bobby. He's not here no more, he gone along the ground to 'nother tree. Too far for him jumping. See here? he said. Gone up again. There were marks in the trunk, too, rough axe cuts and—Bobby showed them how—you put your toes there. He ran up the trunk, toes finding the steps a stone axe had made.

Christopher shook his head, looked into the water for mullet.

Bobby and Christine kept on. Possum home, Christopher heard Bobby say, but he not coming out today. He saw the long white curve of Christine's leg, that she'd tucked her skirt into her pantaloon and that she and Bobby were in a high fork of the tree, limbs and leaves like a safety net below them.

Christine thought Bobby was funny.

Wabalanginy, he said, the name bubbling on his lips. Bobby. He balanced a honky-nut on his head, and she laughed with him all the more.

She said he should have a real policeman's hat. Like Daddy said Peel's men wore on the sleety cobbles of a London she couldn't remember. She skinned her knee, and when Bobby bent to the wound felt a thrill she'd never known.

Very close to the possum, but held high in strong limbs and dappled leaf light they heard whispering all around them.

* * *

With the possum cooking in hot ashes and earth, and his sister and Bobby down at the river, Christopher read by the fire. Oh yes, books came, sometimes published only two or three years before they arrived, and sent by much-loved family at home.

Home?

Christopher couldn't remember that home, the mother country. Or not in any way removed from what he read. Where was his knife? Christine had taken that, too. That was from home. It folded neatly away, the blade inside the wooden handle. He was like that knife, Christopher told himself: an innocent exterior, the sharp steel blade hidden out of sight. A knight humble, but valiant.

Suddenly the valiant knight almost squeaked in surprise, and fear made his heart gallop. One of the *blacks*—dark beard and hair greased tight on his scalp, ropey scars all across his chest like armour—stood beside the fire.

Hello, Christopher stammered, and then—remembering Bobby—*Kaya*.

The man's face split into a grin, was made familiar by the smile. He lay his spear by the fire, unhitched some other implements from his hair belt and—since Christopher made no move otherwise—crouched beside the fire and began talking. Occasionally he paused and studied Christopher. Awaited some reply.

Christopher nodded, grinned and smiled foolishly. No knight, but a jester. Then voices, and in a moment Bobby and Christine burst from the foliage like birds.

The man said something to Bobby. Bobby laughed in reply, not quite looking at him, and gave him Christopher's knife. And then the man was gone. Three children remained.

A SMILE FOR *KAYA*

JAK TAR HEARD CICADAS and wind in the leathery leaves and even the grass. The unequal crunch of his companion's footsteps. He had not expected to miss the ocean, or to miss the very sound of water, and found himself walking down to the river once or twice a day to listen to it falling and laughing among the rocks at one end of the pool. The water there was dark, deep, and reeds grew around its edge save where the boats set people and stores ashore. The pool was surrounded by trees that leaned as if seeking their own reflections, or perhaps guarding and protecting its secrets.

Jak Tar was not accustomed to being inland, nor was he accustomed to being isolated. In a ship it was hammocks side by side and the sounds and smells of companions all around. Here it was just him, bush, and a taciturn William Skelly, who limped around the clearing, busy from dawn to dusk, and kept a gun loaded and close to hand.

Well, it's not our home, is it? Skelly said, when Jak Tar enquired, and elaborated no further.

Skelly was taciturn, but effective enough at communicating

what was required of Jak Tar. Jak was to assist him in every way. At this stage, as agreed with Chaine, Jak was fed, sheltered and kept out of the way of the authorities. Skelly himself also liked to stay away from soldiers and officials, he said, but did not elaborate.

Jak Tar thought of when he sat up in the sand and seaweed and looked into the face of that black boy staring right back at him. Bobby, as he now knew him. Not only his body, but also his mind must've been numb that day. He let himself be led to a group of huts. A white Jack Russell ran at him, barking, and a man and two women stirred inside the hut it guarded. They were naked, they were black. Jak Tar turned his head, and the boy took him to a small hut, barely large enough to crawl into. He fell prone on an animal skin, and someone massaged him until at last he was thawing, becoming warm. He must've slept for hours, and when he awoke he was alone in the hut with a fire smouldering not far from its opening. He crawled outside and unfolded unsteadily to his feet. A group of natives around another fire watched him stumble away out of sight. What to do now? he wondered, pissing. The little dog trotted up to his feet sniffing, and looked up into his face. He reached to pat it, and the dog spun around and trotted back in the direction it had come. Not thinking, he followed it back to the group by the fire; conversation softly continued. About him? There was food on a piece of soft bark. The senior man said something, and turned his face away.

I take you to your people? Bobby said.

No, not the port, not the village.

Mr Geordie Chaine, then.

The boy had gone, Jak Tar had retreated to the same hut and sleep, and when he awoke again was alone. The fire had gone out. He listened to waves sighing on the beach, and when it was light walked to the highest nearby point. He was on a sandy isthmus, the landlocked harbour to his left, the open water of a great bay with its headlands and islands to his right. There was no sign of his ship. He could see the few buildings of the settlement across the other side of the harbour.

Waiting by the simple huts, he studied the way they were woven together and wondered how long they might last, untouched. Other than the ashes and huts there was little sign anyone had been here, but it was a naturally protected place. Peaceful. He found a spring seeping out of the white beach sand at the base of a granite boulder nearby. He made sure to keep out of sight of the settlement, remain alert. But he was hungry. Anxious. What to do? He kept an eye on the settlement, and watched a boat leave from the other side of the harbour, heading for the channel. It detoured late and came to rest on a beach on the inner side of the isthmus, as close as it could to the campsite from where Jak Tar watched. Bobby leapt from the bow.

*

I don't know nothing about where you've come from, insisted the stocky Geordie Chaine. You've come to me looking for work, saying you'll work for your keep. I've agreed.

It was the same fine whaleboat brought him here—Jak handling it although the boy seemed capable, despite his young age—and its sail had driven them out of the harbour, north across the bay into yet another harbour and, eventually, a river. Trees closed over the narrowing water until it was almost a tunnel, and eventually they stopped at a sort of natural lock where a sheet of granite on the bank formed a fine, dry landing. They tied the boat and walked up an open, grassy slope to a couple of rough bush buildings, a surprisingly neatly manufactured timber home, a small sheep pen, and a rudimentary vegetable garden. A man was hammering at an anvil under a roof of bark and rushes. William Skelly.

*

That was some months ago now. With so much time on his own, in this bush watching sheep, Jak Tar's shipmates often wandered through his mind. He sighed with relief each time he thought of the bullying captain, but for all that Jak Tar missed the sea. With luck, Chaine would want him to command the boat he and Skelly were building so very slowly. There were always interruptions, other tasks: the sheep, for instance, depending who was around to help; the vegetable garden. Often enough Chaine came rushing with orders for fresh food for some ship that had come in, and sent them out for tammar or quokka or yongar. (He was learning the many different types of this bounding animal, kangaroo.) Skelly suggested Jak get Wooral or Bobby, who was really a bit inexperienced yet, to help.

When he tried to enlist Bobby, the boy took him to meet Manit. They did not go to her camp but along a tributary upriver, following a path of coarse, dry sand interspersed with occasional small rocky pools of water. When they reached where the creekbed became a rocky slope, and a series of pools one above the other, Bobby came to a halt and looked around. Dark lines across the rock showed where water, when more plentiful, flowed from pool to pool. The old woman sat alone by a small fire in a clearing among the trees on the bank to one side of the rocky creekbed. The fire was only recently lit, Jak noticed, and the woman was not really alone—he saw figures moving around a pool at the top of the sloping series of water holes, and there were other small fires not far away.

Manit wore a sort of rough petticoat under her kangaroo-skin cloak, and Bobby touched it in his conversation with her, and made sure Jak Tar knew it was worn for him. Respect for his ways. It was hard to know her age. Beyond child bearing, Jak reckoned, but not so old as to be stooped; she moved easily. She poked at the fire with a well-worn stick, and spat, and glanced at Jak as Bobby spoke. Jak guessed Bobby was talking about him, making his case. The boy seemed to amuse her.

Jak, only an object of discussion, looked around him. Through the trees he could see one pool, so blue that it might have been an opening through to the sky behind it. The rocks were a red-orange colour, unlike others he had seen in the region. A crow landed beside the pool and bent to drink. But it seemed very watchful. There were many crows in the trees, and now that they had been noticed they began to speak.

Manit slapped her thigh and laughed. Jak heard *Kaya*.

He repeated the word.

She looked into his face; gave a small, slow smile.

*

Jak Tar had assumed the men did the hunting, but Manit proved invaluable, and with Bobby as communicator they were success-ful in supplying Chaine's order. Manit would slip away before they got back to Chaine, taking enough of the catch to feed her family. Or so Jak assumed, and it seemed fair to him; he wouldn't have succeeded without her help.

In truth, Manit's very presence challenged and confronted Jak Tar. Nothing in his experience had prepared him for coop-erating with an elderly, mostly naked woman who teased and mocked him so. His first instinct was to dismiss her, but he could not dismiss Bobby's obvious respect for her, and Jak Tar was truly grateful to him for the help he'd provided. So he persevered longer than he might have otherwise.

The old woman knew where animals would be and Jak realised it was best to let Bobby handle the rifle, and not only because he had such a good eye. On their first hunting trip together Jak had

189

assumed command of the gun—he was the man, he was white. Manit, through Bobby, told him where to wait and where the kangaroo would rush, and then she and Bobby went to frighten the animals toward him. Jak Tar twisted his head as she unexpectedly returned, and at the same instant a mob of wallabies sprang from the bushes in front of him. *Tammar!* He heard the yell and swung the barrel, fired, missed. In one motion Manit slapped him, grabbed the gun, swung it like a club and knocked one tardy tammar senseless.

Wide-eyed Jak Tar had one hand on his cheek. Manit laughed and squeezed his narrow nose between her finger and thumb. He was shocked speechless. His eyes watered.

He was a gentle man, Jak Tar, and not accustomed to being bossed like this by an old woman.

When he was a child, his Aunty used to bring dripping from the kitchens where she worked. Cooked for the Queen, she told him, and made him memorise the names of all the royal family. When she could, she took him to see them wherever they paraded in public.

In the bush, this arse end of the world, Jak Tar came to think of the half-naked and barefoot woman as Queen Manit. It was clear she was accustomed to command. No jewellery, though, at most a few feathers and some woven possum fur; no rouge on her cheeks, though there might be fish oil and ochre; no bustling skirts supported by whalebone corsets, though she knew well the right whale from whose throat those corsets came. She wore animal skins, sometimes a petticoat or blanket, and carried a possum-skin bag more often than not. She chewed tobacco, kept a wad behind her ear.

So that was Queen Manit, said Jak Tar, who had tried to explain the British monarchy to Bobby. But who was the older man often in Manit's camp?

Menak, said Bobby of the man who turned his back on Jak

Tar whenever he saw him. Got that little dog from Dr Cross, and he speared Skelly!

It was something Jak Tar thought he'd have to ask William Skelly about, but Skelly said they'd best take the sheep along the creek toward the bay; he needed to work on a new boat for Chaine. And the sheep needed new pasture.

OVER THE HORIZON

G EORDIE CHAINE'S PLAN was to take the boat around the coast and explore inland from the many sheltered anchorages of which he had heard sailors talk. He intended to look for good grazing country. Mr Skelly had built him a fine boat, a schooner they called *Grace Darling*, and on its deck there was a very small stable, the walls of which could be moved in tight around.

Bobby led the horse along a wide, cleated plank from a jetty Skelly had also built out from the riverbank. They placed the animal in a sling, supported by the mast, so that along with the walls each side it might never fall, even in a wild sea.

On that fine schooner's maiden voyage, Jeffrey and James huddled together and were hardly any help at all. Not that it mattered because Kongk Geordie Chaine said he and Killam and Bobby (the youngest of them all) could handle such a fine craft grandly between them, and sang out in his fine and buoyant voice that it was a compliment to Mr Skelly how well it sailed, and a tribute to the timbers of this country, too, this ocean and this fine breeze. And the sails filled and all those aboard were well pleased with his words, except perhaps those who didn't care about this country because it was not their home.

After barely more than a day's sailing, the new Skellybuilt boat was well and truly tested: the wind started to batter and roar, to tear at their sails and hair, and the waves grew bigger and bigger. They might've taken down the sails and battened up but the sheltered anchorage of Close-by-island was not far, surely. The boat leaned over, and oh the spray and the tremble as it was hauled along the front of waves with sails stretched. They went far out from shore hoping to outrun the storm coming back because there was no sheltered shore here, but were caught and seized, and could not see, could only fight to stay upon the boat, stay alive. When the horse began to shriek and panic, Bobby had a mind to let it leap, but he didn't, and that we got through at all, Bobby told Christopher and Christine, echoing their father's words, was a tribute to that boat and its timbers and we sailing it.

But you can never know what's in the ocean.

So they saw out the storm and the night and next day were still out of sight of land and racing along; a fine day, the sea and sky blue, and the wave at the bow all foam and lace and bubbles and further ahead, there! Land! They were not sure where they were, not even Chaine who had the charts and journals of those early mariners who plotted the coast or so they say, but as they rounded a headland the boat struck something, hard. A reef, or maybe a whale, though no one never saw nothing, just felt the shocking jolt, and then the boat still going, still going, but so low in the water and sluggish they knew it was holed, knew they'd never even anchor but must run it up on that white sandy beach right there if they were gunna save it.

The wind blew from the land, flicking the spray back from waves they were suddenly among and they were grabbed and jostled and pushed and everyone was swimming *inside* the boat. Frightened excited laughing Bobby untied the horse and it swam powerfully ashore, hauling him behind.

Talking about it afterwards they realised that storm must've got inside their heads, too, and flung them further around the coast than they'd thought or meant to be. Oh, they knew they'd gone past Close-by-island alright, but not how far. They stuck the oars upright in the sand for when they'd come back.

We could save her, I know, Chaine said, or if we have to we can build another from her timber.

He had always wanted to walk back from further east of Close-by-island to get a good look at the coast and some of the bays he'd heard the whalers and Noongar talk about. He wanted to know about them, because so far he only knew King George Town and our home and Close-by-island Bay that our river led him to.

(Did Bobby even know how much it pleased Christine that, when he recounted the tale, he said *our* river, *our* home?)

They hauled things from the boat, retrieved things from along the shore, and of course a lot of the flour was ruined, the gunpowder wet, and even two of the water barrels were leaking.

Chaine took his bearings from a hilltop, trying to determine just how far east they must be, and concluded they'd all go on rations, as a cautionary procedure, because they were further east than expected and who knew how long it might be before they reached a place they would recognise. Chaine looked to Bobby, but Bobby was only a boy and declared he didn't know this country or its people. Bobby could tell that Kongk Chaine and Soldier Killam were worried, maybe a little scared.

You could see where people camped—there was an old fire, diggings, even a very faint path. Bobby was glad they'd left; he didn't want to come across them without signalling their own presence first, but Chaine said, No, if we meet them we'll deal with them, but no need to attract attention yet.

Chaine wanted to send Jeffrey and James out hunting, thinking they were old enough, and there were two of them, and since they were black they must know how . . . But they knew nothing about hunting. They were hungry, though, that's for sure, because Chaine dispensed only a little biscuit and a little water at a time.

It was hard going, just the walking, and there was no water they could find. It was good to have the horse loaded, but it had to be led, and hobbled at night, and needed good food and plenty of water, too. But way out there so far from home (Bobby, recounting it, waved his hand toward the sunrise) there's not so much of those things. He was so hungry for meat! Chaine and Killam, too, and Jeffrey and James most of all. But Chaine said, No, we have many days to go yet and if someone can find and kill something (looking hard at the two young men) then we can eat to our heart's content, but what we now have should leastways get us home if we are disciplined. We will make it last. Mr Killam, I expect more from you, Sir. The husbanding of our resources, the will to stay our course . . . That is what sets us apart, Sir.

For the moment there was energy in his voice, but for all of them it was difficult. Sometimes there were well-beaten paths or dry creekbeds that served as such and gave them shade, where otherwise there was none because of the short and spiky bushes, but as soon as such paths headed inland, Chaine, looking to his compass and the curve of shore, took them back beside the ocean. That salty breeze, the sound of waves, the fetid scent of the dense growth in the valley between dunes and sometimes a soak or spring or ridge of granite solid under their feet, suddenly ringing under the horse's hooves.

They walked all day, and at day's end fell and slept wherever they'd reached. The nights were cold and the wind strong, and they sat around the one campfire, eating their meagre allowance. Chaine and Bobby slept by the campfire once the horse was checked and settled, but the other three moved away and lit a separate fire of their own. They slept huddled closely together.

Sometimes Bobby heard one or other of the boys grunting and moving in his sleep as if tossed by brutal nightmares.

Next morning Jeffrey and James were sulky, not talking with Chaine and staying close to Killam, as if they were family, together, in a strange place. And then they would come apart, all three in separate directions.

The scrub was so dense they had no choice but to walk the soft, sandy beaches. But in places the seaweed banks were so deep they went onto the damp sand between seaweed and sea, even into the sea itself. Then they had to fight the horse to stop it drinking seawater.

Bobby collected dew from the grass and shrubs in the early morning using a long piece of folded bark he'd kept from the day before, and they drank it slowly because it was so precious. Refreshing, but not really enough.

They were thirsty and oh so hungry. Even Killam was angry with Chaine, who said he was also hungry, and so, too, the horse. But we must get by, he insisted, with as little as we can and we will travel further yet.

Killam baked damper. Too much! said Chaine, and now they ate more than he rationed else it spoil and go to waste. Killam said, Sorry, a miscalculation, but seemed pleased enough. Even so there was not much to eat, and Chaine saved what he could along with the biscuits and dried meat for the future.

Jeffrey and James asked Bobby at different times: did he and Chaine eat food secretly, sneak away on their own? Could Bobby get some? For there was now only flour and dried biscuits. Once Bobby recognised tubers, another time some other root; he shook seeds from trees and ground and pounded and roasted them in ashes. It was women's work, he said, because he was not sure how it was done. And they kept moving, on a journey that was dry and hard and sandy and for which there was no path.

Jeffrey went to Chaine as they rested, staring at their feet. Mr Killam was starving them, he said. Chaine looked to Killam, who had charge of their rations, and Killam only said, We might all complain because our rations are small. The two grim men looked at one another, and Chaine said, Mr Killam is responsible for you and for your welfare, not I, or not so directly. Killam told Jeffrey that if his contribution to the party increased, so might his rations. How could he do that? What could he offer?

Jeffrey turned his back, as Bobby had seen Mrs Chaine do sometimes when her husband displeased her, and walked away.

Bobby, busy with the horse next morning, was slow to realise Jeffrey and James were not there. Chaine added that Mr Killam's rifle and several days' ration of food and water were also missing.

There was no sign of the two youths by nightfall, but late the following day Bobby saw two heads bobbing in the distance like corks in the sea a long way behind, and that evening he saw the glitter of their fire. He told Chaine, then listened to the two men talk of compassion and discipline, and what action to take if the boys returned.

Or we could take them at their campfire, suggested Killam, who seemed most concerned at the loss of his rifle.

Next day they came across a kangaroo snared in a noose of some description. Chaine walked up to the frantic, kicking animal, loaded both barrels and held the weapon to the beast's wide-eyed head. Click. The barrel jammed, an unfortunate characteristic of this particular gun. He pulled the other trigger, and the animal stiffened and fell to the ground with all their ears ringing.

Killam took the noose which was made from many neatly woven strands of sinew. He admired the ingenuity of placing it on a thin path a little way into a tight tangle of bushes. Bobby said they could leave at least a leg for whoever had set the snare. But no, they would not. Those runaways might receive it. They lifted the animal onto the horse.

Late that day they saw two figures, it had to be Jeffrey and James, in the distance. They butchered the kangaroo and cooked it that evening, but Chaine kept some in reserve. The party moved off in the morning and saw the faraway figures reach their departed camp, but nothing remained for them. Killam had taken the trouble to carry any excess even of skin and claw out to the rocky point and dump it in the ocean.

Jeffrey and James came within yards of Bobby the next afternoon as he trailed the two men and the horse. You help us, Bobby? This even though he was a boy and they several years older, and should be men really. Chaine affected to ignore them, and Killam turned and sneered, but neither said anything until they stopped and the light began to fade. Jeffrey and James walked a step or two behind Bobby, and came to a halt when he did. Killam held out his hands and the two young men placed his rifle there.

We need to unpack, Chaine said, and indicated the loaded horse. Bobby bent over a fire and the boys attempted to set up camp while Killam and Chaine sat and smoked and snorted criticism, then stepped in to direct the recalcitrants: sent them to collect firewood; showed them (again) how to hobble a horse. And as the small party sat around their fire, Mr Geordie Chaine explained how, in order to teach and train Jeffrey and James, he was going to put them on smaller rations than before, smaller than their own. He still did not know how far they must yet travel. And they had *stolen* enough some days ago to last them a much longer time. You will not die of starvation, never fear.

The party stretched out in a line, became small clusters; Chaine and Bobby at the front, Killam next, Jeffrey and James trailing, dropping further behind. Killam drifted back to join them, came to Chaine off and on over the day, the two men sharing the burden of responsibility, the ingratitude of those boys, their talk of distance and fatigue. Bobby moved away and back, went to higher ground, looking for granite islands on the plain, for hollows of green or level sheets of granite on the slopes . . . But there was no green, no sloping land, and any distant granite islands were dreamed or imagined way over there beyond the horizon. Distances grew between all members of the party except for the two young men, who together stewed and chewed resentment.

In the late daylight it might have seemed they all huddled together, especially if you were to look from some elevated distance across the wide sandy plain, but there were two thin plumes of smoke. The horse was hobbled but needed freedom enough to feed, and because on previous nights it had been unsettled— usually by dingoes, to judge from the howling—Chaine said he'd take first watch, follow the animal for a bit. Killam could take over halfway through the night.

Killam liked himself and his charges a little separate when they slept, and although Bobby was not accustomed to being alone by his fire and sensed a shifting, malevolent energy in the darkness beyond its light, he fell asleep quickly, soothed by clucking tongues of flame and glowing coals. But during the night he awoke startled and no longer alone, because some evil spirit had slipped through the dimming firelight into his roll of blanket and clothing, and was breathing on the back of his neck, palming his belly, pressing itself against his flanks.

Bobby flung an arm back, *Yoowart*! Rolled and leapt to his feet shouting, No! No!

Mr Killam sprawled there, looking up. Some nights ago a dingo, flame-lit on the far side of campfire, had met eyes like this with Bobby.

Why, Bobby, what disturbs you, what brings you to my bed?

No, Bobby said. Not your bed.

Killam looked around, Oh, I . . . Was I sleepwalking, young Bobby? Mumbling, he picked himself up and turned his back. I'd best be back at my camp, those villains'll be going through my bags to find some leather to chew on if I leave 'em or let 'em. They'll be at one another now, and I . . . Spindly-limbed, pale skin gleaming in the light of the newly risen moon and alien without hat or boots or trousers, Killam picked his way back to his own bedroll on tender feet.

Musing on Killam as *djanak* or *debbil-debbil*, Bobby watched the stars shifting so slowly and then just one star falling, falling . . .

Next thing he was sitting bolt upright as a gunshot echoed all around the sandy plain: gunpowder in his nostrils, wind shrieking, frightened clouds scudding across the sky. Two figures standing at the other fire looked down at something on the ground; something groaning, coughing, spitting. A few steps told Bobby it was Killam, and he'd been shot.

Jeffrey was going through the saddlebags while James held the gun, saying, Get the other one, other gun. Their ruthless focus: ammunition, food, water.

Killam writhed on the ground, uttering sounds of some devil, not a human.

Another voice saying, Come with us, Bobby. Leave these bloody white men.

Bobby turned and ran, calling out, Mr Kongk Chaine, Sir, he been shot! The tightly bound mallee all around him was like waves of the ocean. Clouds in waves, too, and the moon a ship, itself plummeting.

Geordie Chaine had been well beyond the firelight, out in the darkness and wind and with the horse as it threaded its way among the many stands of scrub, the crouching mallee, the mounds of rock and stubbled earth. Moments before, he had turned the horse back toward camp. The wiry shrubbery around him jostled and swayed in the wind. Like I'm in a crowd of people who are hostile to me, he thought, and immediately pushed the strange idea away. He looked to where the camp must be, hoping to see the fire, and instead saw a bright flash, and then heard the sound of a gunshot. Startled, he staggered and would have fallen but for the thin, springy boughs and prickly twigs that caught and held him. He was still recovering when, almost like some creature emerging from the ocean depths, a thin figure detached itself from the unformed, jostling darkness between him and the camp. Chaine recognised Bobby by his movements, even before he heard the voice.

Oh Kongk Mr Chaine come here quick, quick!

Bobby gave no other information, only turned and ran. Not understanding, Chaine followed, trying to keep the boy in sight. When they reached camp, it was obvious Killam had been shot. The man lay facedown on the ground, shirttail lifted, and blood, vomit and shit around him. Jeffrey and James were gone and the contents of the saddlebags and packs were strewn across the ground. Most of the food had been taken, as well as two rifles.

Chaine turned to Bobby. Bring in the horse, he said. He gave Bobby the gun Jeffrey and James had left behind. Only then did Chaine prop Soldier Killam up and wrap a blanket around him.

Killam groaned, his eyeballs moving so very quickly in his skull.

Bobby returned with the horse, built up a fire and stayed close beside it while Chaine loaded his weapons and moved out of the firelight and into the cover of darkness. Chaine stayed awake until dawn, and watched Bobby, illuminated as if on stage, fall asleep despite himself and the groaning of the injured man and tormented wind.

Chaine saw no sign of the two villains that night. And even for a long time afterwards, Bobby told Chaine's children and anyone else who might ask that, Yes—choosing his words carefully—them boys never come back and we never seen them again, not ever.

Chaine weighed the situation: two able bodies lost; three, counting the injured Killam, and even fewer supplies than before. What to do, leave Killam, stay until he recovers, or load him onto the horse? Chaine had limited medical knowledge, but he doubted Killam would survive. If Killam were a horse, Chaine would have killed him. (Eaten him?) It would have been a simple decision, although of course not a pleasant task. Killam was a human soul but, logically, it would be merciful to kill him now; he was likely to starve to death, if not die from his injuries. Best to just leave him to the hand of God, then. Could Chaine afford to risk his own life (a father, a husband, a key man in the fledgling colony) to save Killam? If they were to move him, how? And where were those murdering black boys?

Daylight came, but did little to lift his spirits. Bobby answered the problem of what to do about Killam. He dug up some long shallow roots, and hacked them to length. We use them for spears, he said. They were thin and very flexible indeed, but with the help of some sticks across them and some sinew and cord from his own supply, Bobby fashioned a sort of bed, one end attached to the horse's saddle, the other resting on the ground. Man and boy wiped the blood and grime from Killam as best they could—they could spare no water—then rolled him in a blanket and tied him to the crude bed. If he survived, the horse would drag him home. It would have to suffice. None of this was easy. Chaine did not panic, or lose his nerve, and was reassured by this mark of his character. His goal had been to find more good grazing country; now he must survive their mishaps, and return with Killam.

They loaded up the horse, and their reduced party set off with Killam slipping in and out of consciousness, clearly in pain, but there was little they could do to soothe him, save a sip of brandy and a taste of water now and then.

They travelled in silence almost all day and saw no sign of James and Jeffrey. Even the flames of their campfire were nervous and apprehensive as the light fell away. They slept fitfully, dreams corrupted by Killam's groans and perhaps by fragments of the evening before: waking to a gunshot; a sprawled and soiled, half-naked body.

Next day, after some hours of silent walking in file with their horse, Bobby pointed to two pale vertical objects shimmering on the otherwise featureless scrubby plain. The objects, at a distance, moved parallel to them and Chaine gradually made out Jeffrey and James, each wrapped and hooded in a blanket.

Bobby slowed, and Chaine came alongside of him. He had hoped not to see the boys again, but had wondered what they had planned. He had thought they would go on ahead, hoping to reach King George Town and escape before their crime was determined. He had no fear of them; not while he had his rifle and pistols, and not while daylight persisted. But at night, or in less open country where there was cover for an ambush? The two boys had taken the majority of the food supplies, but Chaine believed they would be unable to ration themselves; more likely they'd already feasted and again had nothing to eat. They could not hunt to save themselves. He reasoned that it was only a matter of time before they attacked.

Chaine called a halt. Telling Bobby to remain with the horse, he advanced toward the two black boys with rifle in hand. Closer, he saw that each held a double-barrelled rifle, and each rifle was pointed at him. Each young man rested the barrel on his left arm. Chaine could get no closer, for they retreated to maintain their distance.

Can you survive this alone, boys? He waved his hand at the desolate blue-grey mallee that stretched in all directions around them.

They said nothing. Mallee leaves clattered in the stiff breeze. Something squawked: a wounded sound, not a song. A bird, or Killam?

It's a long way, a still unknown distance. Have you water? Food remaining?

Nothing.

Did you sleep well last night?

The heads turned to one another. The blankets formed hoods over their skulls, and their faces were in shadow. Chaine faced the sun, squinting. The grainy light; late afternoon already.

One spoke. Chaine could not tell which. James? We don't want you, Master. We want Bobby.

We can be together, Chaine said. All five of us. Bobby chooses to stay with me! He turned to Bobby. Bobby nodded, remained holding the horse.

Chaine stepped toward James and Jeffrey again, and again they retreated. Time was precious; they needed to find water, to continue moving, to get closer to King George Town. Chaine turned his back on them deliberately and walked back to Bobby and the horse. This was their chance to shoot him. When he reached Bobby he put a hand on his shoulder, and looked to the others. They had not moved. He squeezed Bobby's shoulder. Those boys did not have the nerve. He gave Bobby a nod and a little shove and they continued on as before.

At intervals Killam groaned. Otherwise there was only the horse's footfalls, the swish of its tail, the clattering leaves and the wind moaning with Killam. James and Jeffrey stayed at the same distance, picking their way through the scrub, and began calling out.

Bobby. Leave him. Come with us, Bobby. You think you a white boy now?

Often just their heads and shoulders showed above the bushes, as if they were seals in the water, curious. But those boys weren't barking like seals, they were calling out to Bobby like wild dingoes; those boys who hardly even spoke to him earlier because they thought they were too good for people like Bobby Wabalanginy.

Their voices became plaintive and wailing. Why did they need him so, when he was only a boy?

Bobby did not so much as turn. After an hour or maybe it was three, Chaine called to pull up the horse. He patted Bobby on the shoulder and made his way again to James and Jeffrey, rifle in hand. When he got to a distance beyond which they did not want him to come, and at which they raised their guns and stepped backwards, he threw down his rifle and kept slowly walking toward them.

We must work together, together is the only way we will survive. God will forgive; I'll say nothing. You are two; I've thrown down my gun. What do you fear? And he kept walking toward them palms open. The boys trained their guns on him. Slowly, he kept walking.

James let his rifle fall to the ground. Chaine was closer now, he walked to one side of the two of them, his hands behind his back. The boys turned as one, eyes on Chaine who was keeping James between him and Jeffrey, who held the rifle still.

I've put my hands away, Chaine said, looking down. His arms were folded awkwardly behind him. How can I shake hands with a rifle? Put it away and let us shake hands again, and travel together. We are all under God's eye . . .

James, unarmed, turned to his brother. Their eyes went to one another, as if to discuss, and in that split second Chaine pulled his pistols from where they were tucked into his belt and shot James. Jeffrey lifted the barrel, and pulled the trigger but no shot came. Just a click. The jammed barrel.

Chaine shot him, too.

One or both of them was grunting, crying. A leg convulsed; it was all Bobby could see of them above the scrub and yet he could still hear Killam, and the wind, moaning softly. Smelled gunpowder. His ears were ringing, and after the explosion of the gun the space around him seemed vast. Chaine stood over the two young men. Pushed one with his boot, and then returned to Bobby and the horse. He put an arm around the boy, so that Bobby might after all learn at least something of fear, and what it meant to be strong and protected.

Onward, Bobby, onward.

*

Walking walking walking. The sea on their left, following a straight line except when they had to go around something be-cause of the horse and the man it dragged along. Bobby was beside Chaine; he was in front, behind. Sometimes Bobby felt as tired as Chaine looked but then he'd be moving lightly again, enlivened and happy so long as he did not fall behind the party and have to trail Killam, to listen and observe him. He could no longer walk behind, driving the horse, not with Killam stretched out before him, shaking and groaning in his delirium. Flies gathered at the man's mouth. His pale, lined face, his reddened eyes and beard made him seem like a stranger. But we must all of us look a sight.

So Bobby stayed beside Chaine or went further ahead. He patted the horse, ran his hand down that long face, the curve of jaw, talking to it softly. Its ears twitched as if he offered some surprising, though comforting news.

What are you telling that horse, boy? Chaine's voice almost a whisper.

How strong she is, Kongk. Helping us.

The horse's ears twitched.

Chaine turned back to his silence.

Bobby speared some mullet at a tiny, salty estuary and rubbed its oil into Killam's burnt skin.

At times it seemed Chaine could hardly lift his legs, keep his forward momentum. The horse followed, skins stretched over its jutting hips and shoulders and falling in folds. It looked like badly upholstered furniture, and moved as stiffly. There was scant life left in it, and it dragged a dying man behind. Perhaps the dying man drove the horse, and Killam and it were pursuing Chaine and Bobby, goading them on, insisting they lead them to where there was food, water, somewhere worth resting. The horse's hooves dragged, flicked, pressed into the earth again; it needed re-shoeing. Chaine looked like he could do with new boots himself.

They persisted, slowly pursued by a horse and a dying man who, mumbling and groaning, gave them no rest. And further back, the restless spirits of the two black boys that must be left behind at all costs.

They came to a small stream, and Chaine and Bobby carried Killam across, one at either end of the rough stretcher. The salty, brackish water was near chest-high for Chaine and Bobby struggled to keep his head above water, let alone the stretcher. The horse stumbled as Chaine pulled it across, and bruised him. Branches lashed and flayed him, broke his skin. He slipped searching for shellfish on rocks beside the sea, and waves leapt and pounded and almost swept him away.

Chaine continued, one foot after the other, showing his learning and speaking of Flinders' journal, and that there would be comfort at The Barrens, at Mt Misery and One Tree Hill . . . He promised Bobby he would climb to the very summit of each blue rise they saw in the landscape and take his bearings. But in truth those few such high points were nearly all inland, and his energy was low. His eyes stared far ahead.

Still they kept the ocean on their left. Birds lifted from the dunes at their approach, resentfully it seemed, settling again on some stunted banksia trees at a distance, watching Bobby carefully as he leaned to the low bushes. He grinned and shouted at them as he returned to Chaine's side, and the birds rose and drifted, complaining, back to the bushes.

The berries were small and round, tough-skinned; they made small explosions of salty moisture in Chaine's mouth.

They kept the sea to their left, and walked on, walked on. Walking.

Bobby and Chaine had been eating salted flesh, insects and parrots, and had long tired of that tucker. So long since they'd seen someone it felt as if they'd come from a dead place. What people stay there? Bobby knew stories of how they drank blood and ate their enemies. Well, they'd left behind some cranky spirits to trouble them. Those boys. He looked back the way they'd come.

Bobby carried a switch of leaves, and waved it over Killam to keep the flies from gathering at his mouth and eyes. A couple of crows followed, flying from tree to trees, sometimes settling on the ground ahead, always keeping a close eye on them. High and circling in the sky, an eagle.

And then Bobby found a sheet of granite, and a small rock hole covered with a thin stone slab and filled with water. He crouched to it, touched the stone, and sensed home. Something in the wind, in plants and land he'd at least heard of, and increasing signs of home. There were paths, and he knew where there'd be food. He tried to open himself to where they were but . . . Perhaps it was his fear, his bad nerves since the other day when those boys were calling out to him like wild dogs, and he stayed with Chaine . . . He couldn't yet relax or trust himself.

*

Chaine had changed as they travelled. Sulky and sullen, he was even more miserly with his food supplies, such as they were. He was muttering to himself, and constantly sighing. What with Chaine's sighing, and Killam raving and groaning, Bobby was glad of the horse's company, glad that its twitching tail helped keep the flies from Killam's face.

Whenever they stopped near the ocean Chaine looked to his book. He'd look from book to land, sky, back to book, and then lift his head again and look all around him as if for his old friend, Mr Flinders. Flinders. Vancouver. Names and words from over the ocean's horizon.

WRIGGLED HIS TOES AGAIN

THEY CRESTED another heath-carpeted rise, one of the ancient dunes running inland from the coast, and suddenly there was the ocean again all the way to the horizon, green and blue and grey and turquoise near the shore, gleaming like a laughing eye as the land breathed across it. Out of habit Bobby looked for whale spouts. None, though they must be here soon. No shadows or glint of salmon; they'd have long left. When was he last close to the sea like this, with the wind and sun just as they were now?

There was an estuary, barred from the sea by only a narrow strip of sand. Among the paperbarks Bobby thought of his family: Manit and Wooral and Menak and others. He thought of a dry creekbed, how speedily he could travel its path of sand, and the trees leaning over him for shade, sheltering him from the wind. He thought of the pools of water whenever you wanted one pretty well all along its length, and then the slope of red rock humming, the pools there welling, brimming . . .

Tears in his eyes thinking of it. He even pulled at Chaine's sleeve, saying, This way, we go this way, follow the creek away from this spring and this estuary.

But Chaine insisted they keep near the coast all the way to King George Town, keep near enough to a straight line, so he could catch sight of the sea every now and then.

Dolphins rolled and waved. Further to the horizon gannets plummeted, smashed the ocean's surface and then—as if ocean spored—rose again into the sky. Lines of swell followed one another to shore, crumbling as they approached.

Sunlight splintered Bobby's vision. A *djitty-djitty* waved its tail, jumped sideways, flew a short distance, looked back over its shoulder at him. A *koolbardi* tilted its head, warbled. Bobby closed his eyes, felt the wind tugging at his hair and rushing in the whorls of his ears. Breathed this particular air. *Ngayn Wabalanginy moort, nitjak ngan kaarlak . . .* Home.

What this? Out on the ocean, not gannets, not whale or dolphin. Light flickering, something splashing white in the sun.

Boat! Bobby called, pointing.

But there was nothing to see, nothing at sea. Spoke too soon. Chaine wanted boats, he was lonely for them, Bobby knew it and thought he'd found him one, but . . . Imagined it? He looked out over the ocean for a sight of sail, for a white tick, a mere nick in the texture of ocean. They gone sunk maybe?

*

Chaine's head lifted at Bobby's call, as might his heart and spirit, too. As if just hearing that shout—Boat!—brought a moment's respite from a relentless dreary wilderness and the sick man dragging behind who would not leave him be. Flies and birds following, following.

But he saw no boat. And now neither could Bobby.

With no boat Chaine felt his loneliness; this despondency and being driven and led all at once. It was land he'd hoped for—pastoral country, with good water and close to a sheltered anchorage. But he had tried and been disappointed. It deflated him. At least on the coast he would not be confounded by forks and tributaries and the way these creeks slipped underground to continue who knows where, or ceased to flow altogether, oozing away into stagnant swamps. He'd hoped for river mouths, but creeks stopped short of the sea, barred by banks of beach sand.

He ascertained their bearings. Soothed himself, as any observant bystander could see, in the handling of compass and paper. The oilskin wrapping and journal.

Again they came over a headland, and there was yet another crescent of sand between granite outcrops, the bright turquoise sea advancing, retreating, its white foamy edge moving to and fro on the sand. His eye, as is wont to happen, followed the curve of sand. Halted. He reached for the telescope in his saddlebag.

Boat! called Bobby again.

Chaine swung the telescope across the sea then back to the curve of the beach. At the far end, where the beach turned and began to follow the headland so as to face both them and the rising sun each morning, there were thin upright posts.

No, not posts: ship's masts. But yet, if masts, they leaned at an extreme angle and were bare of sails and motionless.

Boat, Bobby said again. Kongk, boat.

Dammit man.

But Bobby was pointing. Chaine swung the telescope out to sea. A whaleboat, with its one small sail up, reached the headland, then seemed to enter and disappear into it. Chaine cursed his confusion.

Island there, close to shore, Bobby told him.

Chaine realised there must be deep water between the headland and an island very close to it. The whaleboat had joined what must be a ship anchored there. The mast tips he saw were visible over one end of the island, but now even more dangerously tilted than before. Why?

Chaine slid down the dunes and onto the beach, Bobby and the horse more slowly behind. Having reached the open sand, he lifted his legs and stamped his feet, suddenly energised. Tolerably firm, he said, and looked to the island and headland which he could distinguish from this distance, the one in front of the other. Tolerably firm, he muttered again and led the way around the curving beach.

Killam turned his face to the waves. Smelled ocean? Felt it? The crows came no further than the foredune.

Still only the tips of the ship's masts showed over one end of the island and now they rocked wildly from side to side. Chaine reached for his telescope. As he watched, the masts slowly moved from the vertical to an extreme angle, and then suddenly jerked straight again. But the ship must surely be in shelter, could not possibly be rocked by waves, and waves could not be large or so close together to cause a ship to rock like that. As they approached, Bobby and Chaine observed it happen several more times: the masts slowly lean over to an acute angle, and then suddenly jerk upright, and rock to and fro. As they proceeded around the beach their angle of view opened so that they saw the ship, floating in deep water between the headland and island, heeled over and with her masts slowly moving closer and closer to the water. And then, released, rock violently from side to side until seized and slowly begin to lean to one side.

At one stage, the boat leaned so far away from them they could almost see its keel. Something, some power, was pulling it toward the water, mast tips first. Something was trying to upend and drag it into the water and each time, at the last moment, it escaped and righted itself. And the ship seemed to be winning, because the movements—the angle to which it tipped, the extent to which it rocked to and fro on release—was becoming less violent.

Closer still, they realised the ship leaned toward something large right beside the hull, that the mast tips were drawn toward this as it was lifted partially out of the water, and then when it fell and splashed, the ship again sprung upright and rocked violently.

Eventually they stood on the beach in the shade of the great headland of granite and trees. The late afternoon sun, blocked and splintered by the granite behind them, gave an almost twilight quality to the scene: white sand, deep blue and turquoise water, the island close to shore, and the ship tearing blubber from a whale beside it.

Chaine noted the details: a hook inserted into the whale's blubber, a cable running from it into the mast, a pulley, a winch on deck. As the cable tightened the whale began to lift, the ship heeled over until—suddenly—the blubber peeled away like rind from an orange, and the ship sprung upright, masts madly waving.

Between mainland and island the light was soft, strange; and the dark, purple water had an oily sheen. Two boats moved away from the ship, towing the peeled whale carcass. The men in the boats and Chaine called to one another, their thin voices bouncing off granite and water, and then one of the boats headed for where the two figures and the horse stood on the gleaming white sand. Blue light now, the sky smeared red behind the headland, behind the island, all along the sea's horizon.

Bobby glanced at Killam's pale and lined face, his blinking eyes. Bobby wriggled his toes in the wet sand, anticipating.

FIRELIGHT IN AN EYE

M ENAK HAD WALKED to the ocean, had come down from beneath a jutting shelf of rock and old voices still echoing in the gorge, left his camp with its scent of sandalwood and jam tree ash, come through the peppermint trees and past the pool of the rivermouth over the last white and sandy dune to the ocean.

On this beach, here, they sometimes lit fires and painted themselves up to sing in the dolphin, have them bring salmon massed in the shallows and sometimes leaping onto shore. He walked the couple of hundred yards of beach to a rocky headland, his little dog Jock trotting after the retreating water, running as it rushed back again, splashing in the bubbles of foam.

Menak walked out to the end of the point and began collecting crabs, crushing and grinding them in a tiny hollow in the granite rock below his feet. The rock sloped into the sea, and a headland and another rocky shelf protected him from the swell, but seen from a distance it seemed that he stood among crashing waves. But no, there was deep water right at his feet, and the fragments of shell and flesh he tossed there glinted like motes of dust in sunlight as they descended, disappeared.

Shafts of sunlight at this time of day penetrated deepest, but even so the ocean, shifting restlessly like thick smoke, absorbed and blunted them before they had gone very far at all into that vast beneath and beyond. Who knew how far it continued? Far as the horizon, further? But of course this was inner distance; deep, not far.

Menak waited for a shape to form, expecting to lure a groper to spear. It was a slow job: gently, bit by tiny bit, crushing and tossing fragments of crab into the water. He was humming, occasionally voiced fragments of song. His hands were stiff with salt and gritty crabshell, and he dipped them in the water, singing, as the ripples made faint circles, and he saw—sensed?—a shape shifting in the water. The groper he sought? It was an evocative thing, such a shape in the dark blue depths; a nephew passed through his thoughts, a grandfather . . . The shape shifted: human, fish, nothing. Had gone away again, but not before Menak sensed something familiar with the depths of ocean, something hardly aware of its own self's deep pulse until some melody and rhythm and baited light lured it up to air and sunlight and close to him.

Menak swallowed, took a deep breath, bit his tongue lightly. Someone had called him back to himself, too; a frail and temporary, insubstantial self. Crouching by the sea he turned to look back along the rocks to where his family rested in the dense shade of that tree with its back bent to the weather. Their voices had called him.

What?

They waved, gesticulated.

He turned to the ocean. A whale, almost touching the rock Menak stood upon, rolled to one side with its eye upon him. Menak heard its voice, its moist exhalation. Had he lured this? Crab and shell mean nothing to this one; this whale wants the company of people, wants to be ashore. But—he glanced at the sky, the sun so very, very low—there was not much left of this day. He called for a fire to be built on the beach around near the estuary, not far from the corner of the bay.

Firelight reflected in a whale's eye; himself dissolving there. Be the whale.

SUNLIGHT AND A BLOODY GROAN

B OBBY WAS RIGHT to curl his toes in anticipation, because soon all his friends met one another. But first he had to meet someone else, someone Soldier Killam already knew and from whom Jak Tar jumped away.

The men in the boat rowed the whale carcass from the ship and came back to those waiting on the shore. Behind them the pale body of the headless whale drifted slowly, shapeless flesh gleaming in the failing light. Dark bodies thrust from the water, struck the carcass, slashed like knives, splashed back again. Birds screamed and rose and fell.

Bobby untied Killam from the crude stretcher behind the horse. He was covered in grease and blood caked his shirt. Unable to speak, he croaked, moaned; unable to stir his limbs, his eyes moved from side to side.

The men in the boat were also not well. They tentatively leaned into their oars, and when the boat reached the shore they rose gingerly, as if each movement caused them pain. They hardly spoke; did they worry tongue and teeth might fall from their mouths?

Bobby hobbled the horse and joined the others in the

whaleboat once Killam had been loaded aboard. We have a surgeon among us, the men said, glancing at Killam's grease- and pain-smeared face.

And the captain was very interested in that face.

Killam lay prone on the deck, breath rasping.

I believe I know this man, said the captain. And asked was his back striped, not long healed? Well, yes, Chaine knew it was. The captain shifted on his feet and grunted.

The man suffers more now than with what I did to him.

Killam's eyes were wide in a face that sun and grease and dirt had baked into a bearded mask.

However, I blame the authorities in that port as much as this poor soul. We have a surgeon among us. I remember there were two black boys as well. And his gaze fell upon our Bobby who turned, deflected from Chaine's flashing eyes, and went back to shore.

Ah yes, said Chaine, they were with us when we began this expedition but alas absconded. Doubtless thought they would fare better alone.

Bobby could not see the horse on shore. A dead whale was roped beside the ship and other dead whales floated in the bay, flags in their spouts. Each man was caked in salt and whaleblood, clothing and hair stiff and thickly matted, and hung glowing with the red light of a sunset that seemed to last forever . . .

Chaine talked in that loud, cheerful way he had. Bobby caught only fragments before the men strode away with Chaine, enlivened, having taken hold of the matter and with the captain also in hand. No vegetables, you say . . .

Scurvy, the captain told Chaine. But he could not let them rest from whaling, not now when they were again near land. We hope to grow vegetables on this island. Or perhaps you know there are vegetables here?

Native potatoes, said Chaine. And fresh meat. And we will trade for rum and brandy and these other things, too.

Bobby slept in a cleft on deck that night, but not until late. Left to himself, and weary, he was nevertheless thrilling with excitement. He knew ships, but he'd never known a deck like this; a blazing furnace the whalers called the try-works was its heart. Tongues of flame curled out from behind doors, licked two great pots and lit the rigging and furled sails of the masts so that shadows leapt and danced as men with huge forks flung long strips of blubber into the hissing pots, skimmed the oil with great spoons, stoked and fed the flames with scraps of dried blubber that clattered like dry leaves and old bones. Bobby moved among the men, deftly sidestepping their rush and enormous cutlery. Another dance. Smoke and the stench of burning flesh rolled across the deck. He climbed the rigging through the shifting light and shadows and smoke until he was secure and looking down upon it all below him, the choreography and spectacle of it.

Later, descended once more, Bobby heard a flute of some description, sensed Chaine's jig vibrating the floorboards. The old man had joined the captain in his cabin, had recovered surprisingly quickly. A few seconds later the dancing ceased. Maybe his body was not so resilient as his mind and spirit.

Killam was stored somewhere below deck.

Bobby slept cushioned on rope; timber kept the depths below and darkness thickened all around the ship.

A few short hours later, Bobby was shoved awake to voices and rushing footsteps; boats being lowered, dark hummocks rolling in the dawn light, mist rising from the sea. The bay full of whales!

Boats raced away from the ship, each with a man standing at the stern, and six sick men rowing. Each playful whale sank from sight immediately its would-be harpooner rose from his oar to grasp his great dart, and each boat, rather than waiting for the whale to rise again, rushed for the next whale in its path that was just there, there, but always out of reach. Too many whales for the whalers who, confused in the moving middle of this rolling abundance, lost focus and remembered their aching limbs and swollen joints, worried for their falling teeth.

The sun rising above the land way across the other side of the bay showed a great many two-stemmed spouts blossoming and sparkling on a vast plain of rolling whale backs and sea mist. One moment the whales were gathered together close and touching, the next they were moving apart and leaving the bay. A harpoon struck a trailing calf, and immediately all oars in that boat rose from the water and pointed at the sky as the boat swung away. Bobby saw a whale detach itself from the pod, and come back to the already slowing boat and the small whale it had struck, now rising. A second boat's harpoon hit the mother as she reached her stricken calf. The mother went underwater, the bow of the boat almost followed, but then just as suddenly lifted as the boat took off, skipping across the bay with a bow wave splashing before it. But then it slowed and came to a rocking stop.

Dart's out! said a voice near Bobby.

A group of whales turned back to the bay; a third whaleboat rowed to meet them.

Inside the bay, a man at the boat's bow thrust his lance into the wounded calf. The calf's tail rose and fell, the boat went back and forth to avoid its flailing, to drive the steel in again. The water frothed with blood; the mother whale returned, put itself between calf and boat. A second boat, another man, another harpoon. Now the mother dived, and taut rope sang and it seemed the two boats must collide, their lines entangle, but no; the boat sped toward the horizon. But as it left the bay it swung round in an arc and came back into the wind, leaping waves and with white water exploding around it. Harpooned, dragging a great weight of pain, the mother was returning to her calf.

The silver spear at the bow of the boat stabbed again and again. Sunlight glinted on steel; thick, bright spouts of blood. The mother whale's tail repeatedly rose and struck the water close to her dead calf. The men worked the oars to evade her blows, and each blow was less. The boat's lifted oars were a row of spikes, and the man at the bow drove and twisted his steel spear into the whale.

Bobby groaned, thinking he heard a whale groan, too, and thick hot blood rained upon the boat and upon the men, and in the water a red stain grew larger. The young whale, the mother: each had a flag flying from its spout, and the boat which had killed them was already after another pod at the mouth of the bay. Sick men seemed well again, come alive with whale blood. Whaleboats skipped across the waves, crisscrossed one another's paths.

Smoke billowed from a fire on the beach. A group of Noongar people stood between it and a whale stranded there. Even at this distance, Bobby recognised Menak. Further around the beach waves broke against the pale and murky carcass of yesterday's whale kill.

Not yet officially on lookout, Bobby turned from one sight to another.

PEOPLE'S ATTENTION SCATTERS
LIKE SHEEP DO TOO

WILLIAM SKELLY and Jak Tar began by following the river inland, driving the sheep before them. Months ago, Bobby had suggested it would lead to good grazing country. The river soon became more of a creekbed, really, a soft sandy track connecting pool to pool. Skelly grunted a grudging admiration when Jak showed him the bush Bobby (once again) had told him poisoned the sheep. And but for that poison, the men let the sheep graze where they would, penned them in rough bush fences of an evening and listened for dingoes.

They met up again with Manit, Menak and a couple of boys on the edge of adulthood. There were smiles, and the old couple had a fire going almost before Skelly and Jak were aware of it. Manit lifted her arm and pointed across country, then waved her hand at the sheep. An expressive gesture; the arm was old: ligaments taut, flesh sagging, the skin wrinkled and coarse at the elbow but her thin bent finger was so assured of its direction. It was easy going, and they maintained their way; why change course? They could return anytime.

Perhaps it was his seaman's eye or perhaps it was his nostalgia for ocean, but one day Jak looked back from a granite dome he had spent some hours reaching, and saw other granite outcrops blue in the distance across a sea of mallee. They looked like islands, and the line of trees marking water courses showed him they'd moved across land from one river to its neighbour.

Even the taciturn Skelly found time to talk. And Jak Tar was a good listener. At first Skelly gave only instructions: how to build a bush shelter or fence, the dangers of dingoes. Occasionally the blacks, he added. Mr Chaine encouraged this sort of roaming, Skelly told him, so long as the sheep were well cared for. That old woman (Manit or something they called her) had been introduced to them by Bobby. The boy was a nephew of hers, or something like that. He's got relatives everywhere and they're useful enough, never been any trouble, but you hardly ever see a young woman among them, he said. It was obvious that Skelly would like to meet such a young woman, some female cousin of Bobby's. The old men keep them; and he shook his head. They keep the young men under their thumb that way.

Skelly hated his own people, the 'English'. My white people, he said with a grimace. And the blacks were beneath him; he made that clear. He was going to forge a different life for himself here. Had to, there was no going back. He was a convict, did Jak Tar know that? Had been. Jak Tar said nothing. Not much of a talker, is you? said Skelly.

They reckoned they must now be heading back toward the coast. Closer, they caught glimpses of the sea, and when the landscape suddenly opened up, Jak Tar was first to see the ship. He swore and rushed to put himself away from the view of any who might be aboard.

*

Menak stood waist-deep in water, close-up beside the whale and confident no shark would bother him. The whale's eye dimmed, and yet still it reflected the campfire on the beach, the sky's pale dome, and Menak, too, along with Manit and the young girl. Waiting.

Only in the old stories had Menak ever known of so many whales in the bay. There were old whalebones in the dunes, and sometimes you could walk from one to the other without touching the sand. He was deep in the whale story of this place right now, resonating with it, but there was some new element, some improvisation and embellishment of its well-known rhythm that distracted him, caught at his attention and kept bringing him back to himself, this specific now. Further around the beach something was being savaged by sharks and seagulls. A whale carcass, the inner part of a whale, but still fresh and with the head and thick skin stripped away. What had the ship done to it? And here was young Wabalanginy, rowing from that ship to shore along with the horizon men. Menak knew Noongars would be arriving over the next few days, but he hadn't expected one from the sea. This boy coming to be a man, and bringing strangers with him.

He made an incision in the whale to release its spirit. It was something he'd once done with Wabalanginy's father. But what man stood beside him now?

*

The ceiling was very close to Soldier Killam's head, the air not good. He drifted in and out of consciousness; his misshapen, damaged limb ached insufferably. Perhaps it was the effect of being back on this ship, but the scars on his back were a net that kept pain close and small waves slapped the hull.

STRANDED

F ROM AMONG THE DUNES, Jak Tar saw the boat rowing to shore. Is that Mr Geordie Chaine, Bobby? There was life in the stranded whale yet: a twitching fluke and he thought he saw something in the water move quickly toward a young woman in the shallows. Stingray? But no, it was gone. Bobby had waded into the deeper water to join Menak and the two or three men beside him, one of whom, with spear ready, scanned the water surrounding them. To keep the sharks away? Jak wondered.

Chaine was walking into the gap in the dunes, and Jak Tar, making sure he remained out of the ship's sight, moved to meet him. Remarkably, a couple of nights' sleep, the comforts aboard ship and the prospect of a business arrangement had restored Chaine to something like his best health.

That was your captain, I think? Chaine barely tilted his head in the direction of the ship. He seemed amused.

Jak Tar nodded.

I think we can ensure you two never meet, Chaine said, still smiling. But I'm onto something here, boyo, and it's a fine coincidence you getting here with these sheep. The captain and his men will be happy for fresh mutton, though they're more in need of vegetables. I've a mind . . .

Even as he spoke Chaine was inspecting the condition of his sheep and the rough pen Skelly was constructing to hold them. He bent to taste the water of the patient river, reacted as if it was some rare treat, and rose up and down on his toes the whole time he talked to Skelly.

Not that Jak Tar was watching too closely; he kept an eye on that ship, not keen to meet any of his old shipmates and certainly not the captain.

Bobby came up the dunes. Jak noticed how the sand was loosening already; the low-growing plants had a tenuous hold on the dunes and were not accustomed to so many feet. Like Chaine, Bobby was in high spirits and told Jak Tar that he was not going to eat this whale. He did not eat whale. Plenty people be here soon to do that, but.

Chaine told Skelly and Jak Tar to go with Bobby. He'd explain—or get one of the women to—how to gather and prepare the native foods around here, and he wanted to make some sort of mash for the captain and his men. You know, like those cakes the natives bake. Scurvy, he said. The ship surgeon reckons even if it tastes like muck they can mix it in with their biscuits. They're soaking their biscuits anyway, most of them, lest they drop a tooth.

The old woman lit a fire, and before the men had time to gather their senses it had run away to the river's edge, smoking furiously, and almost as suddenly died out.

Bobby told Jak Tar she was letting people know about the whale.

*

Next daylight released the scent of ash from that fire. Skelly and Jak Tar first gathered, then mashed and baked the seed and tubers. Chaine had hoped these might help the sailors, but the results were disappointing. Over the next several days, as more people arrived, Skelly observed it done more skilfully. See, said Bobby, easy! Is so very easy easy easy. Oh Bobby was proud of his English and the way he made that 's' sound, and never more so than when in front of his Elders.

Skelly and Jak Tar noted that the natives did not take the same trouble to hide their women away as they did closer to King George Town. And weren't there some fine beauties among them, too, smiling and bouncing and not a bit of shame?

*

Smoke streamed constantly from the ship's try-works and soon there were four whale carcasses drifting in the choppy waters of the bay. Jak Tar had made a shelter high up where the old dunes met the granite headland, so placed that he could keep an eye on the ships and the bay. He had used some old canvas and ancient whalebones he had found way up there so far from the water and, protected from the wind and with the ship and its stinking smoke further downwind, it made a very respectable shelter for him and Skelly. Bobby, making one of his regular visits—and he usually brought a companion along—was impressed. He asked how it was made, repeated it all for his companion's benefit.

Chaine offered Skelly's help in manning the whaleboats. Said he could soon have another couple of men. And told Jak Tar to travel lickety-split back upriver to the Kepalup property, and come back with as many potatoes as the horses could carry.

*

Several days later, when Jak Tar returned to the inlet with horses and potatoes, he found his tiny shelter of bone and canvas had been taken over and enlarged by Chaine. A wee bit of a stench on that ship, his boss explained. He'd arranged for a boat to take him out to the ship whenever he wanted, and some of the sailors had been let ashore. Don't worry, he said as Jak left to load the potatoes into the boat, they're too busy to worry about you. The captain has given them a bonus of rum. He'll have as much oil as they can carry soon as this last whale is boiled down. He was right to leave that one—tilting his head in the direction of the stranded whale—to the blackfellas, after all.

The captain wouldn't return to King George Town, but he agreed to put them down in a whaleboat in the sound. Killam was recovering, and they could row him into the settlement. Oh, the whaleboat? I'll keep that, said Chaine. And you know, I think we might move out here, permanent like. Why should these good ships go to King George Town when we here at Close-by-island Bay (he winked at Jak Tar) can take their money ourselves and put them up in comfort?

*

Twilight, or almost, since it was not so much that the sun had properly set but that it had dropped below the headland. Jak Tar sat in its deep shadow. Bone weary, he would've liked the rum and company of some of the crew, but not enough to risk ending up back aboard that ship. There were campfires along the beach starting to glow in the fading light: Noongar figures not far from the stranded whale and, further along, near the gap in the dunes where the river came to halt, sailors.

What with the smoke and the quality of light Jak could almost have been underwater. He saw the stranded whale melting, blubber and flesh falling away, and a long line of Noongar people emerging as if from its wide-opened mouth. No, not only Noongar; Jak Tar's family, too. Naked they walked away and naked they entered the dunes, side by side. Now and then Jak recognised himself in the little pigtail some had tied their hair into. He saw people at the dune crest and also beyond the crest (as if he saw the dunes, yet saw through them), a long line of people disappearing to the inland horizon, all in conversation and attending to one another. And something in the curious light, and their nakedness, and that some had that little pigtail . . . It was hard to tell black from white. Jak Tar tried to call some of them: a son surely, but the boy did not turn his head, and was gone. He tried to call a wife and daughter, but had lost his voice. He wanted to run and grab them, haul them back to himself, but could not move. Son, daughter, wife? Jak Tar had none, not yet. They were faceless, these individuals, but he *felt* them as children and wife, felt the love, felt them as his own.

And still people continued to emerge from the tunnel of the whale's ribs. Daylight was almost gone, but the cold sunset and the campfires showed a glowing membrane adhering to the bones, and people continued emerging from that pink and bony cave, quiet and serene and stepping toward Jak Tar on a red carpet of tongue . . . So many people.

He sat up with a start, that little pigtail of his quivering. The sun must have set. He had slept for hours. He got stiffly to his feet and walked toward the whale. The fires were bright. The great bulk of the animal, the people beside it, all of a kind, dark and glistening in the firelight, disappearing when the flames dropped.

Closer, Jak Tar thought himself a shy savage. Was he dreaming still? He recognised faces, one slicing a strip of the whale, rubbing himself with blubber. Figures feasting, whale fat bubbling from the fire, grease spitting from flesh skewered on a sharp green stick. Could not help but smell the whale blubber.

Dancing, singing. Young men and women glistened with whale oil, their muscles quivering beneath the skin. Pert young breasts, smooth buttocks and long thighs. Would have liked to be closer. Jak recognised an old fellow: Menak? He nodded, smiled, but the man turned away. Jak wanted approval and to be led across the vast space beyond which he was stranded; wanted to dance and sing, make those women laugh and toss their glances his way. Where were those sailors, his old shipmates, and their rum? But he could not risk meeting them, and someone informing the captain.

A little Jack Russell came running up to him, barking.

Bobby's voice: Hey Jak, meet Jock! Oh you already met, unna?

Bobby came at Jak Tar, words rolling from his lips trying to explain something: old people passing, the whales, me them brothers come on the sand to woman return me properly.

Really, there was no following him when he was excited like this and spoke straight at you without adopting a voice like that of your own.

Jak Tar hadn't forgotten how Bobby helped him when he jumped ship, and was constantly surprised not only at what the boy could do and his resourcefulness, but at the things he said. Jak Tar was a good listener, he was reflective (which was just as well, since he looked like spending a lot of time with only sheep and maybe the river for company) and he was observant. He was also lonely.

After a time he started to say, Boys and girls . . . A man and a woman, how do they marry, Bobby, among your people?

Old woman young man might go together, sometimes, Bobby explained, specially like when . . . and he searched for words, dancing, corroboree (he brightened for a moment at that word, but dissatisfied, moved on), party time, we all together, a spree! . . . But old men get all the young girls. He looked at Jak Tar suspiciously, and Jak said he wasn't interested in any girl Bobby fancied, but his cousins and sisters maybe, who would their husbands be?

Bobby tried to explain how things worked, about promised

ones. A man might bring food to the family of even a baby girl who will be his wife when she growed up; he look after them well and good. And when she's old enough she go with him. The family want a good strong man.

You'll have a great many lassies then, Bobby!

No. It was not so simple, because some men and women could not go together. And if a man died before his promised one was old enough, then she would be promised to some other man. Like Binyan, Bobby said, that one dancing down there, her promised man dead. See, lotta people die. Lotta people sick. Some sailor people kill them. And she ready.

So this Binyan, began Jak Tar, formulating the question as he spoke . . .

Before long Bobby was sated with food, and sleepy. Heavy eyelids, voice little more than a husky whisper, he could no longer follow Jak Tar's questions. He curled up and was soon snoring softly, breath leaving the tiny tunnels of nose and throat in regular flurries.

Jak Tar built up their campfire and thought of its smoke, disappearing into the night sky and, somewhere there above, joining the smoke of those other fires on the beach. He listened to the singing, the voices. He'd made his camp on the headland, and at a height that showed the curve of the beach, but not so far away that he could not see the figures flickering among glowing fires and flame, dancing. Sailors and natives together; heavy-footed William Skelly, too, most likely. The sea glittered with the firesticks and moonlight, and he thought he could still discern the dark mass of the whale. Jak Tar looked back over his shoulder to the sleeping boy, and caught the arc of the whale jawbone that held their canvas shelter, and the crescent of moon in the sky. The echoing shapes of whalebone, moon, beach. And how many crescents of white sand stretched between here and King George Town?

The whale's last exhalation was long gone, that forgiving eye had dimmed.

*

Jak Tar made it two days since the whaler had left, taking Chaine and Skelly with it. They'd be putting a whaleboat down outside King George Town Harbour and taking Killam ashore.

A crowd of people (natives, he had to remind himself despite their nakedness and present state) continued moving in and out of the cave of the stinking carcass. Though raised on haggis and sheep's eyeballs, Jak Tar seemed the only one offended by the smell. He kept to himself, upwind and sheltered by whalebone, canvas and a gnarled old tea tree tucked among rock and sand.

The remaining sheep grazed on the green shoots sprouting on the patch of earth Manit had burned all those weeks ago. Jak and Bobby were to let them graze their way upriver to the homestead. As he went over the last of the dunes, Jak Tar looked back on the bay. Far around the beach a couple of shapeless whale carcasses trembled in the waves, attended by sharks and squawking gulls. Closer, people remained just upwind of the single stranded carcass.

The ship had long gone; now the sheep, and Bobby and that Jak Tar, too. Menak gathered up his goods, his *kitj* and *dowak* and *kerl*. Manit was already standing, ready to go with her possum-skin bag on her back and her teasing words about how stiffly he moved in his old age. They walked off together toward the creek, and the young woman Binyan accompanied them, hand in hand with Manit.

They took the opposite side of the river.

ANOTHER WHALE SEASON

BOBBY WABALANGINY—a boy beneath a brow of granite, just a boy sheltering from a wintery westerly wind—watches whales and boats so far away they might be toys and playthings.

Kongk Chaine and the rest push the whaleboat onto the water, splashing, leaping in as it jumps from the sandy shore. Kongk at the stern, steering, the others pulling at their oars, finding a rhythm. Bobby picks them out: his uncles Wooral and Menak and Wabakoolit, and Killam and Skelly and Jak Tar, too, right up front and ready to throw his spear. His harpoo-oon (in his mind Bobby stretches the word out, makes it long and—closing quickly—sharp). The boat speeds past the rocky point, past the island close to shore, and heads for the misty forest of whale spouts out at sea.

There's a ship out beyond the whales (who they on that ship?). Three whaleboats leave it, and immediately its sails fill and it moves away to head off the whale pod.

They will help us, thinks Bobby, watching. His limbs mime the rowing. His back arches. He's with his family and friends, rowing, and he's with the whales, too. The ship will help keep them whales in the bay. Keep them at bay. Oh, too many whales. *(More whales, Jak always says with a laugh, than peas in a pod!)*

One boat heading from shore, three boats approaching from seaside.

They'll drive them to us, thinks Bobby, lightly leaping up and down with excitement.

Already, one of the ship's boats has fastened to a whale. Bobby sees the boat lean to the water and thinks it will capsize, but then it rights itself, the men lift their oars into the air and bend low, and the boat skips away.

Nantucket slay ride, Bobby has heard men say. (Where's Nantucket? What's a slay?)

Another boat fastens to a whale, suddenly speeds toward the horizon. Bobby sees the bucket thrown overboard, the sail flung into the water but the boat doesn't slow down.

Our boat, Bobby thinks, hasn't even reached the whales, but nearly, nearly, nearly . . . The many remaining whales continue, seemingly unhurried, closer to shore, closer to the whaleboat.

The ship also approaching.

Bobby turns to see the foreign ship's third whaleboat accelerate and disappear from sight behind the island. He returns his gaze: the ship has sailed between our whaleboat and the whale pod. He sees men waving angry fists. Can only imagine the curses they shout.

Galeed.

A whaleman's word: galleyed.

The whales turn away.

Save one.

So: the pod of whales heading out to sea, the ship, and between it and the shore a single whale, a single whaleboat and Jak Tar standing ready to throw.

Bobby, up on the headland, throws an imaginary harpoon

and sees the whale dive, Jak Tar fall and the boat lean over on its keel, one gunnel almost under water, and then speed off in pursuit of the ship and the whale pod. The boat skimming the surface, white water at its bow, men doubled up and leaning forward, oars in the air.

Oh! Like everybody—whales and whalers—just wanna be together. One happy mob. One big family.

The other whaleboat appears from behind the island, rowing back into the bay. Musta come unstuck, thinks Bobby, then realises our whaleboat's heading—oh so fast!—straight for it. And now here comes yet another of the Yankee whaleboats speeding back from out near the horizon and the white wave at its bow, its skipping speed, shows their whale has still not tired.

Excited, Bobby stands tall as he can and dances from foot to foot as he watches two charging whaleboats rapidly converging on the slow one—the one powered only by men desperately working their oars. Even the mother ship seems slow and clumsy and as likely as not to be hit.

The whale pod is swimming faster now. Leaving the bay their misty exhalations, caught by the wind and flung with rain and sea spray, are barely visible.

The Yankees lean back on their oars, and the steersman stands tall and our whaleboat wants to go one way but the whale pulling it musta turned the other way so . . .

Bobby sees the crash, expects to hear the collision but it never comes, there's only wind in his ears, rustling vegetation, the crashing surf as Kongk Chaine's whaleboat rides over the stern of the other—the steersman leaps a moment before—and the boat rises into the air and men spill like seed pods, and then the boat is falling, seems headed beneath the water . . . Wallows, the bow rises. The boat bobbing on the waves.

Cut the line! Bobby calls out. But they've done that already, haven't they? Because there's the boat, and heads in the sea also bobbing. Bouncing on the balls of his feet, Bobby sees the men in the whaleboat offer their hands to the men swimming in the sea, and Chaine shouting orders.

*

Wooral shed his clothes, and the dying sun lit the drops of water on his dark and greased skin. He shook his head and his hair sprung up in exclamation marks all round his face. He laughed, teeth bright in his beard. Look at him! Full with ocean, wind and rain, the energy of it, the size and the strength of the whale! Wooral can hardly swim, and yet he speared and seized a whale right out at sea.

Killam was sullen as ever. As soon as the boat was hauled onto the sand he, with trousers rolled to just below his knees and plucking his shirt away from his shoulders the way he did, went looking—Bobby knew—for his grog.

Even in this failing light Skelly ran his hands over the bow of their whaleboat, looking for what damage had been done. He could not believe their luck or the strength of its timbers, and said so repeatedly, limping around the boat, admiring it, patting it like a pet.

Menak stood apart like he so often did, this time between two smaller fires Wooral lit for him in addition to the one they all shared. Only Jock seemed able to get through to Menak, make him smile like a human being these days. The dog yapping and wagging his stump of a tail, ignoring Wooral's entreaties, waited for the signal to jump into Menak's arms.

Only Wooral and Jak Tar looked to Bobby, only they stopped to listen to what he'd seen. Jak Tar put his arm around Bobby's shoulders. You'll be wiv us soon, he said. But his eyes were searching beyond Bobby, looking for his woman.

Chaine said, Six men, seven. And a boy. We can barely man a whaleboat, not really enough.

He looked to Menak, but Menak turned away.

Killam came walking back to the fire, cup in his hand. *Galleyed*, he kept repeating. They have no right. British Law stands here. The scars on his back were stitches binding his anger. A man would be a fey idiot, he went on, to fish while foreigners can enter our ports unchallenged . . .

But Chaine believed they were right to have picked up those Yankees, helped them back to the ship. He wanted to have a talk with this captain, too. They might work together, we could help them top up their ship with whale oil. See how they are for fresh meat, and whether they like kangaroo. His men had a lot to learn yet, he'd seen how the others were so quick to fix to their whales. He thought the boy might be trained up to take steering oar. He had more important things to attend to himself, other ventures.

Killam swore and turned on his heel.

*

The Yankee ship anchored in the shelter between island and headland. Beyond, the sea was all shifting troughs of darkness and the inside of ocean bleeding at each crest.

Furling its sails, the ship seemed to withdraw into itself even as it sent a smaller boat to shore and as the Yankee—Brother Jonathon, Chaine gave him the same name as the one before—spilled onto the sand Chaine was splashing there, reaching out a hand in welcome. Oh loud voices and laughter, these two men. Chaine, arms around the shoulders of Brother Jonathon, led him to his shelter high in the dunes while Jonathon's men drifted away with Skelly and Wooral to the cooking camp and their rum. Killam was nowhere to be seen, Menak was camped in the dunes near where the creek halted, barred from the sea, and Jak Tar had slipped away to join Binyan, Bobby's sister.

Jak had made many visits with Bobby to talk with the family of Binyan and her deceased promised-husband's brother, himself a very old and frail man. Jak had taken axes and knives, a sheep; he'd taken sugar and rum and flour. He continued to tongue-stumble over the words Bobby taught him. He could not keep his eyes off the girl, but she stayed apart. He made a dress for her from an old shirt, and she put it on in his presence. Possess her completely, he told himself. Yes, he would.

So Bobby found himself standing by the boat, on the sand, at the sea's edge. Stranded. He'd studied along with the Chaine's own children back at King George Town, slept under the one roof; he should surely stay with Chaine now.

Geordie Chaine had set his camp apart from the others, and made a shelter of oiled canvas draped over a whale jawbone he'd had the men drag from further in the dunes—God alone knows how it had got there. He found it more than tolerable to stand tall under a roof of canvas, and have plenty of dry space behind him still. He kept a small fire burning at the front.

I'm new to this game, he told Brother Jonathon, thinking the man young to be a whaling captain. You're younger than I, he went on, but I must learn from you. The man frowned, smiled. Even young Bobby knew sweet-talking Chaine was flattering the captain.

You're one boat short, you need men . . .

And so the two men toasted their agreement with rum and the whale jawbone, arching against the stars, gleamed with firelight.

A few more whales and Captain Brother Jonathon would have all the oil he could carry. That wouldn't take long, not with three boats working between ship and shore. Chaine could have all the bone; there was still a market for the fine structures from their mouths, stays and bustles for the fashionable ladies. Captain Jonathon accepted Chaine's assurances that the natives told him countless whales entered the bay this time of year. Once he was ready to head for home Captain Jonathon would offer Chaine equipment he no longer required. All the more room onboard ship for oil then. Chaine had a list of what he wanted: try-pot, whaleboat, harpoons, lances, line . . .

The try-pot floated to shore, as unsteady and strange in the water as a top hat Bobby had seen floating in the harbour at King George Town. Chaine's team waded out to it and Bobby could not help but dive into the water, listen to their muffled voices and hear his own heartbeat loud. He rolled his back, being a whale. It was whale blubber kept him warm.

Over the sand he skipped, barely touching but helping roll the try-pot out onto the rocky point, just in the lee of a small granite headland which sloped gently at its base and touched the ocean, calm in the solid shelter. Killam and Skelly built low walls for a furnace beneath the try-pot, then larger walls and a roof to keep the rain off, stop it spoiling the whale oil. Jak Tar, noting the boy's interest, explained it all to him. Chaine reckoned on melting down a lot of blubber. His grin became a grimace. He told his men how it would be: whales would arrive on the most wintry of days, days when they'd struggle just to get the boats out from shore through the surf; men would fall overboard, get seasick, harpoon one another as soon as a whale; mountains of ocean would rise between boat and whale; rain would bucket down, spill into and spoil the oil, kill the furnace; and always, men would want more rum.

Realism, not pessimism: good planning meant anticipating what might go wrong, and hardened the resolve.

He talked it through with Mrs Chaine, and Bobby listened. Whaling was better than attempting to work this land with its topsy-turvy seasons and poor soil, and there'd be trouble with the natives, farming. The best land was their best land, too.

And they are so many more than we.

Bobby heard his words, and had repeated them to himself. And said, That's true, too: we are.

Whaling was better than arguing with everyone in King George Town, Chaine moaned. And it was easy enough enticing young blackfellas to help.

True again. Menak and Wooral had welcomed those curious few who came to the camp their first few days here and Bobby had them laughing in next to no time, showing them the pitch he was spreading across a boat's hull under Skelly's instructions. They carried some of the sticky stuff away when they left, holding it gracefully in a curve of bark and careful not to let it spill. Took some knives and axes, too.

Chaine said he'd try his luck this winter, then maybe bring Mrs Chaine and the children out this way. Set up a proper house. Who knows, he might be able to persuade some of these whalers to call here rather than King George Town's harbour. It'd be a damn sight easier for them sailing from here, especially with summer's prevailing easterlies.

But Bobby never knew how Chaine's mind, his plans and dreams, ran away from all of them.

*

Late in the night, a yellow moon appearing in the sky from further around the long curve of silver beach, Bobby stood on the sand, whalebones beneath his feet, whalebones in the dunes at his back. He turned, saw Chaine's fire at the crest of a dune, behind it the arc of a great jawbone silhouetted against the stars and his sleepy mind saw whales rising and rolling, following a trail from way out in the ocean to the right of where this moon and the sun also rises. Whales butting into the wind the way a sail cannot go, and spouting bubbles and spray and scribbles of white water like hordes of older brothers.

All them Brother Jonathons came from that way, too, from the ocean horizon somewhere.

Bobby saw the whale spouts sunlit on the grey sea, showing like blossoms, and flowers were appearing, too, all across the dunes behind him, the undulating land beyond. Whales came, and creeks rushed to the sea to meet them; kangaroos put their backs to the wind and their heads inland, toward sunrise; frogs rose from the ground, pulses calling.

Diving into the ocean today, Bobby heard the whales singing. They sang for him.

GLISTENING

WELL, BOBBY WAS HAPPY to be back playing with Christine and Christopher Chaine; happy even doing lessons. You know . . . If it was writing, one of them would hide another's chalk or pen; if it was reading aloud, the others would be asking questions, or correcting them. Or might whistle, eat a lemon even, so the reader's mouth went funny and no way would the words come out right.

There were games with a ball. Games with cards. Games with a spinning top, with bones, with rope. Bobby knew a game of throwing spears at a rolling disc of bark, and games with string, but the Chaine children had a hoop. Just the edge of one plane of a circle, it was all open air inside. Christine spun the hoop around her wrist, threw it in the air, and caught it again. All this Bobby could do, too, and run with it spinning on a short stick. Christopher said it was a girl's game and refused to play. He went to his books and his model ships, the magnifying glass and the pins that held his dead insects. Bobby delighted in the models, but they were delicate things, as Christopher explained, taking one from his hand. The magnifying glass was also a wonder, the lines and whorls of your skin like tree trunks or even some rocks he knew, and the tiny circle of sun you could draw with it and use to make fire. But it was precious, too, and fragile, and the only one that Christopher had. There was no other like it here. Christopher cut leaves from trees, flowers, too, and hung them to dry or placed them inside his books.

Christine spun the hoop around her ankle, one leg going up and down. She put it around her waist and moved her hips around and around in circles, and when her arms went up high, her cheeks flushed with concentration, she made Bobby think of those dancers at Close-by-island, the young women around the whale.

They played hide-and-seek, just the two of them. At first Bobby hid behind doors, under a table, or ran outside. But he struggled to find Christine, and too late found she was hiding beneath the bed or among the bedclothes, or standing up straight in among hanging dresses and coats . . . When Bobby hid, Christopher never found him, but with Christine he would come out into the open as she approached because it was good to laugh, to lose and let Christine be the winner.

In among the bedclothes, or among hanging dresses and coats when their bare skin touched that of the other, or he felt the warmth of her body leaning against him, Bobby felt confused and excited.

Christine was curious. You go naked, Bobby, when you're away from here?

Well, yes, but he never even thought.

The girls and women, too?

He taught her the words *mert*, the male thing; *tert*, female. Down at the river, by the welling spring and still so far from the sea, he sang her songs of ocean and air. The song to the whales: carry me far; the song to the dolphins: carry them to me; the song of the soft down on the fairy penguin's breast: comfort us. Bobby's voice, soft, almost like a whisper but imbued with something brimming, some great depth.

He taught her the word for kiss. There was a song, too, he said, that his old grandfather taught him, long gone now but everybody sang it, they all sang it now. He was up on a hilltop, watching his girlfriend run away with another man, a young man: *boonjining*, Bobby sang, lips pouting and tongue tip just moving between his teeth as he made the words, *boonj, boonj, boonjining*.

Christine learned the word, if not the song, learned to make her lips move outwards, make that kissing pout. They sang the song together, faces close, lips reaching out.

Christine met Bobby down at the pool when he had been away from the homestead and was glistening with the cold, dark water before he dried and put on his Chaine clothes. Jak Tar had a little hut there where Bobby left his good clothes and some other things.

There were always games, so many games.

Christine did not hear Bobby knocking when she was at her bath, and he came in the door and there she was, flushed and glistening, too.

They found one another, glistening.

Another time, he hardly knocked and rushed in almost at the same time but it was Mrs Chaine in the tub, near the fire, with her hair up and her mottled skin pink and glowing. Her eyes widened and she crossed her arms across her chest looking straight into his eyes, hard. Bobby backed away, closed the door softly.

*

Binyan joined Jak Tar in his hut at Kepalup, came with Manit and Menak, who took away the gifts Jak provided: the exotica of clothing, the utility of axes and knives and glass, the supplies of food. He made a hut not far from a spring which ran into the river, the other side of which Skelly had erected a rough pen for Chaine's sheep. The next time Manit and Menak arrived the old woman walked right past Binyan, stood very close to Jak Tar and told him straight to keep sheep away from that water. No hut near tears welling, he thought she said, confused. Manit and Menak called Binyan away, and together they laid reeds and rushes and leaves all around where the spring issued from the rocks. To please them Jak Tar built a rough fence of bushes each side of the trickle of water, and around the spring itself. He wondered why he bothered; Menak's eyes passed over Jak Tar as if he were not there. When they left he let the sheep in to drink again.

Binyan took the sheep away, and Jak Tar could not find her for days. Angry as he was pursuing her, he found himself apologising soon as he found her. Chaine never noted their absence, and yes, it seemed one sheep could be spared every now and then.

Jak showed her how to milk the cow. Knelt beside her and together their hands worked the teats. He sprayed her with milk, and they sucked the liquid from each other's fingers. Binyan made the cow, and the milking of it, her responsibility. The very early mornings were no trouble for her, she would stake the animal out and move it during the day, telling Jak that it looked at her with those big eyes asking like a child that could not speak.

So Chaine had got himself two workers for the price of one, or less than that because Jak Tar worked for not much more than his keep, and shelter from the law. Binyan could shepherd sheep without him, and so more often than not she went alone with the sheep for a day while Jak worked on an old whaleboat Chaine had salvaged. Jak thought that once done, he'd slide it in the downriver side of that stony barrier—which in a way worked a bit like a lock in the rivers at home—and sail it around to the whaling grounds.

No way did Jak want Binyan shepherding sheep all the way to the whaling grounds at Close-by-island; let Skelly do that on his own, or find someone else to help him. Skelly'd take a black woman any time he could. If Jak had his way he wouldn't even be going to the whaling grounds, but Chaine said sail the boat there soon as it was completed, and wanted him away from the homestead. Chaine's wife and daughter couldn't be expected to put up with seeing a white man living like man and wife with the natives. So be it. Jak would go, but he was taking Binyan in the boat with him, and Bobby, too, come to that. They'd be all the hands he'd need. Let Chaine and his missus fret all they like.

Oh, he fairly puffed himself up sometimes, did Jak Tar. Thought he could take on the world. He sewed clothes for Binyan from canvas, using a sailor's skills. He wanted her clothed properly, and undressed for his eyes only. And whatever he thought, for Binyan it was something novel and exotic, to drape herself in cloth, and gave her a greater power over the man.

Word was Killam was already at the whaling grounds, having learned a few tricks from a Chinaman. He reckoned they'd have a fine vegetable garden ready this season for any Yankee or even Froggy whalers that turned up. Skelly'd be there also by the time Jak Tar arrived.

WITHIN AND UNDER THE SEA

ONCE-WAS-A-CONVICT William Skelly limped still, and did so for the rest of his life. It became a way of perversely cherishing the memory of his spearing, more than something caused by stiffness or pain in the limb.

And so he limped as he paced the dimensions of a shed Chaine wanted made around the forge at the whaling grounds, planning how he might get himself even more into Chaine's employ, make himself nigh on indispensable, and get ahold of the tools and equipment for all that would need doing, not so much here or at Kepalup but at King George Town. There'd be—there already was—a need for boats, for carts and wheels, for a jetty, a church, for huts and shearing sheds . . . And where was the man and skill to provide all that? Skelly tapped himself on the chest. Him. He was the only man.

Except now Chaine was all for whale fishing, and left less time for building things up or laying good foundations. Said he wanted a return for his investments and he wanted it now. Only got so many years, he said. Last whale-fishing season he'd partnered a couple of American whalers, splitting the work and the profits, and done well by trading this and that: fresh food mainly.

He reckoned on setting himself up nicely at the bay for future seasons. Had told anyone who'd listen that he'd make it more than a fishery, make it a port to rival King George Town and no ship need ever again go into King George Town, especially with the fees and charges they stuck with despite the advice of merchants like himself. That damn fool Governor, Chaine swore repeatedly with no need for provocation.

So now Skelly was dragged to Close-by-island Bay yet again, out of whale season and all, because Chaine wanted him to erect another of those easy-to-build houses of his, along with less permanent buildings for the men, and a hut to store the barrels, and a shelter for meals. Chaine said he'd employ a cook next season. There'd be a garden, and already they'd cleared around the soak. But it wasn't just Chaine and Skelly: it was like a caravan, a flock of gypsies, there were so many of them, and a wagon and all. It amused Skelly to see Jak Tar treating old Manit like she was really something; Tar was even learning her language and making a big show of it. It must've been the old girl who'd given him that young woman; why else was she tagging along? Skelly wouldn't mind that young thing himself and who knows, just as likely he would, there were plenty of them to be had in between then and now.

Killam was with them as well, but so quiet and withdrawn like he was all the time these days that you hardly noticed him. So altogether there was Chaine, Tar and his woman, Killam, Manit, Skelly and of course the boy, Bobby. Only Mrs Chaine stayed behind in King George Town, because even her children made the trip. As things turned out she'd never forgive herself for that.

Manit, Bobby and Binyan had wandered off somewhere near the soak. Skelly, Tar, Killam and Chaine had their heads together over one of the whaleboats, and the two Chaine children were playing in the tiny stream which ran from the dunes, across the sand and into the waves. Only a few flowed deep, it flowed surprisingly fast and as it reached the sea seemed to lift itself clear of the damp sand, cords of water woven together, and cast some spell upon the ocean. No waves broke, and sand was stirred up in the water. Someone should have noticed that, especially when the Chaine children began playing in the shallows there.

Not even all heads turned immediately when the two children's voices began crying out together. By the time Chaine looked Jak Tar was already many steps away, and Bobby was running across the smooth damp sand, water splashing at his feet. Chaine saw his daughter, waist-deep or more, leaning toward the shore and behind her Christopher's bobbing head and arm. Even heard his choking cries. Chaine set off fast as he could, and cursed his oh so clumsy body.

Bobby had the girl by the hand, and Jak Tar—taller than both—was splashing toward them. Christine slipped and Bobby went over with her; they struggled, the force of the current sweeping them off their feet, then Tar had Bobby's hand, and Bobby had Christine's but neither was on their feet. Tar held on to Bobby's thin arm as the waves rose against him, unbreaking, and he tried not to stop them lifting his own feet from the ground. Chaine was next into the water, and he in turn grabbed hold of Tar and pulled him close to shore. He glimpsed Christopher, already a long way out, head bobbing, an arm lifted. There were four of them in a line for a moment, and Chaine pulled himself past Tar and Bobby, grabbed Christine and headed back to shore. The girl was already on the sand, vomiting, as Tar and Bobby left the water, looking over their shoulders. Chaine ran to the whaleboat, which Killam and Skelly and some of the others were dragging across the sand. They had not expected to be dragging boats to the water quite so soon. Chaine was screaming, Tar, Bobby, get here, too!

A head bobbing in the waves, gone. No, there again. Was that his voice on the wind, faint? Or birds?

Manit and Binyan were with the girl and Bobby.

Eyes scanned the water. Where was Christopher? Must be somewhere in this bay, must be somewhere floating . . . still.

*

Mrs Chaine sat by her daughter's bed, stroking the girl's hair, her unlined skin like porcelain. Her husband was away again, unreachable since the accident even when he stood beside her. So often silent. They had rooms where the roof was only sheets of bark, and she listened to the wind moaning in the trees, the branches tossing wearily to and fro. Through the open window sunlight danced brightly on the harbour and shone on the hills enclosing it, as if to spite the daughter who lay muttering and tossing her head from side to side. Even here in town Mrs Chaine could hear the malicious croaking of frogs, the shrill voices of cicadas and crickets, the harsh shrieks and mutterings, sometimes, of birds. She pinched her skin, hard. It could not be real that she was here, like this, alive, when her son . . .

Geordie had brought their daughter back to King George Town by boat. It must have taken forever, his clammy daughter awkward in his aching arms, and to arrive to a shrieking wife . . . But who else could be blamed?

Skelly and Killam came back more slowly with the wagon. Manit and Bobby began with them, but slipped away. The men were in no great hurry, and wandered when they could, either hobbling the horses or leaving them to slowly continue on their own. There were only so many ways the horses could follow.

It was a hot, dusty journey. The men complained to one another, cursing imprecisely. A throbbing heat, and the constant pulse of what must be cicadas and bees, and dangling leaves turning slowly on their axis even as the breeze shook them so that they clashed like cymbals. A man's own breath heaving like an animal's. Where were the women, the black bitches? That fucking stupid boy. Their bodies found gaps in the bushes, their heavy feet followed those of another and another and another . . . Here, in a steep valley among smooth rocks, a deep blue pool, irregularly shaped, as if the rock had been torn apart. They had water, it was not thirst that compelled them. Strangely, no one even tasted the water. Killam lowered a long tree limb into the pool but couldn't tell how deep it was. Then Skelly was undressing; he plunged in, and came back to the surface gasping, a hand held out, pleading, and when they pulled him onto the rocks he was already blue with cold. Shivering and dressed again he looked into the pool with the others and they saw a dark form pass across it. The two men stepped back. It was salt water, yes, but can ocean be beneath earth this far inland? Each thought of the boy. Drowned, gone underground? Some spirit of water, of ocean, even here? The dome of sky might have fallen, crushed them to the earth with no space between.

SOMETIMES A WHALE'S PATH

B OBBY WAS ALONE—a rare thing among his people, really—
and he stood beneath the old trees on the line of rocks that
crossed the river just down from Chaine's homestead, his bare feet
disturbed a thin sheet of water as it went over the edge, turning
silver as it fell. The water was dark because of the shade of peppermint trees, their leaves falling now and then, drifting until
they reached the line of rocks his bare feet straddled. Some caught
for a moment there, and the river brimmed, and brimmed again
so that the leaves must move, and fall, inevitably, to the water a
handspan below. They floated in little circles then, those leaves,
agitated for a bit, and there were small bubbles and squiggles of
foam. Like someone spitting.

Cold here, but not so cold as Chaine's house. They built it
with stone walls, and the sun never hardly got in there no more.
And their boy, he, too, was no more, at least not a live boy. They
should've moved away when he passed on. Mrs Chaine, her skin
all grey and she like an everlasting flower, dry, tiny and just as
likely to blow away in a wind, even by the wind say made by
someone's laughter. And so Bobby didn't laugh; you couldn't

laugh when you were with her now. Not that she was really no-
ticing much of the world about her.

Bobby went back to the lessons with Mrs Chaine and Christine. Christine? Same thing, she was not like she was, at least
not when she and her mother were together. The boy was there,
it was just that you couldn't see him. But he was there alright,
and he was sick and he was unhappy and everyone was still
ashamed. He never wanted to be here and he never wanted to be
dead.

Yes, they returned to their lessons, but it was very careful letters, and say if you wanted to write the letter 'd', well, then in
the slow time it took writing it—took Bobby, anyway, but not
Christine—there was all the time to think those words like
dead, like decay and death and then don't, desist . . . It slowed
Bobby right down. And don't even think about the letter 'c'. He
didn't know how the sister could even write her own name.

It was cold and quiet in that house, and behind the sound of
his own footsteps going through some of those rooms there was
the sound of another footstep, someone following close. Sunshine hardly ever touched them inside those walls. Voices moaned
and complained all around the house right in the middle of the
day when the wind was up.

Back to lessons, and they read the Bible. Oh yes, that book was
always within reach. Bobby remembered Jonah, and the disciples
and their supper, and Samson with all his blind strength. Lazarus
was one he never heard before: the man who died walking out of
a cold, stone cave. After that Bobby had to stop himself hesitat-
ing each time he had to open a door to the Chaine house. Who
might walk out to greet him saying, I come back now?

Mrs Chaine's chin dropped sometimes and she seemed to
bend a little more, as if she was trying to look inside herself, and
went very quiet, and when she did try to speak her voice was weak.
Then she would wave a hand, and go out of the room just like

someone they could not see was pulling her. She went away and left them to their own lessons.

Mrs Chaine appeared as Bobby was about to leave with Geordie Chaine for a second season's whale hunting, and gave him an oil-skinned paper journal.

A gift from Christine and myself, she said, placing it between his hands, and her hands around his. Keep up your lessons, Mrs Chaine told him. But she could not be so friendly as she once was. Christine smiled, looked to the ground.

Later, on lookout, the thought of Christine made Bobby sad and happy at the same time. He ran ink over the pages of that journal; made lines, prints, laid traces of what was happening. It was like he was moving, following, making tracks of time so that later—further along—they'd tell him, if not where he was, then what he'd been doing. Even if he stepped onto a rowboat and left no sign and ended up somewhere altogether different, where not only the prints on the sand, but the sand itself, the wind and plants and air, the birds rivers insects were strange, and no pattern or rhythm, no sound he knew to move and be a part of . . . Well, even then he could backtrack maybe . . . He could, he could. Bobby knew he could do that.

So this moon—May, some say—the air chills quickly soon as the sun sits on the land, ready to go away. Bobby looked at that setting sun sitting, and felt the wind blowing from his left-hand side, not the writing hand side, like it did, even late in the day, this time of the year, after the salmon been, before the whales came. A chill land breeze early tempted you, then it was a warm breeze, the land breathing out and its breath blowing across the sea.

Going where?

The breeze rippled the sea's surface, but even so it was gentle enough and quite smooth, even when there were lines of swell pulsing beneath it. The sea might be blue, might be dark grey and looking thick like blood with dark cloud making one single coat of fur across the sky. A few salmon slid in the shallows, and herring closer still. Across the sand the mullet made circles with their tails, their bellies on the sand floor of the estuary, wishing the sand away, waves breaking not so far but a world apart. Foam on the sand like clean mouth-spit. Rain like human tears, and the smell of earth and moist leaves in the warm air. Frogs call out from where they're buried, sensing rain, saying move inland move inland move away from the sea.

But Chaine stays. And Bobby stops right with him.

Fun. Chaine says, Let's race. It's one boat against the other and Bobby with Jak Tar in the boat this year, on the rudder—steerer—and Jak Tar is boss of men and boat and harpoon, too.

The boys run—Bang! says Chaine or Jak Tar—and they're off! Grab the whaleboat, drag it to the sea. You might be behind, but you can still catch up, rowing out past the rocky point and back. Pull your weight against the oars, lean forward lean back (you and your brothers' legs arms backs drive the boat) and the hull slices the sea's skin, spurts froth and foam.

A new rhythm.

Some of the boys go with Killam and Skelly. They break up the ground with steel shovels, open the earth, shit and dig it in. Put seeds in the damp ground.

Skelly takes the sheep walking, with that woman that come along this time. They walk the sheep around the poison bushes, keep them near to water.

Slow and easy.

Chaine gives everybody rum. A tot, boys. A tot. He sings in the evening and there's always food. All the boys, same as brothers. Bobby and Jak Tar special brothers now, ever since Jak got Binyan.

* * *

The whale jaw was planted in the ground to make an archway, and Bobby went through it to get to Chaine's hut. He came up the slope, walking with the wind but knowing that the winds when the whales started dying here would keep the stink of their death and the try-pot away. He would go under the arch of whale jaw and it would seem so grey, the sky would be grey, the ocean, too, and most often it was raining and blood everywhere. But today he looked up and saw the curve of bone—bright, white—arching against the vault of sky, and the bright whale teeth, and the sun behind so biting and stabbing at his eyes it brought tears.

A path of bone began at the arch. It was all rectangles and circles; whale vertebrae, cut in half, with flat surfaces uppermost and sand packed solid in between. Bobby stamped his feet as he walked to see if the path would shift. It didn't. He looked back over his shoulder—the white sandy beach, the slope of granite to one side with the whale hauled up on it, and the headland rising above that—and remembered blood flowing down the granite, and the sharks, their fins and tails above the surface, cutting and slicing to and fro. The try-pot, and the dry blubber fed to the fire, and the black smoke rolling away in shredded clumps.

Already the Yankee whaler had anchored inside the island, furled its sails, and men were rowing to shore across the many shifting surfaces of grey, green, turquoise sea, preparing themselves to walk again on solid ground.

Bobby raised his hand to knock.

Used to be there was no archway, no path, and the hut was tarpaulin and kangaroo skins, so there was no need for knocking; you just pushed the door aside and walked in, and see the *wadjela* missus looking startled, excited. It made you feel strong, and sorry for her, too. He heard the stories.

Boss got the soldiers, that place. Rifles and horses.

It's different, things change. Bobby stands on whalebone (oh yes, he who will stand on a whale's back, and have a gun of his own and food given him by the bosses) and pauses, fist raised ready to knock, to marvel once again at how the tiny holes in this door rescued from the sea have merged with the bevels and curves made by a man like Skelly, somewhere.

The door opens, and Bobby almost punches Boss Chaine on the nose.

Seen it, Bobby. Chaine shoulders him aside in his rough and familiar way. Boss Chaine, all beard and glittering eyes and bulky like a bullock.

Chaine knows what he wants. Profits, not prophets. Knows what he wants done because he writes it down first. Some of it, least-ways. Him and his lists. They will build a stand for the try-pot; they will make a garden, then tend and weed it. They spread pitch on the boats the Yankees left them. They shepherd sheep, make fences to keep sheep in and kangaroos out. But those *yongar* leap clear over the fence. Chaine gives Bobby a rifle, and Bobby comes back with a kangaroo and puts it in the fire. He singes the skin first, then buries it in the ashes.

Now—though the precise boundary of *now* remains unclear—trees bloom, and a few late salmon can still be seen in the waves. The crests flutter, torn by the wind to look like Missus Chaine's lace, and you see the fish silhouetted clear and separate from one another. The wave breaks and Bobby thinks to run along the beach, forever and forever beside the breaking waves, the rolling miles and miles of spit and bubbles maybe all the way back to King George Town.

Of course you couldn't keep going fast all that distance be-cause of the rocky headlands in between and the soft sandy beach, unless of course you can maybe travel like a fish, and not even Bobby with so much family out there in the sea can do that.

From the lookout Bobby sees fish in a solid mass, indistinguishable from one another under the skin of sea. He sees how a shark can't join them, can't merge because soon as he moves into the school, they break apart. Another thing altogether, shark.

Bobby knows there's life under the sea still, like there was at the cold, frozen time. *Nyitiny*, he thinks: cold time. *Nyitang*: cold with. *Wadjela*: white man, away very? The spirit of all those from the cold time still there under the sea's skin, and their shapes change because the light is different, the sounds are different. Dolphins wave to him as they journey by, show themselves racing the waves, leaping and twisting in the air. Air suddenly all around you as you hurtle from the back of a wave, the fear and thrill of that, and then the crash, bubbles, the world pulling itself close again and hearts beating and the calls of brothers and sisters moving through water thicker than air. Outside and inside, ocean and blood; almost the same salty fluid.

Bobby crested a dune with his uncles and cousins, and there were fish spread out across the beach; the water left them, suddenly shrank away, pulled back. Uncles said don't eat them fish. Mullet. *Merrderang*. Nearly the same word as the word for penis, his people said so, anyways. Dick. Never realised that before. A lot of dicks lying on the ground. Like Chaine's dick that he wave around sometime, but never with his wife close by.

And big-dick Chaine (a bubble of laughter bursts from Bobby in his solitude), big-dick Chaine wants whales. And if he wants whales then Bobby knows this is the place where they come close to shore, close enough for him and the other men to leap into a boat, row quickly to them with spears.

Madness.

Bobby was excited just thinking about it!

All the life and spirit under the sea's skin and out past the horizon, and Bobby gunna bring it back, give it air, haul it onto the sandy shore.

Every time Bobby walked through the whale jaws he still thought of Jonah, from the Bible story, and that old people's song. Grab the whale's heart, squeeze it, use its eyes and power to take you where you wanna be. He sings to himself, that song with one man on a rock next to deep ocean, and a whale scraping its barnacles on the rock. True. He on a rock and right next to him in the water, bigger than the rock he's standing on, is a whale, breathing and groaning. He steps onto its back and into the spout; he slides down into the cave which must be inside each and every whale. And in that echoing cavern of flesh he sings and hurts its heart, he dances around, driving it to that place further along the coast he heard in story and song. Never been there, never seen it. The whale comes up to breathe and the man looks out through its eye and sees only the ocean, and birds in the sky. No sign of land. But he trusts the song his father gave him, and he makes the whale dive again, and again, and makes the whale take him deep and far. Until the whale takes him onto the beach, and the women on the beach love him and bring all their people there, and they all feast and altogether party.

In that story the man returns home, his children with him and their two mothers, pregnant again the both of them.

Daadi man, him. Everybody love him.

Jonah woulda been alright if he was a Noongar man.

Come back home rich and your people gunna love you.

*

Bobby seen them by their smoke first, and went closer to greet them. Wooral and Menak and Manit and some other old ones who he not seen oh since before his uncle died and he went to live with Dr Cross and now Kongk Chaine. They were in a grove of paperbarks, near the edge of the dance ground, and not far from where the creek rested near the beach, waiting for the rain and the storms to join them all up again.

They hugged him, one old woman nearly crying to see him. She was so old and grey, so wrinkled and tiny and Bobby was so much taller now that she rested her head against his chest, tapping her palm against his cheek. Wooral and Menak stood close, patting his shoulders and touching him. Manit came and stood beside her old sister. He was tall as her, too.

Oh! Manit had him by the nose! Had her fingers inside his nose, pinching the flesh between his nostrils and Menak and Wooral held him by the shoulders, and they wouldn't let him go, none of them. Granny Manit's fingernails hurt. She held him like that old bull was held. And something very sharp was being stuck into the skin inside his nose.

They let him go and he jumped away. Looked at them, and fingered the piece of bone in his nose. Understood there were other people he must also be with on his way to becoming a man.

Jak Tar told Chaine that Bobby wouldn't be back, not this season leastways. But he reckoned they'd find some other fellas could help with the whaling.

But not my boy Bobby, too? Chaine first thought of Christopher, then: Oh, you mean he's gone with the Yankees? Not with that captain!

No, Jak Tar said, with his own people.

Chaine felt somehow betrayed.

PART IV

1841–1844

BOBBY CAME HOME ON HIGH

BOBBY CAME HOME on the shoulders of brothers and uncles and cousins and, coming home high, held in the sky, he saw things with new eyes. They carried him because he was important, because he was boss and too solid, and (if truth be told) because he couldn't yet quite find his feet. Eyes, feet; he was different.

He travelled from river to river and what seemed from island to island until there were trees he'd never seen and family whose names he'd never heard. In these years he learned hard things, and had his strength and nerve tested.

He ran until he was breathless and his limbs turned to stone, and then ran easily again downhill with limbs flailing, never falling. He lay in icy creeks, stayed with no food or company until he heard voices all around him. Frogs called that rain would spill from the sky like a ruptured bladder. Magpies sang to him and the goanna said, Time to dig yourself out again. When birds moved away he went, too, following them. An eagle in the sky was only a circling speck, and then there it was, just the other side of a steep gully. Bobby looked across the narrow space between him and the eagle, and the eagle looked back at him, held his eye.

Returning home with new friends and family, he was massaged with oils, and his fine, strong and supple self was decorated with feathers, with twigs and tiny nuts, with fur and skin, and he was lifted into the air and supported by those resolved to show him his importance. Bobby trusted, he was supported and held up high. They carried him to await the welcome home of Menak and Manit and laid him on soft animal skin with women either side, and everybody just so happy to see him back again. People filed past in a long line just to see him, speak to him, tell him oh how wonderful to have him back again until Bobby Wabalanginy thrummed with pride and pleasure just being him.

After days at the centre of this strong circle, he heard an English voice, one he carried in his head but so long since he'd heard its sound saying Bobby. Bobby.

He thought them all: Christine Chaine. William Skelly. Soldier Killam and them two boys . . . Kept his thoughts moving: Mr Boss Kongk Chaine. Missus Chaine. Menak and Manit then, but not them because they did not have the sound of the voice he heard, and he realised he was thinking in letters, too, doing the names of people and here MENAK and MANIT did not fit either, and soon as he tried the letters the memories would not come, and the letters broke or moved apart like a boat hit by the whale's tail, when all its planks just fell apart, floated separate and the best you could do was tie an oar crossways . . . Jak Tar came into his mind then. JAK TAR, the picture of the letters written like that came along with the memory, his bare feet and stiff pigtail and the grin wrinkling his face up.

And then as if underwater and heading up to the surface there was light and the skin of the sea and he broke through . . .

Jak Tar was sitting on the ground beside Bobby's campfire,

smiling at him, and the lines of his smile led to the pool of each eye. Jak Tar called to him. Bobby, he said. Whales.

Jak Tar wove rope: a fine line for the harpoon, a line to go from boat to harpoon to whale. The line had to be strong, yet flexible, and being three strands each of sixteen threads it was slow work. Jak not only liked to make it himself, but he liked to stack it, too, since because of a loose loop or tangled line he'd seen men lose a limb or plunge clumsily overboard in pursuit of a sound-ing whale.

Jak Tar had always taken pleasure in being methodical, but his present happiness was thanks to Binyan. Who'd have thought, a native woman at that, and at an age when he might have been a sun-dried and salty thing pressed in with his own kind. The only thing worse than sailors in a ship was whalers in a ship; maggots in a floating abattoir.

Instead, he was beside the sea only a few months of the year. *Beside* the sea, not *on* the sea. True, they were wintry months, and not the most comfortable to be at the seaside. True again, it was no Brighton or Nantucket, but it was nonetheless a place where he helped take the mightiest harvest the sea provided and met and mingled with those who sailed her. The rest of the year was his. He was as independent as a labouring man could be, and lived what he called a life of comfort: it was easy to earn his keep, put bread upon the table (though there was not always a table!), and he had the comfort of love.

Binyan appeared now, entering the tent Jak had made of whalebone, tree limbs and sailcloth. Its roof fairly soared, and when he rolled up the tent's sides he had shade, a cooling breeze, and a view of the bay to rival Chaine's. It was a home that served him well for the whaling season, and could be dismantled and stored if need be.

And Binyan herself! Not a princess, to be sure, not with a name like Binyan and dressed in old sailcloth, cloth she was ready to throw off with hardly a thought for modesty but clever enough to know what a thrill it gave an old mariner like himself to unfurl.

She was a young woman but worked like a man. Could lean into a shovel or hoe, had learned as much as he knew of horses (which was not much) and then had them doing whatever she wished without ever raising her voice, let alone a whip. She'd led him to more sandalwood trees than he could count, and helped cut and load and cart enough to see them through a month of idle loving; she could provide more shelter than any man with such a lover required, and it was she who found the best grazing when they were shepherding, where poison bush ran thickest, and where dingoes were least likely to trouble them.

Her hands were cool and, especially given how hard she worked, surprisingly soft. Perhaps that was the sheep's fleece, or the oil she rubbed into her skin.

Laughing, she was always laughing, her body rocking with it as she leaned against a horse, or grabbed his hand with her own, as if to make him dance with her.

They lay in one another's arms in their high-ceilinged tent with the sides rolled down for shelter and the front opened to a view of the bay and the island below. It was mostly just the two of them at the whaling grounds this time of year, though her family might drop in at any time. It seemed he had no say in that. He preferred the place to themselves.

Not much chance of that, since Chaine was planning a fine home here where he'd lost his boy and until now been happy with canvas and whalebone. Reluctantly, Jak admired the man's ability to acquire and develop. This was a fine anchorage, and if

Chaine's boasting was to be believed, the extent of his trading would soon rival that of the Cygnet River Colony, let alone King George Town. It was all due to him, he'd tell you with no need for prompting—the force of his will and his energy. He could be a regular pain in the arse, Chaine. Of course he'd profited from Jak Tar, same as he had from everyone he knew. The thing was, without him, none of them would be able to make a living here except, of course, the blacks. Binyan's people. Well, if they needed to *make* a living, and not just live.

Ships called in all year round because the sleepy government-fed port of King George Town charged such exorbitant rates (theft, the sea captains called it) for its anchorage, and yet was nervous of sailors and rum and almost any flicker of life that sailed into its drowsy hollow.

Jak liked it here, but this woman-girl of his wanted to be up and gone. These past few weeks, ever since they'd come back to the whaling grounds, she'd suddenly up and disappear. And now she wanted to be gone again.

He be back maybe, was all she said. Wabalanginy Bobby man now, your brother. Him a man now. Young man. Them girls lost their promised mans, 'cause too many old people—young ones, too, but—dying. He a clever man Bobby Wabalanginy *baal kaditj koombar booda mabarn ngan demanger wanginy* . . .

Jak Tar had to slow her down right then. He might be a good listener, and even learning her lingo, but he couldn't understand everything.

You him brother, she said. Manit say . . . She was laughing in his face: delighted, excited. The detail of it made no sense—he guessed it was something to do with the way old Manit had adopted him, Jak Tar, and arranged things so he might get together with Binyan. It was hard to follow; anyone might be brother or sister, any uncle also a father, any aunty a mother. They were such loosely applied appellations.

Appellations! As he followed Binyan, Jak Tar congratulated himself on the use of such a word. He might be living at the very bottom of the world, and among those others would happily call savages, heathens, Indians or blackfellas . . . (Nobody except they themselves said Noongars and there were far more names than understanding.) Jak may have learned something of their tongue—more than most bothered—yet had lost none of his way with English.

If they were to stay together, Binyan would need to have less to do with these people, her people. For the sake of the children they would have. A surprise, really, that she was not yet pregnant. But Binyan was leaving, and he called out for her to wait. She turned, smiling, her head tilted.

Biirdiwa, she said. Not a word he'd want to write down; how the blazes would you spell it? Though in his mind the boy he remembered became Biirdiwa Bobby, though she used the name Wabalanginy. A mouthful of sound, that one. But how long since he'd seen the boy? Or was he a man now, as Binyan seemed to be saying? As a boy he'd been as quick with his mind as he was on his feet. What would he be as a man?

Anxiety flickered in Jak Tar's gut. What about his own yet-to-arrive children? What opportunity would they have, with a black mother and a runaway for a father? Jak Tar knew enough of British ways and, as much as he'd all his life loved its people and its institutions and its justice and in his childhood had run home with lard from the royal kitchens where his Aunty worked and . . . Well, he knew what he knew and Jak Tar would wager that whatever Bobby's talent there'd be precious little place for a black man as the settlements grew. Though it was a wager he'd gladly lose.

It was Jak Tar's responsibility to make sure their boats were well maintained, well manned and well stocked. It was a responsibility he revelled in and took seriously. He'd run his hand over the boat, tracing each of its long, thin curved planks and was embarrassed to notice Bobby copying him. He wondered if he was being mocked, but it was just that Bobby was trying to see things as Jak did. That was Bobby for you: trying to get into other people's heads.

*

Jak Tar trained Bobby, and oddly enough began with description, putting the boat and its equipment into words. The boat was as long as about four or five tall people laid down in a row; its width about the same as an older child (say you, Bobby, just a couple of years ago) laid across it. Twenty-six feet, by four feet ten, Jak Tar told him. The other men, experienced in whaling, noticed the precision and the care he took. Six men to a boat, Jak reiterated, as if Bobby had not seen them hunting, and then pointed at the bow. The harpooner up front, see? And the steerer at the stern, with his great long oar, and probably four men between them, rowing.

And what was in each boat?

Jak Tar wondered if Chaine was using Bobby to keep an eye on his own dutifulness, or wanted him to take over his own role.

There was a tub between the centre seats—thwarts, Jak had told him, and Bobby afterwards always used that very word— and in it some four hundred feet of very flexible line, carefully woven and tarred and thick as a man's thumb. Near the tub was an anchor, and in some boats a cross of heavy wooden planks to be lashed to the end of the rope if the whale was strong enough to have taken its entire length. A barrel contained some weight of biscuits, and another held fresh water. (We might finish up a very long way from shore, my boy.) There was a ship's lantern, and candles, flints, steel and tinder sealed in a tin box. There were bowls for baling, one or two buckets to be thrown overboard as sea anchors as the whale hauled them along, a hatchet, a knife, and a small mast and sail. The sail might also serve as a sea anchor. And of course there were harpoons and lances with their wooden handles.

Jak Tar knew the feel of the lance's wooden handle like the hand of a lover; better, because it was not his lover's hand that he was most taken with. The wooden handle had taken the shape of his own hand. Jak Tar knew the boat very well, since it was from the ship he'd escaped, and the steerer's oar fell easily to his hand. In fact, Jak had Bobby in mind as steerer, since he was quick-witted and so lightweight he'd be no handicap to the rowers.

Jak was the boss of these two boats, and this whaling team. It was his, set up by Chaine. Previous seasons Skelly and Killam had been part of the team, though there'd also been ship escapees or labourers ready to try their luck. A man didn't pry into another's background unless it was offered. Some of the local Noongars joined them, young men, usually. Menak had tried it early, but walked away. Wooral had proved himself invaluable.

The men practised early in the season, not only rowing hard and fast, but also manoeuvring to and fro, as they would need to when close to the whale. The boat's pointed stern meant that, with the steerer's oar lifted from the water, she'd reverse as easily as go forward. And we'll get to know one another as a team, Jak told Bobby, you shout the orders when we row.

Jak would be on harpoon. Headsman.

Chaine wanted to enter into partnership with a Yankee whaler as early in the season as possible. This had proved a convenient and profitable way to operate. The Yankee would take the majority of the oil, and Chaine the whalebone from the right whale's throat. It was right whales they sought; they came in so close to shore and particularly, it seemed, to this very bay. The bone was for women's dresses, Jak Tar told Binyan and Bobby. Oh? Both wanted an explanation of what was beneath the ladies' skirts.

But it was too early yet for the whales: the salmon were mostly gone, but schools of herring abounded, and the wind had not long shifted so that it blew softly all day from the north, inland, and there were days of fine rain and low dark skies where sea and sky seemed the same, almost merging.

Not long now, Bobby told him. And Jak Tar, remembering the last couple of years, agreed it'd be another few weeks before those southwesterly gales, and the whales, arrived. Chaine himself was due any day.

WHAT'S NOT IN A WHALE SONG

B Y SEASON'S END Bobby had a song of the whale hunt, and his voice offered it as the ship left Close-by-island bound for King George Town. Fittingly enough, the song began with what was happening just then: the shoreline shrinking and the home-fires flickering smaller and fading as their ship, like the boats in the song, pulled away from shore. The song was a search for whales as the sun our mother rose but even before that the sky was upward drawing the light from deep blue water and oh look here come the whales . . .

Wooral and Jak Tar added their voices and the whalers smiled and laughed, recognising the mime and also, among the incomprehensible words and infectious melody, the names of their tools and hunting cries. But mostly they delighted in the sinewy energy of the song, the resonating voices, the way it lifted you like an ocean wave, and they felt the gathering energy about to take them on a ride like that behind a whale racing from the harpoon's sting.

This last season Bobby (and by now only Noongar knew him by another name) and his team hadn't needed him or anyone else perched high on the headland calling out, Whale! Whale! There she blows, we rose a whale! Somehow he seemed to know when a whale was in reach, or else they went searching for them on one or another of Brother Jonathon's ships or the little schooner Chaine now owned. But truth was they rarely needed to venture beyond the bay, though sometimes a whale hauled a boat so far it was a day's rowing back to camp.

The schooner proved ideal for blocking the path of rival shore-based whaling boats, for there were other men from King George Town who wanted the wealth Chaine was gathering from the sea. Chaine's successful alliance with the Americans stirred his jealous rivals' patriotism: this was a British dominion, Sir! It stirred their resentment, too, because a man would indeed be a fey idiot to fish with a land party if foreigners are allowed into our very own ports . . .

Bobby's song did not touch on such rivalries. It captured the experience of the whale hunt in a series of verses that did not always follow the same sequence. It was how he relaxed and re-vitalised himself and even now, at season's end as he lay on the deck of the American ship surfing across the backs of waves with the easterly wind of summer filling its sails, he was com-posing and refining verses in his head. The words of whaling: harpoon and lance, sleigh-ride and bucket, blankets and book-pieces and skimmers and spoons. *Galleyed* almost made him laugh out loud, even in the dark and his almost-sleep, as he remembered the frustration and fury of other hunters as the schooner slipped between them and the whale.

Lowering in and out of sleep, Bobby saw the smooth slick sur-face which showed a whale beneath the water. The whale rose, dived, and the last glimpse of its tail showed Bobby where it would appear next. The boat glided there, the men rowing under the guidance of Bobby who would first see the change in the wa-ter, and the whale bursting back into their world. The lance struck home and Jak got two turns of rope around the boat's loggerhead before the whale reacted, and then the rope was hissing, uncurl-ing as the men shipped oars and clung to their seats and the boat was skipping across the sea's surface like a thrown, flat stone. Foam flew about them, the rope hummed, the boat vibrated and leaned dangerously if any man shifted his weight, and Jak doused water where the rope wound around the loggerhead, adding steam to the smoke of its heat.

Early in the season, Bobby and Jak were in the one boat. Jak thought it fitting, since old Manit insisted that not only were they brothers, they were brothers to the whales as well. Least that's what Jak heard her say. His very first throw of the season fixed them to a whale, but its dive did not send them streaking toward the horizon; instead it circled, and towed them back toward its fel-lows. Jak Tar stood poised to cut the line at the first sign of trouble, if it caught on another whale or . . .

Obligingly, the whale slowed as it reached the edge of the pod, and across the rolling backs and spouts of this crowd of whales they saw other boats in explosions of foam and spray, their tumbling bow waves testament to how big a whale they had harpooned. By contrast, they went slowly, gently towed deeper and deeper among the elegantly rolling backs of what seemed hundreds of whales. The men in the boat looked all about, ner-vous. What if a whale rose beneath them? In front? What if a tail . . . ?

At the bow Jak Tar waved his sharpened steel this way and that, and it was as if the harpoon were a magic wand. They slowed even further, and now the water was a smooth, rich brew brim-ming with bubbles. Then the line fell slack: the harpoon had loosened; oh, their whale was gone. Frantic activity; another harpoon? Amazingly, the whales slowed, rested, were apparently waiting as the men wound in the rope, and wound it in a dripping coil. Surrounded by whales, the men could pick and choose. Jak readied himself to drive in the dart.

But think: how would they escape the pod, towed by a panicking whale? The whales were packed closely, their very motion carrying the boat along with them: any acceleration from here would smash and sink their good selves into a deep watery grave. Best not to try a harpoon just now; best wait until things cleared a little. They could see the sense in that, but each man was also in line for a percentage of the total take—his *lay*—and here was money all around them.

The whales closed in tight. Whale eyes held them, whale breath descended like warm mist, and the men felt a solidarity so far out to sea, surrounded by the very mass of these mammals. It was like being in the shelter of a headland, except that the headland was in motion.

Eventually space opened up as the whales slowly moved along their ocean road. Space cleared, and so did the hunters' heads. Jak Tar went to seize the moment; this was their opportunity. Look what was to be had. He lifted his harpoon. No! Why waste it on such a whale? And swung to another rising to the surface, but once more held his arm. Poor Jak Tar was a flurry of indecision, and the men in the boat, usually leaning into their oars and moving with one mind like a school of fish, pointed in all directions and insisted on various targets. The men were cursing and accusing even as those targets moved out of range.

Jak Tar threw. The harpoon stuck, the whale shook itself . . . the harpoon came loose. Tails waving goodbye, the whales were gone. The men sat at their oars, bowed heads shaking as whale backs rolled into the distance, breath tolling, their spouts a semaphore of farewell. Perhaps with a ferocious Chaine barking from the steering oar, or an equally fiery and wilful harpooner pointing the way they might yet have won themselves a whale. But not today, not this pod, not this Jak Tar.

*

Bobby grew into the role, and by season's end, as the two or three whaleboats raced one another to the whales, his voice was heard urging the men to land me on that whale's back, boys, I'll fix a whale and take us for a ride. He stood, legs bent, on the rear thwart, watching the water for sign of a whale, its reappearance, or change of direction. Heave, heave, my strong men. Land me on that whale's back and I'll steer him home.

One day they succeeded: landed Bobby on a whale's back, but not from the momentum of headlong pursuit; it needed the whale's help. The harpoon had stuck, but unusually the whale did not dive and race away. In fact, it hardly reacted. It seemed more curious than in pain, and shifting its tail around in what seemed an exploratory way, struck the boat a glancing blow so that Bobby was catapulted into the air. He landed on the whale's back and was on his feet in an instant, arms out wide and feeling a deep trembling through the soles of his feet; and then the whale dived. Bobby felt the angle shift, and the soles of his feet stuck for a moment, gripping the black whale skin as water rushed around him and there were bubbles and silver and below him the great shape dwindling, shrinking, disappearing into the blue darkness. He felt the bright whip of the harpoon line cutting past him, taut as a long silver spear, and when he came spluttering to the surface his steerless boat was already distant and skipping toward the horizon. He raised his arm, called to the other boat rowing his way.

Jak Tar leaned over the gunnel. Need bridle and saddle for riding whales that way, Bobby!

* * *

No longer needing the risk of try-pots on a ship's deck, they set them up on land. Dead whales floated in the shelter of the headland, and the sloping granite was a ramp up which the whales were hauled, their blubber peeled from them. The try-pots sat just above, boiling and belching smoke. Wooral (Bobby's song told) slipped on the blood that flowed down the rock in sheets. Sharks waited. Wooral went screaming into the bloody water, and in an instant heads turned to him see him silhouetted on the headland high above them all. He held a shark in his arms. So ended another of Bobby's verses, and another man joined the refrain.

Bobby sang, and it happened just as in the song: the boats left the shore and home receded, but the singer was on the boat, not on the shore like in the old songs, not on a hill and watching others leave, not scanning the seascape for a first or last sight of whale spout or tilting sail. Singing, Bobby thought of the marks he'd made when he was on lookout: his pen on paper, his chalk on slate, his *roze a wail* and the like, but there was no getting those marks into song, though sometimes he wrote letters in the sand, to show whaling men he knew their schooling and way of being civilised, too.

There was a cook with them only a short time. First time Wooral and Bobby came for their food, the cook said it wasn't his job to serve Niggers. Kongk Chaine was there and Jak Tar, too, and they rounded on him like sheep dogs. Said we are one here, we judge people on what they do, not their skin. This is not your home. Chaine sent the man away soon as he found someone who could take his place.

The business of a white man thinking he was too good for a Noongar was not in Bobby's song, but instead the men onboard ship, black and white and a Chinaman, too, if we want to keep saying people are this or that, and Yankees and convicts and froggies and soldiers . . . They all joined voices with Bobby as the melody grabbed them, held them, hauled them along behind. For some it was recognising the words—their whaling language in the midst of all the blackfella talk—and they called out, putting their voice beside the singer, trusting him and themselves to get to the end.

Asked to describe the song many would have struggled. One of those blackfella songs, they said, but with some of our words in it. They caught familiar words and snatches of melody, but something in the sound and the rolling momentum of liquid syllables moved them, put them at sea again and full of spirit.

Chaine was reminded of Indian flutes, or even a fiddle, the way the melody wavered in quavers. Toward the end, each verse suddenly dropped an octave and men eagerly joined their voices to the rumbling refrain, proving they were as one, together, even if not knowing all the words, and even if only for the singing of this small part.

And such solidarity strengthened when Bobby and Wooral and Jak Tar mimed what they sang: the harpoon throw, the men crouched in the boat with oars raised, and then that relentless octave-down drone at each verse's end. Other voices joined theirs, and once more Bobby on steerer had them tap-tap-tapping across the sea, wallowing, bouncing and tumbling at the heart of spray and foam, helpless and taut with excitement, until the bright focus of the glinting lance entering the whale again and again stilled them. His song had them in a boat suddenly made small and frail, dodging tail and fins and a great head as waves and whale threw them about and showered them in clotted, hot blood and they heard a brother whale's low-down dying groan . . .

Bobby sang of the long rowing, of towing the whale back to the beach or ship, and their red selves covered alike in dried salt and thick blood (Bobby planned dancers covered in thick red

ochre, their bright white eyes shining at the audience). Finally—
and here voices joined him as he sang small pieces of many of
the songs people had brought to the campfires—he sang of the
whalers sharing their songs of celebration back at the campfires,
singing bits of the very verse he now sang, and the rum and the
voices of different brothers and the congratulations and love
of Noongar people made them lose their selves, drew them
together . . .

Bobby's song had little of cutting up the whale. It did not say
the whale's blubber was peeled and sliced into long strips. It did
not detail the 'blankets', or 'leaves' or 'book-pieces' into which
the blubber was further cut. Only the verse about Wooral referred to the clanking of the windlass hauling the whale from
the water and onto the granite slope. There was little of the thick
blood that ran in rivulets, the driving wind and rain, the pink
and gory water, the black gritty smoke of the try-pots, the stench
and the sorry shapeless whale carcasses floating in the bay. These
things were not in Bobby's song.

Bobby had no part in these things. He could find whales, and
could chase and run with them. But his hands could not kill a
whale. He was only steerer. And when it was time for cutting
and boiling and for stepping through bloody gore and smoke he
often went to where his people and their friends were feasting
on the whale carcass on the sandy beach. He sought out Menak,
wondering why he kept so distant, but that man was getting too
old and grumpy, too set in his ways and angry about how things
had changed from the years of his youth.

Some of these people came from far away for the bounty of
whale meat, and not all respected the Noongar whose country it
is. Menak growled if you so much as spoke English near him
and, with his little yapping dog, kept a sharp lookout. He didn't
want strangers rushing close.

The old man snorted his contempt for Bobby's song: those

foreign words, that horizon people's bleached and salty tongue and prickles of strange melodies held in a familiar sound. There are too many whales ashore, he said, and too many people come from all around, and do not greet us when they arrive or say goodbye when they leave. We are pressed by strangers from the sea now, and from inland, too.

Menak and his little sailor's dog camped on hilltops so they might see anyone coming, and not rely on their signal of approach. Because these days there was not always a proper signal, was there? The old man stayed at a distance, waiting for a whale to come ashore alive, to come die under his hand. But no whale came to him all that season.

Bobby sailed with Brother Jonathon's ship from Close-by-island Bay, and sang of the shore growing smaller and fading even as it happened, and sang of people feasting—as indeed they still were—and was glad to be leaving. There were people on the journey ahead who were waiting to meet him, and old friends, too. By and by King George Town would be appearing before him. Appearing for him.

CHRISTINE AND HIS LAY

THE CHAINE FAMILY were at their town house, dwarfed by the one being built next door that made Christine realise what a shabby hut this one was, without even what you'd call a proper floor. Thank God the building next door would be theirs, and that Papa was in good spirits despite going through his accounts and expecting word from the harbour.

Everything was so tedious. She had begun reading a new book, *The Last of the Mohicans*, which must've arrived on a recent ship and been passed around the community. But even this could not tempt her when she felt so heavy, so congested and lethargic. A curse indeed, that women had to put up with this trial for . . . She shrank at the thought of the decades of monthly strife that lay before her, of retiring as Mama did to privacy until the bleeding ceased. She could not accept that being a woman meant also becoming an invalid. And Mama was an invalid, it seemed, since the loss of Christopher.

She heard footsteps and Papa's voice in conversation with someone else; all too easy to eavesdrop when you lived in a hut. She walked out of the shade cast by the hill on the slope of which they lived, and followed Papa as he entered the new house, unable to resist inspecting its progress. Their footsteps rang on the new floorboards, bounced off the stone walls and the high ceiling. The smell of earth—Papa said it was the white clay they used—refreshed her, and with no door and no glass in the windows the building was so light and open and she could see the bright blue of the harbour, the sails, and the sunlight this sparkling day. Her father had his back to her, was a heavy shadow turning away from the window at the sound of her steps.

My Yankee captain is in, Christine.

His voice resounded in the empty building, and she no longer had the view of sunlight and sea, but only of him, her father. Who took her hands in his.

Join me in an hour or two, my darling, he said, once I've seen to things and taken some of my men to the store.

Christine had caught him in one of his better moods. Congratulating himself, perhaps, on his expanding business: the schooner, the store, the tavern. Accepting a woman's lot despite herself, she smiled in reply, touched his arm and acquiesced.

I'll send someone for you, her father said, bending to kiss her cheek. And your mother, if she feels ready.

But Christine's mother had retired to a darkened room with one of her headaches, and it was her father who came to collect her, not one of his men. She took his arm and they followed a sandy track, keeping the harbour on their left until they reached the cobblestones near her father's tavern and the store.

Mr Killam, hampered by his withered arm, was struggling to unlock the Sailor's Rest. Christine wondered how he would react if she shoved him aside (with a long-repressed sigh of exasperation!) and performed the task herself.

Expect a busy day today, Killam, her father said.

Yessir. But did not cease his struggles. The store next door was locked. Her father's loud voice informed all within earshot that he had already moved a great deal of merchandise today. Paid each man his lay, and they were free to buy from me what they wish, he said. It is many a day since I moved so many axes and knives and even ladies' dresses . . . The Yankees would be off the boat any moment now, he continued, and Mr Killam will find himself needing hands to help him; a wench would be best, if he can find her, because these sailors will be desperate to slake their thirst.

Billy Skelly's finished at the jetty, sir. I thought perhaps he might . . .

As you think best, Killam. Perhaps he can find a woman to help.

The two men laughed as Killam finally mastered the lock, and father and daughter resumed their walk. They crossed the footbridge that spanned the muddy earth where sometimes a creek ran, and doubled back. A group of sailors approached from the direction of the jetty. Clearly excited and happy, the men quietened (except for a few comments meant only for themselves) as they drew close, and bid her father and herself good morning in their strong American accents. And then, at their backs, became uproarious again.

Christine's attention was on a number of people gathered at the foot of the jetty. At this distance she guessed it was whalers, but there also seemed to be quite a few of the natives. Bobby was in a whaling team, Papa had said. And there were more people moving from the peppermint trees.

Oh, it was certainly an animated group. Closer, she saw that Bobby and another native were at the heart of the commotion. They were handing out gifts: clothing and jewellery, axes and knives. And Bobby . . . Christine had only known him in her family group, and most often only in the company of her brother and herself. How many years ago now was that? Four? She had not seen him in a larger group of people before and she realised he was a performer. But of course, he had always been that. And a leader, too.

Bobby held up an axe, glinting in the sun, and brought it down in a chopping motion; she could not tell if as weapon or tool. He spoke in Noongar language, and Christine could not follow him. There was something different about it, too; more like song than conversation, though there was something in it of banter, the to and fro of it, and Bobby leading. There was a lot of laughter. He held a woman's dress in front of him, wiggled his hips and sashayed; shrieks came from the women. And when he lifted the dress in one hand and held it above his head the women called out and seemed to be competing more for Bobby's attention than for the dress.

Lean-limbed and broad-shouldered, Bobby's white and open-necked linen shirt showed the strong tendons of his neck and the hollow at the base of his throat. His skin shone with health, and he wore a blue dresscoat of impeccable serge, fine riding breeches and new boots. Stepping about, playing and dispensing gifts, he was the very picture of a hero. Not realising the extent to which she herself had matured, she marvelled at how much he had grown, and changed. Oh, if only they were both children still, and alone together. But of course . . .

Christine looked about. Other than her father and William Skelly, who'd probably come down to admire his jetty, there were no older men in the group surrounding Bobby and his companion. And how very odd: Skelly had himself apparently bought a box of women's dresses. Papa nodded at him and said, Killam reckoned you'd be down here, helping.

I'll be there very soon, Mr Chaine.

Chrissy! A strong voice, cutting through, demanding ears.

Bobby left the centre of the small crowd admiring his gifts, gently but firmly moving people from his path until he reached

Christine and her father. He shook hands with Papa, in a way so unlike Mr Killam and Mr Skelly: respectfully, but without subservience. And turning to her, nodded a greeting so gracious it might have been a chivalrous and sweeping bow the way it surprised and melted her, and then he suddenly clasped her hands that were wavering ridiculously in the air between them.

Bobby! Christine pulled her hands away as Papa playfully slapped Bobby on the back and put an arm around his shoulder. Bobby wriggled from his grip, but Geordie Chaine had inserted himself between them, and all three were so close that Bobby had to lean and look around the man as if he were a large boulder or tree that moved as they moved and kept them apart.

Need a new dress, Christine?

That laugh again; she couldn't help but join her voice to his. Bobby called out something to the others who were still admiring their gifts, and then they were walking away, Bobby the other side of Papa. Ahead of them Mr Skelly had two native women by their hands, each wearing one of the colourful dresses and a hat. Mr Skelly must be giving out presents as well. He and the women were walking very quickly, and entered the Sailor's Rest long before Christine, her father and Bobby got there.

ROWING

BOBBY ROWED PEOPLE and luggage between ships, and to and from the shore. Some of the men hid rum away for Chaine's tavern, and after a while Bobby went back to the small dinghy, rowing alone. There were several ships in the harbour, he had not seen so many at once. As he rowed, daylight thickened and leaked away; he drew a dark line between ship and shore, and silver laced his oars and bow. Ships faded, disappearing as darkness closed. Bobby trusted his judgement to find his own ship, but the others became mere maybe-ships, except for one—glittering brightly with lamps in its rigging, and candles—around which golden light lay like broken glass. He detoured a little to observe the glittering ship, to better hear the music and voices, the tinkling laughter and greetings falling on those shifting fragments of the sea.

Collected from a ship (A most fruitful meeting, Bobby!) a red-faced Chaine was buckled and buttoned-up; bright and shiny lace frothed at his chest and wrist. Bobby rowed him ashore, pulling up beside a larger rowing boat resting in the shallows. Two figures came across the sand toward them and although it was dark and hard to see, Bobby recognised Killam and Skelly.

They were carrying something, carrying . . . They entered the shallows; they were carrying Mrs Chaine and Christine. In long dresses and jewellery, their pale breasts almost bare.

Eyes passed over Bobby. Voices spoke to Chaine: Darling. Papa. Sir. The men placed the women in the larger rowboat, holding it while Chaine stepped unsteadily from one boat to the other. As the men pushed the boat afloat Christine smiled briefly at Bobby; the men gave another push, two, and then pulled themselves aboard and took the oars.

Chaine, over his shoulder, said, Come pay us a visit sometime, Bobby my boy.

Bobby lowered his eyes from the glittering ship, listened to the oars entering, dripping, the hull slicing the water, the little waves lapping the sand.

He had beached the dinghy on the sand and was sitting on it when the other boat returned.

You come back? he asked. Bobby thought they'd stay with the laughter and voices, the music and light and clinking glass.

Not for the likes of us, Bobby. They did not quite laugh. Killam plucked at the shirt around his shoulders with his claw of a hand. Skelly silently walked the anchor up the beach. And then Bobby was with them, because Killam was all for rushing back to the tavern, and Skelly also. A tot of rum, Bobby? Killam had suggested. Just like at the whaling camp, see.

Bobby—small and wiry, not really tall at all—had to duck his head as he stepped down into the room. The ceiling was low and as his feet touched the old wrinkled planks he thought of some of the worn ship decks he'd walked upon. The ceiling was higher at the bar and there were glasses and bottles stacked on shelves within the vast arched bone of a right whale's jaw, a jaw so wide a horse and cart might be driven beneath it.

289

On one wall an array of spears: long, short; varying barbs; different colours. Bobby saw a hunting spear, a fishing spear, a digging stick, a thigh-piercing spear, a ritual fighting spear, a fighting club . . . There were harpoons and lances, too: all the points and blades for killing and stripping whales.

Grinning, Killam offered him a tot. It burned like always going down his throat. Just like the whaling camp. It always made Bobby want action, and to be like fire, burn. Skelly held up another glass. Oh, another one! This was not so usual. And another. Oh, he was full of energy, full of fire. Another glass. Again. He was grown too large for this space, and smoke wreathed him like mist about a mountain. Stood tall like a mountain. Dizzy. And cool air was on his cheeks, there were cobblestones and mud, and it must be somebody's piss he was sitting in. He met the eyes of an aunty as Mr Skelly took her arm. There was another woman here in one of those bright new dresses and he must not meet her eye. Peripheral vision: she was staring at him.

Bobby stumbled away from the Sailor's Rest with some devil working his legs, and vomited just like a bullock shitting. Hands out for balance, he staggered away from his own muck.

Must've had a good sleep, because he felt much better when he woke. The harbour still calm, the ship still glittering. He drank from the spring near the footbridge and walked down to the jetty. Mr Skelly was fussing over a boat.

Give us a hand, Bobby, he said.

Mr Killam was busy at the tavern and Skelly was a man short on the oars, so Bobby had to help him row to collect Mr Chaine and family.

Yes, Bobby could do that, and the cool water, the fresh sea air in his lungs and the feel of the boat gliding over the water soothed him. They pulled up beside the ship and the light kept shifting on Mr Skelly's face, and broken slabs of it were bobbing all around them. No more music now, but braying voices and women shrieking, and here was Mr Chaine coming backwards down the side of the ship, his broad beam blocking the light. Skelly reached out to steady him as his weight came into the boat, and for a moment the boat rocked almost as wildly as beside a thrashing whale. Chaine sat down heavily, and belched. Mrs Chaine was halfway down the rope ladder, and Skelly took her waist in his hands and lifted her into the boat. He turned to assist Christine but she, with one foot on the bottom rung, swung lithely on the pivot of Bobby's hand and into the boat. Her bustling, whalebone dress made her, for a moment, like a bird, settling.

That Gov'n'r . . . a scoundrel and a fool . . . Chaine's tongue was clumsy, seemed thickened. But his son, he continued.

Oh Papa, Christine murmured.

The men rowed silently. It was clear to Bobby that Chaine and the Governor had had what Missus called a difference of opinion. Missus talked about the dresses, the jewellery, the gallant captain, the music. Christine? Nothing. She trailed a hand in the water, looked over her shoulder at the boat once, twice, more, twisted the gloves she held in her hand.

A full moon had arisen and its light shone on the faces of Christine and her mother. Shone even on their breasts, forced high and together. Bobby and Christine had swum together as children, innocent. He wondered about doing the same now. Push her into the sea, maybe? They'd gone high among the limbs of trees; he remembered the strong tendons at the back of her knees, the long muscle of her thighs.

Slurring, thick-tongued Chaine could not leave the topic of the Governor's son, Hugh: his attentions to Christine, their many dances together. The fine companion and partner he'd be. Money, inheritance, alliance.

Eventually they reached shore, and Missus Chaine held out her arms for Skelly to take her. Chaine clumsily hauled himself out of the boat, the remaining men holding their oars against the sandy bottom to steady the boat. But not Bobby; he leapt into the shallow water and turned back for Christine and she, confidently, fell into his arms. He breathed that very sweet scent, and beneath it the earthy acrid smell of her sweat. She blew some hair from her cheek, and he had her breath.

Mmm.

Put her arms around his neck.

I'll take my daughter.

Swaying, Chaine stood before them, the solid darkness of the peppermint trees and granite hill at his back.

Alright, Kongk, nearly there.

Chaine grabbed at his daughter.

Papa!

Her arms tightened around Bobby's neck, and Bobby stepped forward, moving their combined weight against the older man, and then to one side. Pushing back, Chaine only brushed them as he fell to his hands and knees in the shallow water. Bobby walked to shore, and set Christine on her feet. Watched Skelly help Chaine to his feet.

Damn you, Bobby. You are not children anymore.

No, not children no more.

Christine turned away with Missus's arm around her shoulder. Chaine pushed Skelly aside and stumbled after them into the shadows.

JUST FOR HIM

Bobby awoke. A woman slept beside him, soft hands pressed together under one cheek. She was wrapped in woollen blankets and kangaroo skin, and Bobby could smell her and the two of them and the sandalwood oil on his own skin.

Later today, he'd join the other men and it'd be a brother or uncle rubbing oil and ochre into his skin, but not like a woman would. His shape would be consolidated, as if he were wood being carved, or stone chipped and ground and polished. Except he wasn't wood or stone and the oil and ochre and strong hands made him more alive, loosened his muscles so he felt how they were anchored to strong white bones, and how the blood surged in his veins and his lungs filled. The ochre had been carried and passed from person to person until it reached him, had begun with a hand cupping it far east of here.

The smell of earth in the ochre and oil, his increasing sense of the fine and delicate paths of blood and nerves and the many fine sinews connecting him to this place, this perpetual moment. Fingertips tingled, and his body hummed with the voices all around him, of bees, cicadas and crickets; of whispering wind and rustling leaves; of bird song and wingbeat; the creak and hiss of reptiles; the breath and various footfalls of animals; the murmur of waves upon the sand; the exhalation of dolphin and whale; of water welling and spilling playful paths across rock, through and beneath the sand . . .

A day for singing, for decoration and embellishment; a day of strength rising in them all, and of women and young men in the evening, dancing together.

Bobby breathed close upon the neck of the sleeping body beside him. Who murmured. As Christine had murmured to her drunken father that night. Bobby lifted the rugs, let them fall softly so that the air moved gently across them. Ran the back of his hand across the fine grain of her skin, felt the vertebrae of her neck, shoulders, continued down the vertebrae of her spine with his thumb and fingers, and with his open palm, the pads of his fingertips brushed lightly across her flesh. The woman moved against him. Smiled, welcomed and wanted him, opened her limbs and drew him in. Christine must move like this, too. The two of them might also move on deep currents like this, opening and plunging, and breathing deeply, rhythmically, be lost like this in salty air, ride rolling waves from far away and call out to one another.

And yet fall away. Christine.

*

Bobby woke a second time and looked again at the sleeping body beside him. He ran his fingers through his wispy beard, took a strip of softened kangaroo hide and wound it round and round his skull to hold his hair.

Later today he'd be among bodies adorned with feathers, leaves, the fur of possum or dingo, all their voices and spirits so close there was no need for thinking or choosing but only for moving together like grains of sand rolled by water, like the flowers blossoming from their armbands and hair, and rooted in their heart and guts.

A woman in his dream had called from the other side of the campfire, moist eyes reflecting the flames, following him as he sang and leapt. Could a blonde woman be at his campfire? He had walked away from her and the warm mass of granite which sheltered their camp, just as if something had nudged him, as if some story had left a space into which he might venture. His bare feet trod the warm sand, the scent of the oil and ochre enclosed him. Who knows how long he walked? The sun was like a shiny coin, grass trees shimmered, life hummed. Just for him.

BONES AND CHILDREN

WHAT WITH HIS TENT, and all these dark-skinned people around him, Jak Tar felt like an Ar-ab: the sheik of Close-by-island Bay. No harem for him, though, thank you very much; he had quite enough trouble keeping his one woman in sight and under control.

It was a fine life, and this season leading up to the wintery whale season he thought the finest of all. Not yet the strong ocean wind and rain, but past the heat of summer, and the ocean smoothed by a land breeze blowing gently all day long. He expected to have seen more whaling ships by now. But not a one. He wondered if there were any even at King George Town.

Chaine would be at King George Town, of course. Had a house here at Close-by-island Bay, too, overlooking the estuary. Follow the river inland and you'd reach his third house at Kepalup, and his sheep grazed between here and there, and beyond. Chaine had sheep and shepherds, teams of kangaroo shooters, men employed cutting and carting sandalwood, and all of it came to this little private port here at Close-by-island Bay. He traded with the whalers and ran whaling teams as well. You had to admire his acumen and pluck.

His workforce was ex-convicts and soldiers, a few labourers he'd imported from India and China even and men like Jak Tar himself (not all of them runaway sailors) who just wanted to keep out of the way of the authorities. Noongars worked for Chaine, too; one or two on roo-shooting teams even had their own guns. They were invaluable to the sandalwood axemen and carriers. Jak Tar saw how working with white men helped young men like Bobby and Wooral get out from under the Elders' control and become aware of other possibilities. Noongar people were already arriving, anticipating feasts and festivities like the last few winters and Jak Tar had seen smoke wisping from campfires the other side of the estuary.

Menak's little dog strutted into the clearing, looked back over its shoulder, and gave a few short barks. Menak and Manit appeared moments later, the old woman stooped and limping. And although Jak Tar remembered Menak as a man who could speak English, he had trouble following their conversation with Binyan because Menak refused to use that tongue. It was obvious they were both unhappy. Their gestures had an anger he hadn't seen before, perhaps because of the violence they recounted. Jak Tar picked up words here and there and, from the resentful glances occasionally cast upon him, began to feel he was classed with the perpetrators. He kept himself busy: stoked the fire and set up the spit for the sheep he'd slaughtered (he knew what losses Chaine would tolerate).

They were talking about whales; Jak Tar recognised the vocabulary from parts of Bobby's song. Stroking and patting the little rat-catching dog, Menak spoke of whales rising from the water; of whale tails beating the water, striking men and splintering whaleboats; of whales charging, and energy from beneath the sea's skin bursting forth . . .

And then he was speaking of there being no more whales. No more ships. No more white men.

Day after day the gentle land breezes persisted. Some days were bright blue and sparkling and the white sand shone; other days were steel-grey or black, and sea and sky merged so that there was no horizon; or it might be that a fine, misty rain fell all day . . . but always the wind blew from land to sea. No ships came. No whales.

The wind?

No, said Jak Tar, this wind won't stop a ship getting here. Perhaps they've found themselves another whaling ground, one closer to home.

But what about the whales?

Maybe we fished them out.

But no one could know for sure.

The men were done with coopering barrels for the oil. The boats were sanded and oiled, spread with pitch. Boat crews raced one another: pushed the boats across the sand, rowed out to a bay and back again. Harpooners challenged one another to target practice, sharpened their weapons. The card games grew longer. They waited.

In the evenings singing came from the Noongar camps at the estuary; came on the wind, headed out to sea. Jak Tar would not increase the whalers' allowance of rum.

Bobby walked a path that ran through the dunes from the whalers' camp to the estuary. Then walked along the beach; he liked to look for the silhouette of fish in the waves, the flash of silver he might at any time see. Who knows, maybe even the spout of a whale.

Menak thought it unlikely.

What was wrong with that old man? When Bobby was a child Menak made him laugh, speaking English in different accents;

French, too, just playing. Now he grumbled if you spoke any-thing but Noongar language. Jak Tar was the only white person he talked to, and he was cranky with him, too.

It was a calm day, the tide so very full that the sea on the beach seemed to be brimming, was like water in a bowl about to over-flow. Seaweed floated, not moving, as if the sea, too, had lost di-rection, was also waiting.

Bobby stopped. Far out at sea, almost on the horizon, he saw a whale spout. He took a few long strides and shouted, but his voice was so feeble. No one to hear him here. Oh, a few Noon-gar children in the dunes looked up and waved. Bobby began to run back along the beach, speeding up when—yes, the boy on lookout must've seen the spout, too—he saw the tiny figures of men running to the boats. Someone would have to take his place: the cook, or even Chaine himself if he was down at the camp. Bobby wished he hadn't wandered away . . . But the grey day was closing around him. He was running in fine rain, feet slapping on hard sand the ocean lapped. He could no longer make out men or boats, and in a few moments could barely even see the headland.

Would they find a lone whale?

Panting. There was no one, and he could not see any distance in this damp fine rain. The water beside the headland was smooth; wind must've shifted. Finally, the beginning of the winter pattern.

The boats returned just on dark, the men wet and miserable. The wind was up now, and rain came over the headland in ir-regular and violent forays against the huts where the men huddled grumbling, snarling, muttering. Jak Tar allowed a second and third tot of rum to help fight the cold and their disappointment. Bobby and Wooral slipped away, their kangaroo skins turned fur inward and well greased against rain and cold, to visit some of the Noongar camped in a sheltered hollow of paperbark trees over the other side of the estuary. The strong wind at their backs lifted them, their cloaks rose like wings, their feet were light. Jak Tar had given them half a sheep, exotic food still to those they were visiting, and they bottled their share of rum as a gift. The old man and his young wives would be pleased. So long as they did not bump into Menak.

People usually moved inland this time of year, and despite the last few years most had renewed that habit. Those who remained had withdrawn into small groups, the wind and rain making it a bad night for singing and dancing together. Menak had told everyone the whales would not come, but what would he know? He reckoned sheep was no good food.

Bobby and Wooral found a friendly campfire in a sheltered grove among the dunes, and late in the night listened to the sound of the wind in the trees joining that of the sea, and slept curled in the warmth of their people.

Not long after dawn they walked back around the littered beach. The air was washed and still. Not only driftwood and weed and dead things, but also a lot of old whalebones had been washed ashore during the storm. Bobby thought he could hear bone rattling against bone.

*

Weeks passed: a succession of cold fronts, with barely a day between them. Rain, winds strong and always cold, the sea ragged and torn. The try-pots were ready, the lookout tower manned. The men slept and played cards. Empty barrels awaited their whale oil, and the boats sat on the sand without the weight of men or feel of the sea.

No ships came. Occasionally a lone whale was seen far out to sea, and the whaleboats gave chase but never got close enough to use a harpoon.

The cook got drunk and wanted to fight. Jak Tar sacked him, and brought Binyan in to cook for the men. She knew how to feed Jak and could cook like he wanted, but they required bigger quantities now. The camp was not happy, and where were the whales? If none came, some were thinking, how would they live beyond the season?

William Skelly kept a few men working on the gardens, still hoping for trade with visiting whalers. But he had to set a guard now, because the gardens had been raided. Bobby and Wooral studied the prints. Said they didn't know who'd done it, but yes, the people at the camps were getting hungry, too, and these last years there'd always been plenty of whales. Skelly's job was to oversee the garden and sheep, and the animals he penned each night. He wanted to give Wooral and Bobby a gun and have them stand guard. But no, they could not, not here. Of course these people were unhappy, because there were no whales, see?

Skelly and Jak Tar didn't want anyone coming close to the whale camp, only Bobby and Wooral.

On a still day Bobby heard whalebones tock-tock, moving with the waves. Skeletons of the carcasses that had been towed away from the headland these last few seasons were scattered over the floor of the bay, and each storm washed more bones up onto the beach and among the rocks. Children played at the edge of the sea among bleached and weathered whalebones, and thin stems of smoke rose from among the dunes where camp dogs snapped and snarled.

Menak's dog, Jock, swaggered right into the rough bough shed where the whalers waited. Bobby called the animal, but it ignored him and a little later Menak appeared. He looked very old and, standing almost naked before the men, began speaking passionately of something they could not follow.

Some of them turned away almost immediately. Jak Tar, who might have listened, was not among them. Someone laughed.

Menak shook his fist, and Wooral and Bobby got to their feet and went to the old man who, shaking with rage and feeble in his old age, flailed his arms at them.

Kokinjeri mamang ngalakatang . . .

Bobby tried to translate: My people need their share of these sheep, too. We share the whales, you camp on our land and kill our kangaroos and tear up our trees and dirty our water and we forgive, but now you will not share your sheep and my people are hungry and wait here because of you . . .

Bobby realised it was true what the old man said, it was all true.

Skelly muttered, You'll get a ball in the skull, old man.

Get him out of here, said another.

But it's true. Bobby saw the whalebones on the shore, and the children playing among them, the dogs snapping, the thin stems of smoke in the dunes . . . At King George Town, too: the old men trading their daughters and young women for food and rum.

Chaine suddenly appeared. Chaine was prepared to brook no opposition from his men. I'm breaking up camp, there's nothing to . . .

He had barely registered Menak, who stepped toward him with boomerang raised and Chaine, hardly faltering, grabbed and twisted the old man's arm. The boomerang dropped to the ground and Menak fell back into Bobby's arms. The little dog snarled and leapt, but Chaine's boot sent it rolling among some empty barrels and, cringing, whimpering, it limped back to Menak's side. It was the three of them and a wounded dog against the others; Skelly had a lance in his hand, Killam a hatchet. One whaler had a musket. The others had also risen to their feet, excited. Bobby was glad Jak Tar was not among them.

Chaine flung the boomerang away contemptuously, and it flew a surprising distance across the scrub, low and spinning, before it curved up into the air and hovered, turning and turning and turning . . .

All the men looked, couldn't help themselves. Even Chaine, even Skelly and Mr Killam; they just stood and stared as it spun, so fast it blurred and seemed to almost melt and become a pool of water in the sky.

Bobby and Wooral and Menak looked at one another. They had thought Geordie Chaine would stand with them, and not against Menak. And Jak Tar? With the others still distracted and staring, Bobby and Wooral led Menak—injured dog in his arms—back to his camp.

The boomerang fell with hardly a sound; cushioned, suspended by the mallee, it was gently lowered to the soil, twig by twig. The men looked at one another, looked around. What? And they began to pack up their things, moved to another game of cards, another tot of rum on Chaine, who said, See me in the morning, I always have need of good workers elsewhere.

SHEEP, SUGAR AND KNIVES

L OOK, THE ESTUARY WAS WELLING, brimming; the river already running faster, frogs singing out . . . *Wetj* would be nesting and reluctant to move far, *Yongar* would turn their backs obligingly and not expect you coming at them against such a wind. There would be no whales. The Noongar left the coast and soon no one at all remained at the whaling grounds.

Bobby knew most of the shepherds, none better than Jak Tar, and found him in some shade overlooking a flock of sheep. Jak looked up from the book he was reading as Bobby, rolling on the wind, was almost upon him and Oh! Bobby saw the little fear in his eyes, then relief. Bobby lifted the book from Jak's hand, read its title.

The Last of the . . . the . . .

Mohicans.

Jak said, Err . . . about the other day, Chaine's temper and all that . . .

But Bobby laughed it off. Menak was always too bossy, wasn't he, like that dog of his. Binyan? She was with the sheep, and Jak walked away a little as he spoke to get a view of her and the flock. She'd be glad to see you, he called back to the young man, waving to get her attention, but she couldn't see him and so he walked a little further. Kept walking, kept walking and still she didn't look but just kept moving further away.

Eventually he reached her. They hugged, they kissed; he might not be a young man anymore, but oh yes, they were very happy to see one another. When they finally got back to Jak's resting place there was the book, facedown, but no Bobby.

Jak Tar and Binyan were so fond of each other it was quite some time before they thought to again check the sheep, and when they did about a dozen were missing. Binyan assured Jak there'd been none missing before.

But where are they, what happened?

Binyan looked around her, reading the ground, and pointed the way the sheep had gone.

Jak Tar rushed along their tracks; he could read the prints enough to follow, they could not be far. And there were other shepherds in the vicinity with their own small flocks.

Jaky! Binyan called out to him; he turned but would not wait.

Within twenty minutes, seeing about eight Noongars driving his sheep, he called across the distance, Leave those sheep be! He didn't recognise any of the men, but kept striding in pursuit. Jogging. As he reached where the river ran, shallow and rapid over some rocks, he realised he was the one entrapped, because the others had turned, and were now quite close—he had entered a half circle they made—with their spears ready to throw. He stopped, surprised. He had never thought. The river tugged at his ankles.

Kaya, he said, *ngaytj wort koorling yey.* Hello, I away going now.

But another voice called, and there was William Skelly higher on the other bank, aiming his rifle. Where'd he come from?

If you spear that man I will gladly shoot you.

Skelly's voice seemed so very thin. A bird called something scornful. The moment stretched. Skelly would be speared many times over in the time it took to reload after his first shot. Eventually, each Noongar man unshipped his spear and, with spear and spear thrower in one hand, lifted the other waist high and palm down in front of him, calming. Jak Tar heard his name called, caught someone's eye. Some small laughter. The long spears shifted, and the Noongar men turned their backs and walked away.

Jak Tar and the two other shepherds in the vicinity penned their sheep together and took turns keeping watch. Jak kept Binyan by his side.

In the morning half the flock was missing.

Jak Tar and Binyan stayed with the flock, and a spare revolver, while the other two shepherds searched for the missing sheep. Jak was alert and anxious, and spun around at the sound of Bobby's voice somewhere behind him.

You look bit shitty-arsed, Jak Tar.

Jak told him about the sheep being stolen, the spears held against him. Bobby looked surprised, and Binyan interrupted: They far-away men. Bobby reminded Jak that many people from further east had come visiting over the last few years, because of all the whales, you know.

Bobby stayed for an hour or two, conversing in Noongar language, slowing down and repeating himself at times for Jak's convenience. But of course Jak struggled, especially because Bobby often moved into that sort of singsong manner the Noongar sometimes used. Binyan was at times helpless with laughter. The third person in a conversation dominated by the other two, Jak was perhaps more observant than usual, and he noted that Bobby lifted his head at the sound of what Jak assumed was a bird call, and took his leave just a little later.

The other shepherds returned, shaken and agitated. They had

survived a shower of spears, and been driven away from their own hut and the ton of flour and three bags of sugar it contained. They had seen thin columns of smoke in the distance. Natives signalling one another?

The men looked at Binyan, who shrugged. They would again keep watch, and return to the farmhouse in the morning to alert Chaine and the others.

When Binyan came back to her and Jak Tar's tiny bush shelter she found a large possum-skin bag packed tight with fresh mutton.

THE OCEAN FLOOR

A MONG THE PEPPERMINT TREES, upon a floor of soft sand and leaves, Bobby Wabalanginy, a brother and friends, shared a meal of mullet from a sheet of paperbark. The fins and tails of the same fish broke the surface of the shallows only a short walk away, and stirred the ribbons of seaweed floating there. It was very still. Outside the harbour the ocean had been rolling for days, some of its energy even coming through the granite channel and into the harbour. A pale moon hung in the blue sky, a reminder of yesterdays and days to come. The foamy bubbles and weed in the still settling ocean; the fragrant leaves at their feet, the leaves falling, the leaves hanging from the trees waiting for a breeze Bobby believed was just about to arrive; that thin old moon: Bobby felt himself at an intersection of many different rhythms.

Smoke lifted into the sky the other side of the harbour. Someone hunting? *Kaya, Wooral,* a voice confirmed. Between the smoke of that hunt and Bobby's companions, the unfurled masts of two ships at anchor pointed to the sky. So very bare, like trees after a fire. Thin and straight like giant spears.

Bobby moved away and was alone. Wabalanginy, Menak had recently said to him, means all of us playing together. But you often go alone. And we cannot always be playing.

Bobby turned his back on the harbour, and as he did the wind ruffled the water's surface and gave him the gentlest push up the slope toward the morning sun. It pleased him to read the wind so well. The loose sand shifted under his feet. Soft sand often meant graves, but there was only the one grave here. He paused. In later years, long after Bobby Wabalanginy and the span of this story, we might call this a *significant* site, a *sacred* place, and that's just how it was for young Bobby, standing there thinking of Wunyeran and Cross.

Dr Cross had arranged his friend's burial, allowed Menak to instruct the soldiers how to prepare the grave. Dr Cross had cried and years later, as he lay dying, had asked to be buried with Wunyeran in the same grave. Bobby Wabalanginy imagined their bodies rolling toward another as the flesh fell away, bones touching, spirits fusing in the earth.

He worried for them because of all the digging for buildings and rubbish that went on in King George Town. He thought of those two boys Geordie Chaine shot, their skeletons lying somewhere toward where the sun rises.

But the shooting was a memory Chaine had bidden him put away and never mention to the people of King George Town.

Floods would carry away the bones of Wunyeran and Cross. All along this coast of ours, bones were plucked from riverbanks and tumbled together to the sea. All those bones of ocean.

Bobby continued walking against the flow a flood might take, onto the granite hilltop and along its ridge. Saw The Farm, its buildings and fences. And oh how the storybook tree he and the Governor planted had grown. Although still tiny at this distance, it was tall beside the hut of The Farm.

He went across the edge of the old yam field (fenced) and up among the granite boulders and their bubbling spring. Beside a small fire, Menak was attaching a shard of glass to his spear. As grumpy as ever, the old man sat in the smoke, rolled the spear across one thigh of his crossed legs, hardly acknowledged the presence of Bobby Wabalanginy. He did not look up as Bobby said goodbye.

Boodawan djinang.

Coming up to The Farm Bobby smelled smoke, saw Manit being unusually attentive to a barely alight fire beside one shed near the house. She must be waiting for flour or sugar for herself and Menak.

He moved toward her. She was still distant, beyond anything but his loudest shout, when he saw the Governor's son rushing from the house. Hugh? Looked like he was shouting, angry. Why? Hugh slapped Manit, and she bent away from him. Bobby was running now, and Hugh was kicking dirt over the fire.

The grass around them was very dry, though Manit had cleared it in a wide enough circle around the fire. They must have been carting straw also, Bobby guessed, because pieces of it littered the ground.

Satisfied he had extinguished the fire, Hugh turned to Manit. Bobby, his arms around the old woman, saw the surprise register on Hugh's face, the more so when Bobby slapped him, once, twice. These were ceremonial slaps, not blows, and Hugh's head barely flicked from side to side, but he was shocked, into rigidity apparently. Very deliberately, Bobby went to the fire and took a longer piece of kindling from among the dirt and ash and blew upon it until it began to glow. He made eye contact with Hugh. Bobby moved a few steps away from the fire. Hugh's eyes flickered back to where Manit, crouched beside the fire, was obstinately coaxing it to life again.

It was only the three of them, an awkward sort of triangle, with Bobby at the greatest distance. He lowered his firestick and ignited a piece of straw at his feet. Hugh looked to the nearby paddock and its growing crop, the thin flames spreading, and turned and ran to the farmhouse.

The yard between Bobby and Manit was alight with thigh-high flame when Hugh reappeared from the farmhouse with two soldiers and Killam. Only Killam had a rifle, but even with a good arm he was never a decent marksman, let alone at this distance, and Bobby felt safe. The men ran to the shed, and out again with shovel and wet bags and bucket of water ready to douse the flames. Already the flames were diminishing as Bobby and Manit, because of the dying wind and the still-green crop, knew they would.

They looked across the lightly scorched earth at the men with their bags and implements. What makes Hugh the Governor's son walk with soldiers at his side?

*

There were no whales.

Not at Close-by-island Bay.

Not at King George Town.

And, as Bobby now realised, King George Town was a growing village, spreading upward from the shore of the harbour. Might not need whales, the way its people were. He paused at the Sailor's Rest. No longer was this the only drinking-building. Along with huts of wattle and daub, there were stables and water tanks and buildings of stone. There would be a church, so he'd been told. Further still up the hill he came to the grave of Wunyeran and Dr Cross: one grave for a black man and a white man. The difference in their skin colour had seemed just one among so many other things—but maybe it was the most important, after all. No one said Noongar no more; it was all *blackfellas* and *white-fellas*. The grave was surrounded by holes for rubbish. A man with a shovel was poking right into their shared grave.

Wunyeran's body, buried in not quite a foetal position, must have begun to dissolve into the earth along with ochre and leaves and ash. The gravedigger's spade, working its way around Cross's coffin, broke and chipped Wunyeran's bones, exposed and disordered the skeleton. It was not like the passion of flood, or a persistent wind lifting the soil to expose bones at the core of country. It was deliberate and careless all at once.

Of course there was a very bad smell. Bobby told the man to stop and, when he did not, he shoved him. Slapped him. The man left immediately. Bobby sat beside the grave, arms at his sides with forearms lifted and palms raised just as if he were a set of scales, weighing the balance. The gravedigger returned with men of authority, and Bobby rolled crumbs of earth between the thumb and forefinger of one hand, and with the other stroked and smoothed the soil beside the grave as if it were the pelt of an animal. They came at him angry and with loud voices. Hauled him to his feet. Gave him a shove.

Bobby was alone, and vulnerable.

None of Wunyeran's people were present when Cross's decaying, coffined body was reburied in the new town cemetery, not far from the great granite boulders near where Bobby had once rescued Skelly. Skelly's bowed head was one of those around the patch of earth where Dr Cross's coffin was laid and which was marked by not just a cross, but a railing and a headstone engraved:

DR JOSEPH CROSS

1781–1833

SURGEON PIONEER AND LAND OWNER

1826–1833

KING GEORGE TOWN WESTERN AUSTRALIA

It seemed Geordie Chaine and Governor Spender had for once agreed: this was more appropriate to Cross's important role in the history of King George Town.

The original, still raw grave was hastily filled. A town dog scurried away with something in its jaws; a cat, hunching its back and showing its teeth, would not be moved. Small bones were left to grey in the sun, be trodden in horseshit and piss and vomit as the town grew and bright moons waxed and waned.

Bobby roamed the ridges the other side of the harbour, where limestone broke through the thin, sandy soil like enormous old skeletons, and the ocean moaned and spat in the hollows and tunnels in the earth beneath his feet. The moon was old bone in a blue sky, dissolving as the sun rose higher. Clouds gathered in the southwest, drifted to meet a plummeting sun and spread across the dome of sky so that by dark-time there were no stars or even a moon, only a soft and drizzling rain. *Mitjal*: a rain like tears.

Deeper in the night the wind lifted and rain began to drum the earth. It fell and fell and fell; it gathered in the hearts of grass trees, in forks of branches and cups of leaves, in clefts and cavities of rock and small indentations in the earth. Fell, overflowed, and began to move together again.

Bobby entered a rock shelter flickering with firelight. The little dog leapt to its feet barking so wildly Bobby thought it might burst, until Menak growled it into silence. Bobby had travelled alone and so at first Menak and Manit looked around for his companions, before realising there was no one. Menak's two younger wives and an assortment of children, mostly asleep, were beside another small fire.

Manit raged for a while. Call yourself men? She spoke to Bobby, but included Menak somehow. *Winyarn*, she said, *Noonook baal kitjel don.* You coward and weakling: spear them! But after a while her abuse slowed and she relented. The white man's guns, for one thing, and all these strangers and the other Noongars they will turn against us. Fighting will not help us; we would need guns like them, and they are now more than us.

Bobby had brought his brooding silence into the camp with him. The raw grave, the hollow in the damp earth that had held Wunyeran, his bones. They all felt Bobby's diminished spirit. He could not smile. He did not dance, he did not speak.

Menak wanted to know nothing of the white men, anyway. Sadly, he could see their fires from here. On calmer days you could even hear their voices from way over there across the water. He was absorbed, was singing about rain. It was easier to sing with him, softly, than try to speak of this, of all that was happening in their lives and the terrible change of it. That they were spiralling down-ward, like leaves from a tree, yes, a tree that had already fallen. Cut down.

Manit—over her rage—struck the fire so that sparks rose and tongues of flame grew and multiplied, greedy in the dying light.

Menak sang, Manit too, and Bobby, barely moving his lips, traced his finger across the wall of granite beside him, drew something of the trajectory of the tune and the words. Rain ran down granite slopes either side of the valley floor. Water streamed from she-oak slate roofs into earthenware pots, and over the brim, over the brim flowed . . .

The open gutter one side of the path sloping down to the har-bour spilled over, and the path itself became a growing stream. Rain fell in great bodies, slamming the earth, then recovered, collected its many selves and flowed, chuckling, past flimsy houses and pubs of clay and twigs, swirled around the footings of the stone church awaiting construction, rushed beneath the foot-bridge built across what was usually a tiny stream at the bottom of the slope. Not a tiny stream today, but. The footbridge—no longer spanning the stream but isolated at its very centre—tilted, leaned, rolled over on its side and was swept away.

What had been a path was now a torrent carrying twigs, branches and household rubbish. It pushed pieces of building rubble and stones and similar things, rolled them over and swept them to the sea. No trouble at all then, taking bones to the ocean. Always been this way. Bones from riverbanks washed down toward the sea, and only a kindred spirit and tongue can find them, maybe bring them alive again, even if in some other shape.

The wind scuffed the ocean into whitecaps, and waves raced across the harbour to fling themselves at the torrent rushing to meet them. Fresh and salty water jostled, swirled . . .

Did all those bones reach the sea and join a path of whalebones across the ocean floor? Or years later become part of the foundations of the town hall and its clock with ticking faces looking north, south, east and west and, right at the very steeple top, that very great weight: a nation's fluttering flag?

But forget it. That's long after this little chapter of a single plot and very few characters, this simple story of a Bobby and his few friends.

HAD WE BUT

G OVERNOR SPENDER WAS DISTURBED, and said as much. Disturbed and very concerned. The arrogant defiance his son, Hugh, had reported in the incident with the old woman and that boy, you, Mr Chaine, claim to have raised. We might all, along with our property and what we stand for, be put in danger.

Chaine raised his hand against the accusation. Inserted his other hand between the buttons at his chest. I gave him a little education, that is all. He might still be an asset.

Hugh, the third at this gathering, reminded them that some three hundred sheep had been stolen from Chaine's coastal property. Driven away and slaughtered. How many natives must there have been to have devoured them?

The three men looked into the fire. Raised their heads, met one another's gaze.

When I first arrived at this place, said Chaine, we were on friendly terms with the natives, although they were largely disrespectful of our habits and considered their right to enter our huts to be the equal of our own. And they were very numerous. I was the first settler to make a stand against them in this regard. Not Dr Cross.

They all nodded thoughtfully, the rhythm of Hugh's nodding head more enthusiastic than that of the two older men.

It may have been that in the past, the Governor said, we did not dare take steps to secure the offenders. Dr Cross's reports to the Cygnet River colony say that the natives could muster two to three hundred while he had but nine military. That is not the case now.

Their numbers are not so large, said Chaine.

We have police and military and able-bodied men.

They might have said it all at once, or been led by young Hugh, with Chaine and the Governor merely giving their voices in support: steps must be taken.

THE SETTING SUN A STONE

B AA BAA BLACK SHEEP, have you any wool . . . Bobby was
walking alone, as was his way, and walking beside one of
the creeks feeding into the river of Kepalup. Already the waters
were slowing, the level dropping. The coarse, soft sand between
the shrinking pools was crisscrossed with the prints of many
beings, and Bobby moved quickly along it, sheltered from sun
and wind by the trees on either side. He came down the rocky
slope of water holes, and stayed to clear some of them of reeds,
and lay a carpet of leaves not far from the eagle's nest. The old
bird studied his efforts.

Not much further and the creek joined the river, and Bobby
kept to the old path along the riverbank until he reached the
tiny bubbling spring that fed it, and that little stone wall Skelly
had built so that come summer it might be closed off for Chaine's
sheep. On one bank their footprints had cut away all the earth.
Chaine's horses would drink here, too. His hunting dogs and his
workers. But what about Noongar people?

The old trees still leaned over the riverbank. Further upstream
he saw the eagle watching from its bough. A mallee hen emerged

from the dense forest of jam tree the other side of the river, and returned his gaze for what seemed a long, cheeky time before it retraced its steps, disappearing into the close ranks of trees. Bobby turned up the bank and again paused as a family of emu studied him, and then—it seemed a little resentfully—strode off and vanished into the trees. So he was known here still, in this place where his people had always walked. Not so alone then.

But what about those people up in the farmhouse he'd known pretty well all his life? Did they still want to know him?

Neither William Skelly nor the man helping him saw Bobby until he was within a few steps. It was a very large hut they were building; the stone walls rose two or more times the height of even a tall man. Skelly's companion tapped him rapidly on the shoulder, pointing.

Nigger, he said.

Skelly's heavy body turned slowly, his head even lower in his shoulders than Bobby remembered, so that when their eyes met Skelly seemed a glowering bullock.

Mr Skelly, Bobby said. But Mr William Skelly did not hold out his hand.

Bobby, said Mr Skelly. The third man watched them closely.

Are Mrs Chaine and Christine at home, Mr Skelly?

I'm not too sure, Bobby. But they'll not be wanting to see you nekkid like that, boy. Hairy balls on show and all.

Skelly sent away the other man who, looking back over his shoulder a couple of times on his way to the house, seemed about to break into a run.

I'm going to King George Town, Skelly.

You'll need clothes there, too, Bobby, and no spears with you. Them's the new rules, see.

But Bobby knew all these things, and because Bobby was a friend, Skelly went to find him some clothes.

Bobby shook out the crumpled rags he received. How worn they were. Smelled of mould. Bobby had lived long enough with the Chaines and Dr Cross to know they would not wear clothes in this state. These were used for polishing, or patches.

They'll let you in town with these, Bobby.

Skelly seemed particularly pleased with himself. His companion came jogging back, happier but still nervous by the look of him. He had a gun, primed and loaded.

Mrs Chaine and her daughter are indisposed.

Bobby's people said he should be with Chaine's daughter; look how Chaine favoured him, and hadn't Bobby himself helped that family? But Bobby knew old Boss Chaine had his own laws. Chaine and them, they seemed to divide the world up into black and white people, and despite what they said, they put all black people together, and set to work making sure they put themselves in control, and put their own people over the top of all of us who've always been here. When Bobby was a child, he and Christopher and Christine . . . They were together, and they shared. But not now. Christine come close then run away, went back and forward ever since they could be man and woman together. Why? Because he was with the black people? Because he was black? Could only be outside and not at their dance, nor with the horses and wagons and big house?

Bobby remembered the change in Mama Chaine after the death of her son.

And Christine? She is also now indisposed? He remembered the girl climbing the tree, the strong tendons behind her knee and the long muscles of her thighs. They said bone from the whale's throat was used to lift skirts away from such legs, yet still conceal them.

Bobby took the clothes, walked diagonally across the rectangle they were building, leapt a fence (one foot touched the cap of a post), continued across a paddock where as a baby he'd gone with the women as they dug for yams, and walked down to the river crossing near what Chaine called 'a set of natural weirs'. There was still a path on either riverbank, but the other side was loose and worn deep from hooves and iron cartwheels. Bobby thought of following the river to Shellfeast Harbour; a boat might save him a day or more. But even if he did find one, it'd be too large for him to row alone, and the chance of finding one with a sail was remote. He wasn't too good with a sail, anyway. And he didn't want to steal.

The yapping dog announced Bobby's arrival at Menak and Manit's camp, and shied away from Bobby's every quick movement, its wariness somehow emphasising the old couple's isolation.

Too many strangers, boy. *Waam nitjak.* Cheeky young ones, they friends with white man.

Their food was a few tubers, nothing more. Bobby had wanted to bring something more substantial, but had seen no meat, no emu or kangaroo all day. He set a snare for quokka or tammar but come nightfall, there was nothing.

Manit laboriously ground seeds between two rocks, baked a damper in the ashes. They shared a bitter and meagre meal, and drank from a small water hole in the granite sheet nearby. Someone had broken the flat slab that had always capped it.

The walk to King George Town next day was very slow, because the older couple were now so frail. Not so long ago a blow from Menak was feared, but he was harmless now. Kangaroo shooters occupied his old campsite: one Noongar boy, a few women, and some older white men. All had rifles, and although some listened, visibly chastened, to Menak's insults, and invited him to remain with them, none of them would be moving from such a choice site. Menak and Manit put themselves the other side of some large granite boulders that marked the camp. You could see how The Farm had grown since the Governor chose it as his home. Bobby thought about last night's seed cakes, wondered if King George Town would still offer flour to appease Menak.

Bobby climbed the fence surrounding the yam grounds, and was still quite a long way from the house when a soldier yelled out for him to halt. Bobby had not seen the man, and now he waved, friendly-like, but the soldier gesticulated angrily and raised his gun to his shoulder. Bobby stooped and dug up a couple of yams. Studied them. They were not ready, and he threw them to the ground and turned back the way he had come.

Horses and carts of various kinds began arriving a little later. Under a full moon the buildings of The Farm huddled, surrounded by tethered animals, wagons and sulkies and carts. Soldiers moved around its perimeter, and the windows were small rectangles of brightly glowing amber. The high tent beside the house shone like a lamp, human figures flickering and flowing within it. Bobby fell asleep to the sound of music, laughter, and thin, increasingly excited voices floating on the wind. The Chaines had arrived as the sun was setting, and from his vantage point, Bobby, leaning his cheek against a great, grey granite boulder, imagined that boulder—with just a little shove—rolling down the slope, clearing a path through the vegetation, smashing the house. Crushing.

In the early dawn those who had stayed at The Farm were rudely woken, and they rushed from the buildings to cleared land near the road leading back to the harbour. The crop beside the buildings was on fire, the flames deeply coloured in the early light, smoke rising and rolling into the lightening sky. The Governor and his son, and some soldiers and other men, threw buckets on the buildings and the ground surrounding them, but when the fire reached the ground burned by Bobby and Manit just a little time ago, it rapidly dwindled. The wind dropped, too, and the men looked across burned stubbled earth and smoking ash at the rising sun.

IN THE GAOL DANCE NOW

C HRISTINE CHAINE BRUSHED her hair: twenty-three, twenty-four . . . One day, Hugh, the Governor's son, will watch her prepare for bed like this. She was a woman now, and they were a good match. Even Papa said so, and although he had very little time for Hugh's father's pomposity (Oh, how many times had she heard this!) if she was in her heart fond of him, well . . .

Hugh would be her lover, and also a very steady friend. She did not have many: a consequence, she supposed, of growing up in such isolation. Her governess of the last few years, a woman not much older than herself, had been a friend—no matter that she was paid for her companionship—but had now married. Her brother had been a friend, too. She thought again of his death, his face that one last time above the water's surface, and their hands parting . . .

Bobby Wabalanginy had been a friend. Fancy, a native as best friend! How isolated they were in this backwater. She had been a child, innocent.

That childhood friend was in prison now, Papa said. He'd even been to see him. Bobby had got into some sort of trouble at the Sailor's Rest, which was really no surprise to Christine, who always took to the other side of the street when she passed the tavern, because of the mess, and because of the people. People affected by liquor were unpleasant, but it was the natives that most bothered her: men and women alike dressed in rags, and sometimes scarcely dressed at all. The women were quite shameless, she thought.

Laws were being enforced now, thankfully. Natives must be clothed and without spears if they were to enter town. It was only decent, and if we are to civilise them, as Papa said is the only way, then clothing is an important precursor.

Papa believed Bobby had got into trouble because the policeman and his native constable had tried to prevent the old man with Bobby from entering town. The old man claimed it was his right, that it was his town! Papa laughed recounting it, said it was true in a way. And it was also true, as Bobby apparently claimed (shouted, she'd been told, and slapped the policeman), that the old man had received a ration of flour from previous authorities, and had even been dressed, accommodated and fed at government expense. Why? Because he was the landlord.

It might even be true, in a way, but to what use do they put this ownership as against what we have achieved in so short a time? Papa could sometimes explain things so well. It may have been expedient at one time, but was no longer necessary.

Christine's hair shone in the lamplight, and the mirror reflected her serious face back at her. She smiled, but just as quickly her smile fell away.

Bobby and one of the other natives had apparently attacked the native constable who tried to arrest the old man, and it was only with the help of Mr Killam (who of course was both publican and gaoler) and some visiting merchant sailors, that Bobby was arrested.

Once in gaol Bobby had sent word that he wanted to see her,

Christine, and her father. She had been quite surprised, and quite touched, and thought to render what charitable assistance and comfort she could, but Papa had gone alone. He had used his influence with Killam and the constable to arrange to have the old man released. In truth, he laughed, the old man's wife had set up camp outside the gaol wall, lit a little campfire and all, and there might have been another diplomatic upset if, as Mr Killam threatened, he'd beaten her within an inch of her life for creating a fire hazard! He'd had them escorted along with their dog to a native camp away from the town buildings and had made them a present of appropriate clothing.

Papa said Bobby had to be taught respect for the rule of law. He was a good boy. There was no doubt that, with firm encouragement, these people were capable of being civilised. Bobby certainly was. Furthermore, there had been trouble with natives stealing sheep and spearing cattle at some of the out-stations, including their own. There had been a number of fires—bush fires, perhaps—but Papa said it was no coincidence, and they had seen how the natives controlled fire. The fires had come to the edge of huts and buildings. Like a warning. Bobby may not necessarily have been involved in this or any such trouble, but it was important that he understood the situation. He is a young man of some influence.

Hugh said he and his father were also talking about the native problem. The fathers were united in that at least. How very peculiar that her friend (soon to be fiancé) Hugh Spender and herself should be the children of two men so often opposed to one another. The man's an oaf, Papa often said (and worse), but the family has connections. Especially here it would be a good marriage. She had blushed. Capital, blood, name and alliance, he said. Papa was so very pragmatic, but knew nothing of romance.

Spend her life with Hugh? He was well mannered, cultivated,

and shared her love of this place, backwater though it might be to some. Hugh and his father had acquired property well suited to grazing and had already arranged to import some fine breeding stock. Papa had advised him accordingly, and was most impressed. A practical man, but also refined; he knew music, painting, the latest literature, and what a shame it was that there were so few—apart from herself and Mama—with whom he could share these pleasures. And he held himself so very well that even Papa had commented on his fine *military bearing*, and despite the way their circumstances limited him—limited them all, when it came to fashion—he dressed impeccably. He was always very masculine, but fashionably so. Her mind wandered. How would *he* look in native costume, in—what had Bobby called it?—a cock-rag?

What was Bobby really like now, Christine wondered. Once he had combed her hair with a banksia cone. He had been a very good-looking boy, intelligent and funny. Still was, perhaps. It showed what they were capable of, given a chance. Papa said he had proved an able member of the whaling crew, and invaluable in preserving good relationships between the blacks and themselves. He seemed popular.

Christine remembered seeing Bobby distribute presents at the end of the whaling season. Dressed like a young rake, he had shone among them all, black and white, with his wit, his sense of humour and the joy he radiated. Incredibly, she had even felt a little jealous. And she had felt his attraction when he rowed them to shore after the shipboard ball. It was disturbing, if one allowed oneself to follow that line of thought.

*

Locked in a gloomy and crowded cell with only Wooral as a friend, Bobby Wabalanginy might have felt defeated. At least old Menak had been released and had Manit to soothe him. But where? Oh, there were policemen, merchants, citizens of all sorts living in the old man's home, and they chased away their . . . what was the word? Landlord.

Even Jak Tar turned his back these days.

Some of these other Noongars were no better than the policeman. Come onto Menak's land and pay him no respect. Hide behind Chaine. Behind his gun. Chaine and Governor, and Killam and Skelly . . . But Killam did whatever Chaine told him and followed, suffered . . . He had power now, a gun and the lockup key, but he worked at the tavern to please Chaine, and locked people up to please . . . the Governor, Bobby guessed. Working for rum? To keep the gun? For money?

Killam had written all the names in a heavy book and signed his own and the policeman's name, too. The helper—that Noongar policeman from far away—never even had his name written there. Bobby could write more than his name, though he never got so good with pen and paper and reading and writing as he might have. What was that Noongar policeman doing here, anyway? Old days, he'd be talking sweet and soft to Menak, but not now. He could put away a man and take his woman if he wanted. Go wherever he liked, with a gun and the policeman beside him. The gun.

Like those boys Chaine shot, all those years ago. Jimmy and Jeff. Chaine just shot them. He should be the one in this gaol. If the Governor knew . . .

Killam came back with food. The air was bad in the cell because of too many people and a bucket of everybody's shit and piss in the corner. These other ones had all been sick from grog, but they wanted to be gone now. Bobby too. Killam unlocked the outer door to bring in the trays of food. It was a struggle for him because of that bad arm. Them Governor boys did that. Them ones Chaine shot. Killam put the trays of food on a little table, but he couldn't bring them all in at one time.

Give you a hand, Mr Killam?

Hmph. No. Just stay, all of you, back against that wall.

As he came in, awkward because of the tray and his arm and the lack of space, Bobby stumbled forward just like someone pushed him. Killam stiffened and nearly dropped everything, and Bobby looked back at the others with a hurt expression, as if blaming one of them. He sensed Killam relax, readjust his balance, and then Bobby leaned against him and grabbed his good arm. Bowls and food spilled, and Bobby pushed Killam to one side and the others all came around him. Killam didn't struggle.

Bobby simply danced them all out of the gaol, and they locked all the doors behind them. There was no sound from Killam. Bobby knew what he'd been through, why he was frightened. The escapees went in different directions. Bobby and Wooral looked at one another.

Menak.

Only then did Killam begin shouting for help.

*

Several sheep were missing; Skelly counted once more and confirmed the loss. Was this the same thing as at Close-by-island just starting up? He'd had no news from there, nor from King George Town for how long now? Days? A week or more? Chaine would expect to see signs of progress when he eventually arrived.

Skelly stomped around the pen, looking for a hole or some sort of break in the brush fence but there was nothing, and they'd been counted in last night.

He found Bobby patting the dog at the shed where Skelly had rigged up an anvil and workbench. So much for the guard dog, thought Skelly. Maybe he needed to get a dog like that one Cross gave Menak all those years ago, that barked at everything.

Bobby looked up, surprised. Grinned.

I been see some fellas eating your sheeps, Mr Skelly, he said. And I wanna help you and make friends again too many.

Clearly, the black boy's English was reverting to type, probably because he was spending more and more time with his own kind. But yes, of course Skelly wanted to see such evidence. It'd be even better if he could catch them red-handed. He had Bobby wait a moment while he fetched and loaded his rifle.

Gunna shoot them, then?

If need be.

But just one sheep maybe, when you killing all the kangaroos far as people walk.

Skelly didn't answer.

Bobby showed him where the brush fence had been dismantled and then repaired. He pointed out tracks, though Skelly could see nothing. They from far away, this mob, Bobby reckoned. Well, no surprises in that, thought Skelly. He's not going to blame his own family or friends, is he?

Bobby led the way, barely glancing at the ground.

Will they still be there, Bobby? Did you actually see them with the sheep?

No, I just seen the ashes and the eaten-up sheep.

Not too fast, then.

Skelly had his eyes peeled. Was wary of where he was led. It was a convoluted journey, and an area of Chaine's land that he did not know.

You sure you know where you're going, Bobby?

They found the ashes of a fire, but no sign of sheep.

So they ate it up, bones and all!

Sheep here this morning, Bobby said and pointed to the ground. Someone carrying something away on his shoulder.

Well, what good is this? Will we chase nothing all day?

Okay. *Boorda.*

He was gone, quick as that. Damn.

Bobby!

But there was no answer.

It took Skelly most of the day to get back to Chaine's shed and sheep-pen, and he had only found his way back after recognising part of the river near some land Chaine had sold him. Surprised and relieved to find the sheep still penned, he returned to his work, and did not discover until evening that the storehouse had been broken into. There was no sign of entry, but bags of flour and sugar and knives and axes had been taken.

Bobby.

*

At first light next morning, Soldier Killam found his storehouse had been raided. Rum had been poured onto the ground, the empty barrel rolled into the shrubs. Careful not to disturb the footprints, he sent word to the policeman who brought his newly-appointed black tracker. Personally, Killam thought him worthless, but at least he was from another district.

The policeman arrived with William Skelly, who had come to town because of thieving and trouble at Kepalup. Chaine had suggested they combine resources, since this was clearly strategic and premeditated. We have been too lenient, Killam agreed. The policeman and tracker talked to some of the natives around town, and Skelly showed him the tracks from the day before.

Surely Bobby wasn't involved in something like this.

That boy might make a fine native constable.

The tracker identified Wooral's footprints at both scenes, but was less sure of who the other people were. They were carrying heavy loads. Killam pointed out he was well aware of this, since they'd taken rice and sugar and all the biscuits, things they'd developed a taste for from their trade with the whalers over the last few years. But of course this year there were again very few whales, and hardly a whaler to be seen. No one knew why. Very likely the whales had been fished out. Or had the whalers found a source closer to home? Unfavourable winds? The weather was odd this season: today, for instance, the low and heavy clouds, and the wind gusting.

It seemed another set of footprints had joined those they'd been following. The tracker did not want to continue. He was tired, he said.

Frightened more likely, said Killam.

The policeman pointed his loaded gun at the tracker. I'd hate this to go off, by accident, like.

The tracker looked at each of the men, who returned his gaze steadily, and then went back to the task.

After a time they came across a fire and a large pot of rice. The men looked around. This fire was recently deserted and fresh tracks led away.

They must've heard us coming.

The men knew they were close. A gust of cold wind whipped at their clothing and tongues of flame lifted from the fire as they followed the trail. They would be upon the thieves in no time. But the wind sprang up, trees lunged, and hailstones pounded them as if they were under attack. The men scurried for shelter and, when the storm passed, the tracks they had been following were gone.

*

Some nights later, many small scattered fires and the smell of various foods roasting; thin smoke and tapping sticks and voices singing, and flame-illuminated dancers within a clearing surrounded by paperbarks. They wore jackets and trousers, feathers and white paint in different combinations, and in that flickering light people and shadows and gleaming trees shifted from one thing to another: tree person shadow, painted-skin tufted-bark flapping-clothing.

There were the old dances—hunting, ancestral beings, memories and legend—and they did the Deadman Dance, with its refined display of a gun and a fierce, strategic intention that people now understood so much better. And there were new dances—crowds of coughing bodies, hands brushing clouds of flies from around mouths, barking rifles and falling bodies and stiff limbs. Bobby was at the centre, the others falling back from him like always as he came alive in the Deadman Dance and gathered together all their different selves. So impressive, so unpredictable: what might he be next?

Bobby danced the sea, jumpy and barely restrained, and the surprise of a dolphin or whale bursting into the air, the sudden clear shape of a groper emerging from the depths, a salmon in a wave face. He offered them surprise and sudden revelations.

Bobby danced many of the people in the settlement of King George Town, and it was as if they had all come here to join in the festivity. Here was the quick-striding Soldier Killam, with that twist to his torso and the bad arm; the hulking Convict Skelly; Dr Cross (oh poor thing, remember him?); Chaine, bouncing up and down on his toes, throwing commands with his arms; Gov'nor Spender, nose up, hands going up and down, patting heads . . .

It was like Bobby *was* them, was showing their very selves, inside their heads and singing their very sound and voices: . . . *intelligent curiosity . . . delighted by music . . . extravagant prices of the necessaries of life . . . the natives the natives the natives* . . . He mimed playing a fiddle so well that everyone heard it, then the singers made the very same sound and tune. Bobby barked like a dog, and Jock joined in. Bobby could look through the eyes of anything. It made everyone unstable, surprised and hardly trusting, but everyone was laughing. Here was Bobby ballroom dancing on a ship's deck as the swell rolled beneath it: one two three, one two three, ooh . . .

Jak Tar could not believe his eyes or ears. Fretting for his Binyan, he had come to take her back to their hut. She saw him slinking around the edge of the firelight, beckoned him, grabbed him, hauled him in among the dancers just as they began to deflate, to slow down, to hold one another, laughing at themselves. And pleased, secretly relieved that the terrible beauty of Bobby's spell had been broken.

ABOUT A NATIVE GANG

Governor Steeling Sir,

It is with great regret that I must inform you of several depredations committed by a number of Natives, led by two in particular, within the last month or six weeks and which Natives baffle every attempt of the constables in taking them. There are warrants for their arrest.

Allowing these natives to be at large only tends to induce others to become thieves and hardens them in their daring attempts.

There not being a Native Constable upon whom we can depend is a great drawback to the white constable of this place.

On the 18th of August Mr Chaine was robbed of sheep, and had his storehouse broken into while the native Bobby pretended to show him where the natives had been eating a sheep of his. The storehouse was broken into by digging under the foundations and 100 cwt. of flour stolen therefrom, and two bags of sugar, knives and axes were also taken away. The footmarks of Wooral and Menak (a very old man of hereabouts) were identified.

On the 26th of August Mr Killam's store was broken into and taken therefrom one Bag of Rice and 20 lbs of sugar. The footmarks of Bobby,

Wooral, Menak and others were identified, and when traced by the policeman who came on their fire at which they were boiling a part of the rice, and recovered the major part of a bag of rice but owing to heavy hailstorm he was not enabled to track them further.

On the 4th of September Mr Chaine's storehouse was again broken into although every precaution had been taken to secure it, and taken from his premises were 4 cwt. of biscuit. On this occasion the footmarks of Bobby, Wooral and Menak among others were identified and the policeman tracked them for a considerable distance but was not enabled to come up with them owing to the Native he had with him refusing to go any further.

From the above I hope His Excellency will see how desirable it is this Gang of Natives should be broke up more especially as they are those who know our habits, and are more civilised for having been so much with the Europeans, and will therefore sanction a further contingent of police and soldiers experienced in these matters to be sent here for the purpose of taking the natives by whatever means are most expedient.

Yours . . . E Spender,
Governor-resident
King George Town

WITH FRIENDS LIKE THESE
WE BREAK APART

THE CHAINE FAMILY WAS CAMPED inland from their
homestead, Bobby heard, at Bandalup Pools, not far from
Kepalup. Old Chaine himself, his missus and Christine and
Skelly. Governor's boy, Hugh, was with them, too, but not now.
No sheep, no cattle, just their horses.

Strange. Not an expedition, then.

Several people had gone out of their way to tell Bobby this, and
said they'd been camped many days now. Why? Waiting for him?

Bobby walked the coarse, dry sand of the creekbed barefoot,
skirting the occasional pools that remained at this time of the
year. Trees on either bank leaned and sheltered him from the sun
and wind, soothed. Expecting to find the Chaines camped around
the next pool, he slowed, listened, smelling their fire as he approached.

From among large boulders grouped almost like buildings,
Bobby looked through a veil of leaves across the granite slope
down which the creek sometimes ran. He recognised the boulders patterning the far riverbank, and the suspended thin slabs
of lizard traps. Pools of water stepped down the slope, a wavering black line linking them.

The eagle was not in its nest.

Christine, cushioned by the cloth of her dress, was sunning herself on the warm granite beside a pool thick with green reeds. A fallen tree left by some past flood stretched its limbs toward her, so smooth and white and tiny-dimpled. Her mother was close by, reading. A small bird splashed at the side of the pool, tail held high and dancing. Christine turned her head, and her unseeing face floated to Bobby through a sparse cross-hatching of saplings, leaves and spider web. A sleepy racehorse goanna backed itself under some bushes not so far away. Must have just dug itself out of the earth. Another goanna was silhouetted on a branch against the sky. Bobby walked the rocky sheet of the creekbed to stand the other side of the small pool beside which Christine lay.

Mrs Chaine got up and came to stand beside her daughter, book firmly closed.

Oh, Bobby. You startled us. How dashing you look.

Bobby smiled. He'd taken care with his dress, adding boots and shirt to his costume not long after he smelled their smoke.

Mrs Chaine turned. Geordie!

But Geordie Chaine was already striding toward them, footsteps sounding on rock.

Bobby, my boy. Arms out in welcome, he paused to offer a hand so that Christine might haul herself to her feet. Geordie Chaine kept his eyes on Bobby, and his grin did not go away. He put his arm around Bobby's shoulders as they walked back to the tent.

We needed a holiday, to get away from working all the time. You know what I mean, just to get out in the bush and have a good walk about. You've always been like a son to me, Bobby, you know that, don't you? And oh, after the whaling season, coming into port, remember when they first come across that ship and we were dragging poor old Soldja behind us? Why, if Bobby liked to give people dresses and food and axes and knives he could do that by roo-hunting, or sandalwood cutting, or helping the police, even, and there'll be another whaling season, for even without our Brother Jonathons we can take the Leviathan on our own . . .

Christine said he sounded like the Bible now, and wasn't this almost like when they were children and Christopher was still alive. She stopped talking then and Bobby didn't know what he could say.

A sip of rum, Bobby? Rum in your tea?

No.

Christine and her mother went to pick flowers.

Suddenly Soldier Killam was right beside Bobby, Convict Skelly, also. They held Bobby's arms. Must've been watching from Mrs Chaine's tent.

Chaine was very close, face to face, noses nearly touching.

I mean what I say, Bobby, but must make certain things clear.

There was a horse ready for him, and they let him ride but his hands were tied and the policeman's friend who led the horse was no one Bobby knew or trusted.

*

Christine Chaine glided, felt like she was floating among the bright gleaming walls, the high ceilings, the paintings and furniture and the drawn curtains that spilled light and the trembling blue of the harbour into the room. The flung-open doors, the bright air moving through the house, so refreshing.

Poor Bobby was in prison. The ringleader maybe . . . She'd been surprised to hear he was so involved in all this trouble, and Papa was, too. A son, Papa said, he'd treated the boy like a son.

She'd been like a sister . . . Or had she? There'd been Christopher, herself and Bobby, but even when Bobby shared their lessons . . . Oh of course, they welcomed him into their house, treated him no differently than if he was family. The native girls they kept now, the servants, might almost be family also and yet one must—as Papa said—impose one's will. They were forever laughing and playing without purpose, and it was almost impossible to get things done. To help and civilise them.

Common theft and disrespect, Papa said. The boy was capable of so much, had so much potential and remarkable influence over his own kind . . . He had fed his friends and family from our stores and enterprise and now his influence was so much the greater. What would happen to us if we allowed that to continue? Cross had begun this, he said. But Christine was not sure she could remember Mr Cross. He encouraged ideas of entitlement, Papa said. Not respect and a work ethic; not the necessary discipline to defray one's immediate and short-term gain, and understand self-sacrifice . . .

Christine had rarely seen Papa so upset. He kept at it so long, on and on he went . . .

She was startled when one of the native girls interrupted (a relief, really) with a message from their visitors, who were almost immediately in the room. Really, this was of course rather more informal than one need be. She knew the man as Jak Tar, one of her father's workers, and he had a native woman with him. Bold as brass they were. Christine may have blushed. She should not be here with him at all. Jak Tar had the good grace to look uncomfortable, but the woman—in gloves and a bustling dress quite ridiculous in this town—appeared amused. Jak Tar wanted to see her father. This business with Bobby. Something has come up that he must . . . that her father needs to know.

Fortunately, Christine was able to manoeuvre them to the parlour (this without the help of servants . . . those girls behaved more like guests) where they might await Papa's return. Since they were so insistent. She was pleased to excuse herself. Really! As if they were a married couple. What if they were all to . . . what if she were to be with a black man? She imagined Bobby on the dance floor, sweeping her across the deck at one of the too-rare shipside balls.

Ridiculous.

But she could easily imagine him dancing, and dressed for the occasion.

Had Bobby really committed these break-ins and thefts, these depredations? He was brave, she knew that. Clever, as a boy at least. Not evil.

What on earth could Jak Tar have to say to Papa that was so important?

*

Not wanting Bobby's court appearance to be in kangaroo skin or the rags the prison made available, Jak Tar had rushed to the prison with a set of clothes as soon as Binyan told him of Bobby's capture. He'd found Killam at a heavy and roughly made desk, helping the constable complete the paperwork. The constable was barely literate. A small opening in the door showed Bobby's face, his hands gripping the bars, watching the two men. Jak Tar had expected to leave the package with Killam for Bobby's court appearance, whenever that might be, but Bobby called out.

Mr Tar, my good man.

Jak Tar knew how Bobby could move into performance, how he could give a recitation, foregrounding and mimicking the speech patterns of others. Jak Tar felt himself begin to tug his forelock, to bow to this voice of the ruling class. His reaction angered him. Was he bred to obey that sound? And angry with himself, he was also angry at Bobby. And he was Bobby's friend. What would it do to others, such a voice coming from a black man?

Bobby's hands were tight on the bars, and so was his face behind them.

Mr Killam, Constable, need I write that report for you?

The two men ignored him, and turned to Jak Tar who held up the parcel of clothes.

I fancy he'll be a good witness, he said. The Governor presiding?

Yes. Governor Spender will adjudicate.

The men's speech seemed particularly formal: Bobby's influence, perhaps.

They brought the men out one by one to make their statements; Killam and the constable helped ensure they were brief. Eventually, it was Bobby's turn. Jak Tar remained. Killam and the constable must've thought him an ally. Bobby tried to see what had been written, but could not. Yet he was not cowered, showed no remorse.

Yes, he said, I broke into Mr Chaine's property on whatever that date you tell me it was, and I stole his sheep and I stole the flour and the sugar and the knives and all we needed.

Yes, he said again when it was put to him, yes, I took the rice and the sugar with me from Mr Killam's place. He was smiling.

Yes, I took a lot of biscuit from Mr Chaine. Not all of it, because he has too many biscuit. But I took it and gave it to people who were hungry.

And—last time, yes—I speared some cattle and took some sheep and yes, the rice and treacle, too, and we all slept with full bellies.

Although he might bluff the constable and the gaoler, Bobby knew he was not the reader he pretended to be. Nevertheless, he could make out some of the long and twisted phrases scrawled across the pages: *depredations, break-in and stealing, impudent, native-gang* . . .

Yes, he said. I did all that. Guilty. Yes, yes and yes again. And I ran from the gaol because I was frightened, see.

Why were you frightened, Bobby?

Almost immediately, Killam regretted the question.

I was frightened, Bobby said, because years ago I seen Mr Chaine shoot dead those two boys that came with Governor Spender and he might do it to me, too.

Jak Tar, watching, listening but not saying a word, saw Killam's head lift. The pen stopped moving.

That is enough for now.

And Jak Tar got to his feet and rushed away to see Mr Chaine, probably for Binyan's sake, really. Wanting him to think him a hero.

Mr Chaine listened to Jak Tar.

Mr Tar, you endanger yourself in speaking up for the boy. You are yourself an alien, are you not? One who jumped ship?

Jak Tar ignored the threat implied. He went to see the Governor.

Chaine, the Governor and Jak Tar met with Bobby at the gaol-house. Killam and Skelly had agreed they might also withdraw charges if Mr Chaine saw fit. And charges against Bobby would be withdrawn when he signed the statement Jak Tar had collected from him:

> In 1836 I left King George Town with Mr Chaine and Mr Killam on the boat and also two lads named Jeffrey and James belonging to some other country but come here with the Governor.
>
> After we were shipwrecked we had to walk back a long way. We did not know the country and did not have much food and after we had been walking James and Jeffrey often told me that we should never get to King George Town as we would die in the bush and they wished me to leave

Mr Chaine behind and go with them more quickly to my country and then to King George Town.

One night Jeffrey and James and myself were sleeping at the camp when Mr Chaine was away from us watching the horses which we used to take turns. I was asleep and then I woke up to the noisy gun being fired and I jumped up frightened and ran to Mr Chaine calling out 'You hear a gun?' but he was already running the other way to the sleeping place and said what was the matter?

We went to the tent and there was Killam lying on the ground breathing heavily and his arm smashed up from the ball that got him. We thought he might die.

James and Jeffrey were gone from the camp and took away with them dampers and some tea and sugar and water and two guns and some ammunition and also tobacco and pipes.

We left soon as we found what was done for King George Town. Next day James and Jeffrey were following us. Jeffrey had a double-barrelled gun and James had one also.

I heard them crying out for me like dingoes. Mr Chaine asked them to come with us but they ran away amongst the bushes and we never saw them again but kept on our road to King George Town. Anything else I might have said about what happened is not true.

Bobby looked at the page carefully, bluffing he had the gist of it. And, bluffing still because he had been practising this very phrase, wrote in his careful hand *I attach my signature to affirm that these are my very words* . . . But then stopped, lifted the quill.

I will only sign this, he said oh so very theatrically and looking around at those awaiting his signature. I will only sign this if . . .

Jak Tar was irritated; it was a foolish risk. But the conditions Bobby set did not seem onerous. And there was no dissuading him.

Chaine thought it pride, and Bobby often had this wilful, play-fulness about him. Simplest to humour him. Chaine retained a genuine affection for the young man.

Bobby had wanted them to gather in the gaolhouse so that he might also have the other prisoners as his audience, but instead they brought him to Chaine's house. It was the only condition on which Bobby relented. He would have preferred a larger au-dience, but he knew not all the townsfolk admired Mr Chaine and at least this way he had enough witnesses to ensure justice would be carried out.

The doors and windows of the largest room of Chaine's new house were opened so that the light shimmered on the walls, and the air was raw-earth fresh. Bobby glanced around him: a coat-stand in the corner, with no coats on it; no furniture, no rug, the room so new and never used and our fresh white ochre on its walls. Bobby faced his audience: Mr and Mrs Chaine, and Christine, Soldier Killam and Convict Skelly. The Chaine women were seated together, but Mr Chaine had inserted his thumbs in his waistcoat, and was bobbing, rising up on his toes and dropping to his heels again. Skelly leaned against the corner of the fire's mantelpiece, favouring his bad leg. Mr Killam looked about restlessly, clumsily plucking again and again at the back of his shirt.

And finally, Jak Tar and Binyan arrived with the Governor and Hugh, though immediately Jak and Binyan moved to one side and a little apart. It might not seem an auspicious audience, Bobby knew, but it was mostly friends and family.

Menak had waved a hand, dismissed him. Manit had sworn and sneered when told of Bobby's plan.

Bobby laughed. Hadn't he escaped the lockup just from a few words on paper? Child's play. What was that against dance and song? They'd seen how people fell back before him, joined their voices with his.

It is like the dance to dodge the spears; they cannot match us.

Bobby Wabalanginy knew that he could sing and dance the spirit of this place, had shown he could sing and dance the spirit of any gathering of people, show them what we gathered together here really are. He reminded them he was a dancer and singer, what Dr Cross called *a gifted artiste*, and by those means and by his spirit he would show them how people must live here, together.

Afterwards, he'd sign their paper. We will sign a paper with them about how we might live. There will be no more gaol. We show our talent and good grace, and Wooral and them no longer need use fire and spears and fight them and their guns.

The old people shrugged. Let him try it his way.

*

The sun had almost reached the hills on the far side of the harbour, which seemed to have absorbed the blue of day even as the sky grew pink and the soft light trembled in the whitewashed room. They could hear one another breathing. Be sincere, Bobby told himself. Speak straight like a spear.

He began. My friends, you here are all my friends, *blackfellas* and *whitefellas* I hear people saying, but we are not just our colour. His eyes rested upon Binyan, moved onto Christine, moved on . . . Years from now, our grannies' grannies will be old people and our same spirit in them still, but maybe they won't look like us or know about us or . . . I'm guilty taking food from you but that's not stealing and I did no wrong. I can't be sorry I share and look after families and friends and many of you sitting here today. In my language there is no need to say please and thank you. My old uncle knows this language I am speaking now, but he keeps his tongue away and says it is not worth the sound of it. He would not understand the spirit of words on paper, only in their sound.

We all different from when we babies, you and me too. I change, doesn't mean I forget all about my people and their ways. But some people come to live here, and wanna stay like they never moved away from their own place. Sometimes I dress like you people, but who here I ever see naked like my people?

No one laughed. Binyan's little grin was just as quickly gone again.

One time, with Mr Cross, he share his food and his beds with us, because he say he our guest. But not now, so we gotta do it ourselves. One time we share kangaroo wallaby *tammar quokka yongar wetj woylie boodi wetj koording kamak kaip* . . . Too many. But now not like that, and sheep and bullock everywhere and too many strangers wanna take things for themselves and leave nothing. Whales nearly all gone now, and the men that kill them they gone away, too, and now we can't even walk up river away from the sea in cold rainy time. Gotta walk around fences and guns, and sheep and bullock get the goodest water. They messing up the water, cutting the earth. What, we can't kill and eat them? And we now strangers to our special places.

Ngaalak waam. Naatjil? Why?

Bobby saw figures at all the windows of the room, watching. Figures he thought he recognised, but somehow too faint and obscure for him to be sure.

These shoes, he said, looking down and moving sideways without moving his legs so that the shoes seemed to carry him, and his audience had to smile at the way he waved his arms as if he was about to lose his balance. *Djena bwok warra booja kenning.* These shoes might stop me feel the dirt I tread.

He stepped lightly out of the shoes, and left them balanced

on their toes, propped against the base of the naked hatstand in the corner of the room. *Booja djena baranginy.* Sand can hold my feet instead.

Noonook kaatabwok koorl baranginy. Take this hat . . . He bowed, and as the hat fell he caught it and, straightening, flicked his wrist so that it went hovering across the room and gently landed at the very peak of the hatstand. Oh!

The hat up high, the shoes balanced on their toes, no body between.

Naatjil kaatbwok. Why wear this hat? *Ngayn yirra yak koombar maar-ang kaat koombar.* Clouds around my head just like a mountaintop; *Ngaitj nol-ok darrp koorl, dabakan, dabakan, dat nyin.* I want shade? Slip beneath the big trees, slow down, stop.

He took off his jacket and, dancing across the room as if with a ballroom partner, left it buttoned below the hat. A human form was taking shape.

Nitjak bwoka. My shirt.

Bobby pirouetted, and the shirt spun from him; he gave a flourish and there it was within the coat, buttoned and secure as if there were still a body within. Oh this was going even better than he'd expected.

Bwokabt, ngaank ngayn maarak ngabiny. No shirt means the wind and sun caress you better.

In moments, Bobby wore little more than a thin belt made of human hair, with blonde strands woven through it. A mysterious, well-dressed human form hovered on its toes in the corner of the room like a ghost, a silent witness, a hanging man; like all those things at once.

Bobby was singing softly.

Now look here, began Chaine, but fell silent as Bobby—somehow staring into all their eyes at once—held his arms out to each side and made the muscles under his glistening skin quiver and jump.

On his feet now, Chaine glanced around; Christine had turned away, but only a fraction, and Mrs Chaine's cheeks were flushed.

Bobby leapt into the air, landed smartly on a single foot and Chaine sat down again.

Bobby knew his audience felt animal fur and feathers brush their skin, so softly, knew they breathed the scent of sandalwood smoke wisping across them . . .

A fine bright bone pierced Bobby's nose, brightly coloured feathers bobbed in his hair, and a cloak of soft animal skins hung from shoulder to shin.

He looked at his audience. Smiled. Knew he'd won them.

Wunyeran and Dr Cross were at one window, nodding and grinning their pride and their pleasure. Manit and Menak, too, little dog in his arms, its alert ears turned and leaning forward. Wooral?

Boodawan, nyoondokat nyinang moort, moortapinyang yongar, wetj, wilo . . . Nitja boodja ngalak boodja Noonga boodjar, kwop nyoondok yoowarl koorl yey, yang ngaalang . . . Because you need to be inside the sound and the spirit of it to live here properly. And how can that be, without we people who have been here for all time?

Bobby saw a scene spread before him like a sandplain, and he on lookout: guns and horses and flour and boats and people shimmering plants animals birds insects fish, all our songs and dances mixing together because here in this place we are like family: friends, becoming family. Binyan and Jak Tar doing that already. Who knows, maybe he and Christine next despite all old man Chaine's worry.

This is my land, given me by *Kongk* Menak. We will share it with you, and share what you bring.

Boonj boonj boonjinying. He sang the sweet melodic refrain and lyrics of the kissing love song, pouted his lips so that sound and gesture were united.

Bobby knew he was storyteller, dancer, singer, could dance around a spear and make a song to calm any man. Yes, Bobby Wabalanginy believed he'd won them over with his dance, his speech, and of course his usual tricks of performance-and-costume stuff. He was particularly pleased with the red underpants, worn as a concession to his audience's sensibility.

Suddenly, he felt not fear, but a terrible anxiety. Faces—other than those of Jak Tar and Binyan—had turned away from him. Bobby felt as if he had surfaced in some other world. Chairs creaked as people stirred, coughing. Chaine led them to their feet. Figures at the periphery of Bobby's vision fell away. He heard gunshots. And another sound: a little dog yelping.

AUTHOR'S NOTE

This novel is inspired by the history of early contact between Aboriginal people—the Noongar—and Europeans in the area of my hometown of Albany, Western Australia, a place known by some historians as the 'friendly frontier'.

I'd like to acknowledge my debt to historians and other sources. Neville Green's *Nyungar—the People: Aboriginal customs in the southwest of Australia* brings together most of the significant colonial diarists, including the notable Alexander Collie, and Green's collaboration with Paul Mulvaney to produce *Commandant of Solitude: the journals of Collet Barker 1828–1831* has revealed insights that would otherwise have been virtually inaccessible. Neville Green is also largely responsible for *Aborigines of the Albany Region 1821–1898*, which provides, as it were, 'snapshots' of many Noongar individuals, albeit through the coloniser's distorting lens. Tiffany Shellam's *Shaking Hands on the Fringe: Negotiating the Aboriginal World at King George Sound* is a much more recent work, and I wish to thank her for its cogent argument that Noongar people saw ships as 'vehicles for significantly extending kin networks and enhancing geographic knowledge and perspectives of country'. Similarly, Martin Gibbs's *The Historical Archaeology of Shore Based Whaling in WA 1836–1879* demonstrates the extent of Noongar involvement in the nineteenth-century shore-based whaling industry, and also pointed me to examples in the Daisy Bates collection of English language and colonial experience contained within an historical Noongar worldview. Edward Eyre's published reports and journals also inform parts of the novel, along with research by the late Bob Howard (www.kiangardarup.blogspot.com). The advice of the poet and academic Dennis Haskell was also invaluable.

Most importantly, I wish to thank the Wirlomin Noongar Language and Story Regeneration Project; most especially Edward Brown, Iris Woods, Ezzard Flowers, Roma Winmar and, of course, the talented Mary Gimondo, Marg Robinson and Lefki Kaillis.

I say the novel is 'inspired' by history because, rather than write an account of historical events or Noongar individuals with whom I was particularly intrigued, I wanted to build a story from their confidence, their inclusiveness and sense of play, and their readiness to appropriate new cultural forms—language and songs, guns and boats—as soon as they became available. Believing themselves manifestations of a spirit of place impossible to conquer, they appreciated reciprocity and the nuances of cross-cultural exchange. In the earliest months of colonisation, the Noongar man, Mokare, is reported as interrupting a conversation with soldiers to sing out to an arriving brother, not some traditional Noongar song, but, 'O where have you been all the day, Billy Boy?' This is as witty a cross-cultural performance as any I have encountered. But Mokare was not exceptional. According to an observant colonial diarist, a verbal account by another Noongar guide—Manyat—exploited structural characteristics of the 'expedition journal', a popular literary form of the time. The military drill Matthew Flinders's marines performed on the beach was transformed into a Noongar dance. That Noongar choreographer's grandson, Nebinyan—one of the Noongar men forming some 40 percent of the nineteenth century shore-based whaling workforce along the south coast of Western Australia—composed a song cycle around the novel cultural experience of rowing a boat out to a whale, spearing it, and being taken for a 'Nantucket sleigh ride'.

Also important to this novel are the lively, late-nineteenth-century letters of Bessie Flower, and English phrases such as 'King George Town' and 'captain on a rough sea' that blossom so strange and alien among the rolling Noongar sound of songs composed by members of her Noongar community. Other Noongar heroes of mine are Nakinah, Gallypert, Wylie, and the many individuals given the name 'Bobby': Candyup Bobby, Cape Riche Bobby, Doubtful Island Bobby, Gordon's Bobby . . .

Of course, there were admirable colonists at the 'friendly frontier', too, including Alexander Collie and Collet Barker.

I have used the names of my own Noongar ancestors— Wunyeran, Manit and Binyan—and modelled a fictional geography around places today referred to as Princess Royal Harbour, King George Sound, Torndirrup National Park, Cape Riche, the Kalgan River, Mandubarnap, Balongup, Cocanarup, Pallinup, Bandalup and several easterly-facing headlands, bays and small rivers of my ancestral Noongar country along the south coast of Western Australia.

A NOTE ON THE AUTHOR

Kim Scott was born in 1957 to a white mother and an Aboriginal father. His first novel, *True Country*, was published in 1993. His second, *Benang: From the Heart*, won the 2000 Miles Franklin Award and the Western Australian Premier's Book Award. He again won the Miles Franklin Award for *That Deadman Dance*, as well as the Commonwealth Writers' Prize for the South East Asia and Pacific Region.

Scott has also published short stories and poetry. He currently lives in Western Australia with his wife and two children.

mL   2-12